Dracula's Guest

Dracula's Guest

BY

Amaya Tenshi

www.penmorepress.com

Dracula's Guest by Amaya Tenshi
Copyright 2022© Amanda Thoss
Published by Penmore Press LLC

All rights reserved. No part of this book may be used or reproduced by any means without the written permission of the publisher except in the case of brief quotation embodied in critical articles and reviews.

This is a work of fiction. The characters and events in this book are fictitious and any resemblance to persons living or dead is purely coincidental, with the exception of historical personages as described in the Author's Note.

ISBN-13:979-8-9855298-4-5(Paperback)
ISBN-13:979-8-9855298-5-2(e-book)

BISAC Subject Headings:

FIC009060 FICTION / Fantasy / Urban
FIC010000 FICTION / Fairy Tales, Folk Tales, Legends & Mythology
FIC051000 FICTION / Cultural Heritage

Cover Art by Neutronboar

Address all correspondence to:
Penmore Press LLC
920 N Javelina Pl
Tucson AZ 85748 USA

DEDICATION

*In loving memory of my loving husband.
May we meet again.
And many thanks to all my friends who believed in and encouraged me, especially to Ileana for her support and Mike for his help.*

PROLOGUE

WHERE DO WE GO FROM HERE?

In October 1451, just a few years before the fall of Constantinople and the following Siege of Belgrade, Bogdan II, a successor to Alexander the Good, was assassinated by one of that illustrious ruler's many sons. Not an unusual event in the Balkans during that timeframe, which was marked by turmoil and political flux. Serving on a throne often conferred a very short reign, if not a life expectancy to match. This particular assassination turned two specific young men into political refugees. The older of the two was twenty-one, the other was three years his junior. The older one was accustomed to living on the road, having done his fair share of that since he was born, and also accustomed to exile. In fact, he had spent almost the entirety of his young life in exile or as a political prisoner. This more recent exile was just one more turn of the screw, given that he had fled to Bogdan II for protection after he had been ousted from his own throne not long before.

They were still well within Moldavia's borders, but out of sight of its capital, Suceava, with the Carpathians to the west when they stopped to deliberate and consider their course before they lost too much light. Bears and wolves roamed the wilderness, and they were not prepared to camp in the chill night on a pile of stinging nettles with leaves rustling overhead.

The older hid his mouth behind a fist to think, his brows low over his deep-set eyes, casting them entirely into shadow. Some of the menacing aspect of that scowl was practiced artifice, while the rest was natural to a young man who had lived a hard, hard life bereft of much joy or comfort.

His younger companion, a dear cousin, came up alongside, studied the distance his cousin glowered at, then scanned the horizon all about. Fall had turned the verdant landscape to gold and copper. The younger man fought not to be overcome by some emotion, gritting his teeth and wrestling to keep his breath steady. It was not the fear of death that had the younger so troubled. Both of them had participated in a military campaign against an invading Polish force and driven them back the year before.

Hearing his companion's struggle, the older took a moment to regard him. "Catch your breath," he instructed. The younger answered with a little nod and did his best to obey. Seeing his cousin's continuing distress, the young man's hard look softened. His eyes wavered a bit as he struggled to find the right words. "We are not killed yet, and God willing, we shall live for many years longer. If so, we shall find a way to avenge your father."

"Memory eternal," the younger murmured. He crossed himself and turned his face the way they had come. The last few rays of sunlight caught in his gold hair.

The older one crossed himself also and resumed ruminating on their predicament. His younger companion prayed voicelessly for a space of time.

"We haven't time to waste, I suppose," the younger said at last. "By God's grace we have come this far. Let us pray for His protection and guidance. Where can we go?"

"Ștefan, let me think a moment."

"I suppose we could...flee to Poland."

"Poland? Why?"

Ștefan turned away to hide his flush. "I could ask for backing to take back the throne," he said in a low voice.

"You would become a vassal?"

"Vlad, where else can we flee? The Sublime Porte? You still have the Sultan's backing for your throne—"

Ștefan fell silent when he caught the cold fire in Vlad's eye at the mention of the Ottomans and their sultan.

"I suppose that settles it, then," Ștefan said. He crossed himself again. "It is a long way north."

"Don't go to Poland. You will have to make promises you ought not. They"—Vlad's hate-filled eye turned south—"always ask a great deal of you in exchange for support for your birthright. Too much. You should continue to distance yourself. Own your own land. Walk on it as a proud lord."

"I can walk on nothing I own as it is, and neither can you," Ștefan pointed out. "And what good is it to talk of ownership and birthrights while we both stand at the edge of a wood with no prospects before us and enemies behind us?"

"I told you, let me think."

"What is there to think about?" Ștefan demanded. "Our course is clear: we must flee north and seek support, or else south to the Turks. We can follow the Siret well enough."

Vlad's baleful eye remained fixed southward, as though he could see something even from this distance which he reviled. He played with a ring on his fist absently.

"West," Vlad said.

"West? Across the mountains?" Ştefan asked, perplexed.

"We are going to Count Hunedoara," Vlad said, with finality. He turned westward.

"You intend to flee to Transylvania?" Ştefan blurted, starting after his companion. "You mean to tell me you stood here wasting time thinking of some solution *other* than the Sublime Porte and you landed on *John Hunyadi?*"

"That's right."

"Have *you* gone mad?"

"He is a strong military commander, a firm Christian, and knows the role of voivode. He also honors the customs of hospitality."

"Oh, he's a splendid commander," Ştefan agreed, "save for... that doomed campaign...." Ştefan dared not mention the events of the Varna campaign, when the one-time voivode of Transylvania—now demoted to count of Bistriţa, Severin and Timişoara—had fought alongside Vlad's father and older brother. It had ended in disaster. "He had your father and Mircea killed, Vlad. He hates you—"

"You think I don't know that?" Vlad snapped.

"He surely knows you have the Sultan's backing—"

"We are going to Hunyadi." Vlad turned and stared down his shorter cousin.

"But why?" Ştefan demanded. "Why take such a risk? He might have you killed also."

"We aren't going to throw ourselves on the mercy of those who wish to be our overlords," Vlad said in a tone of finality. "Are you going to be a lord in your own right, or owe your seat to some suzerain's pleasure? So he can sweep you aside the moment another claimant promises him more? Will you not set your own country on a better path than your grandfather did?"

This set Ștefan back on his heels. When he had no retort, Vlad turned westward again.

"Think of your boy, Vlad," Ștefan admonished. "What sort of man will he grow to be if his father walked straight into death's jaws rather than take the cautious, more certain road?"

"Mihnea would grow to be a brave man over whom death held no sway, for he would know his father would prefer to face death head on than throw himself at the feet of some... tyrannical degenerate."

Ștefan considered this.

"Even should we secure Hunyadi's help, can we free our lands from vassalage?"

"We can make the attempt," Vlad replied.

"By the grace of God," Ștefan said, "it may be possible."

Vlad grunted in answer.

"By the grace of God, no one will find us. The Siret is the obvious route to look for us if our uncle believes we are fleeing to the Sultan. No one would expect us to flee to Transylvania."

Ștefan cast a glance over his shoulder, but Cetatea Bistrița was out of sight. Roads were treacherous at best, washed out at less than best. Lawless swaths of country lay between them and their destination, savage wilderness alternating with nearly impassable mountains.

"Outlaws, bears, wolves and bandits lie before us," Ștefan remarked.

"I fear neither outlaws nor animals," Vlad said. "And neither should you." He turned back. "Be stalwart." He considered his words, speaking deliberately. "If, by God's grace, Hunyadi should take us in, and I win back my throne, I swear to help you win yours."

Ştefan's mouth dropped open. "That..."

But Vlad had already turned to their course again.

"Well," Ştefan said. "Should I, by God's grace, win back mine first, I swear to help you win yours."

It was Vlad's turn to be struck speechless. He whirled back, seemingly as baffled by the promise as if his cousin had just spoken Chinese to him. His dark eyes widened, but then the uncertain waver returned. He turned away and gave a short nod of his head. He was accustomed to neither kindness nor generosity, and the unexpected oath cut through his armor to the quick.

CHAPTER 1

EVICTION

Heather came back to the apartment after a morning of bargain hunting, holding a mug with a dog's paw print on it.

"Since we can't afford a dog," she explained with a smile. Heather looked thinner these days, and it had Cammy worried, but she didn't want to push.

"Thanks," Cammy said, and took the mug. It was huge and heavy, and the print looked like a real dog's paw pressed into the ceramic. That was probably why the mug was so big. Cammy smiled at the ugly thing. Heather shrugged. "Saw it at a thrift store. Couldn't pass it up." Her checked shirt hung so loosely off her shoulders that she had to roll up the sleeves to stick her fingers in her pockets.

"What do we put in it?" Cammy wondered, crossing the dingy, ancient carpet to the tiny window above the kitchen sink. Droplets of rain dripped down the streaked pane, sparkling against the pale gray outside.

"We need some flowers," Heather said. Cammy nodded, set the mug on the tiny sill among the other mugs of flowers and seedlings. When she turned around, she saw how truly pale Heather looked, almost like paper. The bones of her wrists stood out.

"You okay?" Cammy asked.

"Yeah," Heather's voice was enthusiastic, but her eyes shifted and she bit her lip. Cammy thought, *Something must be wrong*. But she decided not to say so. She fingered the new mug and watched the points of light as droplets rolled down the window.

"It's too bad you're working tonight," she told Heather. "I was looking forward to you meeting the group. We're going to see a triple feature."

"Aren't you working an afternoon shift yourself? Heather asked.

"There'll be just enough time for me to leave work and catch the opening credits."

Just then her phone began vibrating. Cammy checked the number; her friends usually texted. *Oh no, not now.*

She sighed. *If I don't answer, she'll just keep calling. Better just get it over with.*

* * *

Cammy slid down into the coffee shop booth, fiddling with the most depressing matcha green tea latte ever made while her mother tapped one manicured nail on the table. Drizzle dripped down the window, the drops catching the lights inside the coffee shop and sparkling as they wiggled down the glass. The cluster of lights stuffed into empty glass bottles hanging from the ceiling above them cast dim light across the table.

"Well?" her mother demanded. The lighting cast deep shadows on her face. Cammy's phone buzzed.

"Well nothing," said Cammy, snatching her phone and hiding it by crossing her arms. The foam art in her latte looked like a lumpy pillow floating on light green sheets. She hadn't been in this coffee shop before, but she would never agree to meet with her parents at her place of work, so here she was. Her mother touched her father's arm. He cleared his throat.

"We're worried about you," he said, nodding his head to her mother while his eyes remained on his hands.

"Okay," said Cammy. She slid her eyes down to read the message screen on her phone.

Where are you? It's starting in a few!

Cammy stealthily tapped out a reply.

Trapped by my parents. Don't expect me to be there any time soon.

"What are you doing?" her mother demanded.

"My friends want to know where I am," Cammy explained. "I was supposed to meet up with them."

"Your 'friends'?" Her mother's mouth formed a shape like a smile while her eyes remained unchanged. "You mean that druggie you live with?"

"She went to rehab. She's fine now," Cammy told her.

"Honey." Her mother reached across the table. Cammy crossed her arms tighter. Her mother's mouth uncurled and her lips pressed together. The woman straightened her back and crossed her own arms over the table. "We just want what's best for you. You know that. You're too young to be on your own—"

"Mom, I'm going to be twenty-one soon."

"But you're still working at that ridiculous coffee shop, and you still don't have a major selected?" Her mother's eyebrow arched higher than could ever be considered an expression of real, organic emotion.

"No, I'm still—"

"At that community college." Her mother's expression shifted into something like pity.

Cammy glanced outside at the light rain turning streetlights into glowing halos in the dark. Her reflection was a shadow in the window, no features. She tried to sneak a peek at her phone in the window's reflection, but she couldn't read the screen in it. Instead, she saw her mother's reflection lean back in her seat. The woman hadn't actually drunk her own coffee, though her red lipstick lined the ceramic lip. Her father's cup was empty.

"Yeah, well, it's what I can afford," Cammy said. She sipped her lukewarm tea latte. Something like fine grit settled on her tongue.

With a little Cheshire grin, Cammy's mother reached into her clutch purse and procured a bundle of twenty-dollar bills.

"No."

"Look, the fact that you can't afford a better place to live just goes to show that you don't know how to manage money. You're so immature you can't decide on a major. You're going into debt taking out student loans, and you expect me to believe that you're responsible?" her mother sneered, though she tried to hide it under something approximating sympathy. "The fact that you're slumming with that loser—"

"Heather is *not* a loser!" Cammy stood.

"Camellia Constance Lilly, I am not done talking," her mother said through her perfectly white teeth. Her hand balled into a thin fist with deep valleys between the tendons and knuckles. "Sit down."

"Nice seeing you, Mom, like always," Cammy told her. "Bye, Dad."

Her father nodded lethargically and did not look up from the table.

"Just a minute." Her mother's white teeth glinted behind the red lipstick. "Sweetie, I'm not mad. I just want to make certain you're safe. Your father and I both do. We're just worried, honey. That apartment isn't safe. Something might happen to you because of your loser friend. You can come back home. You won't have to worry about money."

"So you can tell me what to wear and how to talk to people and who I can hang out with again? No thanks. And Heather is not a loser. And Brian and Melissa aren't far away."

"That cop wannabe and his fat slob of a sister?" The teeth were bared now, and the sneer was undisguised.

Cammy snatched her bag and stormed past the booths to the glass door.

"Camellia, get back here," her mother's voice stabbed at her from behind. "You think you're impressing anyone with this temper tantrum? You're making a scene!"

Cammy slammed open the glass door, then grabbed it to keep it from smashing against the wall. It might be a crappy little coffee shop, but why ruin some poor store owner's night just because her mother sucked?

She stepped out into the light rain and the dark. The air tasted clear.

Her mother's thin hand hooked around her wrist.

"Look, honey, just think about it. I'm your mother. I know it's hard out there. I'm not mad, I just have high expectations. You know that. You know you can come back home if you need to, don't you?"

"Yes, Mom."

She hadn't meant so much resignation to creep into her voice. It must be habit. Her mother pulled her into a loveless hug and kissed her head.

"Ugh, you're all wet. Didn't you bring an umbrella? After all these years you still can't plan the simplest thing!"

"Thanks, Mom."

Cammy pulled herself free. She heard her father mumbling something behind her; she couldn't tell if he was talking to her or her mother.

"Take a cab! I'm not going to be sorry if you get yourself raped!" her mother shouted.

Cammy resolved to walk.

The walk in the drizzle cooled her head. She checked the time, figured she'd missed enough of the first movie that there was no point walking in now. Besides, she was short on cash and she'd been considering skipping this movie marathon anyway. Textbooks kept getting more and more expensive. She texted her friends to let them know she was heading home and received no response. They had agreed no phones during the marathon, mostly because Lindsey was glued to hers otherwise, so that didn't bother Cammy.

What did bother her was the sight of all her stuff thrown haphazardly in front of the entrance to the apartment complex. No, not just her stuff, Heather's stuff too. She stood for a moment, flabbergasted, then stormed inside to Mr. Knox's office. She knocked, got no answer, so called the landlord up, after hours or not.

"What?" Knox answered.

"Hello, my name is Camellia Lilly. I'm a resident of apartment 17? Do you know why my things are all thrown outside?"

"You don't pay rent, you get evicted. That simple."

Cammy considered her words, wondering if she should temporize. No, be straightforward.

"I *did* pay rent."

"Well, I never got it."

"You have to give tenants some sort of notice?" Cammy mock-wondered.

"I did. For months. Not my fault if you don't check your mail."

Cammy looked down at her stuff.

"Mr. Knox, I have nowhere to go. I paid rent. I never got a notice."

"Not my problem, I never received cash, and I delivered notices. Unless you pay the six months you owe me, you're going to have to figure something out."

The line went dead. Cammy squatted beside her haphazardly strewn things glistening in the streetlights and keyed up Heather's number. No answer.

"Heather, I swear, if you don't pick up...!"

Ring. Ring. Ring.

Hi! It's Heather, if you know me, just text me—

Cammy tapped to hang up as angrily as she could. It didn't help. She gazed up into the dark sky, blinking. The drizzle seemed to be letting up. Yay.

Seeing everything she owned lying on the pavement made her chuckle to herself. It was practically nothing. Hair brushes, some clothes, some toiletries, little collectibles, a charger Heather had lost a few months ago, all of it lying right there on the sidewalk for everyone to see.

I'm so poor. She giggled at her phone screen.

Wait a minute.

Her mother had known. Known that something was wrong. Heather must have been keeping the rent money, hiding notices. Had to be. But her mother had known, and not told her.

You're a monster, she thought.

She spent the next half hour hopelessly trying to reach her friends. No dice. Just in case, she dialed Brian again. Voicemail, and it had been voicemail the last, oh, fifteen times. She knew why her movie-going friends weren't texting back, but it was weird that the other two didn't. They must still be at work.

Ping.

It was Heather.

We got evicted?

Cammy glared at her phone.

Yeah, you took my money and didn't pay rent! she texted. Heather read the message, but made no reply while Cammy seethed.

Finally, *Ya sorry bout that.*

I'm stuck on the street and we have nowhere to live!!! Cammy wished adding exclamation marks would be as satisfying as screaming, but they weren't. Again, Heather took her sweet time replying. That seemed strange. Heather's thumbs could fly over a touchscreen like hummingbirds on rocket fuel.

Sorry.

Thanks, Cammy thought sarcastically, but she texted, *What do we do now? Where ARE you??*

The answer came slowly, in pieces.

Dracula's Guest

I can't get to you. I can get to that coffee shop near the theater. Can you get there?

I don't have a car and no one's picking up.

Try Green4Life. They're cheap, local. I used them a couple times.

Cammy vaguely recalled Heather mentioning the rideshare, but didn't know much about it herself. New, local, eco-friendly, or something? Probably better than the electric bikes or scooters. It'd be harder to carry her stuff if she had to use one of those.

Fine. I'll bring what I can.

Heather didn't even text a 'thanks.' Cammy ran through all the things she wanted to scream when she met her roommate face to face.

Well, it wasn't going to get any better sitting here. She checked what was left in her bank account. Yikes. She could get a ride to the coffee shop, then to Brian and Melissa's, but it would be tight until payday next week, especially now that she had no fridge, stored rice and beans, or other goods she'd need between now and then.

She installed the rideshare app, then stuffed what she could into her bag. One of her downstairs neighbors must have gone to a farmer's market or something, because she found a sturdy cardboard box on the bushes in front of the building. It must have fallen from a window or been tossed deliberately, and recently enough that it was only damp, not soaked. Cammy was able to fit most of her things in her bag and the box, along with some of Heather's stuff, minus the kitschy three-to-seven-dollar blind bag collectables they liked to accumulate. All the flower pot mugs were shattered, their contents turned to mud on the pavement, except for the dog print mug. It had landed on a heap of clothing and was only broken into three large pieces. She had just placed the pieces in the box when a clean-looking hybrid car pulled up in front of the building. She tapped on the window.

"Hi, are you with Green4Life?" she asked when the insanely pale-looking driver rolled down the window.

"Yes. You Cammy?" he responded.

"Yeah, thanks. Is it okay if I put this all back there?" she asked, showing him the box. He nodded.

"You would *not* believe the day I've had," she told him as she scooched the box across the seat and climbed in. "Wow, this is a pretty nice ride. I thought maybe since you guys were local and little cheaper you'd have, I dunno, older cars or something? I mean, it's practically new car smell in here!"

"I got it detailed," said the driver.

Cammy glanced up at the rundown little apartment complex as the car pulled away. The apartment's sign had that worn sort of ugliness that she found charming, its letters faded and the rust leaving bloodstains down its face. Probably it should be condemned, she guessed. Whatever, rent was cheap. *Had been* cheap, but even that had been too much for Heather, apparently. Well, this would teach her not to agree to pay rent with cash in envelopes handed over every month to be paid along with what Heather contributed.

I hope she's okay. Cammy thought to herself, *idiot*. If Heather hadn't paid the rent in months despite her new job, it was probably because she was on something again, or somethings. Had Heather really thought that if the rent didn't get paid that somehow no one would notice and they could just keep living there? That they wouldn't come home one day to find that the *technically* legal establishment hadn't just dumped their stuff on the street and told them they were evicted? Heather must have been hiding the notices too, because Cammy had never seen them.

Cammy fiddled through her photos while they drove. There wasn't any point bothering anyone now. She and Heather could wait on the Warrens' doorstep until one of them came home from work.

What a perfect end to a perfectly awful day. Ten hours of putting up with customers' petty rudeness, and then her mother wanting to talk to her out of the blue. Maybe if Brian went to sleep early she could sneak some booze from Melissa. Brian was a hopeless case, relentlessly upright since graduating to real cop.

"Wait a minute, where are we?" she asked when she glanced out the window. They had pulled off interstate 5, but it looked like they had passed Lake Ballinger—putting the coffee shop and the theater south of her. The driver had just made a left and they were heading south again. She couldn't imagine that this could be a route to the coffee shop; had the driver missed it and needed to turn around? She looked out the window. The nearest storefront was dark and tarps covered the inside of the windows. Whatever it was, it was closed. The one just beyond it looked like it was under construction. "Hey, um, Caleb, right?" she asked. "Where is this? We're going to Crest Cafe over on—"

"It's fine. This is a shortcut," said the driver. Cammy glanced back out at the shops they had passed. She hadn't taken this street on the bus before. Some of the grass poking up through cracks in the sidewalk was as long as her hair. She realized the reason it seemed so dark; there weren't any working streetlights. It looked like he was going to pull off the road onto a weird, dark, parking lot.

"Hey, um, I think your GPS is wrong. We're on the wrong side of the interstate, and too far north."

"It's fine," the driver repeated.

Cammy looked out the back window. About a hundred feet or more to a streetlight, and there weren't any cars in sight, not even on the road they had turned off of.

"Seriously, I think you have the wrong address or something. Here, I can pull up directions on my phone, hang on..."

She saw his pale fingers take hold of a stylus to poke at the cellphone mounted next to the wheel. Suspicious, she pretended to enter the apartment address into her phone, but watched him type *Got her. B there soon.*

"Hey, seriously," Cammy said. "Turn around."

This time he only glanced at his mirror and kept on going. She tried the door, and heard the lock *tunk*.

Oh no. Of course she'd get murdered for not taking a mainstream rideshare service on the one day she couldn't reach anyone and got evicted. Of course on the night her mother had screeched at her for not taking a taxi. Of *course*. She yanked on the handle but the door would not open.

"Unlock this right now!" she screamed. Wow. Screaming already. It was embarrassing. Maybe it was because Brian's cop training had sunk into her brain when he told her about horror stories and safety precautions. Well, not the training stories, just the scary "everyone is a murdering rapist" parts. The driver had stopped talking to her altogether.

She dialed 9-1—

Dracula's Guest

The driver grabbed her hands in his huge, freezing cold fingers. She screamed in pain. It was like the grip of a machine: relentless, overpowering. She pulled back as hard as she could, but couldn't break his terrifying grip.

"Let me go! My best friend's a cop! I just left like a million messages on his phone! He's gonna come looking for me!" she screamed.

Cammy kicked at the door and the window, only then noticing there were people outside. A lot of them. *Oh no oh no no **no no**!* She bit the driver's hand. He tasted like rotten meat and he didn't even have the decency to flinch. The lock *tunked*, the door opened, and someone grabbed Cammy by the ankle.

"No!" she shrieked as she was dragged from the vehicle. The driver ripped her phone from her hands, watching her as she clawed helplessly at the door, the carpeting, the wheel well, but couldn't hold on. "No! Stop!" More people grabbed her legs, her wrists, and they lifted her up like she was an inflatable pool toy. They didn't say anything to each other, but she spotted one looking into the vehicle at her things as they carried her away.

She was going to die. These people were going to kill her, or sell her on the black market or harvest her organs or all of those things. They were crazy cultists or something. *Is this why I can't reach Heather?* Cammy suddenly went cold. Heather had told her about the service. She must have used it at least a few times. Was Cammy about to disappear into a serial killer's basement and see Heather's head on a dissection table?

"Help! Help! Someone heeeeeellllp!" she screamed.

The hands holding her up stopped carrying her towards the nearest building. She heard something like thick fabric whipping around, then a thud. She heard the same set of sounds again and the hands all released her except for one pair, whose owner wrapped an arm around her chest and pulled out a gun with his spare hand.

She cranked her head around. The gray-faced guy who held her was wearing a green hoodie. She noticed the others wore just whatever, like everyday people; there was even a woman in a miniskirt and heels. The only thing they had in common was their weird skin color, and they all kinda looked sick and disheveled. Then she saw two of them on the ground—*beheaded.*

Her eyes just about fell right out her head and into her open mouth when she saw that.

What was happening? The maybe-cultists waved their guns or knives at the darkness like a bunch of helpless bimbo-stereotypes from slasher movies. One of them, a middle-aged man, fired his gun at a pillar. The noise made Cammy flinch in surprise, and it stabbed her ears. The sound seemed to be echoing in the space.

Then a man in black came out of nowhere and put a sword through one of the maybe-cultists, a hipster-looking chick wearing a handmade knit cap with a penguin on it. The hipster girl's eyes widened. Before she could even look down at the weird, curved blade sticking through her chest, the man in black ripped it out of her and used it to chop her head clean off. Other would-be murderers fired at him, but the man in black seemed to duck and weave well enough to avoid getting shot by these obvious amateurs. He rushed another one of them and performed the same stab-and-slash, killing a Hispanic man in his fifties. Then he went for the next nearest, and the one after that. Some of the pale-faced people were fumbling to reload.

The hoodie guy fired his gun and Cammy did her best to plug her ears. She had never heard anything so *loud* before in her life. Movies did it no justice at all. Hoodie kept firing while she flinched, and she found she couldn't look away from the man in black with the sword. She finally realized why it looked so weird and thick and only half-shiny. It was made of wood. Well, one side was wood. The other side looked like steel.

What the heck?

Suddenly there weren't any more amateur-cultist-serial-killers-whatever-they-were except Hoodie, and the man in black faced him head on.

"Come any closer and I'll kill her," Hoodie warned, pressing his gun to Cammy's temple, then aiming it at the man and black, back and forth several times. The man in black did not approach.

I gotta do something, Cammy thought to herself. That's what Brian was always saying. You had to survive, somehow or other. If she let Hoodie keep using her as a hostage, he might take her somewhere where no one would ever find her. She swung her fist at his crotch, hitting it as hard as she could. He didn't flinch, but she heard a gunshot and felt Hoodie jolt backwards just a little. The man in black had a gun in his other hand.

"You complete noob," Hoodie said, "that can't kill me—"

The man in black had crossed the distance and sliced Hoodie's gun hand off. Cammy ducked, felt wind on her hair, and then Hoodie's other arm simply fell away. His head bounced a little on the old asphalt as his body collapsed beside it.

She screamed and jumped away from his corpse.

There were twenty people or more lying all over the ground, decapitated. Somehow, the man in black had killed all of them without getting shot or stabbed. And done it with a weird-looking, half-wooden sword. She watched him stab Hoodie's headless corpse in the chest with it.

She felt light-headed. Her ears were ringing. She realized she was about to faint. Cammy dropped to a crouch and put her head between her knees. Melissa had told her to do that if she was ever going to faint. She needed air or something. Had she remembered to breathe?

She squeezed her eyes shut, forced herself to take *slow*, deep breaths. In, out, in out. Her fingers were trembling, everything in her chest was trembling.

Finally, she forced herself to look up. The man in black was talking into—of all things—a flip phone. Her ears were still ringing, and it took her a few moments to understand what he was saying.

"...twenty-two, to be exact. There were two inside the building. No, I'll need a new one, this is getting uselessly dull. I *know* you'll have to get it blessed. No, no witnesses." He paused in the conversation and stared straight at Cammy, and she gasped in spite of herself. "Victims?" he said into the phone, studying her. "I didn't see any. *Yes*, I am checking." He held a finger up to his lips.

Cammy knotted her eyebrows together in confusion. "Wha...?" She fell silent when he frowned and tapped his finger to his lips aggressively. The man in black stepped over three headless corpses, coming right for her.

Crap! she thought. He seemed to have sheathed his weird sword; she saw its handle poking out from his long, black coat. She didn't see the gun he used, but maybe he'd gotten it from one of the pale people? Before she could think whether she should try to run or not, he was right in front of her. He gently touched her chin and lifted her head a bit to take a look at her neck on both sides. Satisfied, he smiled and winked conspiratorially at her, then took one of her hands and placed an incredibly wet kiss on her knuckles, lingering just a touch too long.

"No, I didn't find any," the man in black said into his phone. "No. Just a car.... Yes.... Devil take you, you cretin."

He flipped the phone shut and fixed the lapels of his coat with a grunt of disgust. He muttered something to himself that didn't sound like English, and walked away into the night.

"Hey!" Cammy shouted. "Hey! Mister! Hey! Wait!"

The man in black ignored her, so she slapped her legs to get herself moving. She charged after him. When she had come nearly within arm's reach he stopped dead and swung around to face her with a suspicious glower and one hand on the handle of his weapon.

"Whoa! Whoa! No! Whoa! No, I wanted to thank you."

He remained immobile, eying her suspiciously.

"I mean it. I mean, I don't know who you are or where you come from or what all that was about, but—"

"You'll want to get your things and be on your way," he told her. "Sooner, rather than later. Go home."

"Uh..." No, there wasn't any point explaining everything, was there? "Well, I was on my way to a coffee shop. I just got evicted because my roommate didn't pay—anyway, you don't need to hear all that. I just wanted to say thanks." She held out a hand, which he studied like it was a crossword puzzle written in Ancient Greek. "For real. You need a favor, I mean, I don't have a lot of cash or whatever, but if you want, like, infinite free coffees or something, I'm a barista, and…"

He blinked at her with what she thought must be frustration.

"Sorry. I'm rambling, but really, thank you."

"If you like," he said. Hesitantly, he took her hand. It was then she noticed he wore gloves.

"Oh, wait! I gotta call the cops—crap, what do I tell them?"

"I wouldn't," the man in black told her. "This will be taken care of. Just go home."

"My phone—so are you some kind of investigator or something?" She trotted back towards the pristine eco-car. The driver's head was in his lap, and she spun in a circle to settle her rising gorge and catch her breath. Once it was caught, she turned back and kept her eyes on anything else until she spotted her phone on the floor in the back.

"Hey, if you're an investigator, this guy was texting someone earlier. He might have contacts or something." She rubbed her phone with her thumb. No cracks, thank goodness.

She almost jumped onto the car roof when she noticed the man in black standing next to her. He moved as silently as a shadow. She watched him peer into the vehicle and spot the driver's phone. Then despite her trying not to, she saw the driver's severed head had fangs.

No way, she thought, *No frickin' way.*

But the wooden sword made more sense now. Not calling the cops made even more sense. The group of pale-faced creeps living in abandoned buildings made *way* too much sense. And the man in black had *checked her neck* when he was looking for "victims".

"Am I crazy, but are these... I mean, these guys aren't...?"

"Just go home," the man in black repeated. He straightened up, looked at her. She saw in his eyes she was right. He didn't even try to lie to her.

"That's impossible," she told him—and herself. "Impossible."

She stepped away from the car and watched the man in black walk around to the driver's side. He reached in, slapped the severed head to the floor, then took the phone from its mount. He tapped at the cell phone he had stolen with increasing frustration before he pocketed it.

"Oh, crap, is it broken?" she asked, jogging around the car to take a look.

The man in black eyed her, then pulled out the phone and showed it to her. She didn't see any cracks in the screen.

"That's weird. It looks fine," she mumbled. The man in black pulled it out of her reach when she tried to check it herself.

"Right. Fingerprints," she said, before she realized that made no sense. This was a man who had just killed twenty people—people who were apparently vampires. That made him some sort of vampire slayer, and that meant this was something else entirely. He'd said there'd be no police. Some sort of secret group was going around killing vampires, and he was one of them. It was like a movie.

"You saved my life," she told the man in black again. He did not look at her, but she could see he watched her out of the corner of his eye. "And I know what's really going on."

"No, you don't," he told her. She extended a hand to him again, reaching.

"I want to know."

"No, you don't."

She held onto his hand, but his eyes were hard, dark, unmoved. She sniffed and patted his elbow and his shoulder before she let go of his hand once more. The man in black studied her like she was a million-piece puzzle and a few pieces were missing. Then he touched his forehead with a finger in salute and pointed over Cammy's shoulder. She turned, saw nothing, and when she turned back, he was gone.

"Whoa," she murmured.

Cammy retrieved her bag and dragged the box out of the car.

Her hands were still shaky and her legs felt like rubber, so she walked loosey-goosey back to the main street and followed it to a gas station. Once there, she pulled out her tablet, reserved an electric bike, then checked her tablet. In a moment of truly crazy inspiration, she had slipped her phone into the man in black's pocket when she shook his hand one last time, and she could see its location.

This is some crazy Harry Potter, Underworld, superhero hidden-world-call-to-adventure stuff, she thought to herself, and there was no way she was going to let it go. No way.

She found the electric bike she had reserved, discovered she could wedge the box with her and Heather's things between the handlebars with her tablet sitting securely on top of the pile, and set off.

* * *

She couldn't take much more of this. Her phone was still moving, and she had crossed over Lake Washington on Interstate 90 forty minutes ago and now the city was starting to thin out. Heck, all she could see on either side were trees, with the occasional houses sprinkled like bread crumbs along the way. She glanced back and could only see the city's glow against the clouds above. Nothing but trees from here on.

She rode into thicker woods, taking a strangely well-kept dirt road. Her phone had stopped moving.

She came to a pile of stones with the numbers inscribed in Roman numerals. There was a narrow dirt road leading through the trees. Cammy checked her tablet. It said her phone had to be here, and this had to be the address. She peered at the wall of trees and the thick blackberry bushes that would stop her trying to go hiking off-trail. No buildings. The bike was low on power, and probably wasn't supposed to be all the way out here anyway. She sighed and left the bike on the dirt road, taking her box in her arms.

She walked up to the dirt road and spotted two stone gargoyles standing on either side of a wooden archway. Pretty par for the course for a gothic adventure.

Her tablet was hard to use as a flashlight with the box in her arms. She took deep breaths and headed up the path.

The trees grew over the road, blocking out what little moonlight there was through the thin clouds, and her arms ached from the way she was carrying the box and her tablet.

Amaya Tenshi

The wind kept rustling the trees and she felt certain there were eyes on her.

No, you're still jumpy because of what happened. There's no one out here. Just go. She didn't want to turn around and stare at the blackness behind her. She was *certain* she'd see eyes glowing in the dark back there.

The path bent slowly to the right as it climbed a hill. Cammy panted from exertion. Her shoulders ached, her mouth was dry. Was there a *house* somewhere at the end of this? A secret, magical academy, or a dojo or training ground for vampire hunters? She certainly *hoped* so, but she had been walking for what felt like forever and there was still this stupid dark road. Then she saw the pale glow of moonlight ahead. Rejuvenated by the sight, she speed-walked towards it. The trees fell away, revealing neatly trimmed grass, a huge gravel driveway, and an actual freaking mansion standing huge and dark and gothic in the moonlight.

*I **knew** it!* she exulted. She wanted to pass out where she stood, but she forced her legs and her screaming arms and her weary body to propel her towards the mansion. She couldn't see it very well in the faint moonlight, but it looked like just the kind of place a vampire hunter would call home. Four stories tall, gabled roof, the ancient walls covered with ivy and creepers, a thick snake of smoke twirling up out of one of the chimneys. The windows were all dark, except one on the ground floor, and only a soft, flickering glow emanated from it. Nothing electric-looking. She came to a stout wooden door and looked for a doorbell. She didn't see one even after she shone the light from her tablet at the jamb. Finally, she shifted the box to one hand and knocked as loudly as she could. Her knuckles gave a pathetic *dnk dnk*

dnk she felt certain was too quiet for anyone to hear unless they stood on the other side of the door. The wood must be inches thick.

Should she kick it? No, that would be rude. But how could she make more noise? Toss some small gravel pebbles at the windows until she got someone's attention?

It occurred to her she was actually trespassing. Sure, she was knocking on the door and all, but if there was a super-secret vampire hunter inside, he might not be so happy about strangers showing up at his door uninvited. Worse than that, it hadn't even occurred to her to wonder whether he was friendly. He might be a creep, or violent, or something.

The door swung open as she stood biting her lip, realizing this might be the stupidest idea she'd ever had.

The man in black stood at the door, frowning at her in absolute, uncomprehending disbelief.

"Hi!" she greeted him. Nothing for it now but to press forward. "Look, I'm sorry to bug you, but...well, uh..." she had no idea what to say. *You're a vampire hunter and I think that's the coolest thing and I want to be invited into your crazy world.* She couldn't just say that, could she?

"Um, I'm Cammy," she said. "I... you have my phone..." She saw the man in black scanning the path behind her, even leaning his head out far enough to glance to the left and right.

"... so, if I could just get my phone back..." she was saying, when he grabbed her by the throat and hauled her inside.

She found herself sliding across the floor to a wall and heard the sound of the door slamming shut behind her. The box fell to the floor, her clothes and hairbrush and collectibles scattering all around her. She scrambled to her feet, climbing the wall with her hands. She turned to see the man in black coming for her.

Cammy dashed away, following the wall. So he was a psycho. Why hadn't she thought of that? Why hadn't she figured out that maybe there weren't vampires and it was all just some sort of weird, mob turf war or something?

The man in black cut her off. He glared at her so hard she thought his pupils glowed red. Wait, were they actually glowing red? That couldn't be right.

"Who do you work for?" the man in black demanded. "Quick, or I'm going to be creative when I kill you."

"What? No. I don't work for anyone. I'm a barista..." This was such a bad idea.

Her eyes darted to the door. Maybe fourteen feet to her left. Could she reach it in time?

The man in black seized her shirt and shoved her against the wall.

"I'm not accustomed to asking *twice*," he snarled. "Who do you work for? Who sent you?"

"No one! I swear! I'm a barista, I work at this little coffee shop near campus! The Mindful Bean, I swear! Please! I know it was stupid. I'm sorry for bothering you, I just thought maybe I could escape my stupid life and do something, I don't know. Please! Please!" She couldn't breathe, she tried to pry his hand from her shirt, but his grip was like the driver's before. Like iron. She couldn't speak coherently, couldn't think. *Oh, God, please don't let me die. Please, God, I'm so stupid!*

"How did you find me?" the man in black demanded.

"I-I p-put my phone in your pocket," she blubbered between ragged gasps. "I j-just followed it with my tablet."

DRACULA'S GUEST

"What do you mean, you followed it? You followed your phone?" He looked down at her things scattered across the floor. "I don't see anything you could have used. How did you do it?"

"Dude, with—with the app. That's the whole point, so if you lose your phone you can find it again."

"App? What is that?"

What? He didn't look that old. He had a cellphone, he had to know what she was talking about. Sure, it was an old, clunky-looking flip phone from a million years ago, but he had to know what it was. He lived in a mansion, not under a rock.

She flinched when he reached into his jacket and drew forth—not a gun—but his flip phone. He glowered at her between pressing digits before he put the phone to his ear. She could just hear the tinny sound of the rings on the other end.

"Why are you calling me?" she heard a voice say on the other line. Cammy thought she heard music, too. Some kind of synth pop. Her ears were still ringing a little, so she wasn't certain.

"Shut up," said the man in black. "Is it possible to follow a phone when it is lost with technology of some sort?"

Wow. He seriously didn't know? How was that possible? Cammy heard what she thought was laughter on the other end. "Yeah, old man. You've been able to do that for a while. Not with *your* old clunker, but the new ones. Why?"

"Never mind." The man in black flipped the phone shut. He studied her up and down, then kicked at her things on the floor. The pepper spray Brian had bought her came rolling out of her bag. He kicked at the bag again until her wallet came out. The man in black shoved her down on the ground with that same strength she had only experienced earlier this night, and stooped to pick up her bag. He turned it upside down, dumping out her makeup and toiletries. Cammy felt her face start to blush when her box of tampons fell to the floor. He peered into it, reached inside, felt around, turned it inside out, dropped it, then squatted to look over her things.

"I'm really sorry," she told him hoarsely. "I promise I won't tell anyone. I promise. Please let me go."

"Quiet." He snatched up her wallet and flipped it open. "Who are you?"

"My name's Cammy Lilly," she told him. He was looking at her ID, he ought to know.

"Full name?"

"Camellia Constance Lilly. I know, it's stupid. I got two grandmothers' names."

The man in black scrutinized the ID, flipping it over a few times, looking at both sides. Once done, he dropped it.

"You tracked me with your phone?"

She nodded.

He patted at his pockets and found her phone. It had a custom cover she had ordered from an online site from a girl who did that kind of thing, and it was covered in cutesy giraffes and other animals, bubbles, and flowers with smiley faces and googly eyes. The man in black studied it.

Cammy glanced at pepper spray. She kept her face down so he couldn't see her eyes. She could grab the spray, get him in the face, and go out the door before he had a chance to do anything. She hoped she could. She had to do it.

"Why would you do this?" the man in black demanded. "Why follow me?"

"I thought—it's so stupid—I thought it was like, you know, in movies where the weird stuff happens and then the hero or heroine finds out there's like all this magic and they go on a journey and do all this cool stuff...I'm so stupid."

"It didn't occur to you that I might be *unfriendly?*" the man in black asked her. He had crossed his hands over each other, one gripping the other that held her phone. Now was her chance.

She pushed herself forward, grabbed the pepper spray, pointed it at his face, and let him have it. He blinked once, apparently in surprise, but after a few moments of uninterrupted spraying, he didn't so much as wince. Cammy let up, her heart going like a dubstep rave. What had happened? Why hadn't it worked?

She had no way to get out.

She backed to the wall, felt her legs give out, and slumped to the floor. The man in black reached into his jacket and pulled out a white handkerchief. He wiped his face.

"I offer my sincerest apologies," he said. "It seems you really don't have any idea who I am or what you are doing, Miss Lilly."

"Cammy," she corrected tonelessly. She didn't know why she should bother, but she liked the nickname better.

"Cammy," the man in black repeated. "Again, sincerest apologies. Are you badly hurt?"

"I..." she felt faint. "What? I don't understand...what happened? Who are you? What's going on?"

She looked for the door again.

"I wouldn't try that just yet," said the man in black. "Though I would like to know how you managed to get up here in the first place. But first, come. You should sit down."

He gestured behind him to an antique divan. "Are you all right?"

"You threw me into a wall," she grumbled.

"Don't exaggerate," he retorted. "Had I done so you would be dead." He could switch between gentle and condescending and back with surprising agility.

"What do you mean, exaggerate? You threw me into a wall! You were going to kill me!"

"Don't insult me. If I had wanted to kill you, you would be dead and we wouldn't be having this conversation. I am very good at killing people. Please, you should take a seat." The man in black gestured to the divan again.

Cammy stayed where she was, but she looked around. They were in a huge room, with stairs against one wall and beautiful paintings on the others, mostly landscapes, but also some portraits. The floors were marble. There was a stone fireplace, in front of which were the antique divan and chairs with sweeping, curling legs and crest rails. Despite how old they must be, they were in pristine condition.

"I shall get you some tea in a moment, but please, you should sit. Can you walk?"

Dully, Cammy allowed him to lead her to the divan. The seat was hard and unyielding despite its beautiful appearance.

"What's going on?" she asked, when the man in black stood before the fireplace, studying her movement clinically. "Who are you?"

"Forgive me for not introducing myself. I had assumed you knew who I was when you arrived. I do not get visitors or intruders of any kind who do not already know me—"

"So who *are* you?" Cammy demanded.

Dracula's Guest

"I am Wladislav Dragula, one time voivode of Wallachia and Duke of Amlaş and Făgăraş." He offered a beautiful, well-practiced bow. "At your service."

CHAPTER 2
WHO???

"You're *who?*" Cammy demanded.

She saw him purse his lips.

"Dracula," he repeated, resigned. He had said it like "Drrah-koo-lah" with the "lah" almost sounding like "lyah" before, but he adopted the more familiar pronunciation now. It seemed to leave a bad taste in his mouth from his expression.

"Dracula."

"Yes, Dracula."

She squinted at him. Now there was enough light to get a better look at him. He didn't look like Bela Lugosi. She dimly remembered seeing a painting once that someone had told her was the historic Dracula. He didn't look a whole lot like that either. This guy was broad-shouldered with thick hands, heavy eyebrows set over deep-set eyes that weren't black, they were dark green. The firelight glowed in his hair, turning some strands gold. He looked north of forty, but she couldn't gauge by how much. He had one of those faces. She guessed he had that sort of vaguely Eastern European something in his features, like how his nose and cheeks looked. Not very tall, not very short. Not handsome, not unattractive, just worn-looking.

"Are you serious?" she asked.

"Very."

"Come on," she said. "Come on. You expect me to believe you're Dracula? 'I vant to suck your blood'? Are you kidding me?"

"I am not."

"But..." that couldn't be right. "But...so were those guys not vampires?"

"Oh, they were all vampires," he said. "A poor, shoddy sort, but vampires they were."

"But you killed them!"

"Yes."

"Why?"

"Because they've been killing people, and that makes my..."—he smiled grimly—"*employers* quite upset."

"Employers?" Cammy asked.

"Perhaps we'll talk of them later. First, tea."

"But...!" But nothing, he was already leaving the room. Cammy wanted to get up and follow him, but she sat there like a lump instead. She felt dizzy, woozy, weak, wasted, spent. She leaned back against the stiff back of the divan. It felt more like wood than a cushion, to her annoyance.

"Tea will be ready in a few minutes," said the man in black when he returned. She couldn't accept he was Dracula. *That* Dracula. It was impossible. And way too weird.

"Aren't you like, king of vampires if you're really Dracula?" she asked, latching onto the thought as it sprang into her head. She could poke holes in this ridiculous claim.

"I beg your pardon?" he said in that tone wasn't a question, just a sneer of irritation.

"Well, aren't you?"

"No. And I'm not a count, either."

"You're not?"

"No."

"I thought you were."

"Only because a certain Irishman got it into his head to write a book about a vampire count, and happened to find my family name and use it *despite* my expressly telling him not to," he said.

"Wait, you told him not to?" Cammy demanded. "You met the guy?"

"Yes. In a rather roundabout way," the man in black said. "Through his brother Thornley, actually, at one of Lady Wilde's soirees."

"Lady who's what? The book is about you? You're real? All that happened?"

The man in black grimaced in absolute disgust.

"That book," he hissed, as though the word burned him. "That damnable book. No, it is a work of fiction. Mr. Stoker wrote a ridiculous piece of gothic melodrama about a vampire because they were all the rage. As I said, he simply found my name and appropriated it for his own purposes. No piece of it is based on fact."

"But if you met him, you were in England? So you were all Victorian and running around in London?"

"I spent very little time in London. It was an appalling city, and I only went there because Mr. Wilde confessed—but never mind. Yes, I am Dracula, I was Dracula before the book; I will be, I hope, after that damned book is forgotten by the world." He cast his eyes heavenward. "At the least, I pray that one day it goes out of print and ceases to plague me everywhere I go."

"Pray? Wait, I thought you couldn't get near crosses? This doesn't make sense."

No, what doesn't make sense is why a young woman like yourself would go so far out of her way to follow a complete stranger who could be a maniac to his mansion," he countered. "I told you to go home."

"I can't," she told him. "I got evicted. My roommate stopped paying rent—!" she gasped in realization. "I gotta text Heather!"

Dracula—she *supposed* she could call him that—arched an eyebrow at her.

"I... hang on, I need my phone." She leaped to her feet. He mimicked the motion and threw out a hand to stop her. Before she knew what was happening, Dracula had hold of her arm. She thought he was trying to stop her before she realized she had almost fallen right on her face.

"Please take care," he said. "Please, sit until you've recovered." He then held out her phone. She snatched it and slumped back onto the divan to text her roommate.

Heather! You okay? I know I'm late. Can't talk right now. Where r u?

She held the phone in her hands, staring down at the screen. The sound of a tea kettle whistling drew Dracula's attention. "One moment," he said. He went to an adjacent room and returned several minutes later with a beautiful tea set on a silver or pewter tray. The cups looked like real china, beautiful white and blue, with gold around the rims and the handles. He poured her a cup of aromatic, red-brown tea.

"Cream or sugar?" he offered.

"Um, wow," she said. "You went all out."

"I don't see why I shouldn't," he answered. She nodded at the sugar bowl, and he put two lumps in her cup. The tea smelled absolutely marvelous. She noticed tea leaves swirling around at the bottom of her cup. That was a first for her. To her surprise, he poured a cup for himself.

"Wait a minute, can you—?"

He was already sipping tea. Apparently he could.

"What are you, some sort of vegetarian vampire?"

"I beg your pardon?" he asked, sounding confused.

"You know, all reformed and avoiding human blood and all that?"

"I drink human blood," he answered, very matter-of-factly. Cammy stared at him.

"Uh, *what?*"

"Who are you trying to contact?" he asked, as though they had been discussing the weather or the latest show they'd gotten bored of.

"You drink human blood?"

He set his cup down in its saucer and glared at her.

"Couldn't you... I dunno, drink animal blood instead?"

"Indeed I could, but it is not the same. If I hunted animals, I would need a great many of them, and I would have to kill them. If I could easily survive on animal blood, that would have made my experiences enormously less difficult." He took another sip. "But I would have had to take an occupation as a butcher." He shook his head. "Like a *peasant*. No."

She stared at him.

"Now tell me about Heather." He gestured that she speak.

"Heather is my roommate. I was supposed to meet her at a coffee shop since we got evicted."

"Hmm. I recall you telling me that you had lost your residence. What happened?"

Cammy snorted and rubbed her thumb over her phone screen. "Heather stopped paying rent, apparently. I didn't know. Anyway, I guess we were behind. I came home today and boom, no more home."

"But you were going to meet her?"

"Yeah, that's why I was using Green4Life," Cammy said. "She's used them a few times." A thought occurred to her. "Hey, do you think vampires are using that rideshare service as a way to get ahold of people to eat? That couldn't work, could it? They'd get caught."

"I know nothing of that service," Dracula said, "but I suppose they might be. These last few days I have encountered a surprising number of vampires. Even so, twenty of them out in the open is enormously strange. I haven't seen numbers like that outside of wartime."

"You mean the group that tried to... to eat me?" Cammy asked, and he nodded. Cammy looked down at her phone. No reply. Angry, she called Heather.

Hi! It's Heather, if you know me, just text me...

"Are you kidding?!" Cammy snapped. She waited until the message ended. "Heather, I am *not* playing around. Call me back, ASAP."

"Something amiss?" Dracula inquired.

"Yeah, Heather's acting weird," Cammy said. "She wasn't texting earlier, then she was, and she told me to meet her, and now she's not answering." A horrible thought occurred to her. "You don't think they got her, do you?"

"She seemed strange when she texted you?" Dracula asked.

"Yeah, she seemed... I don't know. Rude, I guess. It wasn't really like her." Cammy felt her heart in her throat. Dracula poured himself another cup of tea.

"It seems likely that they did, and she was trying to lure you into their trap," he said, and sipped the tea. She stared at him. Not a whisper of compassion on his face. He might as well have said he saw it was going to rain

"Heather's fine," Cammy snapped. "She's probably just high or something."

"I suppose that is also possible," he said. Same nothing expression, same nothing emotion. Cammy swirled the tea in her cup angrily.

"She's got, you know, a 'substance abuse problem,' as they like to call it. She's been drinking beer and smoking weed ever since high school, and her parents were always on her about that. Sophomore year she started going for other stuff. Cocaine on and off. She's been to rehab, and we're all trying to support her but...anyway, I think she must have picked it up again, because apparently she hasn't been paying the rent for months."

"I see," he said. "So she might be seeking drugs somewhere?"

"I mean, maybe, yeah. I hope so. Wow, I just said I hope she's looking for drugs."

"Do you have a picture of her? I have hunted down several groups of these maggots, and some of their victims. I hope I have not seen her amongst them, but if so I may be able to recognize her. If not, should I uncover more, I shall look for her."

"Thank you." Cammy flipped through her photos and held out her phone. He took it and frowned at the photograph.

"I do not recall seeing her," he said. "Hmm. Someone named Lindsey wants to know 'what's up.'"

"Oh, crap!" Cammy took back the phone. Some of her friends had finally texted her, wondering what had happened and where she was. "Everyone went to see this movie trilogy. The third one premiered at midnight, and the theatre showed them all back to back. Hang on, I'll just let them know I'm okay now."

"Hmm."

He poured another cup of tea and watched her, hawk-like, while she texted her friends she was all right. The look bothered her. Like she was a lab specimen and he was studying her. Before she managed a message to Melissa, her phone screen faded to terrifying, ominous black.

"Oh snap! No!"

"Something the matter?"

"My phone's dead. Crap! I need to charge it."

"I'll retrieve whatever you need," Dracula said when she rose again.

"My charger was in my bag. It's on the floor over there somewhere."

He glanced at the mess on the floor. Undaunted, he made his way over and searched through her things, coming back with the chargers for both her tablet and her phone, and her tangled earbuds.

"Thanks, I just need to plug this in...." She glanced around the room. The wallpaper had flower-like designs, the wood trim was elaborate, highly stylized. There were lamps sticking out of the walls, but they weren't lit, only the fireplace gave any light. Disconcertingly, there were also weird-looking animal skeletons displayed in antique cases. Cammy swallowed.

"Allow me," Dracula offered. She let him take the phone and her tablet. He took them with him to what she assumed was the kitchen, the room where he'd made the tea.

She had her head in her hands when he returned.

"It is quite late. Do you have a place to stay now that you've lost your apartment? I can drive you there," he offered. She blinked up at him.

"You'd give me a lift? Even though I know who you are and after everything I've seen? What about keeping vampires or the Masquerade or whatever a secret?"

"I very much doubt one young woman preaching to the world about the existence of vampires will undo hundreds of years' worth of conspiracy," he answered. "On the contrary, it is humans who want monsters to stay out of sight. More than simply out of sight."

"Wait, so there *is* this whole Masquerade thing going on, but it's not you guys trying to hide and rule us from the shadows? It's something else going on?"

"I don't doubt that most of the monsters that still live are in hiding, but humans are the ones who benefit from the state of affairs more than monsters."

"Oh," said Cammy, not understanding. "Is that why you weren't very careful about not letting me see stuff? You don't care?"

"I assumed you were intelligent enough to know better than to report to the authorities that you suspected you had been attacked by a pack of vampires," he responded.

"Well," she mumbled, thinking of Brian. He was just a baby cop, but she felt pretty sure he wouldn't believe any of this. "Yeah, I guess."

"Then I didn't have to bother. Even if you had, I doubt anything would have come of it, short of a report of some young woman who had taken leave of her senses. You are hardly the first person I've met who has pierced this fragile veil that separates monsters from humans."

"What if the cops come across all those bodies, though?" Cammy wondered.

"They won't. I told my *employers* the location. They'll have cleaned all of that up by now."

"You talked about your employers before. Who do *you* work for?"

Dracula smirked.

"I think it would be better if I don't drag you into that quagmire. But perhaps you can puzzle it out on your own. In any case, where will you stay now? With your parents, perhaps?"

Cammy didn't crinkle her nose, even though she wanted to. "No, I was going to swing by my friends' apartment and see if I could crash there for a while. I don't know what I'm going to do now. I have to find Heather first, but I can't afford rent all on my own, and all my friends already have roommates or live with their parents, so it would be a real inconvenience if I just moved in with one of them. But I think I can stay with someone for a while."

Dracula poured her more tea and refilled his own cup.

"This might be presumptuous, but as I treated you rather badly when you arrived, I feel compelled to make amends. If you like, you may stay here for a time rather than burden your friends."

"Uh..." She bugged her eyes at him. He looked at her, unmoved. "What?" she asked.

"You may stay here for a time as my guest," he explained. "I have room enough, and you can have a key to your own chamber if you are concerned about my intentions."

She hadn't been, but she was now. Did he mean blood-sucking, or the other thing?

"I don't know," she said. She didn't. She had just met a vampire from Europe somewhere, living right here in Seattle. Apparently vampires were real. She noticed one of the specimen skeletons looked like a small, winged squirrel of some sort. So probably other things, too. But ignoring all that, wasn't Dracula supposed to be a bad guy? A monster in real life and in fiction? She thought she'd heard that he was some sort of famous historical psychopath. She looked him up and down. He didn't *look* like a psychopath, but what would a psychopath look like? Brian was always saying you couldn't tell by appearances. Serial killers were charming, weren't they? Well-dressed and presentable, just like this guy was, in his immaculate black suit, sipping tea in front of a huge, gothic fireplace.

"Didn't you used to kill people?" she asked.

"*Used to?*" he repeated. "Hmm. I suppose it's been a while. When did you mean?"

"Whenever you were in Transylvania."

"I was hardly ever in Transylvania in the way that you mean." He pronounced it the way she expected some Eastern European to: "Trahn-seel-vahn-nya." "But yes, I killed people. When necessary."

"So when did you become a vampire?"

"That is an excellent question. I am not entirely certain," he replied. "Sometime after my death, but when and how I cannot say."

"Huh? How? I mean, why is that so hard to figure out? Wouldn't that have been obvious?"

"You might think so, but no, it wasn't. I became aware again and found myself in Turkey. But it seems to me I must have been walking about for some time before that, though I cannot say how long."

"But you did kill people. Lots of people?"

"More than some of my contemporaries, perhaps, though we weren't comparing numbers. If you are worried that I plan to put you on a stake, I have no intention of doing anything of the sort." He grinned maliciously. "Unless you plan on robbing me."

"Uh…" That seemed like a joke in very poor taste.

"I don't think you are a thief," he assured, though she didn't feel very reassured. "You are concerned with being a burden to your friends. That shows some character, and that you are no parasite. You seem brave, besides."

"Brave?" That was the sort of compliment she could get behind.

"Yes. Naïve and foolhardy, but it took courage to track me down. That reminds me, how *did* you come up the road?

There are things in the woods all around my estate that kill intruders."

Cammy felt lightheaded. So when she'd felt she was being watched...!

"Never mind," he said, "never mind. I'll speak to them. You look like you need rest. Do you wish to stay or go?"

"I..." What did she want to do? She had come all the way out here to find out more about how the world actually had vampires in it. She had hoped to convince the homeowner to train her in the ways of the secret world. Like a movie or something. But *this* wasn't really what she was expecting. Still, vampires were real, and she had been rescued by the most famous, most powerful one of them all.

I guess that means I could still learn about what's really going on, she thought, but could she trust this guy? If he had been a regular person, instead of a vampire *and* a famous historical psycho, the choice would have been easy. Well, she supposed if he had been a regular human he might still be a murderer or something. It had just never crossed her mind that a human vampire slayer could be dangerous to humans. A vampire hunter would be working to protect humanity from the creatures of the night. Here was a creature of the night hunting the others because some mysterious people *told* him to.

"Who do you work for?" she asked him again.

"Truly, it may be dangerous for you to pry too deeply," he replied.

"I can't stay here unless I know why you do what you do," she told him.

He grinned wryly. "I have extended an invitation. You needn't accept it if you do not wish to."

He stared into her soul, so she averted her eyes.

But I kind of want to, she thought. She looked around the room. All the antique furniture, the paintings, there were even a few weapons mounted on the wall, now that her eyes were accustomed to the dark. Could she really pass up an opportunity like this? This was better than winning the lottery by miles, wasn't it? No one got a chance to interview a vampire. She giggled at that.

"Okay, thanks," she told him. "I really appreciate it. But just for a little while, until I get another place to stay, and find my roommate."

"Of course." He nodded magnanimously, as though he were conferring a favor by agreeing.

"And maybe you could tell me more about what the world's really like?" she suggested.

"Perhaps you don't really wish to know," he said; then as her face fell, he amended, "Or perhaps you do. But in stages, I think. There is a great deal to know, and you have just survived a very trying ordeal."

When he said that, it all hit her. The feeling of those cold hands on her, the slack-jawed heads all over the ground, her absolute helplessness. She gasped and started to ugly-cry. She didn't want to, but she couldn't stop. Her shoulders trembled, her hands shook all over again, and she couldn't get her breath.

Dracula—and she couldn't get over how weird that was—offered her a handkerchief. It wasn't the one he'd used to wipe the pepper spray off his face with, thankfully. He went to the kitchen while she tried plugging up her stupid tear ducts and blowing her nose.

"Here," he offered her a glass with some sort of clear liquid, just enough to cover the bottom with a centimeter. She guessed it was alcohol of some sort.

"Thanks, but I'm not old enough to drink just yet. Three weeks, though."

He frowned.

"Your birthday is on April 30th?" he asked.

"Yeah."

"Mmm," he said, "*Sankt Walpurgisnacht,*" and his frown deepened. Before she could ask what that meant, he shook off the expression and said, "Go ahead, I won't tell anyone," and gestured at the glass.

She snort-giggled. The whole situation was absurd. She took the glass and sipped at it. It burned. Whatever it was, it was strong, but she liked it.

"Wow!" she coughed. "What is this?"

"*Țuica.* Traditionally offered to guests. I brew my own. Something to keep me busy."

"That's some good moonshine," she agreed.

"Moonshine," he repeated unhappily under his breath.

He helped her to pick up her things, seemingly unperturbed by the tampons she snatched and hid as fast as she could. She hoped that wasn't going to be awkward later, if he really drank blood.

He led her to the enormous staircase, which had elaborately carved pillars as thick as both her arms together supporting a bannister polished so smooth it seemed to glow in the firelight. At the top of the stairs was nothing but gloom and dark shapes, as the firelight couldn't manage to reach that high.

"You know, we have this thing called electricity now," she told him. Without a word, he reached out to the wall and flicked on a light switch. The glass lamps that lined the walls all flickered and took on a warm, dim yellow glow, suffusing the place with an effect like steady candlelight—inviting, and not so bright it burned her eyes.

"For some time, yes," he agreed.

"Sorry," she said. "I just... it was so dark up here...."

"I don't need lights," he explained. "I don't often use them."

"Then why have them?" Cammy wondered.

"For guests," he explained.

"You have guests?!"

"On occasion," he said. "Come." He gestured that she follow him up the stairs.

He showed her to a beautiful room with a real four-poster bed, antique lamps with fringes, and a dresser of polished, dark wood. Everything was spotless and dust-free. Maybe he had servants? There was no way he could keep this whole place clean all on his own.

"This is amazing!" she gasped.

"I have not run the water taps in this wing for some time, so I advise against drawing a bath for the moment. Once you retire I shall do my best to clear them so that they will be ready by tomorrow. There is the wash room." He indicated the end of the hallway. "It is a bit late for a proper tour tonight, but should you need to find your way, there is a lamp beside the bed, and the way to the kitchen is just down the stairs past the foyer. If you should see anyone about who is not me, don't speak to them or interact with them in any way. Will there be anything that you require for the evening?"

"Yeah. Thank you. I have work tomorrow, but I don't have a ride," she confessed. "Is it all right if one of my friends picks me up here? Also, who else lives here?"

He frowned, looking positively menacing. She stepped back in consternation.

"I think it would be unwise to have your friends here. I can convey you to work; what time do you need to arrive? And no other humans. Servants of mine, whom I expect you will meet in due course."

"I work during the day, I don't think—"

"That is no trouble. What time?"

She raised her eyebrows. "You can go out during the day?"

He drew in a breath and let it out in an old-grumpy-dog sigh.

"Yes, I can."

"You don't burst into flames in sunlight?"

"No," he said.

"What about other vampires?" Cammy wondered. Was he special, or was everyone wrong about everything?

"Most of them cannot be awake or away from their graves past dawn, but that doesn't mean they catch fire in the sun's rays. Some do, but that is a new phenomenon."

"Oh. Well, I'm supposed to be at work by eight. I hope I'm better by then; I need the money so bad. I'm still shaky."

"That will pass, but please take the time you need to rest," he said. "I must also warn you not to wander the grounds outside without me. There are things that live in the wilderness that I would not trust with your safety or your life."

"Like what?" Cammy gulped.

"Several things. Wood-wives for one, and satyrs for another. Some other things."

"What's a wood-wife?"

"Heaven above, girl. Do you want to get any sleep or not?"

"Honestly, I don't know if I can. I mean, I watched like twenty people die tonight."

"They didn't die tonight. They died some time ago."

"But they looked like people, and weren't they people? I mean, before? And when you killed them, they still looked like people. And..." Was there anything else she could say? Anything else she could say to *him?* Did he even understand human emotions? She sniffed and blinked at the wall.

"Good night," he said. "Given when you must be at your place of work, we will need to make an early start. It will likely take longer than an hour to drive there." He held out an old-fashioned key for her to take.

"Yeah, thanks. Good night." She took the key. It was heavy and old-fashioned, and it would go really well on her keychain, or on a necklace. She liked the necklace idea better.

I'm so stupid, she thought to herself.

He departed, closing the door behind him. Cammy dumped her things on top of the dresser in an untidy heap. Then she looked down at herself. For the first time, it occurred to her that despite all the head-lopping that had gone on, there hadn't been blood spattering all over the place. Her clothes were damp from drizzle and sweat, but they weren't covered with gore. *Thank goodness.* She rifled through the pile to find some clothes that were clean and more or less dry that she could sleep in.

The bed was like nothing she'd ever encountered. It was huge, and very, very soft. She sank right into it like it was a giant dog bed. Why were those always softer and better than human beds? Someone ought to look into that. The mattress was so warm, and the blankets were so heavy. It was like being inside a giant, toasty sandwich, or an egg, or a hug. She fell asleep almost instantly.

CHAPTER 3

GUEST AND HOST

Brian Warren had totally forgotten he'd left his phone on silent. He was ending his shift when he checked and saw the number of messages.

"What the...?"

"What's the matter, girlfriend miss you?" asked Hendricks.

"No... looks like—hang on." He tapped on the first voicemail, from his sister.

"Hey, BB. Turn your phone on! Has Cammy been blowing your phone too? Something happened with her and Heather and she's on the street right now! I can't get out there. Please, please tell me you can."

He scrolled down. The voicemails from Cammy were hours old, so were the texts. That was *bad* news.

"What's the matter, Rookie?" someone behind him asked. Sounded like Gold.

He ignored the comment and dialed Cammy. The phone rang, no answer. He dialed Heather. Same thing. He dialed Melissa.

"Did you find out what's going on with Cammy?" his sister demanded.

"No. Are you still at work? Did you get a chance to talk to her?"

"No. And yes, I'm still here. It's been crazy since last night. I can't leave. I don't know if anyone else went to get her, either. She said no one else was answering."

"I just got off the clock. I'm heading straight there."

"Let me know how she is, okay? That girl is too cute for her own good."

Brian hung up.

"I gotta bail," he told Hendricks. "I gotta go pick someone up. She might be in some trouble."

"Ooh, '*she*'?" Hendricks teased. "This 'she' someone you're thinking of impressing with your uniform and your—"

"See you." Brian slapped Hendricks' shoulder and headed out of the locker room. Cammy's Shoreline apartment wasn't far away. He considered biking over, but if something had happened.... With Suze's help, he managed to convince the dispatch officer to let him take a cruiser, just in case.

Cammy was not home when he arrived, so he knocked at doors until he got the landlord's number. Leaning against the entrance door, its handle warped from some hooligan kicking it, he punched in the numbers.

"Hello, is this Mr. Knox?" he asked.

"Yes. Who is calling?"

"My name is Officer Brian Warren with Seattle PD. Do you have a moment to talk to me?"

Dead silence on the line. *You monster*, Brian thought.

"Certainly," Knox eventually answered. "What about?"

"Are you on the premises of Great Ways Apartments at the moment, Mr. Knox?"

Another span of silence.

"Yes."

"Would you mind coming down to meet me?"

Knox agreed. When he came out the worn front door, the old man smiled politely.

"Something the matter, Officer?" Knox asked, grinning like a snake. He looked Brian over, obviously noting that he was out of uniform.

"I'm off-duty right now. But I need to know why you evicted two of your tenants last night, a Camellia Lilly and Heather Blake."

"Who?" Knox said.

"Two young women who have lived here for almost a year," Brian reminded him. "A petite girl with curly black hair and another with light brown hair? In their early twenties."

"Oh, them," Knox grumbled. "They didn't pay. I sent notices, they didn't pay. I moved their stuff to the street. The one girl, dark-haired one, she asked me why, said she didn't know about the problem. Wanted an extension."

"Do you realize that you turned two young women on the street with nowhere to go?" Brian seethed.

"They didn't pay."

Brian racked his brain. It was probably illegal somehow, but he didn't remember what laws applied off the top of his head. He would go look it up later, but first he had to find Cammy.

"Did you see where she went?" he asked Knox.

"She got in a car and left," Knox said with a shrug. "Don't know about the other one. Haven't seen her for a few days."

That meant Heather was probably using again. Cammy must have gotten a ride from someone, but Brian didn't have all the numbers for the rest of her friends.

"When was this?"

"I don't know, very late. I was going to call the police to get her off the property. No pay, no stay, that's what I say."

"Thank you for your time," he told Knox, wanting to punch his teeth out. The old man only had half of them; he probably wouldn't miss the rest.

He called Melissa again.

"Hey, BB, did you find her?"

"No. The landlord said she got in a car."

"Did he say where she went?"

"No. Do you have Kenzie's or one of her other friends' numbers? Cammy might have met up with one of them."

"I don't think so. Let me check. Why don't you try her cell again?"

Brian did, got no answer, then got Kenzie's number via text. She might be up; she worked at that same coffee shop, and they sometimes had workers in before dawn.

"Hello?" Kenzie answered in a theatrical, sing-song voice.

"Hello, is this Kenzie? My name is Brian, I'm one of Cammy's friends."

"Oh, hey. I've heard of you. What's up?"

"Did Cammy meet up with you last night?"

"No, but she texted me that she found a place to stay, so we didn't have to freak out."

DRACULA'S GUEST

Brian checked. He had missed the message. That's what he got for panicking and jumping to conclusions, he supposed.

"Oh, I got one, too. Sorry to bother you. If she gets in touch with you, will you tell her to let me know?"

"Sure thing. Bye."

Brian stared at his phone. She had texted that she was all right, but he wasn't convinced. Something could have happened; someone else might have used her phone, or forced her to send that text. He dialed again.

"Come on, pick up," he grumbled.

* * *

She didn't dream; very odd for her. Soft, pale light coaxed her out of her deep slumber. She pushed her head out from under the covers. Her heart leaped in her chest when she couldn't recognize her surroundings and she jumped out of the bed. As she spun around, searching unthinking for an exit, she remembered that she had escaped the pale people last night, come to a mansion halfway up a mountain, and met a guy who called himself Dracula. And she was staying at his house.

She sat back on the bed and took stock of the situation. It had all happened, and she was staying in a mansion. Remembering Heather was missing, she looked at the nightstand for her phone, but it wasn't there. She checked her bag next before she remembered it was charging downstairs in the kitchen.

After throwing on some leggings and her shoes, Cammy timidly opened the door. She hadn't even locked it last night, but it didn't seem like anyone or anything had bothered her. Was that too trusting of her? She didn't know.

Cammy had not realized there was no toilet paper until it was too late. Luckily, for some reason she still hadn't kicked the habit of taking tissues with her everywhere like her mother kept telling her to and had chosen to hang her bag within reaching distance on the bathroom doorknob last night, but she did wonder why there didn't seem to be any toilet paper *anywhere* in the bathroom.

Maybe he doesn't go to the bathroom? she wondered. He drank tea, though. It had to go somewhere, right?

She'd have to replace most of her toiletries. She hadn't managed to salvage them all. Another check on her bank account made her heart sink. Conditioner, or food? Ugh.

She decided against a bath in favor of finding her host and asking about Heather. The hallway was dark except for the faint glow of early morning light that managed to find its way in through the windows at the end of the hall and by the stairway. The mansion sounded abandoned; there was no radio, no sounds of people moving around, nothing. Silent as a proverbial tomb. A chill ran up and down her spine.

There was no sign of her host when she descended the stairs or when she went to the kitchen. She found her phone resting on a counter, next to an old-fashioned taupe-colored phone with the dial you had to turn with your finger. Her phone showed 6:45, which seemed right since the sun was only just up. Later than she had planned, but she ought to be able to get to work with time for breakfast. A cast-iron stove stood in the corner on the other side of a double-hung door with a window for its upper half.

DRACULA'S GUEST

Her friends had texted her back, and she saw that Brian had called a few times.

"Crap." She called him back.

"Cammy! Are you all right? What happened last night?" he shouted by way of a greeting.

"I got evicted," Cammy explained. "I never got a notice. Heather stopped paying the rent, I don't know when. I haven't been able to get a hold of her." The blood rushed in her head. Brian was a cop. She could tell him to look for Heather, and he'd have the whole precinct out looking, but if Heather had been kidnapped by vampires, would the cops be any use against them? Thinking that, she glanced up and saw Dracula standing in the doorway, watching her. She gasped and jumped.

"You all right?" Brian asked.

"Yeah, I just," she glared at her host, "I was just startled. Anyway, she hasn't gotten back to me since last night. I don't know where she is."

"I'll look for Heather," Brian told her. "I know some places. Where are you? Are you safe? Did you have to go to your parents?"

Cammy chuckled and covered her eyes. Despite all that had happened, she could be grateful that she hadn't had to call them for help.

"No. I'm staying with a new..." she studied her host, who still watched her, his hands folded over each other, "friend," she finished. "I'm sorry if I worried you. I was just scared."

"I'm glad to hear you're all right. I'm sorry I missed your calls. My phone was on silent, and I had a lot of—"

"That's all right," she assured him. "I know you're busy. It all worked out, though."

She knew that wouldn't make him much happier, but she couldn't think of anything else to say.

"Okay. Well, so long as you're all right."

"I am. Thanks for worrying about me. Bye." Once she had hung up she looked up at Dracula. "Give me some sort of warning next time! You scared me right outta my skin!"

"My apologies. I am not accustomed to having guests at this hour. I shall make efforts to announce my approach in the future. Did you sleep well?"

"Yeah, like the dead." Cammy caught her breath when she said that. She searched his face for any sign that he was angry. At least he wasn't offended. Wait, "at this hour"? So he had guests at *other* hours? There was a story there...

"I imagine you're hungry," he said.

"You have no idea. Do you have cereal?" she asked, feeling a little silly asking whether Dracula had cereal, then giggling when she realized he sort of already *did*.

"No. I never picked up that habit," he answered. "I cannot bring myself to eat food that lunatics refused unless they had no other choice. I have eggs, bread, pork—"

"Eggs and toast are fine. I'm a vegetarian actually, so no meat, please. Thanks."

He fetched eggs and half a loaf of bread from what Cammy assumed must be the pantry.

"I can cook them, thanks." She looked around the room and set her eyes on the cast-iron stove. She'd never actually seen one in real life before. As she approached, she felt heat coming off the entire surface, all the way down to the feet.

"I lit it earlier this morning so it would be warm," he explained, then gestured to the rag tied around the oven door handle. She supposed it was there so she wouldn't burn herself. There was a cast-iron skillet set on the range.

"You know, I've heard you can do some really great things cooking with these, but I never thought I'd get to use one," she said. "How long have you had this place, if you don't mind me asking?"

"About a century," he answered.

"And you didn't update anything?" She glanced at the old-fashioned phone. Did that actually work? Who would even call him? Did he have friends?

"After breakfast, I can show you around the grounds," Dracula told her. "If there is time, I shall introduce you to some of my servants and tenants."

"Tenants? You're a landlord?" She was trying to figure out how to cook the eggs on the skillet. It didn't look non-stick, and she didn't see any olive oil or coconut oil anywhere. At last, she spotted a block of butter sitting on the table, a silver butter knife beside it. Reluctantly, she glopped some into the skillet and set it on the stove.

"Any monster that has come to me seeking asylum," he said, "and who can cohabitate peacefully with the others and with me, I regard as a tenant, not a guest. They perform certain services in exchange for a place to live."

"Sounds like serfs," Cammy grumped, with a vague memory of some history class or other. He *was* old fashioned....

"No, they can come and go as they please. However, it is my land. They must abide by my rules if they wish to live on it. They must not interfere with any guests who comes onto the property, they must not go out to hunt humans and bring them here, or draw unnecessary attention to me or their fellows, or fight amongst themselves. Or steal from me."

She was starting to think he took stealing somewhat personally.

"So you're like a half-way house for other vampires?" Cammy asked. He raised an eyebrow at her again.

"I don't have any vampires dwelling here with me. Well, nothing that you would call such. I presume you mean European nobility who suck blood and are undead horrors?" His voice had gone flat, with an edge to it.

"Uh... yeah. Are there any other kind?"

"Yes, many. What I just described is a very recent breed. I can count on one hand the number I know who match that description, none much older than two centuries."

"Well," she considered whether it was wise to say, '*but aren't **you** blood-sucking European nobility?*' Probably best to hold off on that. Maybe it was a touchy subject. On the other hand....

"Like who?" she ventured.

"Sir Henry Irving, for one."

"Who?"

For some reason, he seemed amused she didn't recognize the name. He said, "Also Countess Elga, and both Count Saint-Germains, who were the same person after all. I have heard rumors that Lord Byron might have come back after his untimely end, but have seen no evidence. The same holds true for Lady Widow Nádasdy—that is, Countess Erzsébet Báthory. Elizabeth Bathory, I believe she's called in English."

"Oh! She's the one who bathed in young girls' blood to keep her youth, right?" Cammy said. When he seemed surprised that she recognized that name, she explained. "One of my friends is a horror fan. She's also read about serial killers. She said that's what Bathory did. Is that right? Is that how she became a vampire?"

"I wasn't interested in her actions, as I was busy helping Mihai Viteazul—Michael the Brave."

"Was he a vampire too?"

"*No.*"

She detected profound annoyance in his voice at the question, even anger. He sure looked angry at being asked that. *Lots of counts,* she thought to herself. Maybe Stoker had been onto something with that after all.

The eggs were crisping on the outside, so she looked around for a spatula, found one hanging on the wall and fetched it. Before she had to go searching for a plate, he opened a cabinet and procured a delicate china plate for her.

"Thanks. That's beautiful!" she told him, admiring the dainty floral print that rimmed the ceramic—no, porcelain? She couldn't say; it wasn't as though she ate off of fancy dinnerware every day. Even her parents had nothing this fine at home. He said nothing. "Did you get this when you were in England?"

"No. While in Ireland," he told her.

"You were in Ireland?" she asked, sliding the eggs onto the plate. Now she had to find a toaster, but look as she might, she didn't see one. Oh well. She set the slices of bread on the plate along with the eggs.

"I've been in many places," he told her.

"Hey, do you have a coffee maker?" she asked. He pressed his lips together.

"I do not drink coffee. I do have tea, however."

"That'll work," she conceded, disappointed. She thought, *You're supposed to say, "I don't drink... **coffee**"*, but didn't say so. She watched him set an ornate pewter tea kettle on the stove. With nothing to do but wait, she seated herself at the table in the middle of the kitchen to eat. He took the seat opposite her.

"Are you having anything?" she asked him.

"Thank you no, I already ate," he said.

"So you eat breakfast? I mean, real food? Not... you know?" she asked him in between mouthfuls.

"Yes, I eat food," he told her.

She wanted to ask more about that. A vampire that ate and drank like anyone else, and here he was with the sun up and no problems. He'd said he drank blood, but she felt doubtful now. In fact, she was starting to doubt he was really a vampire at all. Maybe this was all some sort of test to see if she was gullible? He was just a human vampire hunter after all, playing some sort of elaborate prank on her, or maybe testing her to see if she could figure out when he was lying to prove her knowledge or something.

"You know, I'm confused. I mean, you eat and drink, and you're all right in sunlight, and I've heard you sigh, but I thought vampires were supposed to be dead? I mean, do you breathe?"

"I breathe, but I don't need to," he replied.

"Huh? Why?"

He shrugged. "Habit, I suppose. Some of the Polish vampires respire, so perhaps that's why." He folded his fingers together self-consciously.

That was weird. It was almost as though he were embarrassed.

"But you drink blood too?"

"When I have to," he said.

"Which is when?" she wondered.

"On occasion. More frequently if I exert myself or don't eat well."

"So you have to kill people if you get really hangry?" Cammy asked, dubious but also horrified at the possibility.

"I can get by on a mouthful at a time if I do not exert myself," he corrected, still angry. Maybe even angrier than before.

She tried to wrap her head around that. If he was telling the truth, he was unlike any vampire she had ever heard of.

"So... garlic?" she asked.

"I find it repellent."

"How about crosses? Are those repellant too?"

"Crosses? No."

"So where did the whole idea that crosses bother vampires come from, then?" she asked.

"From Stoker. And that was crucifixes, not crosses."

"There's a difference?"

"I take it you are neither Orthodox nor Catholic?"

She shook her head. He nodded.

"Are you?" she wondered doubtfully.

"Yes."

"Which?"

"I was excommunicated from the Orthodox faith when I converted to Catholicism, but that conversion was to secure a politically advantageous marriage."

"So you're Catholic???" Cammy boggled.

"Officially, yes," he said, "but I prefer to attend Orthodox services, although I do not participate in their sacraments."

"You go to *church?*" she nearly shouted. "You can go *into* churches?"

"Some strigoi can do as much," he said, "some cannot. There is an enormous variation within that breed."

"What's a, a strigoi? Like that show, *The Strain?*"

"What is that?"

Cammy had no idea how to explain that she had binge-watched the series with her friend Kenzie a few Halloweens prior. Heck, would it be insulting to say she watched vampire shows sometimes? That her friend Lindsey adored vampire romances even though she didn't like to admit it? Surely that would be insulting to him, if everything that everyone knew about vampires was wrong.

"It's just some show I watched. About vampires," she sheepishly confessed. He didn't react.

"Strigoi is the word that best describes what I am," he explained. "They are the native 'vampires' found where I come from. 'Vampire' is a very broad term. It includes creatures ranging from pennagals to maras to alps."

"What are those?"

"I don't think it wise to begin on that topic at the moment. But I would like to show you a little of the estate," he said. "We should leave shortly if you have any hope of being at your place of work on time, and focus on the things you should know immediately if you are to stay here."

"It's going to take a while to explain all that, huh?" she asked.

He nodded. "There are thousands of types of vampires."

Thousands? Cammy was thunder-struck. *Thousands. Hoo boy.*

"So how does anyone learn how to deal with vampires if they are all completely different?"

"There are differences, but there are also general categories into which they tend to fall. Some are incorporeal, some are corpses, some are demons, and so forth. Some drink blood, some steal energy, some require more esoteric sustenance. It would take a great deal of time to explain everything."

The kettle whistled, so he rose to get it. He set it to one side of the stove, scooped some loose tea leaves into a china pot, then poured the steaming water over the tea. Taking up the pot and two cups and saucers on a tray, he set them on the table. She noticed that this tea set was different from the one of last night. This one matched the plate she was using.

"Let that steep for a few minutes," he told her.

"So you said you had servants?" Cammy prompted him. No choice but to wait on the rest.

"Yes, a few," he told her. "The main one is a domovoy who has a wife and children."

"A domovoy?" Cammy repeated.

"A Slavic creature," Dracula told her. "Most of the time they are invisible, but you might see them if you have the talent, or if they suffer a lapse in concentration. He will appear like a very hairy old man without clothing."

"Uh...." Cammy did not like the idea of a creepy, naked old man walking around the mansion invisibly.

"There are also a few brownies, though I can't imagine where they came from. They are small, humanoid, and unclothed as well. You likely won't see them either, but if you do, I would ask that you not offer them any clothing or gifts."

"Wait, like in *Harry Potter*? They're house elves?" Cammy speculated.

Dracula frowned at her as he poured them each a cup of tea.

"It's a book series. And movies," she explained.

"I see," he said, dubiously. "I have heard versions of the story about brownies helping the shoemaker in which the creatures are referred to as 'elves'. Perhaps that's why you know them as such."

"You don't get out much, I guess?" she checked.

"Not anymore," he said, "no." There it was again. The implication that he had been more active once upon a time.

"And you don't know what phone apps are, either."

He looked at her over the rim of his cup as he drank.

"Hey, after the tour, and when I get back from work, I can teach you something about the modern world, then," she suggested with a smile. "We'll teach each other."

"Hmm." He set down his cup of tea. "I would be very grateful, thank you. It seems I have missed something in the last decade... or so."

Decade or so? Sheesh. Who could say how out of date he'd be by this point? The eggs and bread were gone—she'd been hungrier than she realized. Eager to learn more, she tried to chug the tea, but it was too hot.

"Did you find anything about Heather?" she asked him.

"No. I wished to see to your needs before setting out to find her."

"What about that guy's phone that you took? Did it have anything on it?"

DRACULA'S GUEST

She thought she saw his jaw tighten. It occurred to her that if he was out of date, he probably didn't know what to do with the new phones. She remembered him fumbling with it last night.

"Want me to look at it?" she suggested.

"Please," he said, and pulled the phone out of his pocket.

He had been carrying it this whole time? Or had he been waiting for a chance to ask her? She took the phone. It was powered off. She turned it on to find it was locked. Crap. She didn't know how to hack a phone, and she doubted they could ask Brian to do it, because there was bound to be vampire stuff going on here.

She had to figure this out, one way or the other. With no other ideas, she tried the most obvious unlocking pattern, a Z. When that didn't work, she tried it backwards, then on its side. Of all things, that did it.

"Ha!" She showed him.

"What did you do to make it respond?" he asked.

"I had to unlock it. Phones have passwords or patterns so strangers can't use them. We can look at his messages now."

"No, how did you get it to respond to your touch?" he asked. This set her back a moment.

"It's a touch screen, you just... touch it. Here." She held it out. "Tap on that icon, the one that looks like an envelope."

Hesitantly, Dracula tapped at the icon. Nothing happened. He tapped again, and got no response. He frowned, then tried tapping at the rest of the screen, to no effect. Even dragging his finger across it earned no response at all.

"Wow, you've got a bad case of zombie finger, huh? I get that sometimes, when it's cold or when my hands are really dry. You could dry blowing on them..." It occurred to her what she had just said.

"The new phones detect something about your skin?" he checked.

"I think so. Electrical signals or something like that." This was no good. He might not be able to use new phones at all. Not without a stylus. It occurred to her that the driver last night had used one. That must mean that other vampires had trouble with the new technology. Something to remember in the future. But first.... She opened the messages. The two most recent were outgoing.

On my way.

Got her. B there soon.

Cammy's blood ran cold. The driver had been sent to get her. But why? Dracula read the messages over her shoulder.

"Call your friend again," he told her.

"What's going on?" Cammy asked, and her fingers tingled. Her hands began to shake.

"Call your friend again," he repeated. Cammy pulled up Heather's name.

Hi! It's Heather...

"Heather! Pick up!" Cammy shouted into the phone when the message ended. No one picked up. Out of the corner of her eye she saw Dracula watching her, but he didn't say anything. He didn't even try to comfort her.

"You think Heather is dead already, don't you?" she said accusingly.

"I am reserving judgement at the moment. It is possible that she ran into the same group, but it is also possible, as you have said, that she is looking for drugs or working an odd shift."

"You really think so?" Cammy said hopefully.

"I just admitted to not thinking much at all about the situation," he corrected. "At the moment, anything is possible. However," he looked into her eyes, "if you should see your friend again, I wouldn't trust her."

"No," Cammy shook her head. "No, no, no."

He pulled out his flip phone and dialed. She wondered if he was calling his mysterious employers.

"Hello, Malcolm," he said into the phone. "Have you been hunting any of the brazen new-breed vampires that have been popping up around the city? No? Have you heard anything about them? I see. I don't suppose you've heard anything about an, I believe the word is app, called Green4Life? I don't know; some sort of taxi service." He looked out one of the windows. "When do you expect to be here? That's fine. I'll be out, probably in the vineyards. Good bye."

"Who was that?" Cammy asked.

"A comrade of mine," said Dracula. "I have worked with him in the past. Malcolm Marrock. I called him last night about you tracking your phone."

"Oh. You don't work for him?" Cammy checked.

"No. He and I find ourselves in similar positions, though his is less complicated than mine."

"Why is yours complicated?" Cammy asked.

"That will be difficult to explain in its entirety. Before we get bogged down in that, I would like to show you some of the grounds so you don't get lost or worse."

Worse? she wondered. He kept saying there were dangerous things around. Was she really ready to see any of them? *Maybe they'll all be invisible like his servants*, she thought to herself, which did *not* make her feel any better.

But it wasn't going to do her any good worrying, and the sooner she learned about them, the better off she'd be, right? She'd know how to survive. *Survive*. That had a whole new meaning now. Not "survive until the next paycheck" or "survive finals," but "survive in a world full of monsters." It made her shiver, but she didn't want to turn back. She knew what the ordinary world was like. There hadn't been monsters, but it had been a purgatory full of drowning in financial trouble and no hope of a future that mattered. If she learned how to fight back here, she might actually be able to accomplish something.

Cammy finished her tea, except for the bottom with the leaves.

"Hey, do you read tea leaves?" she asked. One of the regulars at the Mindful Bean said it was something she did.

"I was never interested in divination," Dracula said.

Oh, well.

"One more house rule: please be tidy. My domovoy will get very angry if the residents do not do their part." He pointed towards the sink.

"What will he do if he gets mad?" Cammy whispered, terrified.

"He will stop protecting the house," Dracula answered. "He is easily appeased, but he is also easily angered. If you should forget something, please correct it as soon as you remember."

Oh. That didn't sound so bad. She had been worried the invisible, hairy, naked man might kill her or something.

"All right."

Dracula—she still felt weird calling him that—led her out the door she had entered the previous night. He stepped out into the daylight, sure enough, and nothing happened to him. He didn't even squint.

"This is the back door," he told her. "As it happened, you took the road my friends use, and it confused some of my guardians. Your approach was also so haphazard that they doubted you posed a credible threat."

"What friends?" Cammy wondered. *Also, what guardians?*

"Some of my countrymen, among others."

So he had friends. That surprised her. Now that the sun was out, she could see that there was a gravel driveway that led around one side of the house. On the other side the driveway turned into dirt, forming a clearing in the trees.

"As I said last night, there are many creatures that live on my lands," Dracula explained. "Those who have come to me seeking asylum."

"Asylum?"

"Safety and a place to call home. Many have been driven out of their native lands, or have been hunted."

"By humans?" Cammy asked.

"Mostly by my employers."

"Who... are not humans?"

"They are human. And they are most dedicated to eradicating everything that isn't. Ah." He had led her to an old-fashioned well, with a wheel and a bucket and everything. "There is a spirit who lives in this well. Do not look into its depths; she may drag you down and drown you."

"Uh..." said Cammy. This was sounding like a worse idea all the time.

"You can draw water from this well," Dracula explained, as though it should reassure her. "Simply do not look into it."

"Okayyyyy," Cammy said.

"There are wood-wives, rusalki, and vili who make their home in the woods," Dracula continued, leading her beyond the well towards the trees. "They are somewhat similar. They look like human women, and an untrained eye wouldn't be able to tell that they are not. If you see any women out in the woods, return at once. Don't talk to them or try to engage with them at all. Since you are female, they may not bother you, but it doesn't hurt to be cautious."

"Everything that lives here is dangerous, huh?" They came to a stone wall with a wooden gate. He opened the gate and gestured she go before him. It would have seemed charmingly polite except that she wasn't sure there weren't killer monsters on the other side. Hesitantly, she stepped through and saw what looked like miles of vineyard.

"Whoa," she said.

"Not everything that lives here is dangerous," he told her, "though a many are. The nymphs are harmless."

"Nymphs?"

"They also look like human women."

"How helpful," she said.

"You probably won't see them. Much of the supernatural has grown quite shy over the centuries." He pointed at a shady patch of earth beside the corner of the house. Cammy spotted a patch of watermelons growing under the shade of the oak that tickled the eaves above.

"Don't eat those. They are vampires."

"*Vampire watermelons?*" Cammy sputtered. "Wha? How? Do they suck blood?"

"By and large they only harass my cows. But they move sometimes on their own, and bleed if struck hard enough."

"How in the world are there vampire watermelons?" Cammy demanded.

"Sometimes, if they are left out in the moonlight, pumpkins or watermelons can become vampires. But I suspect these became such because that is where I often pour out water with my blood in it."

"Water with... does that happen a lot?"

"If I'm wounded. I think it less risky than to pour it down the drain."

"Your blood turns things into vampires?"

"It can. I must warn you never to come into contact with it."

Good to know, Cammy thought. "You have cows?"

"And chickens. And sheep and pigs. The milk, eggs, and so forth in the kitchen will almost always be fresh."

"Nice," she said, and followed him out towards a fence that separated the vineyard from the house.

"I grow my own grapes and make wine here, especially with the help—"

He stopped as a man carrying a basket stepped out of the rows of grapes. No, not a man. He looked like a hairy man with a full beard, but he had little goat horns, and goat legs.

"Oh, a satyr!" Cammy said, amazed. So it was all true. She had been fighting with the little nagging doubts that she was just fooling herself, or that her host was simply leading her on. Now she knew. Everything she had thought she knew about the world was wrong. The satyr stared at her, surprised, then looked to Dracula, then back to her.

"This is Cammy. She will be staying here as my *guest*," Dracula told him. Cammy wondered about the emphasis he put on the word 'guest.' "Go, tell the others."

The satyr bowed his head and slunk off, following the wall. He cast a glance over his shoulder at Cammy.

"No one wears clothes around here, do they?" Cammy observed.

"Not many," Dracula confirmed. "Do not come out here alone when they are working, do you understand?"

"What, satyrs will try to kill me too?" Cammy wondered.

"No. They might try to rape you."

Cammy stared at his face. Not even the tiniest hint of a smile.

"That's not funny," she told him.

"I wasn't trying to be. If they see women, they can be unpredictable. So long as I am present they will leave you alone. If I am not, I can't say what they might or might not do."

"You have *rapists* living on your property?" Cammy demanded. She could maybe deal with some of them killing people, they were monsters after all, but... rapists?

"That's sick," she told him. "Why would you keep them here?"

"They know wine, and they have nowhere else to go. To be honest, I was surprised that there were any still alive. I had thought them extinct hundreds of years ago. They are nature spirits of some sort, and not well-adapted to farm life or dwelling close to humans."

"I wonder why," Cammy remarked dryly.

"You might not believe it, but they are actually very well-meaning," Dracula told her.

"You're defending them?!" Cammy demanded.

"They are not human," Dracula told her. "They do not think like humans. They are very child-like in many respects, and only interested in pursuing pleasure. They... do not actually understand what they are doing. That is why I warn you to avoid them. They do not understand that what is pleasurable for them may be be unpleasant to others. It is their nature to seek out the nymphs who reciprocate their attentions. As I said, they are creatures of myth, not humans. They ought not to live near humans."

"They don't understand that they're rapists?"

"No. They don't. In the same way that children do not understand how cruel they can be to each other."

Cammy crossed her arms. This did not sit well at all.

"Are there a lot of monsters here that rape people?"

"On my property? No. Just the satyrs. And it has not been a problem before, as I have either been present to monitor them whenever anyone has come up here before, or sent them away to gambol in the wilderness. However, you will be taking up residence here, and I may not be present at all times, so I wish for you to be cautious."

"And you approve of what they do?"

"Approval has nothing to do with it. They are what they are. As are we all. They are not malicious, nor are they treacherous. They have been hunted nearly to extinction and cannot survive by hiding as others can. So long as they abide by my rules while they live here, they have a safe haven."

A safe haven for rapists and monsters that kill people, Cammy thought to herself. This was a mistake.

"Well, I don't know how comfortable I am staying here if you've got a bunch of monsters that want to rape me," she told him, crossing her arms.

"You do not have to stay if you don't wish to," he told her.

"Wow, you really don't get it, do you? I bet you've never had to worry about what it's like for someone like me."

He narrowed his eyes at her.

"You mean to say that because I am male I don't know what it means to fear being raped?" he asked her.

"Obviously."

His eyes narrowed more, his jaw tightened. Finally, he looked away.

"It's a shame my brother is dead, or else you could tell him that. I wonder what he would have to say in response."

"What does your brother have to do with anything?"

"You don't have to be female to be preyed on sexually," he told her. He seemed angry, though he didn't raise his voice. He just spoke through his teeth.

An old-fashioned ringtone drew her attention, and Dracula pulled his flip phone from his jacket.

"We are near the vineyard," he said into his phone. "Come around." To her, he said, "You presume a great deal." He added nothing more, and gestured she go before him back the way they had come.

"You have a brother?" she asked. He glanced over his shoulder at her, clearly still angry.

"*Had*. Several, in fact."

"They're all dead?"

"Humans are not in the habit of living for centuries, but that hardly matters as most of my family were killed."

Dracula's Guest

"By you?"

He glared. "No," he said, and turned away. They went back through the gate as a cherry-red car pulled around the side of the house, making its way towards them. It stopped, and the door popped open. A man in his late twenties or early thirties stepped out, dressed in a leather jacket and expensive, high-top shoes. His jet black hair was styled. Stubble sprinkled his jaw. He had hazel-yellow eyes and bronze skin. He smiled at them. His teeth were dazzling white. He looked like a male model on his way to a photo shoot.

"Hey, Vlad," he said, then pulled a small cooler and a manila folder out of his car. "Hey, hoping you could do me a solid," he said, and walked over. Dracula took the cooler hesitantly, glancing at Cammy before he accepted the folder. Malcolm held out a hand for Cammy to take.

"Hey. Malcolm Marrock, of the Order of Ophois. Who are you with?" he asked. He had a smile to melt the heart of any romantic he flashed it at.

"Hi. I'm Cammy. Who am I with?" Come to think of it, Dracula had wanted to know who she worked for, too.

"Yeah. Which Order or whatever," Malcolm said, his smile losing its shine.

"Cammy is here as my guest," Dracula told him. Malcolm raised his eyebrows, then looked Cammy up and down.

"She's a little young for you, isn't she?" he said.

"Don't be crass," Dracula told him. "She only found out about what the world is really like last night, and she needed a safe haven. And I would never bring a one night stand up here."

Malcolm's eyes widened. He looked Cammy up and down once more.

"Are you *serious*?" He looked from one of them to the other, then clutched his head. "Vlad, are you messing with me? Tell me you're messing with me."

"I am not," said Dracula.

"This is not happening! What is she doing here?" Malcolm demanded.

"Um, *she* came here all on her own last night," Cammy told him. "Because I wanted to learn about vampires and stuff."

Malcolm's eyebrows knotted together. "You wanted to learn about vampires and stuff?" he repeated. "Are you crazy? You don't want to be involved in *any* of this insanity. Trust me on that."

"Well, I think I can make my own decisions, thank you very much" Cammy told him.

"Okay, sure. Has he been giving you the grand tour? You liking it so far?" Malcolm asked her, pointing at the vineyard. "Met anyone you didn't like yet?"

She couldn't argue with him there. Of everything she'd heard about so far, the satyrs disgusted her the most. Malcolm must have seen something in her expression, because he nodded enthusiastically.

"Yeah, you think *they're* bad, just wait 'til his bosses hear about you."

The mysterious *employers* again.

"Why? Who are they? What will they do?"

"In reverse order? Bury you, or feed you to something so they can study the whole process. And they're your government, by the way. Who else could keep a lid on this whole mess? You are in *way* over your head."

Cammy looked to Dracula. He looked back, his face unmoved, unsympathetic, and offering absolutely no reassurance.

"You work for the government?" Cammy asked him.

"Yes. Unofficially, of course. And I wouldn't say 'work,' myself."

"What *would* you say?"

Dracula turned to Malcolm.

"What do you call it?" he asked.

"Free, undocumented labor is what I call it," Malcolm answered. Dracula returned his attention to Cammy.

"There you are. Though that is more diplomatic than I would have put it."

Cammy tried to make sense of the situation. The government? *The* government? Men in black suits trying to keep the supernatural hidden. That didn't seem right. She had assumed it was a bunch of people in hoods and robes, not city council members. Or the CIA. Or the president. Was that even possible? Everyone who got sworn in got told, "Hey, so there's vampires"? That was secrecy on a level she hadn't thought possible. Okay, so she knew people who thought the government was secretly poisoning people, but not hiding vampires and other monsters. What sort of resources would they have to have for that to even be possible? She shook her head. It didn't seem possible.

"Wait, so you *both* work for the government?" That was even more absurd.

"Not him," Dracula corrected. "He works for the Order of Ophois. An occult order founded a few hundred years ago. I happen to be a member of a religious order of knights. Very different order." He showed her a heavy ring he wore on one finger. It was worn almost as bald as an old tire, but she could see an impression like a dragon with a tree or a cross or something on its back. "The Order of the Dragon. Whence I take my name. The order has been repurposed since the 1500s, when it officially ceased to exist. It no longer consists of crusaders fending off the Muslim invasion, and instead defends humanity against the forces of darkness."

"Crusaders?" Cammy asked.

"A very prestigious Crusader Order," Dracula clarified, sounding downright proud, even managing to glow with satisfaction.

"Yeah, you're so proud of that you'll keep that name no matter what, huh?" Malcolm said.

"It was my name first," Dracula growled.

"Your own people don't even call you that anymore," Malcolm pointed out. This earned an ugly glower.

"Thank you for coming all this way," Dracula said, coldly. "If you wouldn't mind, my young guest is worried that her roommate might be in danger. Would you keep an ear out for any word?"

Malcolm tucked his hands under his armpits, but he nodded at Cammy. She pulled out her phone and showed him a picture.

"Her name is Heather Blake. I'm not sure how long she's been missing. We worked different schedules, so I sometimes don't see her for days. She told me about this rideshare service, Green4Life, but when I took them, they were a bunch of vampires."

"Whoa, whoa, whoa, hang on. A bunch of vampires were running a rideshare service?" Malcolm repeated. "Vampire Uber? That can't be right."

"It is a large group. There were twenty-two last night, but I have killed well over sixty so far," Dracula told him. "I've never seen anything like these numbers."

"Over *sixty*?" Malcolm repeated. "And they're using a rideshare to, what, find victims? No, no, no. That can't be right. It makes no sense. They'd get caught, traced."

"It seems the driver alerted others that he was bringing Cammy to them. We haven't learned more than that yet," Dracula told him. Malcolm frowned, chewed his lip.

"Who'd you piss off?" Malcolm asked Cammy.

"What? No one!" she said.

"Doesn't figure that a bunch of vampires would want to pick you up unless there was something personal," Malcolm said.

"Well, I don't know any vampires." She eyed Dracula. "Except him, I guess. I don't know why they wanted me."

"Maybe your roommate told them about you," Malcolm suggested. Cammy glared at him.

"Heather wouldn't do that. Why would she do that? How in the world could she even tell a bunch of vampires what to do?"

Malcolm shrugged.

"Motive is everything," he said. "Tryin' to work out the math."

"Well, you suck at math, then," she told him. Malcolm ignored her comment.

"Tell me more about these guys?" he asked Dracula.

"They're one of the 'Hollywood' types, as you call them."

"Describe them," Malcolm said.

"They can't bear sunlight, they kill every time they feed, and a single bite turns a human," Dracula told him. "Crosses, crucifixes, and garlic do not trouble them. I think these were all thralls. They can be killed by staking or beheading. Do both; some are wildcards."

Malcolm scratched his temple. "That's pretty generic for the modern ones," he said. "Well, if I hear anything, I'll let you know. Though now that you mention it, I've been picking up on some chatter. But you know how it is with monsters. They don't like to talk to me. You've probably heard more than I have."

So Malcolm must be one of the humans who hunted monsters, then. Cammy hadn't been certain before whether he was another vampire.

"I've heard another moot has been called, but I haven't yet heard the location or the time," Dracula told him.

"So there *is* something going down." Malcolm punctuated this by pointing down with one finger.

"Perhaps. A moot doesn't necessarily mean anything specific has arisen, or that anything will be accomplished. Monsters are not so different from humans in that respect. But if I hear anything more you will be the first to know."

At this, Malcolm laid a finger across his lips and nodded.

"Much obliged," he said.

Something about this conversation bothered her. Dracula had been trying to keep her in the loop, but now neither of them were bothering to include her, and it was possible Malcolm's gesture had been some sort of secret sign these hunters used.

"What's a moot?" she asked.

Dracula's Guest

"A meeting called by non-humans," Dracula told her. "It has become much harder to hold them, for reasons that I assume are apparent."

Cammy eyed Malcolm. If moots were for non-humans, then why tell him?

"Are you a vampire too?" she asked. This was driving her nuts.

Malcolm's mouth cracked into a grin and he guffawed.

"Oh, wow. I am not used to people this fresh," he said. "No. I'm one of Ophois' frontliners, and I am what you would call a werewolf."

"Werewolves are real?" Cammy said, then she felt stupid for asking. Why *shouldn't* werewolves be real? "Hang on, what do you mean, what *I* would call a werewolf?"

"You've seen he isn't all capes and fangs and Hungarian accent, right?" Malcolm asked, thumbing at Dracula. "Same thing here. I'm old school, not one of the Hollywood werewolves."

"Well, what are you like?"

"Think more berserker or bloodthirsty doggo and less moon-powered mutant furry," he said.

That didn't sound terribly werewolf-like to Cammy, but then Dracula wasn't very vampire-like so far as she could tell, so it shouldn't surprise her.

"So Hollywood got everything wrong," she said.

"Sure, and now we're stuck with their garbage," Malcolm said, and to Dracula, "Which kind of vampire do you prefer?"

"The modern ones. They are much weaker and less capable than the traditional ones."

Malcolm made a face, and Cammy wondered how tough Dracula must be if he thought modern vampires were 'weak'.

"Well, that's not so true for werewolves. The modern ones are way tougher than I am," he turned back to Cammy, "I'll see what I can do about your friend," Malcolm told her, "but you should seriously reconsider becoming a part of all this. For your own good."

"Thanks," Cammy told him, crossing her arms. Dracula had started flipping through the folder. He closed it and held it out to Malcolm.

"I don't deal with empusas. Get a priest or something."

"We don't work with priests," said Malcolm.

"And I can't fight it. Find someone else."

Malcolm sighed and took back the folder.

"Can't you broker some sort of talk for us? This thing might run rampant."

"That is not my concern," Dracula told him. "But since you've asked, I'll make a call."

Malcolm nodded, returned to his vehicle, and drove off.

"He came all the way up here just for that?" Cammy asked, once his car had gone around the mansion.

"I imagine he, like me, likes the excuse now and again," Dracula said.

The excuse to do what? she wondered. "What's an empusa?"

"A kind of vampire."

No duh! she thought. She eyed the cooler.

"What's in that?"

"It would seem Malcolm is hoping I can broker some sort of agreement between my religious order and his occult one. No doubt he will be rewarded if he should succeed."

"You've got some weird friends," Cammy told him. "So your religious guys will work with his guys?"

"I do not think it prudent to delve into how the different groups interact with one another at this moment. Excuse me, I must put these away," he told her, returning to the mansion. Cammy followed behind. She wasn't about to be left alone outside with monsters that wanted to rape her. It seemed he didn't want to talk about the cooler, so she decided to wait just inside the doorway while he dealt with it.

She wondered what was in it. She supposed the obvious answer was blood, but it seemed strange he'd want to be secretive about something that obvious. Maybe it was something worse? Since he didn't want to talk about it, she let him walk deeper into the mansion and stayed by the kitchen door. She'd have to leave soon, anyway.

"Hey."

Once more, she almost jumped out of her skin. Malcolm stood just outside the doorway, grinning like an old friend.

"What is wrong with you? You scared me to death!" Cammy told him. "Why do you guys all sneak around like that?"

"I'm sorry for startling you," he said, "but I just remembered that I was supposed to get a gift. Some meat?"

Cammy looked over her shoulder, but Dracula hadn't returned.

"Oh, uh, all right? He's putting away the cooler you brought," she told him.

Malcolm continued to grin at her, clasping his hands together. That seemed weird.

"Oh, I wouldn't want to trouble him. Would you just go check in the kitchen? I'm sure there's something there."

"Some meat?" Cammy repeated.

He nodded enthusiastically. "And eggs."

"There's eggs for sure. He said he had some pork..." Cammy said. Malcolm made no move to enter. "Are you not allowed in?" she asked, wondering why he wouldn't be.

"I wouldn't want to impose," he said, "but do you think you could just find something for me? I'm sure it wouldn't be a problem."

Cammy moved to the kitchen, then she hesitated. Most of the monsters Dracula had told her about looked human or were invisible or naked, but this interaction seemed really odd. Malcolm hadn't returned with his car, for one, and his smile was different. It wasn't the smolder he'd flashed at her that first time, nor the hesitant one she'd seen after that. Was he asking her to steal food for him? Considering Dracula's apparent hatred for theft, could that be the reason he wanted her to do it for him?

"You know, I'd feel more comfortable waiting for him to come back," she said. Malcolm smiled harder and began to wring his hands.

"It's nothing to worry about," he assured her. "Just a little food. You won't get into any trouble."

"I'd still rather wait. I'm a guest, not a resident. It's not my stuff to give away."

Malcolm's smile faded. He looked disappointed.

"Oh, well, then—"

A gun suddenly pressed itself up against his ribs. Cammy saw that Dracula was standing outside, wielding the gun. He must have snuck outside and gone around.

"So many intruders," he said. "I really must talk to my tenants. Who are you? What are you doing here?"

Dracula's Guest

Malcolm tried to run, but Dracula caught him by the leather jacket and picked him off the ground.

"Whoever and whatever you are, you don't weigh much," Dracula observed. Cammy felt relieved. She had been worried what sort of frightening superhuman strength he must have to be able to do that to Malcolm. He said to her, "There is a stone on a cord around my neck. My hands are full. Would you mind looking through it at this intruder and telling me what you see?"

Cammy could not imagine why he asked her to do this, but she approached and, sure enough, there was a flat, round stone with a hole right in the middle hanging from his neck. Hesitantly, she took it and looked through the hole. Instead of Malcolm, she saw a small, furry animal that looked like a raccoon with long legs. Dracula had it by the skin of its shoulder.

"It's some kind of animal," she told him, confused.

"Come clean," he told it, "or I'll skin you alive."

"Whoa!" Cammy protested.

The animal wriggled helplessly and she let go of the stone. Apparently it had dropped the illusion altogether, because it now appeared as it had when seen through the hole in the stone.

"I apologize! I just wanted to have a bit of fun!" it said, still wriggling. "Please don't make me into soup!"

"It will be my servants who makes you into soup," Dracula told it. "What are you? Why are you here?"

Wow. There were monsters he didn't know about? She felt less bad about her ignorance, until it dawned on her that this might be the worst news yet. If a centuries-old maybe not really a vampire didn't know about everything, what chance did she have?

"I am a tanuki! I just wanted to play a little prank! I heard there was a safe haven here, and I'm looking for it! Please don't hurt me!"

"There is a place around here, but do you know the owner's reputation?" Dracula asked the tanuki. The little creature shook its head.

"No. Only that there is a place. My wife heard rumors from her sisters."

"I've never seen anything like you; how could your wife know about this place?"

As if in answer, a pair of foxes came skulking out of the brush and bowed. One was smaller than the other, and gray all over.

"Please excuse my husband, great lord," said the larger fox, "he does not know your reputation, else I am certain he would have minded himself better."

Dracula pulled the hammer on his revolver back rather than withdraw it.

"What are you doing?!" Cammy asked.

"If she knew about me, she should have told him."

"He said he was playing a prank! No harm, no foul, right?"

"This creature tried to make you an accomplice to theft while it wished to seek asylum from me. I do not appreciate being made a mockery."

"You're the one holding a gun to a talking raccoon!" Cammy told him. He turned to her.

"A talking raccoon that can change its appearance and impersonate others very convincingly," he corrected. "Do you know what else it is capable of?"

Cammy had no idea. She'd never seen an animal like it before, and certainly didn't know how it could shape-change, but.... "I mean, look at it. How dangerous could it be?"

"If you're asking a stupid question like that, then I agree with Malcolm; you should forget this entire venture and go back to your ordinary life," Dracula snapped. "*Everything* can be dangerous. Suppose it impersonated you? Or me? And asked you to follow it out into the woods only to order one of my tenants to tear you to pieces?"

Cammy watched the tiny, adorable fuzzball wriggle helplessly in the air, then studied Dracula's cold, unfeeling face. He was rude, that was certain, and the tanuki was incredibly cute, but she really *didn't* know what it was capable of. For that matter, she wasn't sure what her *host* was capable of. He had pulled a revolver on a raccoon, after all.

"Please have mercy, great lord, on my poor husband. It is in a tanuki's nature to play pranks. They are stupid and gluttonous and not worth much, but please show mercy," said the fox, inching closer. "As you have said, the fault is mine for not watching him more closely."

"You have a curiously dutiful wife," said Dracula, and he holstered the gun. Still holding the tanuki, he turned to the two foxes. "Where have you come from? And how did you manage to escape detection?"

"We are from Kyoto," the fox answered. "It became too difficult for us to continue living where we were, and my sisters have heard of your estate and of you, so we came seeking a new place to call home. We merely came through the woods last night, when the others were pleased to roam. I apologize that my husband has offended you so greatly."

"I have killed men for less offense." He regarded the tanuki. "However, if it is truly something in his nature, then I shall overlook it—only this once. You say your sisters told you of me? Who are your sisters? I don't know any talking or transforming foxes."

"They go about disguised as humans and live in the city. They heard of you by reputation from the Underground and praised you and your estate greatly."

"That's enough flattery. Speak plainly. Who are all of you, and why should I let you live here?"

Cammy thought he let monsters stay here out of the kindness of his heart. Apparently not.

"Great lord, my name is Aki, my husband is named Komamaki, and our daughter we call Ginko. I have come to this city to work, as my sisters have, amongst the humans. My husband is good at managing money."

"You said he was stupid earlier."

"Nevertheless, tanuki are known for their ability to manage money. We had hoped to provide service to the local creatures as a bank."

Cammy tried to wrap her head around the idea of a shape-changing fuzzball banker. The monster world continued to refuse to make a lick of sense.

"How do you interact with humans?" Dracula asked.

"Pranks only," said the fox. "Some trickery. Neither of us wish them any harm, though they have made living quite hard. We only require game to hunt, or else meat or eggs."

The tanuki made a small squeak noise that might have been an agreement.

"What abilities do you have?" Dracula asked then.

"Shape changing comprises the bulk," said the fox, "and speech. I can create false fire as well."

"Very well. You may stay here. If it is true that you can serve as a *banker*," Dracula said to the tanuki still caught by its scruff, "then I will entrust you with some of my money as well. There are but a few rules, but these must be followed absolutely. Do not bring humans here onto the property; do not kill humans on my property; do not steal from me or the others who live here; and do not fight with anything else that lives here if you can help it. If there is a dispute you cannot settle, come to me with it. Do nothing to draw attention to this place or put me or my tenants at risk. With regards to you in particular," he said to the tanuki, "do not play pranks on me, nor on my guests"—he gestured to Cammy. "If you can obey these rules, you may stay. If you agree to these terms and violate them, your punishment will be severe. Can and will you obey?"

"We can and we will, great lord," said the fox.

"Yes, absolutely!" agreed the tanuki. Dracula set it on the ground and it scurried towards the fox to hide behind it. The three animals bowed to him.

"What sort of accommodations do you require?" he asked them.

"Only a den, great lord."

"There is ample ground you can choose from, then," he told them. "Before you settle in, go seek out Dima, he should be working in the vineyards. Tell him that you have newly arrived; he will give you a bottle of wine if you wish it, and some food as well."

"You are most generous, great lord," said the fox. "We shall never forget your graciousness and hospitality."

Dracula nodded and the animals trotted off towards the vineyard.

"That's it?" Cammy asked.

"You were expecting more?"

"You just treat anyone who shows up really roughly and then turn sweet?"

Dracula eyed her.

"You think me a monster, and ungracious besides." He did not pose this as a question. "That I am cruel."

"Well, yeah, kinda," she admitted. "I mean, you threw me into a wall."

"I did no such thing. Had I thrown you into a wall your skull would have cracked to pieces. I threw you *towards* a wall."

"Well yeah, you *threw me towards a wall*," Cammy agreed. "That's a real relief. Also, you pulled a gun on a talking raccoon!"

"I am master here. I may treat with intruders as I wish. As you yourself have observed, a number of monsters are dangerous and not to be trusted. I have had intruders coming here intent on killing or capturing me or my tenants. Those creatures didn't announce themselves, and neither did you. Good manners would have earned all of you much warmer receptions."

"How in the world would I have announced myself?" Cammy demanded.

"You could have talked to me *before* putting your phone into my pocket."

"And you would have actually listened? I tried! You told me to go away."

"You had done nothing to demonstrate that talking with you further would be worth my time."

"You're a real charmer, you know that?"

"I've never claimed to be. But I might argue that depends on who you ask."

Cammy weighed the events as she had seen them. She still wanted to stay, but it looked like a worse idea all the time. Ignoring that there were incredibly dangerous creatures that lived all around, she still had no idea about her host outside of what she knew from pop culture, which seemed to be all wrong.

"Who would say something different?" Cammy asked. This seemed to take him by surprise.

"My friends, for a start," he said.

"So, Malcolm?"

"And others."

"Who?"

"I told you, some of my countrymen."

"More vampires?" Cammy pressed, and he clenched his teeth.

"No, humans."

"You invite them over for cards on weekends or something?"

He narrowed his eyes at her, his face suddenly frighteningly cold.

"Is it customary to speak so rudely to one's host these days?" he asked.

"Well," Cammy tried to think of what to say. "I mean, aren't you..." she couldn't just accuse him of being a mass murderer. If he was, he might not take it too well, and if he wasn't, it was a pretty low insult.

"Aren't I *what*?" he asked her, his tone blunt, unfriendly. He knew exactly what she insinuated.

"Well, are you?" she asked. He took a deep breath, rubbed his mouth, looked out over the trees in the direction of the city proper.

"I believe you have to go to work."

Before Cammy could say anything else, he turned away and crossed the pebble driveway. She followed him to a two-story brick outbuilding. Unlocking the enormous doors and swinging them open, he entered, and she came close enough to peek after him. Inside were about a dozen cars in models dating from modern all the way back to the Silent Film era.

"Whoa! Look at all these! What's this one?" She pointed at a silver-gray convertible sitting in the back most corner.

"A Duesenberg. I don't take it out very much anymore," he said.

"Oh, for real? It's so cool," Cammy lamented. Dracula eyed her, then the car.

"Well, I suppose it could do with some air," he said, sounding less cold. He walked around to the passenger side and opened the door for her. She crept forward, taking in the leather seats and the wooden paneling and all the little knobs in the dash.

"This is soooo cool," she said.

"I'm glad to hear it."

She carefully sat down and tried to make sense of the dials as he came around and took the driver's seat. He checked the dials and fiddled around with them before starting it up.

"Oh wow, listen to that," she said. He only nodded. He didn't pull out of the garage.

"Something wrong?"

"This car needs time for the engine to warm up," he said. "It will be ready soon."

Cammy listened to the engine rumbling. It didn't sound like a modern car at all. It sounded like a strange sort of growl, like a distant rockslide, or the growl of a giant cat. A little while later, he drove out onto the pebbles, stopped, got out, closed the garage, then returned to the car.

"They have electric doors now," she told him once he had returned, put the car in gear and started off.

"I know," he said.

Okay, so he knew about that, but not phone apps. He also had an old-fashioned phone. She had to figure out where the gaps in his knowledge were.

"Huh, I didn't see this road," she observed as they came around the mansion to the other side.

"That is the front door," he told her, indicating enormous double doors carved with a sort of Tiffany floral pattern, with huge iron bars crossed over them. They were beautiful. He drove them down the driveway away from the mansion.

She watched the trees whip by. The sun rose higher, but the cloud cover only grew thicker. The pebble driveway slowly gave way to dirt, then to a city road. He turned towards the city.

"I'm sorry if I offended you," she said. Probably a good idea not to piss off the vampire whose house you were staying at.

He grunted in answer.

"So," she considered her words. "I don't really know that much about...you?"

He glanced at her, but apparently did not feel like volunteering anything.

"I mean, I've heard you were a real person." She realized how stupid that sounded when she said it aloud. "I mean, not just the book," she clarified, which probably just made it worse.

This did not earn a response either.

"I mean, it's just that I heard...." Considering the responses, she wasn't sure how to proceed. "Are any of the stories about you true?" she asked instead.

"Which ones?" he asked.

Crap. She read the book in high school, just for English class, and apparently that was all wrong. She'd seen some movies, seen the character in cartoons and so forth, but did not know much about the man beyond "impaling psycho".

"About the impaling?" she asked.

"Everyone impaled their enemies back then," he answered. "The Turks especially. The moniker stuck to me, though. One of the voivodes who followed me was called *Țepeluș*. 'Little Impaler' in English."

Cammy tried to figure out if he was telling a joke, but he kept going.

"My son, Mihnea, tried to imitate me and was called *Răn*. 'The Bad' for your clarification."

"Oh." Better not to comment on that, she supposed. Also, he had a son?? "What happened to your son?" she asked.

"Sons. I had more than one. They met bad ends, like most of the rest of my family," he answered.

"Your whole family?" she asked.

"More or less. I inherited chaos; a lawless country and a pack of faithless, backstabbing vultures I had to make use of as allies, and more enemies than I could count. Yes, I was cruel, but it was to set all the crooked things straight if I could. It set things right for a time."

"So you survived all that bad stuff?"

"Me? Not at all. I was assassinated."

Cammy stared.

"You were?"

"Yes. I wasn't really surprised by it, to be honest, but I had hoped I might escape and fix an earlier mistake of mine. The greatest."

Cammy let that sink in.

"What was that like?" she asked.

"Being assassinated?"

"Yeah."

"It was delightful, I highly recommend it."

"What, really?"

"Of course not. I was stabbed in the back and beheaded. How do you think it was?"

"Sorry," she grumped. "I was just curious, I mean, if you *died*, you know..."

She saw him glance at her.

"I can't tell you about what happened *after*, if that's what you mean."

"Well, you became a vampire after."

"I was dead for quite some time, and pretty surprised to wake up later in one piece. But I do wish I had an answer for what happened in the interim. I would like to know..." he fell silent.

Whether there's a hereafter, or where you were supposed to end up? she wondered. Maybe both. The thought of a hereafter bothered her a bit. She wasn't what she would call religious.

"So, how did it happen?" she asked.

"What?"

"You... waking up later?"

"Ah. I have no answer, but I have my suspicions. I suppose one of my enemies might have had something to do with it, but I do not see how, or why. My return would not have been to their advantage. It's especially confusing given that the Catholics seemed to accept me."

"What do you mean?" Cammy asked.

"For my service to Christendom," he said, which meant nothing to Cammy. "Perhaps the Saxons did it."

"Saxons?"

He sighed.

"What do you know of my country, or its history?" he asked.

Cammy crossed her arms.

"Not much. Transylvania's in Eastern Europe?"

"I'm not... my country was called Wallachia. It is now part of a country called Romania."

"In Eastern Europe."

"What did you *learn* in school?" he demanded.

"The American school system isn't exactly known for being great," Cammy told him.

"It seems not. Very well, the long and short of it is that there were many different peoples who settled in Transylvania, including Saxons. For assorted reasons, they and I did not see eye to eye. They spread propaganda that I was a cruel, bloodthirsty monster."

"Oh!" Cammy said. "That's why everyone says you're a psychopath?"

She shut her mouth when she saw the look in his eye.

"Yes," he agreed at length. "The pamphlets they published were well-received by the rest of Europe. It seems that overnight they forgot that they had once liked me."

"They **liked** you?" Cammy said doubtfully. He nodded.

"More or less. I suppose had I succeeded I'd have been remembered as one of the crusading heroes you all seem to have forgotten about now."

"Crusading heroes? I thought the Crusades was all the Christians attacking Muslims and Jerusalem and stealing their lands?" she said.

They hadn't quite reached I-5, but he pulled over faster than was probably safe for his antique car and came to a complete, skidding stop. He turned to her.

"Don't ever let anyone tell you that," he growled. "If it was Christendom attacking them, then what were the Ottomans doing in Vienna twice, and attacking Venice, Spain and Portugal? And my country? Or barely a hundred miles from Paris? Why were they taking my people's children as slaves and soldiers for their war effort so that that pasty, demented *hog* could surround himself with them and protect himself from us and from his own people, who weren't exactly pleased with him until he paid his way into taking Constantinople? Why did they extort our wealth and youth in exchange for not doing to us what they'd done to Bulgaria and Serbia?"

This outburst had driven Cammy to press herself up against the door. This was way more than a touchy subject. There was something still pretty raw here.

"Sorry," she said, just to calm him down. She wasn't certain she really believed him, and she certainly didn't know who he seemed to be specifically referring to, but she was not about to argue with the angry vampire about something that touched a nerve so deeply, and about which she was completely ignorant.

He shook his head and pulled back onto the road. She fiddled with her fingers.

"Sorry," she repeated again.

"You are a product of your environment. I should have known better. My country and I have been marginalized, minimized, and mocked for long enough that I truly shouldn't find it surprising."

That sounded more like the root of the problem. She knew next to nothing about Transylvania, or Wallachia, whatever that was, or Romania, or even him. Nothing about Romania had ever come up in class, so far as she could remember. She couldn't even place the country, or countries, on a map without looking them up on a phone first.

"We didn't really learn anything about you or your country in school," she confessed.

"I know that," he told her like he was lying about how bad a meal she had just served to spare her feelings.

"So tell me about it?" she suggested. He actually looked at her this time.

"Are you truly interested?" he asked.

"Yeah. Tell me," she said.

His eyes stared straight into hers. Then he turned back to the road.

"It is the most beautiful country I have ever seen," he said.

"Really?"

"Really."

"Why are you living in Seattle, then?"

"It wasn't my idea, I can tell you that."

"Whose idea was it?"

"My employers."

Why did the government want him so badly? She wanted to ask but decided to stay on topic.

"Why don't you go back?"

"I've been back several times over the years." He seemed to relax a little. "None of my visits seem to have done anyone much good. And I had reasons to leave each time. Anyone who knows me knows that is the place I would prefer to be most in the world, so they know to keep an eye out in case I return again."

"When were you there last?"

"1885. Bucureşti was being called 'the Paris of the East' in those days."

"Why didn't you stay?"

"I was married at the time and my wife was not ready to make that move. I thought I would simply wait until she had passed and then return."

"Wait, you were married?"

"I've been married several times. Though in the case of that particular arrangement it had more to do with the fact that I had trouble navigating what you would call the 'Victorian Era' as a bachelor, else I would not have entered into it. She also knew what I was, which was advantageous."

"How did she know about you? When did you guys go underground?" As much as she wanted to know about her host, she also wanted to know why and when it happened that everyone agreed that the things that go bump in the night don't exist even though they apparently did.

"She ran into some trouble with the Good People—that is, fairies." He fell silent for a moment and glanced out the window. He seemed satisfied they were still the only car on the road and continued. "Certain mutual acquaintances pointed her in my direction and I helped her out of the trouble. And, as civilized society had decided for some time that vampires were all the rage, it wasn't very difficult for her to acclimate to the idea."

We're still obsessed with vampires, Cammy thought.

"Fairies? Was this when you were in Ireland?"

"Yes."

"So was she pretty?" Cammy asked. He eyed her.

"You mean to ask if I loved her?" he prompted. Cammy hadn't meant to be that obvious, but apparently she'd failed. "I cared for her," he answered. "She wasn't as tedious as the other women of the time, and the arrangement stopped some of the whispering about my Bohemian associates, or at least about my relationship with them."

"So you didn't love her?"

"Not in the way you mean."

Dracula's Guest

"You don't know how I mean it," she asserted grumpily.

"You mean was I head over heels, eyes full of stars amazed at her beauty and her wit?" he said. When he saw he was right, "No. It was a mutually beneficial arrangement. She was too old and too standoffish for the locals to like her, and as I said, my bachelorhood was interfering with my work and my reputation."

"What happened to her?"

He tapped the wheel.

"She died."

Well, duh. It sounded like a boring little blip in his life from the way he described it. Maybe he didn't care much about it.

"Was that the way it was with your other wives?" she asked.

"You are aware I was born in the 1400s?" he said. "As a prince."

"Oh. You mean all your marriages were arranged?"

"Political," he corrected. "Practical."

"How did this whole 'monsters aren't real' thing happen?" she asked.

"It was a long, drawn out process," he answered, "and much of it happened while I was... dead. There had been movements in Western Europe and Asia that I hadn't heard about until the Vatican recruited me. The fact is that human beings had been living alongside or in the shadow of many eerie things since... I suppose since they left the Garden, and for most of human history they thought it simply natural. Eventually some of them decided it might be in humanity's best interest to do something about that arrangement. Secret societies were formed, active hunts were started, alliances were forged with creatures who were willing to collaborate, all that sort of thing. As some of these groups gained traction eradicating, subjugating, or recruiting these creatures, they attracted the attention of people in power. To be honest, it was really just like the politics you see anywhere else; the only reason this proved so successful is because the monsters were never very numerous or well organized, even back when they roamed around freely. I only saw a handful of what you would call vampires during my lifetime."

"Maybe they were the reason you're now...?"

"No. I had them dug up and killed easily enough to get them to stop preying on their families. Back then everyone knew how to deal with strigoi, so it was hardly more tragic than the usual hardships life brought. If someone in your family died and then visited you at night demanding food or sitting on you to suck your blood, everyone knew what to do put a stop to it."

"Is that why you impaled people? They were vampires?" Cammy asked, hoping she had cracked the secret at last. He shot her a look.

"No. Of course not. Contrary to popular belief, my country is *not* overrun with vampires. If anything, *yours* is. And that, probably, because you people can't seem to get enough of them."

Her heart sank. She really wanted him to not be a psychopath, if for no other reason than she did not want to wake up with him sucking her blood.

"You said earlier that everyone did it, but that you were cruel?"

"I was."

"How about now?"

He laughed, which did nothing to ease her concerns.

"Circumstances have changed. I don't impale anybody. I haven't for centuries. There hasn't been any need, and as I said, I only did it when necessary."

"So that's all behind you? You did it because you thought you had to, but if you could go back you'd be less cruel and do things differently?"

"Do things differently?" he repeated, then, "Oh, yes absolutely." He looked straight into her eyes. "I'd be *far crueler*."

CHAPTER 4

ARRESTING BEHAVIOR

Cammy sat silently for the duration of the most intense and terrifying drive she had ever taken. *Far crueler.* Yikes.

"Um, I'm going to have to tell my friends *something* about you," Cammy said, as they drew close to the Mindful Bean. "It doesn't have to be true, but just so they aren't worried."

"Just tell them you met a wealthy older man who is letting you stay at his mansion," he told her. She guessed he might be teasing, but maybe he wasn't. It was hard to tell because his very rare smiles sometimes looked so malicious. Most of the time his mouth didn't even twitch, it was just that little smirk that sometimes lit his eyes that gave away whether he might be amused.

"Can I just say that, like, you know my dad, or you're distant friends with him?"

"If you like," he said. "With any luck, none of them will ask me about your father."

"You want to *meet* my friends?" Cammy said, surprised.

"I rather think they will want to meet *me*," he responded. That was probably true. There was no way she could get away with just talking about staying with a family friend without at least a few of them wanting to check him out at least once.

Maybe this is a bad idea? No, she refused to accept that, despite her nagging doubts. No one got these kinds of opportunities in real life. Certainly never more than once. She had to take this and make it work somehow. What were her options otherwise? College loans and everlasting debt with no job prospects and no idea what to do with her life? Besides, it looked like vampire hunting got you some sweet rides, even if they were probably killing the earth with every mile.

Well, I don't have to get a car like this, she told herself. She wasn't sure she wanted a car anyway.

As they drove, she noticed the people in other cars staring with amazement at their sweet ride. She waved at some Asian American kids whose mouths dropped open *wow* at the sight from the backseat of a car passing by. They waved back.

As they pulled into the Mindful Bean's parking lot, Cammy noticed a patrol car parked outside, and Brian standing at the front door.

Oh no. She didn't know if she could deal with this right now. It took Brian a moment to recognize her, given how he sized the Duesenberg up with obvious admiration.

"Cammy?" he asked, amazed. She tried to smile.

"Hi," she said, "I'm sorry for freaking you out. I was just scared and I didn't know what to do and no one was picking up...."

Brian set his sunglasses up on top of his short-cropped brown hair. He had really bulked up since becoming a cop, but you couldn't quite see that through his hoodie.

"What happened? Is Heather okay? How did you get a ride in *this*?" he asked, stepping off the sidewalk and approaching the car. Dracula took that moment to get out and come around towards the grill.

"Oh, uh," Cammy's mind went blank. She should have thought of a name. Like John, or George, something. But John Dracula sounded so stupid. Something else. No. Just use the first name.

"Hello there, you must be Brian," Dracula greeted with a smile, extending a hand, "Cammy's friend."

"Officer Brian Warren," Brian corrected pointedly. He took Dracula's hand and shook it, confused and very suspicious.

"Brian, uh, this is—"

"Vladislav Dracula," he said before she could finish. Cammy stared at him. He couldn't use that name, could he? No one was going to take him seriously. Slack-jawed, she turned back to Brian, to see him frowning.

"One more time?" Brian asked, disbelief making one of his eyes squint.

"Vladislav Dracula. Vlad to my friends, please."

"Are you serious?" Brian looked to Cammy. "Is he serious?"

"Yup!" Cammy agreed helplessly. The cat was out of the bag now.

"You must have been teased about that in school a lot, huh?" Brian asked, surly.

"The book has made things very difficult for me. And the play. And the film," Dracula agreed, then amended, "Films. But it was the name I inherited. I see no reason to take another."

Brian looked Dracula up and down, then the car, then turned once more to Cammy.

"And you know this guy how?"

"Oh, uh, well—"

"We met only last night," Dracula asserted, "during—"

"Excuse me, Mr. *Dracula*—" Brian interrupted.

"Doctor, actually," Dracula corrected with a smile that was just a touch malicious.

"Oh, you're a doctor too?"

"Yes. As I was explaining, I had the privilege of making Miss Lilly's acquaintance only last night."

"And..?"

"I came to her aid," Dracula was reaching into his coat. He pulled out a black wallet with a gold logo on the front. He flipped it open for Brian to look at.

"You're FBI?" Brian asked, more incredulous than ever. Cammy studied the ID Dracula had just flashed. It looked official. That didn't make sense. He couldn't really work for the FBI, could he? Unless the FBI investigated vampire murders?

Maybe they do? But no, that seemed wrong. Was that why he didn't want to talk about his employers? But if he really didn't, why'd he flash the ID?

"As an officer of the law, you might understand why I am not at liberty to discuss the full extent of the circumstances under which I came to meet Miss Lilly," Dracula said, still smiling that faintly malicious grin. This could not be the best way to explain things. It was like he was begging to have Brian find him out.

"Uh, it was no big deal, really. Just some muggers," Cammy answered. Brian whirled on her.

"You got mugged?!" he shouted.

"No! Almost. Uh, Vlad stopped them. It was really...cool."

"Are you okay, Cammy? Should you even be working today?"

"You're not my mother, Brian," she snapped at him. "I can decide whether or not I want to go to work. Well, actually I can't, because I need money, but even if that wasn't true, I can still make that decision!"

As if to emphasize this, at that very moment Kenzie poked her freshly dyed, turquoise-blue head out the door of the coffee shop to yell at Cammy. "Hey! You gotta get your butt in here! Luna's gonna be here any minute and if you're not clocked in she is going to pitch a fit!" Kenzie squinted through her black-rimmed glasses at the two men. It looked to Cammy like she had a new stud in her lip.

"Sorry, I'll be right in," Cammy assured her.

"Hi, you must be Kenzie. We spoke on the phone. I'm Brian." He walked over to introduce himself.

"Hey, dude, nice to meet you," she said, shaking his hand.

"And this guy is apparently named Dracula and he works for the FBI," Brian added, jerking a thumb behind him.

"Wait, your name is *what*?" Kenzie asked, her interest piqued to 100.

"Brian," Cammy snapped. He glanced at her, abashed. He knew he'd crossed the line. "I don't have time for this. I'm sorry if I freaked you out. Things were crazy last night. I'm sorry. But I really can't deal with this right now."

He nodded. "I'm glad you're all right," he said. She turned to Dracula, who seemed to be enjoying the show from the amusement in his eyes.

"Thanks for the ride. I really appreciate it."

"It was no trouble at all. Will you need to be picked up as well?"

For a second she thought he was being polite, before it dawned on her she couldn't really get anyone to drive her back to his place. It wasn't an offer so much as a reminder.

"I have today off and the car for a while," Brian volunteered, "I can drive you. Where are you staying now?"

"Oh, um, I should be done by four," she said to Dracula. Brian took the hint sullenly and stuck his hands in his pockets. "I'll call you if that changes. Thanks, I really do appreciate it."

"It was my pleasure," Dracula answered. He nodded his head in a bow. "And a pleasure to meet you, Officer Warren. Miss Kenzie."

Brian answered with a stiff nod. Kenzie offered a distance-bro fist and ducked back inside. Cammy glared at Brian and followed after.

"Dracula?" Kenzie prompted, wide-eyed as a kid on Christmas morning.

"Yeah," Cammy sighed. She was never going to hear the end of this now, and her friends were going to have questions she had no idea how to answer. Kenzie bit her lip, her excitement glittering through her glasses, but she took a deep breath and stuck her fists to her hips.

"I haven't finished sweeping yet," Kenzie told her. "Didn't you close yesterday? Why would you do me so dirty like that?"

"Sorry. My parents showed up and wouldn't leave me alone until I agreed to meet them. There was this super late wave of customers and I just didn't have the time."

"Well, lucky for you, I've already got it half-done now." Kenzie grabbed the broom off the pastry case and held it out for Cammy to take.

"I'm really sorry about that," Cammy apologized. She took it and went to work. The half a floor might as well be ankle-deep in crumbs. Kenzie had just been shoving all the refuse from one side to the other, probably to make sure Cammy did her fair share.

"So what happened last night?" Kenzie asked. "Also, that guy's name was seriously *Dracula?* For reals? Or is it like a stage name or something?"

* * *

Brian watched the stranger drive away in his flashy car. The guy even waved at Brian on his way out of the parking lot. Brian narrowed his eyes. Everything about this rubbed him the wrong way. The obviously fake name, the car, the whole "doctor and also FBI agent." No. None of that seemed right. He pulled out his phone.

"Hey, Akerman, is there a way we can check whether someone really works for the FBI?"

"Hello, Warren," Akerman answered tersely. "Why?"

"Can we?"

"Of course we can. You need me to look someone up?"

"Yeah. Just wait 'til you get a load of this name."

He waited for Akerman to laugh when he heard it. Instead, Akerman said, "Sounds like a nut, Rookie. If he's not bothering anyone, leave him alone."

"No, not some lunatic on the street," Brian said, surprised by the response. "He's got a badge and everything."

"Don't bother with every crazy guy running around out there," Akerman said.

"Will you look it up anyway?"

"Will I look up if there's a Dracula who works for the FBI? No. I've got lots to do. Calm down, Rookie. Forget it, leave it alone."

"But—"

Akerman hung up. Brian dialed the precinct and Suze answered. He asked her to check. She snorted and complained he was wasting her time, but said she would.

* * *

So now you're crashing at"—Kenzie pointed two fingers down at the corners of her mouth and snarled. She adopted a fake accent, rolling the R—"*Dracula's* house, wah ha ha?"

"Yeah," Cammy wished he had used a different name. This was going to make everything super awkward.

"For reals, that's pretty dope," Kenzie said. "I bet he gets money off the name alone, yeah? Or is it really his name?"

"It really is," Cammy told her.

Kenzie reached into her pocket and pulled out her phone. Just then, Luna came sweeping in from the back office in her long, bohemian skirt, her wiry gray hair billowing out on either side of her shoulders.

"No phones," she told Kenzie.

"Yeah, one sec," Kenzie mumbled.

Luna made a point of looking the place over before they opened. Cammy supposed that's what owners really ought to do, rather than just sit in the back office ordering everyone around.

"What did I say?" Luna demanded of Kenzie.

"I was just looking something up. Dracula—the real life one—totally had kids." She turned to Cammy, her eyes wide at the realization. "Oh, *dude*, if that's his real name, do you think he's related? Like, he's descended from the guy or something?"

"Now is not the time for your horror movie trivia questions. Are you ready to serve customers?" Luna asked pointedly. Kenzie flexed an arm Rosie the Riveter style. When Luna went to the door, Kenzie sidled up beside Cammy.

"Introduce me, seriously," she whispered. "How did you meet him? Is that why he's rich? He's related to the guy?"

"Uh..." Cammy said.

"Enough!" Luna snapped at them.

Most of the regulars were already outside, so Cammy hurried behind the counter.

"My coffee," said the man who never said anything else. At least, Cammy had never heard him say anything else the entire time she'd worked there.

"I'm doing just fine, thanks," Kenzie responded with the sort of wide smile that working for years in a coffee shop trained you in. Cammy went to work on his soy latte with three shots of espresso. One of the other baristas had had to tell her what "My coffee" meant, since this guy never explained this drink to anyone, new or not. He wouldn't repeat himself either. Kenzie liked to joke that he was some sort of Illuminati hoping to beam his thoughts directly into all their heads. As Cammy set the drink on the counter, she suddenly found herself wondering whether he actually was.

She watched the perfectly business-like business man snatch his coffee, sip it, and leave without a word. Maybe he was a lizard person or something. Crap, anyone she met at any time might be some sort of creature, not a human at all. Apparently vampires could go out in sunlight and eat and drink like normal people. That meant *anyone* could be... who could say what?

"Yo, Cam!" Kenzie called. "Medium decaf!"

Cammy looked down at her hands, the tools. The whole world could be a lie.

"Cam?" Kenzie repeated. Cammy looked at her. The same caramel-colored skin, black eyes heavily rimmed with black liner, but maybe even Kenzie wasn't a human being. Luna might not be, either. She couldn't be sure a single person she knew wasn't really something else.

Kenzie brushed past her to make the drink.

"Go to the bathroom, I got this," she whispered.

Cammy went, forgetting to take off her apron the way Luna always told them to, and locked herself in a stall. She pressed herself against the door. What was wrong with her? She couldn't get enough air. The bathroom stall was so narrow, she pressed against the walls with her hands, but they were still too close.

"Cammy?" came Kenzie's voice. "Cammy, you okay?"

"I'm fine," Cammy lied. It was just what you did.

"Cammy, did something happen? Is Heather okay?"

Cammy had tried not to think about Heather.

"I don't know," she answered. "She hasn't been answering her phone."

"Oh," Kenzie hesitated. "Is that normal for her?"

Heather was one of Cammy's friends from middle school, while Kenzie and her group were from college or the Mindful Bean. Needless to say, the two groups didn't really know each other.

"Sometimes," Cammy said.

"Well, it doesn't seem like you're up to work today. I saw your cop buddy still parked out there. Want me to get him?"

"No!" Cammy protested. She couldn't be stuck in a car with Brian now. She couldn't take it. "Kenzie, I need the money so bad. I can't go. Please, just give me a few minutes, okay?"

Kenzie jimmied the stall door lock open. She looked over the rim of her glasses and crossed her arms across her chest. "You look like a vampire you're so pale," Kenzie told her. "For reals. What happened last night?"

Cammy couldn't think of what to say. Kenzie's horror-movie joke struck her to the quick. It wasn't a joke anymore. Turns out, it had never been a joke.

"What are you both doing in here?" Luna demanded, opening the door.

"Cammy's sick. She needs to go," Kenzie told her.

"Really?" Luna asked, disbelieving. "Even if that's true, you can't both be in here."

"Wheat Bran just got here. It's cool, he's got it," Kenzie replied.

"Get up there, *now*. Cammy, if you're really this sick, I'd like a doctor's note. Go."

"No!" Cammy groaned.

"I know you need money, but you gotta be honest with yourself. You look like you're gonna pop," Kenzie said, placing a hand on Cammy's shoulder. "Sorry we didn't get back to you last night. We made a pact, since you know how Lindsey is. I wish you could have been there, though. We had a bet going whether she could even go five minutes without her phone, much less six hours." She hugged Cammy. "I'm really sorry. You can tell me about it if you want. I'm here for you."

"Thanks," Cammy said, her mouth as dry as paper.

Kenzie walked with her to the front, where she clocked out. Cammy waved to Brandon—"Wheat Bran" as Kenzie liked to call him—before she stepped out of the building. Thankfully, Brian wasn't still there. She debated calling her host for a ride, but thought better of it. She was close to campus, so she could walk there and use the campus health center. It was closer and cheaper than a hospital, and it wasn't like she had regular doctor anyway. Besides, maybe a walk was what she needed to clear her head.

She made her way towards campus, trying her best not to stare at every single person who passed her, wondering whether they were human. No, this wouldn't do. She had to think of something, and at last she did. She called Brian.

"Aren't you at work?" Brian asked.

"Yeah, but, well, I just remembered. You might want to look into Green4Life if you're looking for Heather."

"What's that?"

"It's a cheap, local rideshare. It just got started or something. Heather told me about them, and I think they might have something to do with how she disappeared," Cammy explained. Dracula might not be all that up to date on phones, but Brian was a cop, and he had the resources for that, surely?

"Okay," said Brian. "What makes you think so?"

"Well, the people who mugged me were working with a driver from this service," Cammy said, then took a breath. "Also Vlad thinks so—"

"You're on a first name basis with that guy?"

"Brian." Her tone must have gotten his attention.

"Right, sorry. I'll pass that on. Don't worry, we'll find her."

Cammy certainly hoped so, but she couldn't shake that bad feeling in her gut. "Thanks Brian, I know you will. Bye." She knew Brian wouldn't stop until he'd found Heather. They'd known each other since middle school. He'd even been the one to convince Heather to do rehab the most recent time. The trouble was that the only person who could save Heather if she'd been captured by vampires was Dracula, but the only one with the knowledge to find her was Brian. She couldn't think of a good way to put their heads together.

"Yeah, Suze?" Brian answered once he had hung up on Cammy. He was tailing her "friend" at a distance, figuring the man was a liar and probably dangerous.

"That name was totally fake. Why did you waste my time?"

"I thought it was. I just wanted to be sure."

"Don't double-check every single lunatic's credentials. Or at least don't make *me* do it. You run into some nut in a cape with plastic fangs or something?"

"Not even close. He's well-dressed, clean, driving a multi-million dollar car."

Dracula's Guest

"Wait, you ran into some rich eccentric claiming to be Dracula working for the FBI?"

"That's about the size of it. Also, I need to report a missing person, and if possible, could we run some sort of check on Green4Life?"

"What is that?"

"Some sort of local rideshare. I have reason to believe they might be involved in the disappearance."

"You run into all the crazies all at once, huh?" Suze asked.

"I guess. Right now I'm going to see if I can catch up with this guy."

"Well, if you bring him in, tell me. I cannot *wait* to see how this plays out."

"You'll be the first to know."

He ran the plates first, but all he got back was that the car was legit, and it was registered in that same ridiculous name, though spelled differently than he had expected. On a whim, he looked up the name on his phone, but got about a million hits that weren't who he was looking for at all, not even on any social media platform he tried. He wondered if that made perfect sense or no sense at all. If you were going to go with a stupid name like that, would you even bother going by something else online? He scanned through the first several links, which were historical in context. That took him by surprise; he'd figured he'd get the book or the movies first. Apparently the full name got you the historical figure instead. He didn't like what he saw.

"What a creep," he mumbled. Next he looked up the address, and could only stare. Said creep's house was almost out in the Cascades. There was nothing near it, and when he zoomed in the satellite image he saw a few out buildings, what looked like vineyards, and untouched land. He'd have to see how much of it the guy owned, but he suspected that if the creep could afford a multi-million dollar car, he could afford a healthy little chunk of land. No matter how he searched, he couldn't find anything that told him what the vineyards were; no brands that he could easily tie back to the name.

*Who **is** this guy?* Brian wondered. Then he almost rear-ended the sedan in front of him. *Eyes on the road, idiot*, he thought to himself. He spotted the silver car ahead of him after only a few minutes. The car stood out like a sore thumb. Apparently Cammy's new friend was making his way to I-5, so Brian raced after him. He managed to catch up before the Duesenberg pulled off on an entrance and hoped against hope that he could come up with a reason to stop him before he took off to his secluded home. Luck was on his side: of all things, the multi-million dollar collectible had a taillight out. Brian threw on his lights, doing his level best not to grin like a Cheshire cat as he did so.

Doctor Fake Name glanced over his shoulder, executed a turning hand signal, and pulled off the side of the road. Brian parked and radioed the precinct for the go-ahead to perform the traffic stop. He got it. He shook his head to get the smile off his face, scowled, and stepped out of the patrol car. The nutjob had one hand on the wheel and an elbow on the door.

"Hello, Officer Warren. A pleasure to see you. I did not expect we'd meet again so soon," said Dr. FBI. He must have pulled a pair of sunglasses from somewhere, because he slid them down his nose to look up at Brian. He smiled like a crocodile.

*Please do something, **anything** I can use,* Brian thought. *FBI agent, my ass.*

Doctor Fake Name needed no prompting and had already reached into his pocket for his license, granting Brian a glimpse of something he *hadn't* expected: the grip of a Dirty Harry sized revolver in a holster under the man's jacket. His blood ran cold. Dr. FBI was packing serious weaponry on top of everything else? This was a whole new ball game.

He glanced at the license Doctor Fake Name was trying to hand him.

"Do you have any weapons or anything which could harm me in your vehicle?"

"Is there a reason you asked?"

"That's not an answer, sir," Brian told him.

He could see Doctor Fake Name had figured out Brian knew there was at least one, and was weighing in his mind how he wanted to answer. A 'yes' would give Brian probable cause to search him and his beautiful vehicle. A 'no' was even bigger trouble, and Brian hoped for bigger trouble.

"I don't think you had a reason to stop me in the first place," the creep said.

"Your taillight is out."

"Ah. Thank you for informing me. I rarely take this vehicle out any longer. I'll see to that." He pointed to the license in Brian's hand. "If you would."

"Sir, I saw you are carrying a weapon in plain sight. I assume it's real and functional. Should I also assume it's legal and registered? You have a concealed pistol license as well, I assume?"

Dr. FBI pressed his lips together, sighed, and squinted out his windshield at the entrance to I-5, maybe thinking he had been so very close to being on his merry way.

"I need you to step out of the vehicle, please," Brian told him.

"You don't want to do this," Dracula told him. Brian hadn't expected that response. *A total nut*, he thought to himself.

"Please step out of the vehicle."

Whoever this guy actually was raised his eyebrows in amusement.

"I beg your pardon?"

"Step out of the vehicle. I won't repeat myself."

Doctor FBI squinted at him.

"Step out of the vehicle."

"I thought you wouldn't repeat yourself?" said Dracula, opening the door.

"Hands where I can see them," Brian told him when the nutjob made to put his keys in his pocket. With a look of mild disgust, Dracula held up both of his hands.

"Officer Warren, is this really necessary?" Dr. FBI asked. "I know you've feelings for Cammy, but this hardly seems warranted."

"If you've got documentation for that firearm"—Brian pointed to the gun hidden under the man's jacket—"I'd like to see it."

"I imagine you would."

"Hands on the vehicle, sir."

He tolerated Brian frisking him. The revolver turned out to be a Smith and Wesson .357 magnum. Not the sort of thing a federal agent carried—especially not, now that Brian had a much better view of it, one without a serial number. It looked old, but well-cared for.

"And I guess you've been stuck in a time-warp. The FBI hasn't used revolvers in decades," Brian said.

The creep shrugged.

Next Brian found some sort of spring-loaded antique up the man's sleeve. Then an antique colt strapped to one ankle, a wooden knife, a few bags of plants and one of what looked like sugar or salt. There wasn't any concealed pistol license. Brian had not expected there to be one. *What sort of crazy is this?* Brian wondered, lining all the stuff on the hood.

"Don't scratch the paint," Dracula told him. "This vehicle is worth more money than I'm sure your whole department sees in a year."

"And all this?" Brian asked, waving at the paraphernalia. "Related to an investigation, is it?"

"It is."

"Well, I checked. FBI doesn't know who you are," Brian told him. "So you're under arrest."

He had hoped, deep down, that whoever he actually was might get rattled hearing those words. No such luck. Dr. FBI considered the weapons and other items Brian had pulled off of him.

"I advise you to check again, or else contact your supervisor," he said, and nodded at the patrol car. "It appears you perform your duties admirably. For the sake of your career, I suggest you leave this matter lie."

Is that some kind of threat? Brian thought. He leaned close and hissed, "Listen, friend, you're in a world of trouble. You might want to think more about yourself and less about my career." He donned his professional demeanor again. "Sir, you're under arrest for the unlawful possession of an illegal firearm."

Brian grabbed the man's wrist to put cuffs on him—only to find he couldn't budge the guy an inch.

"What the...?" Brian muttered to himself. He had been working out, and he knew he was in pretty good shape, but this was like trying to move a tree, and no matter how strong this guy was there should be a little give. He pushed harder, only to find he simply couldn't overpower the man. For a moment, his blood ran cold.

"Officer Warren, I advise you to reconsider," Dracula told him. "A call to your precinct won't take very long."

"Stop resisting," Brian told him.

"Resisting?" the creep repeated, a little smile at the corner of his mouth. "Officer Warren, are you having some difficulty with your cuffs?"

That rattled Brian more. This man, whoever he was, and as crazy as he was, was cool as a cucumber. Didn't care he was caught red-handed, didn't care he was getting arrested. Nothing like anyone Brian had ever encountered, arrested, or been trained to deal with.

"You're under arrest. Stop resisting."

Dracula grumbled something Brian couldn't make out, but allowed—and it was clear he *allowed*—Brian to move his arms behind his back and put cuffs on him.

"I advise you again to reconsider," Dracula told him again as Brian read him his Miranda rights and marched him to the cruiser.

Once he was locked back there, Brian secured the weapons and the bags. He wasn't sure they were drugs; if they were, they didn't look or smell like anything he'd encountered before. But he couldn't imagine what else the stuff could be. The wooden knife was the weird part. He took the opportunity to search the car, beautiful as it was. Brian noticed Dracula eying him from the patrol car, so he made sure to take his time. He turned up wooden crosses and wooden knives. In the trunk were more wooden knives, lots of ammunition, and a *sword*. Brian stood there, staring at it all.

What is all this? Wooden crosses and wooden knives? Is he going hunting vampires? Too bad he'd forgotten the irony of his name in that case, and he'd forgotten to bring garlic and holy water along. Maybe there was contraband in the crosses or something. Or maybe he was a member of a goth roleplaying club. That made much more sense. Waaaay more sense. Some lunatic LARPers running around with an even bigger lunatic calling himself Dracula.

It took him a few trips to bring all the weapons to the patrol car, but at last he could collapse down in the driver's seat and call the arrest in. As soon as he was done, he heard the crazy's voice directly in his ear.

"And what is to become of my vehicle?" Dracula inquired.

"It'll be impounded," Brian told him once he had rebounded form the ceiling of the patrol car and caught his breath. He wasn't sure how the lunatic had managed that neat little trick. Just one more reason not to trust him.

"You are making a mistake, Officer Warren," said Dracula as they pulled back onto the road.

"We'll see," said Brian. He felt much more confident arresting the creep since finding all the weapons and weird stuff. He didn't like the idea of some criminal tricking

Cammy by pretending to be law enforcement, but especially not if said criminal was packing serious heat and was maybe an actual crazy person, not just eccentric. Who knows what he might have done to Cammy if Brian hadn't found him out so fast?

In the rearview mirror he saw Dracula watching the Duesenberg as they left it behind.

"Nothing had better happen to that car," Dracula said.

"You just keep worrying about yourself," Brian told him. "Impersonating an officer is a felony. Also, you can't have loaded handguns in a vehicle without a license."

"If you say so."

"No, not if I say so. That's the law. Got it? You are going to prison."

"We'll see."

Don't let him get under your skin, Brian told himself. "You know you're named after a psychopath, don't you?" he said. "I looked it up after we met. A real sicko."

"Oh?"

"Apparently he was a total sadist, impaling his own people."

"Indeed. What else did you discover?"

"Like, impaling mothers and their children, and boiling alive anyone who pissed him off."

The lunatic in the backseat chuckled.

"You think that's funny?" Brian demanded, angry.

"You failed to mention burning people alive. Do they still say he ate human flesh and drank their blood?"

"You sick mother—! You think this is funny?"

"I find the gross hyperbole of the stories amusing. Grimly, of course."

"He was so demented he impaled rats while in prison."

"Wouldn't you if your captor brought people down to your cell to see the great 'impaler'? That's all they came to see. A monster, so show them one."

Brian risked a look in the rearview mirror. Was this guy so deluded he identified with a sicko?

"What, is he like, your personal hero or something? You're related?"

"Hero? No."

"So, what? You admire the guy?"

The lunatic grinned.

"Admire? Perish the thought. That would be vanity. Let's say I feel I understand the man better than most do."

"You understand a mass murderer? You proud of that?" Brian asked.

"I see no reason to be proud of one's ability to understand a man." The creep made eye contact through the rearview mirror. "Or oneself."

You absolute lunatic. He'd said that name was his since childhood, but Brian doubted it. The odds of someone happening to have crazy parents who gave you a crazy name and you growing up to love that crazy name and be crazy enough to deserve it seemed too much for belief.

"I should tell you that Miss Lilly called me just before you appeared. She needs me to pick her up from the college health center."

Brian glared at him through the rearview mirror.

"You've got a bridge you want to sell me while you're at it?" he growled.

"It is the truth," said Dracula. Brian returned his attention to the road. The creep was just trying to get under his skin.

"So what's your deal? You like rescuing girls and flashing your badge at them?" Brian asked. The guy seemed willing to talk even though he'd been read his rights. Maybe he'd just keep talking. That might make the court proceedings go quicker if he said something incriminating. Brian hoped he would. Dracula eyed him, calculating. He looked out the window before answering.

"Not particularly. I only use my badge when necessary, and I've never been arrested for it before."

"You flashed it at me. Was that necessary?"

"To keep you from prying into a matter I am investigating, yes, I thought so."

No good. He was sticking to his story.

"So you're a doctor too?"

"Yes."

"Sure. Where'd you study?"

"Paris and Austria."

"Shut up. You went to med school in Europe?"

"Yes."

"Well, aren't you just full of surprises?" Brian grumbled.

"Oh, you have no idea," said his passenger with a wry smile.

They drove the rest of the way in silence. When they arrived at the station and Brian pulled in to book him, Mr. I-went-to-school-in-Paris said, "Officer Warren, I advise you to check with your supervisor before we proceed."

"Get out of the car," Brian said.

Dracula's Guest

"I have played along with this charade very patiently," Dracula said, "but my patience has limits."

"Maybe you're not hearing me," Brian told him, "so let me spell it out for you: You. Are. Under. Arrest. For committing a felony. You are going to jail first, then you're going to be prosecuted, sentenced, and sent to prison. Now, step out of the car."

Slowly, his passenger exited the vehicle. Brian grabbed him by the elbow to move him, and encountered the same impossible immobility as before.

"Once more, I ask that you contact your supervisor," said Dracula. He looked downright menacing. Something about his eyes, they seemed strangely dark, smoldering with malice. Brian suddenly felt pretty small, which took him by surprise since he had quite a fistful of inches on the guy.

"Do as I say or I will tase you, so help me," Brian retorted.

Slowly, and with enough resistance to let Brian know that Dr. Fake Name was *allowing* him to guide him along, not being forced, they walked into the station.

He didn't recognize the female officer when they got to processing, but Akerman was there. Brian told the officer who he had arrested and why, while Akerman—the precinct's pretty boy, full blond-haired-blue-eyed Scandinavian stock—stood to one side watching the scene unfold.

"Take off your belt, shoes, and other personal effects please," said the officer.

"Some of what I have on me is hundreds of years old and irreplaceable," said Dracula. Brian and Akerman eyed each other.

This the guy? Akerman mouthed and pointed. Brian nodded.

"We will keep them locked up," said the officer.

"Irreplaceable," Dracula repeated firmly.

"It still needs to come off," Brian told him. Dracula turned slowly to eye him. Brian did his best to stare him down.

"Very well, but you will study these. Should they go missing, I will hold *you*, Officer Warren, personally responsible," said Dracula. Brian removed the cuffs and watched the lunatic take off what looked like a high gold-content ring, a very expensive-looking watch, a stone ring on a leather cord of some kind from around his neck. He unpinned a gold pin and set it down as well, then pointed to the items before carelessly flipping his wallet and fake badge on the counter as well. Brian frowned at the gesture. It was as if this guy was telegraphing that his identity and badge were fake while his personal items were not, but he was still sticking to his story; his name did seem to legitimately be Vladislav Dracula, so his ID should still be of some value to him. This guy didn't add up.

Dracula pointed once more to his items so Brian obliged and looked down at them. The ring drew his attention; it looked like a dragon with a sword stuck through it. Goth role playing group with an eccentric and extremely wealthy patron was looking more and more likely, but very surreal considering the lengths this guy was willing to go.

"Pretty neat little museum piece," Brian commented. "Stabbing dragons, huh?"

"Oh, no, no, no, Officer Warren, *impaling* dragons," Dracula corrected, smirking. Brian decided his job was done, and let everything proceed without any more interference on his part. He hated to admit it but he was rattled, and he

Dracula's Guest

couldn't afford to risk doing something that might get this guy off the hook.

"You brought him in?" Akerman asked.

"Yeah. Can't tell you how glad I am I did."

"Oh?"

"Yeah. He's packing serious heat, and so unhinged the gate's on the ground. I'm going to let Suze know, she wanted to see how this went."

Akerman nodded. Brian went upstairs to tell Suze, then wandered back down to see how things were proceeding.

"So I found this guy's address," Brian told Akerman. He'd befriended the senior officer, variously called "Akerboy", "Attaboy" or "Altarboy", just because Brian had mistaken him for a rookie like himself when they'd first met. Though in his thirties, Akerman still looked like a high schooler. "You want to see where he lives?"

He and Akerman retreated towards the locker rooms as Brian displayed the map he had pulled up on his phone.

"I looked him up myself," Akerman said. "Got intrigued. So this guy owns something like a hundred square miles. I'm surprised it's not part of a National Park."

"Who is this guy?" Brian wondered. They scanned the satellite image, but saw nothing that Brian had not already observed.

"I can't answer that, but when I saw that address I decided to dig a little deeper, and you'll never guess how and when this was purchased."

"When? By whom?"

"So in 1926 the Queen of *Romania* visited this city."

"Get out," Brian said. "No way."

"Yes way. She bought the property with the help of a Samuel Hill—not sure if it's *the* Sam Hill—and, get this, turned it over to a Vladislav Dracula, who must be this guy's grandfather or something. It's been transferred a few times, same name every time. They must be some of those folks who like continuity and give all the generations the same name."

"You're saying Romanian royalty purchased this property for this lunatic's grandfather?" Brian repeated. That might explain the fancy car. This guy might be bona fide European nobility or something. Some really old money. He shook his head at the idea of old money from Europe working as a federal agent for the good ol' U S of A.

"So what's the story with this guy? How'd you bump into him?" Akerman asked.

"He saved Cammy from some muggers, apparently," Brian explained. "Or so he says. They're both not giving me the full story. Anyway, he has her living with him." Brian pointed at the image on the screen. "Up there, I guess."

Akerman frowned at the phone.

"How'd she get up there?"

"I have no idea. Neither of them would tell me," Brian said. He stared at the image. "I wonder if he's involved in what happened to Heather, then?"

"Heather?"

"She's Cammy's roommate, and apparently she's missing. Maybe he grabbed Heather first, and was waiting for Cammy and that's how he picked her up?" Brian ran a hand through his hair. This might turn out way worse than he had thought.

DRACULA'S GUEST

Akerman's face contorted. "I doubt it," he said. "If you're thinking serial killer, ask yourself if they both fit a profile. Serial killers usually go for a type."

Brian thought about it. Heather and Cammy didn't look alike. Heather was tall, Cammy was petite. But they were both young women. Was that enough? He hoped not.

"Anyway," he said, trying to distract himself from the dark thoughts that wanted to surface, "that's not even the weirdest part. He was carrying the biggest magnum I've ever seen, and all these wooden knives and crosses and plants in bags."

"Sounds like you've got a lot of cataloging to do, then," Akerman told him. "I've got to get back. Best of luck with all of this."

Akerman clapped him on the shoulder and returned to the bullpen. Brian was pretty elated; maybe this arrest would improve his career track.

Some of the other officers snarked at him about his mystery suspect as he went to put everything in order. Then he heard a voice steamrollering over the general din of drunks and druggies shouting, and cops trying to manage the chaos.

"Which one of you clowns wants to explain to me why the Director of the FBI just crawled up my ass saying we've got one of his agents detained down here?!"

Brian froze in place. It couldn't be; Suze had checked. If the FBI said no, why would they keep checking? It couldn't be who he had just brought in. He turned to see Chief Deble —Dibble when he was out of earshot—glowering at his men.

"Anyone?"

Brian saw Akerman glancing at him. He shook his head. The chief noticed the exchange and came storming over.

"Rookie, you better come clean right now, or so help me you're suspended," Deble told him.

"I checked, sir. They said he wasn't one of theirs," Brian explained.

"Well, I don't know who you contacted, but I have their top brass on the line telling me the opposite." Deble pinched the bridge of his nose. "I don't need this right now. I have to talk to the press in an hour about the city councilman found floating in the Sound. Some damn clown at the medical examiner's office is sensationalizing the death." He shook his head and muttered under his breath, "Exsanguinated. The periodicals would have a field day. The last thing we need is the word 'vampire' in every headline tomorrow." He glared at Brian. "So where'd you leave FBI guy?"

Exsanguinated? Vampire? Brian thought, alarmed. Could the LARPing goth psychopath with the sensational name he'd just arrested be responsible? He sure hoped not. "But sir, he didn't have a standard issue weapon," Brian said. "He's packing like he thinks he's Dirty Harry, sir. And heading off to a Buffy reunion."

"I don't care if you found a rocket launcher stuffed down his waistband along with a whole convention of jailbait cosplayers. You're coming with me. We're getting this straightened out."

Brian accompanied him back to processing, trying to keep his head from spinning right off. No way a federal agent had a multi-million dollar car filled with goofy LARPing props and three non-standard-regulation guns.

"Which one is he?" the chief demanded.

DRACULA'S GUEST

As they approached the waiting area filled with other arrestees, Brian caught sight of probably-a-cult-leader himself sitting perfectly still at one end of the rows of chairs, and pointed him out. Some greasy-looking guy in a torn sleeveless flannel shirt, tighty whities and nothing else was pacing around and carrying on. Two other officers were trying to pacify him.

"You don't have the right to keep me here! I know my rights! You can't prove that was mine! You can't prove I did anything!" the guy was yelling.

"Sir," said the female officer who worked the desk. "Sit down, or you can go to that holding cell and wait until tomorrow before you see a judge."

He answered with a string of amusingly incoherent profanity.

Brian quickened his pace. This guy looked like he hadn't bathed since grunge was invented, and from his red eyes was probably not going to calm down until whatever was in his system had worked its way through.

Flannel man swung his arms wildly, taking up a position near Dracula. He probably hadn't noticed his neighbor because of how still he was sitting. His presence clearly irritated Dracula, whose eyes slowly came to rest on the tweaker.

"I get a lawyer! I know my rights!" the tweaker shouted. "Get offa me, you pigs!" He batted his arms at the air, fending off officers.

Dracula reached up with lightning speed, grabbed the tweaker's flannel shirt, and yanked him down to the floor with strength that took Brian by surprise.

"Listen here, you human trash: no one cares what rights you do or don't have. Sit down and shut up or I will *break* you, do you understand?"

The tweaker emitted a confused and terrified moan. Dracula shoved him against the wall, then dusted his hands off and fixed his cufflinks. Flannel man slumped to the floor. The other officers ran to check on his status.

"For that, you're going to go cool off," one told Dracula. "We handle these guys, not you."

"No! leave him," Chief Deble shouted. Brian couldn't believe his ears.

"But, Chief, you saw what he just did! He just threatened, no, assaulted—"

"I don't care. We're getting him out. He's the guy you arrested, Rookie?"

"Well, yeah, but he—"

"Hey, your name Dracula?" the chief called out. This question turned every head within earshot, including the man Brian was utterly convinced was a sociopath. Dracula nodded, spotted Brian, and smiled like the devil himself.

"I tried to warn you, Officer Warren," he said.

"I apologize for this misunderstanding. What are *you* doing?" Deble demanded when another officer approached.

"We need bloodwork," said the officer, "to test for—"

"It's fine. I'll take it from here." Deble extended a hand for Dracula to take. "This is all a terrible misunderstanding."

"It certainly is," Dracula agreed, then looked at Brian. "But I think the fault lies on my side, not yours. If you would please return my effects, I need to retrieve my vehicle."

"Once again, I apologize—"

"That isn't necessary. Only return my effects."

Deble glared at Brian.

"What do you have to say for yourself, Rookie?"

"*Sir*," Dracula cut in. "Your officer merely executed his duty. Zealously, I'll admit, but that hardly demands you humiliate him for my benefit. However, I do hate repeating myself, so this is the *last* time I will ask for my things."

"Of course, right this way," said Chief Deble, leading them back to the desk. That didn't seem like right procedure to Brian either.

Dracula inspected every single item he had been forced to part with. When he retrieved his wallet he spent the time to count every single bill inside, despite not sparing a second on it earlier. Brian swallowed when he noticed how many bills were actually in it, and the denominations. Franklins all the way. As Dracula recovered the FBI badge, Brian saw the name on it.

"Sir, that badge is stolen," Brian told Deble. "Look at it, the names don't match."

"Never mind the badge," Deble snapped.

"But—!"

"I said *forget it*," the chief snarled. Brian's mouth dropped open. This couldn't be happening.

Dracula made a show of putting the stolen badge back in his coat, eying Brian smugly the entire time. Once done, he nodded to Brian.

"Lucky for you, Officer Warren, it's all here."

"Hey, are you threatening me?" Brian demanded.

"That's enough outta you, Warren," Deble snapped. "Cool it. We'll be having a nice chat tomorrow when you come back in, and I'm writing you up"

Brian gulped.

"Now my weapons and other effects, if you would, Officer Warren?" Dracula asked him. Under the red-faced glower of the chief, Brian went to pull the bagged items out of Evidence. He returned the guns and the little bags and wooden knives and the *sword* to Dr. FBI-After-All in the bullpen so that none of the suspects in the waiting area could get at them. The unusual sight drew lots of curious eyes, but everyone also assiduously tried to mind their own business to avoid the fallout.

"Again, on behalf of the precinct, I apologize," said Deble. "I don't know how—"

"Enough," said Dracula. "I need to retrieve my vehicle." He checked that the magnum was snug in the holster he wore under his jacket before looking up at Brian. His eyes smiled cruelly.

"I believe you're off-duty at the moment. Perhaps you would like to provide me with transportation? As way of apology, of course, and to prevent Miss Lilly from having to wait even longer for me to pick her up."

Brian's mouth dropped open again, but the chief gripped him hard around the arm, so he nodded. Fine. This might give him a chance to get to the bottom of all this. So for the second time that day, Brian put the man in the patrol car— this time riding shotgun.

His passenger was grinning smugly as they left for the impound lot. It took all Brian's self-control not to punch the guy in the mouth.

It was just possible that the car hadn't been towed yet. The roadside where they'd left it was on the way to the impound lot, and if it hadn't been picked up they'd be spared the hassle of the mandatory 12-hour holding time. If it had,

Brian figured he'd be in more trouble. Any damage to that car might have to be paid for out of his pocket. Gulp. He stewed behind the steering wheel and hoped they'd get to the vehicle before the towers showed up.

"Have you been a policeman for very long?" asked Dracula. Brian took it for a veiled insult.

"Going on two years."

"You seem very dedicated."

Brian decided that was another insult.

"How about you? You been an agent long?"

"A long time."

"But you were also a doctor?" Brian reminded him. The creep didn't look young, but he certainly didn't look old enough for that kind of career leap. Brian wondered about how much time he had to spare serving as FBI if he'd gone all the way through med school and practiced as a doctor first. Especially if he'd also been in the FBI "a long time." He didn't look like he'd hit fifty yet.

"Yes."

"Why'd you quit? Doctoring pays better."

"I never did it for money."

"Just out of the goodness of your heart, huh?"

"Hardly. It was a beneficial arrangement. And I imagine I did more good than most of my colleagues." Dracula eyed him. "Given your enthusiasm, I imagine you do more good than yours as well."

"Let's not talk about me, huh?"

"Very well." Dracula pulled out his ancient cellphone and laboriously punched a number. Weird. "Hello, Cammy," he said into the phone, causing the blood to pound in Brian's head. The creep had been telling the *truth* about Cammy asking for a ride? Why couldn't Cammy see that everything about this guy was wrong? She was smarter than that! "I apologize, I ran into your friend, Officer Warren, and I was delayed. Yes, I will be there as soon as I am able. Hmm?" Dracula side-eyed Brian. "You think so? I see. Well, I will ask him, then." He placed his hand over the microphone and turned to Brian. "Miss Lilly seems to think you would be of some help. Would you like to help?"

"Help with what?" Brian demanded.

"Looking for her friend, Ms. Blake," Dracula explained, smiling that creepy, malicious smirk of his.

Brian glared at him. No way he was doing this. Playing the FBI card and then just casually inviting him to investigate a missing person with a civilian sidekick? If it was something that involved a federal bureau then Brian had no business being involved, and Cammy *certainly* didn't.

"You want me to poke around in a federal investigation?" Brian demanded icily.

"Not at all. Local law enforcement is looking for Ms. Blake, I presume? My efforts would be in a purely informal capacity. Cammy is quite worried about her friend."

"Aren't you investigating something right now?" Brian reminded him. "You've got the spare time to drop that and help Cammy out of the goodness of your heart?"

"It would be in a casual capacity, certainly, but I have reason to suspect that her friend's disappearance may tie into my investigation. No proof yet, of course. But I would be killing two birds with one stone, I believe it is said."

Believe it is said? This creep had no accent, but now he wanted to play at English not being his first language? If everything else Brian had found was true, then this creep was blue-blooded old money, and he'd said he went to med school in Europe, so Brian had no idea where he was from. He wasn't even sure whether the FBI only hired American citizens or not. He'd have to check later whether a foreigner had any business working with them in the first place. Brian glared. Every second this creep opened his mouth he made less sense, but if he was going somewhere with Cammy *alone* Brian certainly intended to come along.

"I'm in," he said, and Dracula grinned wider.

"He is interested," he said into the phone. "You don't think so?" he went on, sounding confused. "I think it would help to—well, if you think so, very well. Take care, good bye."

"You're not sore about the fact that I just arrested you?" Brian asked once Dracula flipped the phone shut.

"Are you saying you did it without reason?" Dracula replied, slipping his phone back into his breast pocket.

Brian gripped the wheel tighter. He wasn't sure. He'd been so worried about Cammy, and this guy still didn't add up, but maybe he *had* jumped the gun. All he really had was Cammy's say-so that this guy acted as an authority in a crime, no direct proof. Apparently he actually *was* a federal agent. Brian hated to admit it, but his confidence was shaken *hard*.

"Look, I'm going to be honest here: none of this seems kosher, all right?" he said. "I mean, your name, where you live, your car, and Cammy is a friend of mine. She's been my friend since we were in middle school. I mean, can you blame me for being a little suspicious?"

"Not at all," said Dracula. "I would have done the same in your position."

He seemed genuinely unfazed by the turn of events. That didn't make sense. Brian's head hurt.

"Go towards the college."

"What about your car? You couldn't stop talking about it five minutes ago."

"If it has been impounded I presume it will still be impounded once we are done," said Dracula.

"We're hoping it hasn't been. Because if it has, we won't be able to get it back out for another twelve hours. If you want it, we should get it."

Dracula tapped his lip with one finger to think on that revelation.

"I would not leave Miss Lilly waiting," he said.

"You're all right leaving your car there?"

"For the moment. Drive."

Brian eyed him, but put on his blinker and changed direction. What was he missing? There had to be a puzzle piece he wasn't fitting together that would solve this little mystery. This man was probably descended from snobby European blue bloods, loaded with cash, had been a doctor in Europe, and was now helping the FBI as a special agent, one known only to the director and maybe a few others. But the man wasn't old enough to have spent time doing all that stuff, at least he didn't look it. Brian had glanced at the birthdate on the ID, but he hadn't bothered to commit it to memory so he had no idea how old the creep actually was, assuming the ID wasn't fake. But if it was fake, why would the Feds bail him out after he'd been arrested? On that subject, who had told the director he was arrested in the first place? Brian hadn't called anyone, and Suze had only checked the name.

A lightning bolt shot clear through his brain. *It's way worse.* This guy was probably a government spook. Someone much higher than FBI using that as a cover. That's why Deble didn't care what the man did. That's why nothing added up. That's why he wanted an older phone, one that was hard to trace or hack. This was much bigger than Brian could conceive. Some sort of national security issue? That's why Cammy couldn't come clean, perhaps?

That was something else. Cammy was wrapped up in all this somehow. That's why she was living with the guy. It might be for her protection. She'd called Brian so many times, called all her friends. Had something really big happened and then someone in the CIA or Homeland Security had showed up? Worse, maybe the creep didn't work for the US of A at all. The European connections seemed legit. Akerman had said something about Romania? They had connections to Russia, right? Eastern Europe, former Soviet Bloc stuff, right? The creep might be a bona fide spy for all he knew, working for some foreign country, not Uncle Sam. But then why the high profile name? And why the bail out?

"Your hair is going to catch fire if you keep on like that," said Dracula.

"Shut up," Brian told him, which earned him a smirk. *Shut up, whoever you are. I'm going to figure this out, just you wait.*

"So your place is pretty nice," Brian said.

"To some, perhaps," was the reply.

"It was a gift, or something?"

"It was."

"Why?"

"Why?" Dracula repeated, amused.

"Yeah, why? Why'd royalty buy that property for whoever it was that got it back then?"

"For services rendered, of course," said Dracula. "During the First World War. And for public relations, friendship, and so forth. Do you know anything about the queen who purchased it?"

"No."

"Truly?" Dracula inquired, then he sounded genuinely saddened. "Pity. Everyone knew her when she toured here in '26. I heard that at Roosevelt High School they cheered her by name. She personally greeted a group of red-headed girls who had corresponded with her before her arrival." He glanced almost wistfully out the window.

Toured here in '26? The guy was playing like he was old enough to have been there, saying it so casually. "Why? What has Romania ever done that we should know about it? Besides providing the world with vampires, that is."

"An *Irishman* provided the world with vampires," Dracula corrected, sounding insulted. For the first time, it sounded like Brian might have rattled the creep right back. Maybe he was a dyed in the wool nationalist or something. "And I'll have you know Romania was an ally of the United States in the Great War—that is, the First World War. There's that for a start."

Brian had never heard that before.

"Romania also gave us a famous psychopath."

"Ah, that tired story," said Dracula.

"You don't believe he was a psychopath, I take it?"

"Perhaps to your modern mind," Dracula said, pensively, "and to his enemies, I suppose. The Saxons, I mean, not the others."

"Saxons? Like Anglo-Saxons? WASPs?"

Dracula shook his head but did not answer. This guy.

"So I'm right? You *do* admire him?"

"Hardly. He was a fool," said Dracula. "A damnable fool."

Brian detected bitterness. Something personal, perhaps? Maybe he resented the name after all?

"Why?"

"Sundry reasons."

"What reasons?"

"It would take time to explain in full," said Dracula. "Suffice to say, the greatest was simple bad luck."

"You can't blame someone for bad luck."

"You can when absolutely everything is on the line."

"You're not going to convince me a man who liked to torture people for fun just suffered from some *bad luck*," Brian told him.

"I agree," said Dracula.

"That I'm right?" Brian wondered, surprised.

"No, that I will not be able to convince you."

Whatever, creep, Brian thought.

CHAPTER 5

MISCONCEPTIONS

"Camellia Lilly?"

Cammy looked up at the nurse who'd called her name. The nurse waved for her to follow, so she slipped in through the door to the clinic. Once they had gone into the examination room and the nurse had taken her blood pressure and temperature and all those things, the campus doctor came in. The doctor was a rail-thin, short woman with short blonde hair in a long lab coat.

"Hi there, I'm Doctor Glass, what brings you in today?"

"I threw up. I just need a doctor's note for work—"

"Here's some pamphlets for you," said Glass, handing her a stack. Cammy looked down at the glossy packets in her hands. They were for a family planning clinic.

"Um, I'm not pregnant," Cammy told her. "I just feel ill."

"You need to be careful and use protection, you know," Glass told her. "They'll be able to help you." The doctor started to leave.

"Hey!" Cammy shouted at her. "I'm not pregnant! I got sent home from work, and I need a note!"

"Some girls throw up in early pregnancy," said Glass.

"Excuse me!" Cammy shouted, slapping the pamphlets down on the examination bed and jumping off it. "Are you listening to me? I'm not pregnant! Can you at least give me a note, though? I'm just stressed out, so could you *please* do your job?"

Glass rolled her eyes.

"Fine."

The thin woman left the room, leaving Cammy shaking with rage. What was wrong with her? Sure, that doctor was the rudest person she'd ever met, but the shaking was new. Cammy tried to catch her breath. Was this all because of last night? She'd never been so frightened in her life. That must be it. She glanced at her shaking, tingling fingers. No. That was only part of it. She was worried about Heather. She had to find her.

Then she remembered she still had the driver's phone with her. She pulled it out. If she knew doctors, Glass could be gone for a while. She unlocked the phone and looked through the messages again. She didn't see anything else useful, and nothing in the contacts either. Frustrated, she closed the contacts list and stared at the cell phone's wallpaper. It was a custom picture of her vampire driver taking a selfie with a girl who must be his girlfriend. Well, may have been his girlfriend. For all Cammy knew, he'd eaten her since that picture was taken.

The thought made Cammy ill, so she squeezed her eyes shut and took deep breaths. She wasn't going to let this get to her. Heather needed her. She had to keep it together. She looked again at the phone. There had to be something useful here, right? There were the usual apps, plus the Green4Life app, but right next to it was one she didn't recognize. It looked like a smiley face and was simply labelled "Don't Forget." She tapped it.

The icon blinked, *clicked*, but that was it. She looked over the wallpaper, but she couldn't see what it had done. She checked what apps were running. Messaging, contacts, "Don't Forget." Weird.

Well, that's useless, she thought. Just then Glass reentered, so she hid the phone in her bag.

"Here. You'll also want these in the future." Glass held out a note and a handful of condoms. Cammy tore the note out of her hands and knocked the condoms to the floor. She stormed out the door.

She just wanted to go home, but there was no home to go to. She could call her host back and ask him to pick her up, she supposed. She didn't have a lot of other options. Glumly, she dialed.

"Hello?"

"Hey, Vlad—can I really call you that? I got sent home. I'm really sorry to bother you, but can you come pick me up?"

She heard the sound of the Duesenberg engine in the background. Was he seriously answering the phone while driving that? "I'm on my way," he said.

"Well, I'm actually on campus now, can you meet me there? I'm at the health center right now, but I'll meet you at the entrance."

"Certainly. I shall see you shortly."

That was taken care of, she supposed. She walked to the college entrance to wait. She had to stay focused. She pulled the phone back out. Nothing. But that app might be a clue, right? She opened her own phone to look for a download of it, but her search turned up nothing. Whatever it was, it must be some sort of proprietary thing. Which meant it had to be a clue.

In looking over the phone, she saw it had lost three percent of its power. That couldn't be right. She checked what apps were running. Messaging, contacts, and "Don't Forget." She closed them all and stared at the power. It remained exactly where it should. She pulled out her own phone for reference, then reopened "Don't Forget" and watched the power. She had to wait a few minutes, but sure enough, it fell faster than her own. Whatever it was, it ate up a lot of energy. It was definitely doing something.

She checked settings. What did "Don't Forget" have access to? Then the answer became clear: "Don't Forget" had access to the microphone and the camera. It was recording what happened. She checked the videos stored on the phone and found nothing from the last few minutes. The most recent was of the girl from the wallpaper baby-talking to a pit bull puppy from two months ago. But she herself had accessed the app twice now, and there'd been that click; there should be something on the phone.

Unless it was just uploading the video elsewhere, like some sort of livestream or something.

She closed the app and stuffed the thing back in her purse. If that had transmitted video from the camera, someone else had just seen her face twice.

Some vampires might have just seen her; did they know who she was? She scanned the parking lot for any sign of the silver Duesenberg, but of course it wasn't there. She dialed Dracula again but got voicemail. Strangely, he hadn't set up a message, it just went straight to the mailbox. He'd answered it before even though he was driving, so what was going on?

She bit her thumbnail. This was bad, right? If other vampires could go out in sunlight and everything, then who could say whether they could track her down? She tried dialing again and got the voicemail after it rang for what felt like forever.

She didn't know why, but she called Heather next.

Hi! It's Heather, if you know me, just text me, if you're a boomer, leave a message—

"Aargh!" Cammy hung up and pressed her phone to her forehead. *Stop panicking, stop it! Figure out what to do!*

But nothing came to her. All she could do was gasp the thin, thin air, feel her insides trembling. She put her forehead against her knees, focused on her breathing. *Get it together, get it together.* Inexplicably, she thought of her mother. The woman would scold her for certain, for losing it. *Over your stupid druggie friend?* she heard in her mind, *Get serious. You're not a child. Grow up.*

Screw you too, Mom, she thought. She squeezed her eyes shut and shook her head to banish the specter in her mind. *Think*, she told herself. She forced herself to take deep breaths. In, out.

A while later, her phone rang. She fumbled her phone in sweat-slick hands, then got a grip on it and checked the call. It was absolutely absurd she had a contact on her phone that said "Dracula."

"Hello?" she said, her voice strained.

"Hello, Cammy." She realized he had no accent at all. That seemed funny to her all of a sudden. She was so used to the Bela Lugosi speech in movies, but he just sounded like everyone else. "I apologize, I ran into your friend, Officer Warren, and I was delayed."

"Delayed?" Cammy repeated dully. "But you're coming now?"

"Yes, I will be there as soon as I am able."

"Wait, you were talking to Brian? If he's still there, maybe he could help. We need to find Heather," Cammy said. *I need to find her. Right now.*

"You think so? I see. Well, I will ask him, then." She heard him speaking, and thought she heard a reply. "He is interested."

"We can't tell him about the vampires, though," Cammy said. But these vampires couldn't be out during the day, right? Would Brian find out about them if helped right now?

"You don't think so?" Dracula checked. "I think it would help to—"

"No, trust me. It'll make everything weird and impossible."

"Well, if you think so, very well. Take care, good bye."

She felt relieved, somehow. Even though she couldn't deal with Brian being worried about her, she wanted him to come along. He knew Heather, had always helped when he could. He'd know what to do.

Dracula considered Officer Warren stewing beside him. Precisely why the young man was so smitten with Cammy was beyond his comprehension, but that was no matter at the moment. What mattered was that an unprecedented opportunity had presented itself when Cammy had sneaked her way up to his home. It had become clear to him years ago, when Boese had allowed his release, that the world had leaped far beyond his expectations and experience. Especially with regards to technology. Refusing to be daunted, he had gone out and purchased the new televisions, a computer that a salesman at an electronics store had recommended, as well as other devices. Special Services had given him a phone and pager that they had seemingly forgotten—he still had it stashed in a drawer in his office—and prohibited him from leaving the United States without their permission.

Land of opportunity it may have been once upon a time....

The change in people had proved the most difficult hurdle for him to overcome, and he had begun to think he might never be able to make a solid contact who could truly help him navigate the modern world. He had no particular wish to associate with the horde of degenerates that wandered pointlessly over the world now.

Malcolm had been the closest thing to such a resource to date, and a poor one at that. The young man might as well be a child; he had no virtues or qualities to recommend him, although his lack of loyalty or ideology had made him willing to work with Dracula in the first place.

Then Cammy had come along, seemingly abandoned on his doorstep like a stray cat. This was such a clear sign that he would be the greatest fool to ever walk the earth to let it pass. A chance to observe one of these modern folk up close and learn what the culture had become. To see their souls, if he could.

Though Cammy was proving insufferable, he thought Brian had some promise. Fire, at least. Perhaps he'd be useful in the future. Dracula would have to see. See, and wait for Cammy to help him catch up. He was already regretting

DRACULA'S GUEST

that he'd extended an invitation to her, but he was determined to fulfill his obligations as host. It may be that she might improve with time—though he doubted it.

Her hands had stopped trembling by the time a patrol car pulled up. To her surprise, Dracula and Brian stepped out. Brian hurried towards her, while Dracula came at a relaxed pace.

"Are you okay? I thought you had to work," Brian said.

"I do," Cammy said, "but I couldn't. I just couldn't." She eyed the patrol car. "Why are you driving him around? Did something happen to his car?"

"Uh...." Brian said.

"There was a misunderstanding," Dracula explained. "No matter. You said you wished to look for your friend? I agree that this seems a good time. But where should we begin?"

"Have you talked to her parents?" Brian asked. Cammy shook her head.

"You really think they'll know anything?" she asked.

"Dunno, but we have to start somewhere," Brian said. Cammy eyed his car again.

"So I guess we're taking *that?*" she asked. Brian looked over his shoulder, as though he had forgotten what sort of vehicle he was driving.

"If we are asking Ms. Blake's parents, then that vehicle will likely be best," Dracula said. "It will look very official."

"I'm doing this *unofficially*," Brian snapped.

"Indeed, but people are likelier to cooperate when they think that an official of some sort has come to speak to them."

Brian narrowed his eyes at Dracula.

"You saying that from experience?"

"Yes."

Brian's eyes narrowed some more.

"Okay, if we're talking to her parents, let's get going," Cammy said.

They rode in awkward silence. Dracula had simply taken shotgun. He hadn't even offered to let Cammy sit up front, even when she and Brian stared in disbelief. He seemed blissfully unaware that he was making things weird. Cammy hated sitting in the back of a police car. It was like she was under arrest. The seats were hard and horrible, and she couldn't stand the grate that separated her from the front of the vehicle. She wanted to throw up. She saw Brian glancing at his two passengers, looking worried about her, and glowering at Dracula.

"What happened after you guys left?" she asked.

"Nothing," Brian said.

Yeah right. Cammy said, "You were all suspicious cop, weren't you?"

"Nothing happened," he repeated. She kicked the back of his seat.

"Don't lie to me."

He looked over his shoulder at her. Though he didn't say anything, she saw his eyes saying the exact same thing back at her. She crossed her arms over her stomach. She knew how the situation looked. Weird. Way weird. But she couldn't explain it to him. He was so straight-laced, like the king of boy scouts. He'd never understand. She looked out the window.

Dracula's Guest

They drove to Phinney Ridge, where Heather's parents lived. In middle school Cammy and Heather had walked Heather's elderly, scruffy little terrier mix to the many parks to escape both of their families. In high school, Heather had run away from home a few times and gotten arrested for minor, stupid things. She and her parents had given up on each other, so far as Cammy knew. They parked on the narrow street, under the dogwood tree that grew just on the other side of the fence. She saw the tiny lawn still had the little ceramic windmill and a golfing gnome in front of it, the glass panel of the door with a window to a darkened foyer. They exited the vehicle. Cammy tried to lead the way, but Dracula stepped in front of her and strode up the steps to the door. He rang the doorbell.

Cammy glanced at the tiny driveway. No vehicles, but Heather's father couldn't work anymore after whatever that injury had been at work, and his car might be in the garage if he still had it. He was probably home.

A shadow shuffled to the door, hesitated as it peered out at the visitors, then unlocked the door and swung it open. The heavyset, middle-aged man who answered studied Dracula first, then took in Cammy and Brian. His eyes hardened.

"What did she do now?" Vernon Blake demanded, scowling.

"Hello, Mr. Blake," Brian said. "Actually—"

"Mr. Blake, my name is Vladislav Drăgulescu," Dracula said, pulling out the FBI badge to show Heather's father. "Your daughter is missing, and I would like to ask you a few questions."

"*Dragluescu?*" Cammy heard Brian repeat behind her. The name was news to her, too. If he could go by that instead, why didn't he? It was still a weird name, but it wasn't as weird as *that*.

"What kind of name is that?" Vernon demanded. "Wait a minute, sounds familiar..."

"You may be thinking of the Romanian Olympian with the same name," Dracula said. "It is Romanian. May I ask you a few questions?"

Vernon accepted this explanation, and nodded. "I need to sit," he said, and waved them inside. He led them to the living room. The faded greenish carpet looked more worn than the last time Cammy had seen it, but that had been in middle school. A lot of the room looked the same: the same clock on the mantle with the swinging crystals that hid under a glass dome, the plastic plants, the one real plant, one of Vernon's trophies from college. The only two differences were just how *dark* the room was now, and the family photos were all gone. Nothing with Heather anywhere.

"What happened to her now? Why'd they send a fed here to ask about her?" Vernon demanded, sitting down hard on the sofa that sagged even without him sitting in it. He must sit there all the time.

"There is no reason to worry at the moment," Dracula assured him. "She seems to be missing, though she does occasionally answer her phone. We wish to know where she might have gone. Has she contacted you recently?"

Vernon shook his head.

"Haven't heard from her in over two years. She told us—Kim and me—that she was clean. I didn't believe it. I think she and Kim were talking occasionally on the phone over the years, but it wasn't frequent. If she's answering her phone, why don't you ask her?"

"She won't say. Is that like her?"

"When she's high?" Vernon demanded. "You never know what she's going to do. Run off, like always. That's probably what she's done." He looked to Cammy and Brian. "Ask them. They know how it is. She finds some junkie at his apartment, shares some weed to start, and she'll hole up with that total stranger for a while until she gets kicked out. It's not the first time; I bet it won't be the last."

"So she has not been in contact with you?" Dracula pressed. Vernon shook his head again.

"If Kim talked to her, she didn't mention it to me, either. Mark my words, she's holed up somewhere chasing the next fix of whatever she's into now. It's what she does." He tapped one knee with a thick finger. "But I guess that's not what she's doing. They wouldn't send a fed for that."

"If you think of anything else, will you contact one of her friends?" Dracula indicated Cammy and Brian. "They know how to reach me. And I will let you know if we find her."

"Don't bother," Vernon grumbled, and he pointed to the door. "It's hard for me to get around. You can let yourself out?"

Dracula nodded, thanked him, and led the way out.

"I figured he wouldn't know anything," Brian muttered when they left. He glared at the back of Dracula's head.

"Is there no one else who might know her whereabouts?" Dracula asked. "Another friend, or family member she might have contacted?"

"No. She never got along with her family," Cammy said. "I think her parents gave up on her. She didn't ever talk about them."

"Boyfriend, perhaps?"

"I don't think so. She's never had any luck with dating."

Dracula turned to Brian.

"Where might she go to get drugs, if she was looking for them?"

Brian narrowed his eyes.

"I know a few places. Don't know how much luck we're going to have driving up to them in that." He nodded at his car. "Or yours."

"Hmm," Dracula agreed. Something occurred to Cammy. But she couldn't tell Brian. He'd blow up.

"Brian, you know more about this than we do," she said, "and I'm really sick. I think I need to go rest."

"Okay," Brian said. "That's fine." He glared at Dracula again. "Where are we going?"

"Why can't we get Vlad's car?"

Brian balked rather than answer.

"Excuse me a moment," Dracula said, pulling his phone from his pocket. He walked up the sidewalk a way, dialing as he went. Cammy and Brian exchanged a glance.

"Was he in an accident or something?" Cammy asked. "That's why you picked him up?"

"Uh," Brian said. She squinched her eyes at him. He studied the rows of houses, clearly trying to find some sort of answer plastered on one of them.

"There isn't any trouble," Dracula said, walking back towards them. "We can fetch my vehicle from the impound lot."

Brian stared, surprised.

"Your car was impounded?" Cammy asked. "What happened?"

"As I said, there was a misunderstanding." He pointed at the patrol car. "We're wasting daylight. Let's be off."

They drove to the impound lot and got the Duesenberg out. Cammy wondered what the heck had happened, but neither Brian nor Dracula volunteered any information.

"You want to crash at our place?" Brian offered, when the silver car rolled up beside them. "It's fine. Melissa and I aren't home all that much, so it won't seem so crowded. I'd feel much better knowing you were there."

"That's all right, thanks," Cammy told him. "I'll think about it."

She saw him clench his teeth, but he opened the door for her. He opened the trunk to reveal a bunch of Medieval weaponry and vampire-hunting stuff. Cammy blinked at it, and then realized it was all Dracula's.

Wait, was this the misunderstanding? Cammy realized. That pile of stuff looked illegal to her eyes.

"I think it prudent for Miss Lilly to rest," Dracula told Brian. "You can return my things at a more convenient time."

Brian looked like it was only the strain in his forehead that was keeping his brain from exploding. "You want me to hang onto this stuff?" he demanded.

"I'm certain you won't let anything happen to it," Dracula told him, wearing an uncharacteristic grin. "We have an understanding now, don't we?"

* * *

"So what did you think of?" Dracula asked Cammy, once she'd bidden Brian good bye, and they had turned back onto the road. So he *had* noticed.

"My mom called me up out of the blue the night I was evicted," Cammy said. "She knows something."

"This was something you didn't want Officer Warren to come along for?"

"No. He hates my mom, my mom hates him. It would just escalate."

"I see," he said. "I'll get a less conspicuous vehicle."

By the time they had switched cars, it was late enough that at least one of her parents might be home. Her mother didn't work late on Fridays, so odds were good it would be her. *Yay*, Cammy thought to herself.

The leather seats of the black Mustang were very nice. Extremely comfortable. Apparently Dracula's cars were as immaculate as his mansion. Cammy wondered if the hairy naked house elf took care of the cars as well.

"I should warn you," she said, "my mother is a narcissist. Like, certifiably. Never been diagnosed, but it's not like she's going to let you drag her to a psychiatrist or anything."

"I see," Dracula said. She wondered what a psychiatrist would say about him if anyone got to ask him how he felt about "cruelty". Scary as that was, his presence reassured Cammy. Bad as her mother was, she was bringing an honest to goodness monster with her.

"She's going to try to push you around."

This won a tiny little smirk.

"I mean it," Cammy said. "She's the world's biggest control freak."

"Do you think she orchestrated this whole matter?" he asked. Cammy stared at him. Getting her own daughter evicted was going pretty far, even for *her*. But her mother had known. S*omehow* she had known that Heather wasn't paying rent. Had her mother done something to Heather? Would she stoop that low?

"I infer you and she have a strained relationship?" Dracula said. "After all, you took up residence at my estate rather than go to her."

"You could say that," Cammy replied.

They returned to Phinney Ridge and arrived at her parents' house. The paint was immaculate, the tiny lawn—the little strip of grass behind the brick wall at the sidewalk couldn't really be called that, but her mother wouldn't hear otherwise—neatly mowed to the precise two inches she liked. Her mother's sedan was parked on the tiny drive, so Dracula parked the Mustang on the street in front of the house. Cammy wanted to scream. She had never wanted to come back here. She wasn't drowning in college loan debt for the fun of it. Once she figured out how to escape her mother's stupid gravity well, she was gone.

They walked up the clean sidewalk in a moderate drizzle. Once they stood under the awning, she grimly grinned at the idea that she was here to talk about Heather, whom her mother despised, with an actual monster in tow. What a weird day. Dracula rang the doorbell.

Her mother answered the door, still wearing her pencil skirt and dress shirt from the office, her black hair tied tightly back, her lipstick immaculate. The woman stared at the stranger dressed in a perfectly tailored black suit, and it occurred to Cammy they had similar taste in clothes—dressy, clean, neat. Then her mother's eyes landed on Cammy. Cammy stiffened, expecting a barrage of "Oh, sweetie, don't you know you worried us! Why did it take you so long to come home?! You can't do anything right without my help, can you?" but nothing came. Her mother smiled coldly at her, and returned her attention to the stranger.

"Hello? Can I help you?"

Dracula made his FBI introduction. Her mother stared at the ID, scrutinizing it for flaws or imperfections. Her smile remained fixed, unchanging, losing no edge.

"I'm confused," her mother said through the smile. "What possible reason could the FBI have for bringing my daughter home?"

"I'm here to ask about Heather Blake, your daughter's roommate."

Cammy saw the smile twitch, almost imperceptibly.

You're a monster, she thought.

"I don't understand," her mother said. "I haven't seen Heather in, my word, it must be going on four years, now. She's a vulnerable girl, you understand. Her parents weren't very supportive."

"I have reason to believe you were in contact with her," Dracula said, and gestured at the open door. "May we come in to discuss this?"

Cammy wondered if he needed an invitation. Vampires needed to be invited in, didn't they?

"No, I'm afraid you may not," her mother told him, accentuating the refusal with a little, off-putting laugh.

"What is this about? Why would anyone think I know anything about that poor, lost girl?"

"You called her a loser," Cammy reminded her. Her mother flashed a hateful glance her way, then smiled all the more at Dracula.

"Has something happened to her?"

"Have you spoken with her recently?"

"I told you I haven't seen her," Cammy's mother said, "and unless you have some better reason for harassing me, I'm afraid I'm going to have to ask you to leave."

"You knew she wasn't paying rent," Cammy snapped. "That's why you called me up and offered me money. You *knew*."

"Honey," her mother admonished, "I was just worried about you, that's all. I just wanted you to come home. It's not safe in that area of town, you know. The *riffraff* that lives down there. I mean, who knows what might have happened to Heather?"

"What did you do?" Cammy demanded. "Did you contact her? Offer her money? What?"

"Camellia Constance Lilly," her mother scolded. "I won't be talked to in this manner. You're always so suspicious. It's wrong to accuse people without proof."

"You were always going through my stuff!" Cammy shouted. "Always snooping around, trying to tell me who I could and couldn't talk to online or who I could hang out with at school."

"And no wonder! You made friends with a drug addict, honey." Her mother's tone had lost all semblance of politeness or sweetness. "If you had any sense picking friends, I'd have left you alone."

"This is a serious matter," Dracula interrupted, "and I need you to be truthful. This concerns your daughter's safety."

"Excuse me, Mr. Dragulescu, but as you can see, I'm having a conversation with said daughter at the moment—"

"No, you are having a conversation with *me*," he said. Something about his voice sent a shiver up Cammy's spine. "And I am losing precious daylight. So I will give you one more chance to be more forthcoming with me. Have you been in contact with Miss Blake, or do you have any idea where she might be?"

Her mother stared icicles at him.

"Have I told you that I work for Lewis and Associates?" she asked through her teeth.

"No. Nor do I care who employs you."

"It's a law firm," her mother added. "I'm a legal aide."

"You are not cooperating with me. In fact, you are prevaricating. I take it that you *have* been in contact with Miss Blake."

"You can't accuse me of anything," Cammy's mother hissed. "You've got no proof. No warrant, no proof. You can't just waltz up here and harass me. That stupid little whore was a druggie. She's probably OD'ed in some alley somewhere with five cokeheads crawling all over her. Now, if you'll excuse me, my daughter and I have a great deal to discuss."

Her mother reached out, and Cammy stepped backwards. Dracula put out an arm.

"Excuse me! What do you think you're doing—?"

"For your sake, I hope you have not been in contact with Miss Blake," he said. "If what she is connected to comes back to you—"

"Don't play the heavy with me, Mister. I'll have your *job*."

He chuckled.

"You think that's funny?" Cammy's mother hissed. "You're the one coming harassing a defenseless woman on her own property. You think you're invincible, don't you? Suppose I accuse *you* of something, hmm? Your superiors wouldn't like *that*, would they? Cammy, honey, come here."

"Touch her, and you die."

Cammy and her mother both stared, flabbergasted.

"What the—did you just *threaten* me?!" her mother demanded.

"No. I don't make threats. I gave you a warning. I explained what would happen if you touched her."

"You do **not** threaten *me*!" her mother screeched. "That's it! I demand that you give me your badge number!"

He turned and walked away, leading Cammy by the elbow to the Mustang.

"Get back here right now!" her mother shrieked behind them. "You can't take her away from me! Camellia Constance Lily, come here!"

Cammy dropped down into her seat, and he got into his seat as her mother came towards them, screaming obscenities. He turned the key, pulled away from the sidewalk and out onto the single lane between the sparsely parked cars on both sides.

They rode in silence while Cammy hugged herself.

"So there you have it," she said when they had gone about five miles.

"She undoubtedly contacted your friend," he said, "but I don't think she's involved with the vampires."

"You threatened to kill her."

"I don't make threats," he repeated. Cammy looked at his face. He was scanning the horizon. It would probably be dark by the time they got back to his mansion.

"So you *would* have killed her?"

"I wouldn't need to. If my employers discovered that she was interfering with my work, I have no doubt they would see to it themselves. I am an asset to them, and she would be a liability."

"That's my mother you're talking about."

He looked at her.

"You wouldn't care."

"That's my *mother*," she insisted. "You can't just *kill people*. What's *wrong* with you?"

"You would avenge her death, were she to be killed?"

"What? No, of course not."

"Then you wouldn't care," he said.

"Just because I wouldn't try to kill someone else doesn't mean I don't care!" Cammy shouted. "What is the matter with you? You can't just kill people!"

"It is absolutely possible to kill people," he said. "People are very easy to kill, as a matter of fact."

"But it's *wrong*. You can't do it!"

"Always?"

"Always," she insisted. "Only a psychopath doesn't think so."

He glared at her.

"Don't get mad at me," she told him. "You're the one who's crazy. Only psychopaths kill people."

"*Only* psychopaths?" he repeated. "No one else? There is never reason to kill a person?"

"Of course not," she told him. "I'd never do it."

"You only say that because you've never been tried," he said.

"No, I say it because it's *wrong*. I don't hurt people. I don't even hurt *animals*. That's why I'm a vegetarian."

"And I say you haven't been *tried*," he said. "You've never been tested. Nietzsche looked down on people like you."

"What does *Nietzsche* have to do with anything?"

"He disdained those who think themselves kind because they have no claws. You have no claws."

"You're a psychopath!"

He glared at her.

"So you say there is never a reason to kill a person?" he asked again. She shook her head.

"Never."

"Would you, say, be able to look a young girl in the eye and tell her that when the men who are coming to rape and kill or enslave her that she shouldn't fight at all, and should let them do it?"

"What? What does that have to do with anything?"

"Is that what you would tell her?"

"What does that have to *do* with anything?" Cammy demanded.

"What would you tell her?"

"To call the police, obviously! To run away!"

"Suppose there are no police. There is nowhere to run. Then what?"

"I'm not going to sit here and let you argue with me about some stupid situation that isn't real," she told him.

He looked away.

"*Isn't real*," he grumbled to himself.

She folded her arms and glared out the window. Once more, she stewed in a silent car ride. When they were most of the way there, having left the city behind, she couldn't take it anymore.

"Did that happen?"

"What?" he growled.

"Did you have to tell some girl something like that once?"

"*Once?*" he repeated. "You've never seen hardship. You don't know what it looks like."

"Oh, and you do?" she said.

"Yes."

"How? You were a prince, or whatever, right? So you had servants waiting on your every whim and you took everyone else's money and—"

"I'm going to ask you to stop. My patience is wearing *very* thin."

Cammy shut up. It was his tone. The one that made her shudder. The one that made her think he could—and would—absolutely kill a person. It wouldn't even bother him. So far as she could tell, he didn't regret a single thing he'd ever done. Best to keep that in mind and not let her mouth run.

Maybe she *should* stay with her mother instead. Her mother was crazy, but wouldn't kill her. *Except maybe she tried to get Heather killed*, Cammy thought. *Just so she could get me to come home.*

Maybe not.

"*La naiba,*" she heard him mutter. She looked up at the mansion, which had finally poked its face out from between the cedars and other trees, and saw that there was a car in front of it. Some nondescript black car, but as they came up near it, Cammy could see it had government plates.

Oh no, she thought. "Who is that? That's the people you work for, right?" she asked.

"Yes."

"What are they doing up here?"

"Nothing good," he said.

"What do I do?" she asked. "Should I hide?"

He shook his head. "Let me handle this." He drove to the garage, parked the car, and came to open the car door for her. He was weirdly chivalrous for a psychopath. She rubbed her knuckles on the hand he'd kissed. She flinched. Her hand hurt for some reason, but maybe it was just from when the driver had clamped his creepy, cold hands on her. She shivered.

They made their way from the garage to the mansion, with him leading the way. He entered through the front door —it was unlocked, though Cammy couldn't say if it always was or if his employers had a key for some reason.

"Director, good evening," Dracula said into the foyer. "What a surprise to see you here, in person. How long has it been?"

"Where have you been?" someone demanded. A pale-faced man with a clean-shaven head and chin came storming towards the front door. He had watery blue eyes and scars on one side of his face, notching into his ear. Two other men stood behind him like a cliché of secretive government bodyguards. "We have a serious problem, and you're out driving around getting arrested?"

"Arrested?" Cammy repeated, drawing the man's attention. He stared at her. Looked to Dracula. Pointed at her.

"What is that?" he demanded.

"Excuse you!" Cammy said.

"It looks like a young woman to me," Dracula said.

"What. Is. That?" the bald man demanded again.

"This is a guest of mine," Dracula said.

The bald man stared at him.

"Are you being funny with me right now? Right now? When there's an empusa running loose, and you *still* haven't tracked down the last of those other rats? Why do you have a *guest?*"

"I often have guests," Dracula said, affecting a sweet, innocent tone that also sent shivers up Cammy's spine. Nothing that saccharine should ever come out of that man's mouth.

"Not right now you don't. Get back out there, and don't come back until you've got the rest of those things. *Capiche?*"

"What you demand is impossible to do all in one day, or night," Dracula explained, as though to a child. "I am only one man. I cannot be in every place at once. I will certainly see what can be done tonight, of course."

"You're talking about those Hollywood vampires?" Cammy interjected. She heard Dracula let out a long hiss of a sigh.

"A guest, you lying sack of snakes?" The bald man turned on her. "You know something about this? Who are you? Who do you work for?"

DRACULA'S GUEST

"I don't work for anybody. I'm a barista."

"What do you know about this? Who are you? *What* are you?"

"Okay, wow. *Rude.* I know about this because I got kidnapped by these stupid vampires. None of your business, and I'm human, btw. How about this: who are you, who do *you* work for, and what are *you*?"

"This is Director Roger Boese, of the ridiculously named Special Services Department," Dracula answered for the man before he could say anything. Dracula nodded to the others. "And Abbot and Costello, I would guess."

"Your employer?" Cammy checked. He snorted.

"After a fashion."

"What the *hell* are you doing?" Boese exploded. "You picked a hell of a time to go AWOL. Your freedom is *contingent* on you doing what we tell you. You disrespect me again and I'll throw you back in that hole, you understand?"

"Of course," Dracula said. "But I have spent the better part of the day looking for the source of your so-called *rats*, so I find this unexpected—and rather hostile—visit quite surprising. What on earth could bring *you* up here, in person?"

"The fact that you got yourself arrested," Boese said. "How's that for a start?"

Dracula shrugged.

"I'll endeavor to avoid being arrested again in the future. As it is, I can do nothing about what happened this morning. If that is all you came to say"—he nodded to the door and stepped aside so Boese could get to it—"we're both wasting time."

"Actually, if you're the government," Cammy said, and pulled out the driver's phone, "the vampires who grabbed me were using this app. It's on this phone. I don't know if it's related to Green4Life, or whatever, but this app streams—"

"What are you talking about? What phone?" Boese demanded. She waggled the one she had taken so he could see it. He looked to Dracula.

"You took a phone from the scene. You stole *evidence*, you shifty, devious relic. And you brought a victim up here?"

"I did not tell you about the phone because I did not know about it when I called you. I also took no victims. If she was one, I'd have beheaded her by now."

Boese tried to stare Dracula down. Cammy noticed that although Dracula wasn't all that tall and both Brian and Boese could look down at him, it didn't seem to bother him. He just stood in the foyer, hands in his pockets, eying the director levelly.

"I think you need some time to think about what you're doing," Boese said. "You're coming with me."

"I don't think so," Dracula said. "These new vampires reproduce at an alarming speed. If you are busy trying to banish an empusa, I think it unwise to remove the only asset you have capable of stopping their spread. These creatures are able to turn multiple people a night thanks to your demented movies. Think how quickly you'll be overrun with them."

"You don't tell me what to do."

"I'm merely informing you of the state of things, Director," Dracula said. "But by all means, if you wish to let them run rampant, take me in. I'm certain you have the manpower to keep an eye on me while your men run over the rest of the city." Something about his tone sounded like this was a threat, but Cammy couldn't say how.

Boese tried to stare him down again, once more to no effect.

"You're pushing it," Boese said, jabbing a finger in his face. "You're *really* pushing it. If you don't make progress by *tonight*, I'm going to put you back in there, you understand?"

"If I don't make progress I hardly think putting me in a holding cell will help the situation, but you are the director," Dracula said. "Surely you know what you're doing."

"I'm going to cut out your tongue this time. I don't need to listen to this."

"Thank you, Director, for showing me the respect of coming all this way," Dracula said.

"*Hello?* I just mentioned there's an app or whatever that these vampires are using," Cammy snapped. "Are you going to look into that, or what?"

"How do you know anything about it?" Boese demanded.

"I tried turning it on. It doesn't seem to do anything, so I assumed—"

"Listen," Boese growled, "I don't know who you are, or why he's brought you here, but let me be clear: you don't know what's going on. You're trying to tell me that a bunch of vampires are *livestreaming* each other?"

"No, I don't know what they're doing. But you have resources, right? Like, you can run some sort of techno-whiz stuff on this and figure it out?"

"Why would they do that? For jollies?" Boese demanded.

"I don't know!" Cammy said. "How should I know? They're the ones using this rideshare to trick people—"

"What rideshare? If they're any kind of smart they're not going to leave a trail that easy to follow," Boese snarled. "They'd know we'd be all over them. It'd be easy to trace them."

"Well, it's called Green4Life. The driver texted ahead to say he had me and was going to bring me to wherever. He knew the people there."

"Give me that!" Boese snapped, and snatched for the phone. She swung it out of his reach.

"*Please*," she said.

"How about, 'Give me that, or I'll shoot you?'" the man growled.

"Do, and I'll put you on a stake," Dracula told him.

"You threatening me over there?" Boese demanded. "You can't—"

"Director," Dracula said. It was that same cold tone he'd used on her mother. "I make no threats. I will put you on a stake. You will take hours to die, and I will set up a chair to watch."

"My people will burn this place to the ground, with you in it."

"I suppose that will be of some comfort to your corpse," Dracula said. "But that is a guest of mine you are threatening. You will speak cordially to her. If you think that phone will do you or me some good, then by all means, take it, but *politely*. She is a civilian, after all."

The two men eyed each other. Boese turned to Cammy, considered the phone.

"Never mind," Cammy said. "Seems like you don't really need it."

Dracula's Guest

He looked about ready to pull a gun on her, but Dracula beat him to it by speaking first.

"It seems I am not familiar with the modern technology. Perhaps that has hindered my investigation. Since Miss Lilly has offered to bring me up to speed, it seems in all parties' best interest that you and your people handle the empusa, while I handle the modern vermin. I expect I will come out of this more effective than I went into it."

"You try anything funny, anything at all, and you're going in a box," Boese snarled.

"Yes, yes, where you'll chop me up and contrive further pointless tests and punishments. Surely an excellent use of your resources. In the meanwhile, it sounds to me like you have your hands full, and I would never dream of wasting precious time, so I will let you go to your task," Dracula told him, and gestured once more towards the open door. Boese pointed a finger in Dracula's face, received no response, then stormed out the door followed by "Abbot and Costello." Dracula swung shut the door, but did not bother locking it. Perhaps Boese didn't have a key, then.

"Chop you up?" Cammy asked.

"Yes. He's done it before. It is a tedious waste of time."

"That doesn't hurt?"

"No. It is an inconvenience only."

"Do you grow limbs back, or something?"

"It's possible," he answered.

What a weird way to answer that, Cammy thought. "So what now?"

"Now, I think, you should get some rest. We shall resume searching for your friend at a more civilized hour."

Cammy considered the time, the setting sun.

"But—"

"I shall head down into the city to see what I can find," he said. He looked to her. "Are you hungry?" Cammy hadn't thought of it. It must be close to six.

"Actually, yes," she admitted.

"Do you like pizza?"

She squinted at him. "*You* like pizza?"

"So long as they are careful not to use any garlic," he said. She spotted the shadow of a smirk around the edges of his eyes.

*Oh, so you **can** joke around, just a little*, she thought. "Okay, but vegetarian."

"I'll have something brought up," he said. "In the meanwhile, I wish to make my... evening ablutions."

"Your what?"

"Instead of performing them in the morning," he said.

"No, I mean, what the heck is ablutions?"

"My toilet?" he suggested. When he saw her look even more confused, he said, "Shave, wash, all that."

"Oh. We just say we're getting ready. Hang on, you need to shave?"

"Certainly."

"But, I mean, I thought you were, you know, dead?" she said.

"The hair and the nails keep growing after death."

"That's an old wives' tale," Cammy countered. "Brian's sister is a nurse. She told me that once."

"Be that as it may, mine grow."

She squinted at his face. He was right.

"How do you do that if you can't see yourself in the mirror?"

He let out one of those long, world-weary sighs.

"Oh, that's another thing that everyone got wrong?"

"That is something Stoker, and by extension, everyone who took to his book, have gotten wrong, and have now inflicted on the world," he said. "I imagine he misunderstood something he was told through his Hungarian resource: that you should not let a corpse reflect in a mirror, for fear it will become a vampire."

"I've never heard that before," Cammy said. "So funeral homes shouldn't have mirrors?"

"It doesn't always create a vampire," he said. "Nothing is that consistent."

Cammy gave that some thought. Her eyes roamed to the heavy door. It could probably withstand a car smashing into it, but he didn't even bother to lock it.

"If you need nothing more, then excuse me," he said, and left the room.

CHAPTER 6

MALCOLM

She waited in the kitchen, wondering what sort of pizza delivery person would come all the way up here, and why he'd let someone come up here in the first place. Until then, she'd been ignoring her phone, fearing the barrage of messages that she wasn't certain she could handle, but she decided it was time to take a breath and get on top of it, so she scrolled through what she had received.

They all wanted to know if she was safe, and whether his name was really Dracula.

Surprise, surprise.

Kenzie must have told the rest of them. There was no way the Hammer Horror fan in their group was going to pass that up. Cammy huffed. Brian had gone and arrested him. For what? Having a stupid name? She shook her head. Brian had become a full-fledged cop; she didn't know if she could still talk to him anymore.

Nothing from Heather. She gritted her teeth.

Mother of the year, she thought sarcastically.

Kenzie wouldn't let it go, and was still asking when she'd have a chance to talk to the guy to find out if he was related to the historical figure—Cammy still had no idea how he would answer that if she asked him point-blank—when he came out whatever downstairs bathroom he'd used.

She considered him again. He looked like a not-so-handsome, well-dressed snob. She had thought he was overweight at first, but had finally realized he was barrel-chested, and probably very muscular, instead. Not a snob, actually. An image popped into her head of some sort of mafia thug who had finally squirreled away enough money to retire and pretend like he had class.

He had shaved. The faint shadow coming in earlier could have escaped notice at a quick glance, but now that it was gone she could definitely see the difference.

Her phone pinged, drawing her attention. Lindsey was wondering if she was going to make it to their dance class in a few days. Cammy chuckled at the idea.

"Something amusing?" he asked.

"My friend wants to know if I'd make it to dance class," Cammy sniggered. "Wow. That's a hard no, I think."

"You dance?" he asked. "I had thought young people had abandoned that diversion."

"Not really," Cammy said. "Lindsey said I should try it." She considered him and his suit. "Can you?"

"Of course."

She didn't even want to think about that, and shook her head.

"You say that the phone can send a video to someone?" he asked her.

"I think so," she answered.

"Will you show me?"

He sat beside her at the kitchen table, and watched her unlock the phone and point to the app.

"Will you use it? If it does transmit, I would send a message," he said. She raised her eyebrows.

"Is that a good idea?" she asked.

"I imagine that, if there is someone behind this outbreak—and I suspect there is—this person will be desirous to meet the man who keeps exterminating his minions," Dracula said. "So I will provide that opportunity."

"But is that a good idea?" Cammy asked again. "What if this person sets a trap for you, or something?"

"That remains to be seen," he said. "But in the absence of other moves, this seems the best play I can make at the moment."

"If they're like Hollywood, would they know about you?"

"They ought to," he said. "I am well known in the Underground here, and, I imagine, throughout much of the world that deals in monsters."

"So would they know how to, you know, kill you?"

He shrugged.

"Perhaps," he said. "Many people over the centuries have known how to do as much, yet no one has succeeded."

She wondered how hard it was to actually kill him then. If Stoker was wrong, then stakes through the heart might not work. And if that didn't, then what would? If crosses and churches didn't work, maybe holy water didn't either, and obviously sunlight didn't hurt him. Maybe he had no weaknesses? Not being able to *eat* garlic was hardly a real weakness. No wonder he thought the Hollywood type were lame. She wondered how humanity had come up with weaker and stupider vampires over the centuries.

By pretending they weren't real and falling in love with a stupid story? she thought. But there was something that had been bugging her. Dracula and Malcolm both implied that because beliefs about vampires and monsters had changed over the years, the monsters had, too. How could that be? She asked him about it.

"I don't know," he admitted. "It is a troublesome thought. I am concerned that, because of changing beliefs about me, I might also be affected. So far, few of the changes have troubled me, but it is true that human belief seems to shape the supernatural. Perhaps there is an effect in the other direction, but if so, I am not aware of it."

"That doesn't make sense," Cammy told him, "I mean, scientifically—"

"*Scientifically?*" he repeated. "Does any of this fit any study of science as you know it?"

She shook her head.

"Then I must ask why you think that science should be able to explain this?"

"Well, because," she said, "I mean, everything has to be explainable, right? That's what science is."

"Science studies the natural world," he said, "not the supernatural. I think the modern man's obsession with science is what led to this nonsense about viruses creating vampires—as though a virus could animate a corpse under natural laws!"

"Well, but, look how much science has done for everybody," she pointed out. "We went to the moon, and everything."

"You could have gotten to the moon on a *Táltos*, if any still remained," he said.

"What's a Taltosh?" she demanded.

"A creature that was rare enough when I was young, and priceless. They seem to be gone, now."

"Yeah, but what *were* they?"

"A kind of magical steed in the Magyar tradition," he replied. "I had hoped to find one, when the supernatural was more vibrant and varied." He gestured at the phone. "If you please."

She held the phone towards him, hoping to avoid being spotted, and tapped the icon with her thumb. Hesitantly, he took the phone from her, but did not look to confirm that this was the correct move. She doubted he understood the front-facing camera, but he addressed the phone all the same.

"Good evening. I am growing weary of killing vampires, and I think it is high time we spoke. I shall be at Skyline in two hours." At this, he tilted the phone just a bit towards her, so she reached out with one finger and tapped the icon off.

"Where is that?" Cammy asked.

"It's a restaurant in Bellevue," he said.

"I thought we were eating pizza?"

He looked to her. "I prefer to dine out."

"So you're leaving me here?"

The back door *thumped*. Cammy jumped out of her chair, but Dracula calmly rose and went to open it.

"I had to cancel a date for this, I'll have you know," Malcolm said as he came inside, two boxes of pizza in hand. He wore high-top sneakers that looked brand new and fatigued jeans and a heavy jacket, as though he'd pulled the look right out of a magazine and thought he was going to be on an album cover. He liked his chin fuzz, unlike his supernatural friend, and copious hair products and cologne. Cammy could smell it the minute he walked in the door. It overpowered the pizza.

"And yet here you are," Dracula observed. He pulled out his wallet, thumbed through some bills, and passed them over.

Oh, you've gotta be kidding me. "You hired a *sitter?*" she demanded. "I'm not *five.*"

"But you're new to this whole mess," Malcolm replied. "So you're a soft target."

She glowered at him.

"Don't take it personal. It's just a fact," Malcolm told her.

"Be on your best behavior," Dracula told him. "She is a guest of mine."

Malcolm nodded and tried to walk past him, but Dracula grabbed him by the elbow.

"Your *best* behavior," he repeated.

Malcolm looked him in the eye. He nodded. Satisfied, Dracula gave Cammy his attention.

"I shall inform you if I find anything."

"I want to come with," she said. "If we find Heather—"

"I am not looking for your friend this evening," he told her, "I am looking for the progenitor of these creatures."

"But Heather could be in dan—"

"If she is, all the more reason for me to find who is behind these strange occurrences. If there is any chance left to save your friend, this seems to me to be the best and quickest way."

Cammy mulled over that.

"If you find her, what will you do?" she asked. He checked a cufflink. "Seriously," she said.

"That will depend on the state in which I find her," he said.

"She's fine," Cammy told him.

"Then there is nothing for you to fear." He stepped to the door.

"When will you be back?"

He paused. "By the morning, God willing," he said.

It still weirded her out that he was religious. Also that he didn't seem to notice how his psychopathy didn't jive with the whole "love thy neighbor" message. She wanted to point this out to him, but his not-threats-but-warnings still lingered in her mind. From what little she'd seen, he seemed to be the "do unto others *before* they did unto you" rather than "as you would have done" sort of person. That had saved her once, but she still didn't know what might tick him off just enough to reverse that rescue.

"Here you are," Malcolm said, setting down the boxes. He went to the immaculate fridge that must date from the nineties and looked inside. Clearly there was nothing he wanted, so he took one of the fancy tea cups and poured himself some wine from one of the cabinets. "Want some?" he offered, reaching for another tea cup. She shook her head. "Suit yourself." He chugged the tea cup, poured himself another, then spun one of the antique kitchen chairs around, swung one of his long legs over it, and plopped down at the table. He flipped open one of the boxes, revealing a deep-dish, extra, extra, *extra* meat pizza.

"Um, I'm vegetarian," she reminded him. He flipped open the other box, revealing an equally overloaded vegetarian option. She eyed him pointedly, then retrieved one of the china plates from a cabinet before seating herself at the table and helping herself to a slice.

She did her best answering her friends as she ate. Malcolm wolfed—*ha*, she thought—his own pizza.

"You like meat because you're a werewolf?" she asked.

"No," he said. "Because seven days without meat makes one *weak*." He cracked a winning smile. She didn't. He made a face. "You always this fun?"

"My best friend from middle school might be kidnapped by vampires," she told him icily. His honey-colored eyes searched hers for a moment or two, before he returned his attention to his greasy heart-attack-in-waiting. Like Dracula, he made no attempt to reassure her.

"You think she's dead?" Cammy accused.

"No." He shook his head while speaking through his mouthful. "I think she's worse than that."

Cammy gritted her teeth.

"Well, I don't," she said. He nodded noncommittally.

"Suit yourself."

"So you're a bucket of sunshine, too," she noted.

"Nah, just more experienced than you," he said.

"So how'd you get into all this?" she wondered. "Get bitten by a berserker?"

He shook his head. "Not contagious. That's something new. I'm born and bred. Got some extra modifications thrown in for good measure."

He didn't look like anything supernatural. He looked like a jock who had graduated to pro sports, or perhaps modeling.

"Such as?" she asked.

"Such as of your business," he said, looking up from his pizza menacingly at her.

Maybe being a supernatural creature meant you were obligated to be unfriendly.

"Okay," she said, and rose to wash her plate. "Good night."

"Wait, hang on," he said. "Look, I'm not used to talking about all this, all right? Everyone I know already knows all the nitty gritty, or they're just a date and I get to talk about movies or whatever, all right?"

She crossed her arms. He shook his head and wiped his mouth with the back of his hand.

"I'm sorry, okay?" he snapped. "I wasn't trying to be rude. It's just not something I like to talk about."

"Any particular reason why?"

"It's not like all this is my choice, all right? The job, the... berserking thing, none of it. All that was set in motion hundreds of years ago." He spread his hands. "I'm just along for the ride."

"Okay," she said. "Sorry for prying. I'm just curious. No one tells me anything."

"Probably for the best," he said. "A little knowledge can be more dangerous than no knowledge."

"How's that?"

"You know, if you don't know anything, you're likelier to keep your distance. You know a little, you think you know enough to handle yourself." He shook his head. "But you don't really. People in this line of work have to study for a long time. If I told you that you could kill a werewolf with a silver bullet, you might go out there with a six shooter with custom bullets, but that wouldn't do you any good if you ran into something else, say a weretiger."

"There are *weretigers?*"

"There's a lot of weres," he said. "That's the point. There's a lot to take in."

"So what about empusas?" she asked.

"What about 'em?"

"You tried to get Vlad to deal with one, and Boese said there was an empusa running around."

Malcolm's pizza slice drooped back into the box. He frowned.

"Director Boese?" he asked. "Of Special Services?"

"That's the one."

"You *met* him?"

"Yeah, he came up here to threaten to throw Vlad in a box if this whole vampire thing wasn't wrapped up by tomorrow."

Malcolm crossed his arms on the table and leaned on his elbows. He squinted up at her.

"What did you do?"

"*Me?* Nothing! I just got rescued from these vampires."

"...And now you're living *here*," Malcolm finished, and nodded at the kitchen. "Yeah, I can see why'd he be suspicious. Why'd Vlad take you in?"

"I don't know," Cammy confessed. "I thought maybe he was old-fashioned and chivalrous, or whatever. But now I don't know."

"At least tell me you were as fun-loving with the director as you've been with me?" Malcolm asked.

"I was worse." She grinned.

He pointed at her. "Hey, I might just be starting to warm up to you."

She decided she could manage another slice if Malcolm wasn't going to be rude, but let him have his space. She had a thousand questions, but he wasn't very forthcoming. She'd have to gain his trust first, it seemed.

"So empusas are a kind of demon-vampire," Malcolm started explaining. "They're like succubi. They prey on men and have one brass leg and the other has a cloven hoof. They used to be the daughters of Hecate, but folklore has changed so now they're more run-of-the-mill blood-sucking evil spirits. You can drive them off if you insult them."

"That seems easy enough," Cammy said. "Why didn't Vlad go for it? It seems like he's good at killing vampires. Plus he really knows how to be insulting."

Malcolm shook his head. "You can drive them off with insults, but that doesn't kill them. I'm not sure how to kill them, and it would only be a waste of time and resources to have someone following this thing around to keep driving it away. As far as Vlad..." Malcolm searched for crumbs left in his box, then shut the lid. "I don't know if it would be a good idea to send him, honestly. He's a strigoi, you know, old school. So he's more vampire than incubus, and he's probably not well-equipped to actually fight one of those things. He might even be susceptible."

Cammy took a moment to parse out what an incubus was. Oh. *Oh.* So when he gave her the key, was it really for the *other thing?* Was that why he was okay with having satyrs around?

"So, strigoi...*can*...?"

"Oh, yeah," Malcolm said. He poured himself another cup of wine. "It's one of their more infamous features, actually."

"But, *how?* I mean, they're dead aren't they?"

"They walk and talk and run businesses and eat *food* even though they're dead," Malcolm pointed out. "A lot of food, actually. And not all of them are dead. There can be living ones. I suppose they're a flavor of hungry ghost."

"Hungry ghost?"

"That's a specific term from Buddhism, but I like using it to describe some of the things I've encountered. You don't see that kind of revenant too much anymore: the kind that are ravenously hungry all the time. I guess that famine isn't the specter it used to be, so people aren't worried about it so much these days. A lot of cultures envisioned the afterlife as being everlasting hunger, or that ghosts would be ravenous." He shrugged. "Same with strigoi, though they also go for blood."

"Human?"

"Sure. Animal, whatever," he said. "It's not really my area of expertise, mind you, since I've never seen a strigoi except for Vlad. The old school don't seem to be popping up anymore."

"So what is your area of expertise?" she asked.

"Mostly I do recon stuff," Malcolm said. "Investigation. I don't usually deal with ethereal stuff or demons. I'm not equipped for it. If it bleeds, though, usually I can kill it."

"So what kind of stuff have you killed?" Cammy tentatively asked. He huffed and crossed his arms. Leaning back, he scanned the living room adjacent to the kitchen.

"Does he have cable?" he asked.

"Uh...." Cammy said, nonplussed by the non sequitur.

Malcolm rose from the table, crumpled his pizza box and stuffed it into the trash can by the fridge. He walked into the living room. Cammy rose to follow, but remembered Vlad's warning about his domovoy, so stored her box in the fridge—she had plenty of pizza to live on for a while. She might be able to make it to pay day now!—and quickly rinsed and wiped her plate before leaving the room. She found Malcolm wandering towards the hall, his hands thrust into his pockets.

"Is it safe to wander around?" Cammy asked.

"I've been up here a few times," Malcolm replied, then wiped at his nose with his thumb. "Haven't seen the whole place yet. I saw a TV once with those old rabbit ears. Don't know if he has anything newer than that."

"Why doesn't he know about new stuff?" Cammy asked.

"Not sure," Malcolm said. "He never seemed interested."

"Well, Boese said he had kept him in a box. He was chopping him up or something."

"Sounds about right," Malcolm said, and he opened a door to look inside. He poked his head in, glanced around, and shut the door. "From the stories I hear, they do all sorts of Frankenstein experiments down there."

"What? Why?" Cammy demanded.

"To figure out what they can about the remaining supernatural bugaboos, I guess," Malcolm said. He looked over his shoulder at her before opening another door. "How do you think they got a vaccine for vampirism?"

"There's a *vaccine* for vampirism?"

"Yep. Ever since the whole virus thing became a staple, there've been incidents. Lucky for us, injecting a little ridiculous science into the supernatural gave Uncle Sam a chance to get ahead of that curve. Everyone gets vaccinated against it these days."

Cammy boggled at the thought.

"How?"

"I guess they mix it in with some standard ones or lie about what one of them is," Malcolm said.

"If that's true, then how are people getting turned out there? Shouldn't everyone be immune?"

"To the viral version, yeah," Malcolm said. "Thing is, vampirism was spreading long before the 'virus' idea. So anything slightly older isn't affected by the vaccine." He wandered through the door he'd opened. When she followed, she found a room with a similar layout to her bedroom upstairs, except there was a couch set before an old-fashioned TV with the bunny ears that Malcolm had described. He stood before the darkened set.

"Looks like no cable," she observed. "Are you really going to be here all night?"

"Yep."

"Why?"

"I guess he must be worried," Malcolm said. "Also, he paid me about ten thousand."

"*Ten thousand?*"

"It's my going rate," Malcolm said, "and this time it's all mine."

"Hunting monsters pays pretty well, huh?" she observed.

"Eh, sorta. Probably not better than being a PI. Usually I don't see any of it, so I do odd jobs here and there. I think Vlad gets bored by some of what Boese has him do and he delegates to me instead."

"How'd you guys meet?"

"Oh, my second time out I was hunting this ghoul," he said. "I was cocky, got in over my head. He was out patrolling for monsters, happened to be there." Malcolm shrugged. "That's basically it."

"You became besties just like that?"

"We're not *besties*," Malcolm snapped. "Comrades in arms. He's bumped into the Order of Ophois more than once. We have files on him."

"Really? What sort of files?" she asked. She rubbed her thumb over her hand. It throbbed a little.

"What happened to your hand?"

"The driver grabbed me. I guess hard enough to bruise," she said. "I've also got a bruise on my ankle and my hip, too."

"Just be careful. If the skin was broken, you don't want anything getting in there when it comes to vampires," he said.

She squinted at her knuckles. Just a bruise, so far as she could see. Malcolm reached for her hand. She flinched, seeing the size of his palms. They reminded her of those big, dead hands.

"May I?" he asked, seeing her reaction. She offered her hand. He leaned in to look at it, and seemed to sniff it.

"That's odd," he murmured. "Why would he—?" He glanced up at her and cut himself short.

"Why would he what? Why would who what?" Cammy demanded.

"Nothing." He shook his head and put on his winning smile. "Never mind."

He let go of her hand and she stared at it again. If it was unusual, why was it unusual? The driver had grabbed both her hands, but only this one was bruised, and down near the knuckles, just above them, where you could just see the veins rippling the skin.

This was the hand Dracula had placed that gross kiss on, now that she thought about it. Just above the knuckles.

No way, she thought, *No way*. "You mean, you mean this is…Vlad did this? What did he do? Is his spit infectious or something?"

"No, that's not—I mean, we should probably ask him when he gets back," Malcolm said. "I'm sure there's a reason for—"

"*What did he do?*" Cammy pressed. "You said it's bad news if anything gets in a wound—"

"But there's no wound; don't worry about it," Malcolm assured her. "We'll ask him when he gets back, okay?"

"But what did he do? What is this?"

Malcolm's mouth screwed up somewhere between a snarl and a grimace of discomfort. His eyes wandered the walls.

"That looks kind of like the sort of bruising, you know, that strigoi make."

"What do you mean? Make how?"

"They don't precisely need to bite you to suck your blood," he explained through a wince. Her mouth dropped open, and she stared at her hand.

"He… *sucked my blood?*"

Malcolm winced harder, and nodded. "I think so," he said.

She scrutinized the bruise. Nothing. No punctures, no teeth marks, no scrapes. Just a bruise. But somehow he'd sucked her blood.

Is this why he's letting me stay here? Did he infect me? She felt her head spinning, her chest throbbing. "Is it—what do I do?" she gasped. "Am I going to turn? What do I do?"

"Shh!" Malcolm hissed, and slapped one of his big hands over her mouth. She wrestled with his fingers, but he pressed them harder, his head towards the door. At last, he released her and stalked to the door to listen to the hall.

"What is it?" she whispered.

He gestured she stay put and slipped out into the hall. She came to the door and saw him power-walking towards the far end. She hurried after him. He heard her coming, despite the lavish carpet on the wooden floorboards, and glared over his shoulder at her.

He opened a set of double doors to a grand room full of guns, swords, stuffed animals—the taxidermy kind—and a *cannon*. Malcolm went in without flipping the lights, so she searched for the switch and turned them on herself.

One of the taxidermy animals was a griffin—an actual griffin! With wings and everything!—and there were bits of armor and weird-looking tools or weapons.

"You're going to want to grab something," Malcolm told her. He grabbed a double-headed axe with a long pike on the end and felt the heft of it. That seemed to satisfy him, so he headed back out.

"What's going on?" Cammy whispered.

"We've got company."

"Should we call the police?"

He frowned at her.

"Not that kind of company," he said.

Her stomach tried to vibrate its way right out of her body, and her fingers trembled.

"Okay, so here's the deal," he told her, licking his lips. "You're going to stay up here, in the house. I'll be outside. Whatever happens, don't get close to me. When I go, I'm liable to kill anything that moves. Stake 'em, behead 'em, got it?"

"Do what?" she asked.

"Kill 'em," he said. "You understand? If any of them come after you, kill 'em before they get to you. If these are the same guys as before, standard weaknesses don't apply, so you've got to kill them."

"I can't," she told him. Her voice was so small. "I can't, I can't—"

"Or you can die. Your choice," he told her, and shrugged with one shoulder. "They'll be here soon. Sounds like they're having trouble with the things that guard this place, though. Weird. They didn't come prepared."

"What do you mean?"

"I mean, everyone knows Vlad has his little monster sanctuary up here. If you were going to storm the place, you'd case it first and make sure you had stuff which could fight his little buddies."

"Like the satyrs?" Cammy demanded snidely.

"No, like the vili and the rusalki," Malcolm snarled at her. "You know, the vampire-ghost-women things he's got."

"Vampire-ghost-women?" Cammy repeated. Dracula hadn't described them that way. "Are they dangerous?"

"Are they *dangerous?!*" Malcolm repeated. "Listen: I don't have the time to tutor you in vampire-ghost-ladies 101, all right? But here's the Cliff Notes: *yeah*. Now stay inside." He turned and stormed to the backdoor, swung it open, and glanced outside. Cammy expected him to step out, but instead he pulled his phone and called from his contacts list.

"Yo, Vlad," he said into the phone. "Bad news. We've got company up here. Sounds like they're struggling, but there's a lot of them." He leaned out the door. "Hard to tell. I think your friends are holding the line." He glanced at Cammy. "I told her to stay inside. If anything happens, that's not my—" He flinched. "Oh, really?" He chuckled nervously. "Remind me not to babysit for you in the future, then." He hung up, considered Cammy, and wiped one palm on his pants. He tried to smile. "Stay put, yeah?"

"What'd he say?" Cammy asked. Malcolm shook his head, adjusted his grip on his weapon, and went out, swinging the door shut behind him. Cammy ran to lock it behind him. She pressed her ear to the wood, but didn't hear anything. Some stupid part of her wanted to throw open the door and see if she could spot the danger, and another part of her screamed that was even stupider than her coming up here in the first place. Then she realized she had no weapon. Her hands were shaking. Malcolm had told her she would have to kill them, but could she? Could she look someone in the eye and hack them to death? She squeezed her eyes shut, and saw in her mind's eye the crowd of vampires Dracula had rescued her from, all lying on the ground beheaded. She tried to picture herself doing that, but her head shook all on its own. No way. No way could she look someone in the eye and chop their head off. She wanted to throw up even thinking about it.

Then she thought that Heather might be out there. Out there, with a whole pile of vampires, dangerous vampire-ghost-ladies, and Malcolm, whatever he was like. She threw open the door and scanned the darkness. She hadn't realized how dark the night was. Just beyond the tree tops, she could see the city winking through leaves, sprawling out on either side, but darkness beyond where the city met the water. The trees were black, the ground was black. The night sky was overcast and caught some of the city light and reflected it, glowing a little in yellow, dark blue, and violet.

In the black she couldn't even see Malcolm. The warm light from behind her shot out in a rectangle across the gravel driveway. Her shadow inside that rectangle was the only thing she could distinctly make out.

She held her breath and strained her ears. Lots of wind, leaves rustling. Malcolm had very sharp ears. Must come with the whole hereditary werewolf thing. Unless he was pranking her. But he'd also called Dracula. She knew he wouldn't take kindly to being pranked.

She was feeling pretty exposed standing in the lit doorway. As she turned to close the door, she heard something. She hesitated in the doorway, her ears straining. Now she definitely heard it. Distant screams that were only vaguely human. She couldn't tell how many. Like Malcolm said: lots.

She darted inside and slammed the door shut, then locked it. Malcolm had told her to get a weapon. But what? An axe? There was no way she could wield an axe. No way she could swing it and take off someone's head. She glanced around the room. The kitchen wasn't too far off. She hurried to it and made a quick search of the drawers. There was a real big kitchen knife, and she snatched it up and gripped it tight in her bruised hand. Then she dropped it and clutched her hair. What kind of idiot was going to defend themselves against a bunch of vampires with a kitchen knife?

Or you can die. Your choice, she heard in her mind. And, *There is never reason to kill a person?*

No, she thought at the voices. *No, you can figure a way around it. No.*

You only say that because you've never been tried, she heard in response. Good ol' Mr. Sunshine and Rainbows himself.

She looked out the window, but didn't spot anything. Just more blackness. She did hear a distant scream that cut short just as it started.

Was that Malcolm doing that, or the vampire-women? She thought back on the group that Dracula had so effectively cut down. Malcolm had said this new group was struggling. That was weird, wasn't it? Like they were baffled that this group didn't behave like they knew what they were doing. Cammy supposed even vampires had to get their starts somehow.

A window beside the front door shattered and she jumped straight in the air. Glass crunched across the floor, and her heart rattled inside her. She wanted to move, but couldn't. Her feet refused to carry her anywhere, not that she knew where to go. Her hand refused to take up the knife again.

You've never been tried.

The glass stopped clinking, and her heart throbbed in her brain. Her eyes remained frozen, nailed in place, staring at the space that separated the kitchen from the room with the fireplace and the foyer. Her eyes kept waiting for a dark shadow to walk into that empty space.

A million years passed, and the fireplace kept throwing out its flickering light, but no one walked in front of it to obscure its light. At last, she managed to force her hand to slap her thigh, and she jumped into motion. She grabbed the kitchen knife and slowly, agonizingly slowly, trembled her way to the other room. Empty. Silent. She trembled further and glanced at the front door. Someone was halfway through the window, one arm draped down to touch the floor. She stared, but the someone didn't move, so she timidly crept forward. After a moment, she could understand why they were so oddly bent over—the rest of the someone was missing from the middle of the torso down.

She covered her mouth and turned away. The air was thin again. She squeezed her eyes shut and listened to the blood inside her ears.

Then she realized it was quiet outside. She turned to the window, strained to listen, but there was nothing.

As she stood debating going closer to listen for more danger, the front door swung wide open and she nearly jumped out of her skin to see a shadowy silhouette standing there, an axe over one shoulder. Malcolm said nothing, just loomed in the doorway for a moment. He seemed *bigger* than when he had left, but maybe Cammy's eyes were playing tricks on her. Malcolm stalked inside, came near enough to the fireplace for her to see him. She stepped back. He *looked* different. Not like the playful jock from before; he looked like a thug, like a barbarian. She thought that even his face looked different, but she couldn't say how.

Malcolm crossed over to the very uncomfortable divan and flopped down into it, his wrists on his knees, the axe still in his hands, its blade streaked with sticky blood.

"You okay?" Cammy asked.

"Don't talk to me right now," he said. His voice was different, too. Gruffer, unfriendly.

She left the room.

* * *

Colston Terry rose from his chair and stalked towards the window. He'd been over the footage his minions had recorded several times and had learned nothing new. Cautiously, he pressed himself against the wall and with one finger lifted one window-blind slat to peer outside. The sun would be up soon; perhaps its fingers of light were already tickling the horizon. He pulled down the extra sun protection he had purchased several months ago for privacy and to help him sleep. Technically, he still used it for that purpose, but his circumstances had changed.

Four months ago he'd woken up because a ray of sunlight had snuck past the thick, black sheet and cut across his forehead. It had set his face on fire and woken him immediately. Then he was in the bathroom trying to put himself out and beset by an absolutely irresistible and unmistakable thirst for human blood.

It had taken looking twice into the mirror for the revelation to sink in that he didn't reflect anymore. No amount of pawing at the glass had brought his image back. That had proved a bit of a problem; he could definitely feel that his face was in bad shape, but couldn't tell how bad it was. Luckily, it didn't take him long to realize he healed up fast, especially if he drank blood.

Colston had never wrestled with the reality of what had happened. Thinking back on it, that seemed strange. It should have taken him at least a little while to come to terms with the fact that vampires were real, and he had somehow become one. It hadn't. He was only surprised not to see himself in the mirror, not confounded, the same with sunlight searing like a blowtorch.

He'd checked his neck; no bite marks. He'd tried to think who he had met and when and how this could have happened. There'd been some girl or other from a club about a week before he'd had over. She'd given him a hickey, among other things, but he wasn't sure she was the reason. Even if she was, he didn't exactly have her name to look her up.

At first, getting blood had been really difficult. He'd wandered the streets in the dark, nervous, alone, and found people who seemed vulnerable and equally alone. Then one of those people tracked him down after he had tossed them in the Sound, and he simply knew he had command of this person. And that a lot of the people he'd preyed on before might also be up and running around as well. Options started presenting themselves. He could experiment and find out what killed the vampires he made—he presumed he'd be killed by the same methods—what they could and could not recover from, how far he could command. He was pretty sure he was immortal now. Some kind of super human, a totally apex predator. What else would you call something that preyed on the otherwise obvious apex predator of planet earth?

So he'd carefully reached out to certain people in power he figured might want a slice of the pie. Sure, starting up a rideshare was nice. But it hadn't taken him long to think to himself that immortality would have its perks and its downsides, and that he ought to think *real* long-term about his future. He'd need lots of power in case police ever came knocking at his door. He'd need fake IDs going forward, the works. A few people came on board once he proved to them he was legit, not some nut. Some were less impressed, and one had threatened to out him. That man had been fished out of the harbor a while ago—liberated of his very valuable blood first, of course.

He was being as careful as he knew how, given he had a steep learning curve and no one to show him how to survive as a bona fide vampire. But he was a smart guy, an innovative guy, someone who liked challenges and thinking outside the box. He never had his minions hunt right out of the vehicles, oh no. That would surely come back to him eventually. They scoped out rides, asked questions. Were these people alone? Visiting? Had lonely relatives out somewhere? Then he collated a database of people who might be best picks, or who had routines he might be able to exploit. Still, he was careful. Some of the victims had to be chosen randomly just to spread blood out thick enough for him and his minions. Quite a few were going very hungry, and they misbehaved when they were hungry. They even defied him—or bent his orders to the breaking point—if they got hungry enough.

He liked to talk to the people who got turned, just to see if he thought they could be useful. If not, minions could easily be destroyed. He hadn't meant to keep that one addict, except she promised her roommate wouldn't be missed, and their landlord hadn't been paid, so her roommate was likely to be evicted soon. He'd agreed it seemed like an easy enough hit and had let her be, planning to get rid of her once he had the roommate. She was only likely to be helpful in the event that people *did* come knocking, since the roommate's mother had some ties to some law firm or other.

The thing that had been driving him nuts was that his minions kept turning up dead. He'd slapped "Don't Forget" together—under the excuse that it protected his drivers from groundless accusations—in the hopes of seeing who or what it was, but it wasn't until the roommate that he got a look at the mystery murderer. Some older man who hadn't even bothered with the phone.

Now Colston knew more about this man. He'd looked him up, his address, whatever he could find.

Having no idea how it was he himself had turned into a vampire, he had puzzled for a long time over the man's name. A few months prior, he'd have laughed at it, but not now. Colston supposed there must be other vampires somewhere; he hadn't sprung into existence from nothing. Perhaps he was in someone's territory and had been cutting into this established person's chosen food supply. Perhaps he'd committed some sort of vampire faux pas. But he'd heard enough from the phone and "Don't Forget" to learn this man, this *true* vampire was simply hunting Colston down to kill him.

Colston chewed his thumb. Though his teeth did considerable damage to the meat, it didn't hurt. That sort of thing didn't cause pain anymore.

He assumed that all the minions he'd sent to that mansion had died trying to take out this clearly superior vampire. The one sent to spy at the restaurant had also been killed. Colston had no idea how it was this enemy had so outclassed him. Maybe vampires got stronger with age. This enemy was no doubt cream of the crop when it came to vampires.

And coming to kill him. He chewed a little on the bone in his thumb.

His phone rang, and he glanced over at it. His CFO. He strode to his desk and swiped up the phone, took up the stylus he'd been forced to purchase, and answered.

"Awful early for you to be calling," he said. "Everything okay, Janine?" He started lazily tracing a path around the room; he liked to pace while he thought.

"I'm fine, but there are federal officers at the office. They'd like to talk to you."

Colston froze in his tracks.

"Feds?" he asked. *The murders*, he thought. But which one? Or all of them? Maybe they thought there was a serial killer operating in the area. Had he still been alive, he supposed his blood would be running cold, or his heart would be racing. Not now.

"Yes, I told them you were on vacation, just like you said, but—"

"Janine, I *am* on vacation," he hissed into the phone, then, "Did you tell them where?"

"No, just you were out of town."

Colston drew in a breath to breathe it out as a sigh of relief.

"What do they want, Janine?"

"They said they're investigating some murders. That they want access to anything we've recorded on Don't Forget. They think maybe our drivers recorded something."

"We don't keep those records long-term, Janine, you know that."

"I told them, but they thought maybe you had some kept, or maybe the drivers…?"

"Janine, we purge that data. It's in our Privacy Policy. Tell them to read that again if they don't believe you."

The line was silent. Colston squinted, imagining she was chewing her lip and debating saying something she knew he wouldn't like.

"What is it?" he demanded.

"Well, I thought—didn't you keep some of that, you know, personally?"

"Who told you that?"

"I just heard you were still doing work remotely and I know you like having your finger on the pulse of the company and assumed—"

"I don't want to get *sued*, Janine. I don't keep anything."

"But…" He heard her suck in a breath as she debated pressing forward. "I saw in the code—"

"You're not a coder. Tell them we don't have what they're looking for. Get rid of them."

"They're *feds*, Colston. They'll just get a court order if they think that—"

"Then they better go get one!" Colston hissed. "I'm out of town. If they think they have something, tell them to come back after they've talked to a judge. Good bye."

"But Col—"

He hung up and tossed the phone on the bed. He crossed one arm across his chest so he could keep chewing on his thumb. What with trying to figure out who or what was killing his minions, he hadn't had the chance to reach out to many powerful people. He had nothing solid nailed down on that front. If feds were already here, would they be able to trace a string of murders back to him? He doubted it. Even if they could, he ought to have a little time while they ran off to get warrants or collect evidence or whatever they had to do. But they were going to be a problem. Them, and the *big* problem.

He was really up a creek without a paddle. Clearly, his adversary had better abilities, or knowledge, or both. Colston had nothing to negotiate with. If he moved, the feds might follow him. He needed more information before he just packed up his whole operation and tried to figure out how to fly to some foreign country with no extradition without being exposed to sunlight the whole trip. For all he knew, every major city had some big, bad vampire set up in it and he'd be right back where he started. He needed to get a vise around his enemy somehow. After he'd learned the man's name, he'd read Stoker's book for reference. Some of what was in there seemed to line up: the strength, the ability to go out in the day. Non-silver crucifixes didn't bother Colston, so he'd grabbed a few in the hopes that they would work against his enemy, but he hadn't figured out a good way to get holy wafers. He figured he'd have to get a minion to steal some, which would be either time-consuming or tricky. But if this guy was like the one in the book, that meant he could shapeshift into freaking *mist* if he wanted to. He was only really vulnerable if he was sleeping. Or maybe he was worse than the book. Who could say?

The only way he could think to move forward now was the druggie's roommate. The enemy hadn't killed her or turned her, and seemed to be protecting her. Coslton couldn't imagine why. Maybe his enemy had some chivalric habits from yester-century, or maybe he was keeping her for a rainy day; maybe it was like the book and people he really wanted to turn took a while, so she was going to be his plaything in a month or two. But he'd looked after her safety. So that meant she was the only easy target Colston knew about. The druggie had said the girl and her parents weren't on speaking terms. That seemed likely, since she had reached out to a total stranger rather than call on family for help after being evicted, but the roommate was friends with a cop, so he had to be careful there. The druggie had a vague idea of the roommate's other friends, but social media had filled those gaps in much better. The photographer, the horror cinema chick, the hot dancer, the shy guy who never posted but got tagged all the time. Colston would have to try being bold. If feds were already alerted, he'd have to find a new place to hide—just in case. If they suspected anything they'd likely come knocking at his house, so he'd have to find somewhere he could stay without using his name. Should be easy enough. While he was at it, since there were feds sniffing around, he needed someone to take the fall for a few murders. He'd find someone. Maybe he could roll the two problems into one and lay the blame on the roommate's family or friends somehow. Then while the feds and his enemy were tangled up in trying to figure that mess out, Colston could slip out the back door and settle somewhere else. He could pull all the money out of the company and just vanish. Like mist. He smirked. Maybe his enemy wasn't the only one who could do that.

CHAPTER 7

ALL IN THE FAMILY

Brian flipped a pen in his hand. Not that he needed it, since he sat at his computer, but it helped him think.

Okay, facts, he thought to himself. *Supposedly the guy is sixty-four, though he sure doesn't look it. He's got two IDs. FBI didn't verify the other name, but someone called the chief and got him released despite the loaded weapons. He lives in a mansion purchased by a foreign dignitary a century ago.*

So far, he hadn't been able to locate a doctor by either name, but without more than the regular internet he hadn't expected to find anything conclusive, especially not if he was European.

Heather hadn't been at any of the usual haunts where people picked up coke or other serious drugs, and he'd had been forced to concede defeat. Then he'd headed home to see what he could scrounge up about Cammy's new friend.

His real name was spelled Dragulya. Brian had stumbled across the historical figure's signature while looking for some sort of psychological profile. Historical figure spelled it the same way, and the signature on the driver's license was oddly similar. Odd, because if the man wanted to style himself like the dead madman, one would think he'd have practiced getting it closer.

Despite the real weapons, the lunatic also liked carrying around goth props in his multimillion dollar vehicle—which he had already verified was authentic. Akerman hadn't felt like helping him do more, so Brian had approached Suze for a little more digging. The thing that had him right now was the fact that though the house and vehicles had changed hands over the years, he couldn't find birth or death records for the "father-to-son-to-son" theory.

He *really* didn't like where his brain kept taking him.

He heard keys in the lock in the next room, and rose from the computer. It was a small apartment, but now that he and Melissa were gainfully employed, with any luck, they'd finally be able to afford their own places and move properly into the adult world. He wasn't eighteen anymore, but he still felt like it sometimes. Melissa was six years older than he was; did she feel that way too?

She opened the door to their little apartment, two take-out bags in her off-hand. Her hair looked extra scraggly. He knew the look of "I've had the worst day".

"What happened?" he asked.

"Got pus in my hair. Don't ask, you don't want to know," she answered. He took the takeaway bags off her hands. Chinese, her favorite. "Had to wash it off in a sink. How was your day? Cammy started texting again, so it seems she's okay. Who's the weirdo she's staying with?"

Brian pressed his mouth shut. "Ooh, I don't like that look," Melissa said. "You ran a background check, didn't you? He a friend of Heather's?"

"No," Brian told her. "You want the whole story?"

"Am I going to like it?" Melissa called over her shoulder, wandering to the kitchen to get a beer. The two-bedroom apartment wasn't all that run-down, but it wasn't going to win any prizes, either. You could reach the kitchen from the door in about eight steps, and guests walked straight into the living room. There was one bathroom. Melissa had the master bedroom while he had the side one. She was older, and had sprung more money for the place, so it was only fair.

Melissa was his half-sister from before the divorce, but she was more of a mother to him and Cammy than any of their parents had been. She'd been the only one to support his decision to become a cop. Cammy had hated the idea and rarely passed up a chance to dig at him for it.

Melissa cracked one open and guzzled several generous gulps. After wiping her mouth, she leaned on the little island shelf that nearly fenced the miniscule kitchen off from the living room. "Proceed," she said, sipping from the can.

He told her everything that he'd found, everything the man had said, and everything that had happened. Melissa drained the can, belched, and shook her head.

"Wow, I don't like that at all. Is he one of Kenzie's friends? That might explain the prop weapons."

"Don't think so. They got introduced this morning. Why Kenzie?"

"She's the horror movie nut," Melissa said. "Remember? Cammy's told us about her before."

Before. How long had it been since they'd all been able to hang out, just for fun? His new career ate up all his time, and Cammy worked odd shifts during and between semesters. Had it been years already? The realization socked him between the eyes.

"You're going to have to pay better attention than that," Melissa warned him, "if you want a chance with her. Plus, you're a cop now. I thought paying attention is what they paid you to do?"

"Let's not change the subject," he said, frowning. "What do you think about the situation?"

"I think it stinks," she said. She reached for the takeout bags, which he passed over. She opened one of the boxes and began eating sweet and sour pork directly out of the box with a plastic utensil she fished out of a drawer.

He wrestled with the stupid thoughts that kept wriggling around in his brain, telling them to stay where they were, but couldn't help himself and blurted, "I mean, but about him. It's weird. It's like he's got some connection with, you know."

"Know what?"

"With"—he sighed—"the real Dracula."

"Maybe he does." Melissa shrugged. "Maybe he's a descendant, and he's really into it. And a little..."—she rolled her finger in a circle next to her temple—"you know? Lots of European nobility were inbred, right? Hemophilia and insanity. Maybe he's not all there upstairs; too many cousins screwing cousins screwing cousins."

"Maybe," he agreed. "But it bugs me." He struggled to shut the thoughts up, but he could tell Melissa knew he had more to say. He cleared his throat. "For example, this guy is *strong*. I mean, I've wrestled a little with some people who were trippin', and with the guys at the station. Those were all *nothing* compared to this lunatic. He threw this tweaker into a wall like it was nothing. One-handed, I should add."

"Maybe he works out?" Melissa suggested.

"*I* work out," Brian told her. "This guy is something else. And I can't figure out how he was able to skate out of the station today. Makes no sense. I don't know how whoever it was who called even knew he was there. Who would have told them?"

Melissa raised her eyebrows, stared at the ceiling while she chewed.

"Sounds like someone at the station must have made a call," she said.

That was the most logical explanation. But who, and more importantly, *why?* Brian said as much.

"Dunno," Melissa said, and scooped another sporkful. "Money? You said this guy is rich, right?"

Could it be that simple? This guy was so wealthy and eccentric he had bribed some of the PD to look the other way for him? *But it would have to be Deble, too,* he realized, *he let the man go.* While he chewed on that, Melissa grabbed another beer and walked into the living room to flop down on their second-hand sofa.

"I don't know," he said. "I mean, the guy is rich, but I can't imagine there are that many people willing to overlook *felonies* because some loon pays them on the side."

Melissa shrugged. "That's all I could come up with," she said. He gritted his teeth.

"So, um"—he scratched the back of his head, dreading the words that were going to come out of his mouth—"do you think it's possible that, *maybe*, vampires...?"

Melissa almost choked on her mouthful of pork. She swallowed it as quickly as she could and chuckled.

"BB, be serious," she said. "You're letting your worrying run you in circles. He doesn't need to be a *vampire* for him to be bad news for Cammy."

"But *could* there be?" he pushed. Melissa sighed, then chugged another mouthful of beer.

"I mean, if you're talking about Renfield's Syndrome—the people who like drinking blood—then sure, whatever. But it's not like they're vampires, BB, they're ordinary humans who have a problem. There are people sensitive to light, people who think they're dead when they're not, all kinds of stuff. I guess if someone was unlucky enough to have the right—or wrong—cocktail of these disorders all at once, then maybe you'd have someone who would act like one. But they wouldn't *be* one, they'd just be someone who needs help."

"But maybe there's a disease we've never discovered that makes people—"

"BB," Melissa scolded. "This is weird. I agree. I don't like it. But follow the money, okay? Don't worry about monsters and ghouls. Cammy's probably in trouble, and she needs you to keep your head screwed on straight."

"Yeah," he agreed. "Will you call her? She's lying to me about what happened, and I can't get her to come clean. Maybe she'll listen to you."

"I will," she promised. "After I take a shower, okay? I feel like a plague rat."

"Okay," he agreed. "But be really careful about this guy. I've never heard of *anything* this weird in my life. He's running around impersonating a federal agent, and I don't know how, but he's doing it with impunity. He *knew* he was going to get released; he thought getting arrested was funny. And he walks around with enough firepower to down a squad by himself. He's dangerous, *real* dangerous. Please don't play around."

"Don't you worry, I'm not gonna play around," she assured him. She sighed and headed to the bathroom and shut the door. "Help yourself!" she shouted through the wood. He considered the takeout. He didn't feel hungry, but he ought to eat something. After he had spooned out some beef and broccoli onto a pile of rice, he took his dinner back into his bedroom and shut the door. His bed muscled most of the few other pieces of furniture out of the way, so he skirted it to his desk and sat down.

He pulled out his phone.

"Hey, Kenzie? It's Brian from earlier. Cammy's friend. I hear you like horror movies?"

* * *

Dracula watched the legs the Cabernet left on the glass after he swirled it. Despite the price tag, even the "best" American wines were inferior to what he used to drink in France and his home country. It wasn't just that they had changed vines after the blight in the 1800s—he had not cared for the foreign vintage when it first appeared in Europe—there must be something in the process which Americans employed which made wine so unpalatable.

He sipped from the glass and wondered if he'd ever taste good wine ever again.

So far, no one had approached. No one had sent a message. No contact of any kind. He hadn't expected to meet *nothing*. A certain reticence and caution, but not *nothing*. If no one showed soon, he would have to find another method to track the elusive rats down. He'd have to wander the city again, and he'd had his fill of that.

The staff here knew him by face, knew more or less the things he liked, and that he tipped well. Very well. He despised the demeaning practice, but so long as he was stranded in proverbial Rome, he did as the Romans. His money ensured good service, at least. The young man who had brought him the bottle of overpriced wine returned to refill his glass just as his phone rang.

"Yo, Vlad," Malcolm said. "Bad news, we've got lots of company up here. Sounds like they're struggling, but there's a lot of them."

Dracula could scarcely believe the cretins he'd been hunting would make an attempt on his home.

"How many?"

"Hard to tell. I think your friends are holding the line."

"What about my guest? Will you be able to protect her?"

"I told her to stay inside. If anything happens, that's not my—"

"If anything happens to her, I'll castrate you and cut your throat."

The young man pouring his wine flicked his eyes at Dracula. He ignored the look.

"Oh, really?" Malcolm chuckled. "Remind me not to babysit for you in the future, then."

The line went dead. Dracula put his phone away. It would take him the better part of an hour to get back. He asked for the bill. Malcolm ought to be able to handle the problem, especially with the help of Dracula's other tenants, but he wondered why this enemy would make such a strange move.

Dracula's Guest

It felt as though he was playing chess with an opponent who thought himself very clever while having only read half the rule book. Such a bold move would have been unthinkable except for some of the most terrible of the monsters which roamed the world, and so far as he knew, none of those had bothered to visit Seattle.

A man's home was his castle, so the saying went. This enemy had tried to outflank him and take his castle. Whoever he was, he clearly did not find the idea of parlay palatable. So be it. Dracula had been to war before.

He dropped several hundreds on the table and rose to go. As he did, he spotted someone hunkered in a corner table in a not quite properly fitted sports jacket, furtively staring at him. He froze. He could think of no one who would find him so fascinating except one of those vermin.

They locked eyes. The vampire in the corner rose and made for the door. Dracula made after him. In his rush, he bumped a waitress, and one of the glasses on her tray toppled.

"My apologies," he told her. "Bill me for the glass."

She looked confused that he had offered, and only watched him go.

By the time he had gotten downstairs and reached the glass doors which exited to a small courtyard and the street, the vampire had crossed to the far side of the narrow street, passing by a bank. Despite the crowd of passersby, Dracula spotted him; he had abandoned his coat and donned a baseball cap. No doubt he expected this change of attire would throw off his pursuer. But Dracula had had experience disguising himself in life, and knew what to look for. This proved such a fascinating development that Dracula decided to wager. Malcolm ought to be able to hold his own. If these Hollywood rats were all equally ignorant, Dracula doubted any of them stood much chance against his tenants and a well-trained werewolf. He'd fought a few of them over the centuries. They could be formidable if one was unprepared. They could be formidable even if one was prepared. Meanwhile, *this* opportunity was not likely to present itself again.

Dracula used passersby, shrubs and trees along the sidewalk strips as cover as he pursued. Had he known he'd be engaged in a hunt on foot in this manner, he'd have brought something for disguise—he tended to dress more formally than the rest of the folk he saw on the streets—but alas, clairvoyance was not a talent he possessed.

The idiot glanced over his shoulder to scan the street for any sign he was being followed. Dracula had enough experience at this game to conceal his interest by facing the high-end storefront of the nearest building. The idiot did not notice him. So long as Dracula was careful to avoid the occasional dog-walker, he should be able to continue undetected. Dogs often growled or barked at him if he drew too close.

This was proving so easy that Dracula began to wonder if this was some sort of trap. Perhaps his opponent did know the game, but convincingly portrayed an amateur. Even so, he resolved to remain on his target. The idiot ducked down a side street, and Dracula had to cross the thoroughfare in an unsafe manner, given how dark it was and he being clothed in black. He managed to avoid being hit, though two drivers honked and swore at him out of their windows. Dracula passed through the side street to come upon an underground parking garage between two office complexes. He listened, caught the sound of feet, and did his best to follow them despite the ambient street noise and the echoing. He found the idiot hurrying down some stairs, his keys in his hand. Now the idiot saw he had been followed, actually gasped in surprise, and then sprinted. Dracula ran after him, only to find the idiot was faster than he was. He reached for his gun to try to cripple his prey, thought about his run-in with the police and Boese's sour mood.

He pulled one of his knives and threw that instead. It caught the fleeing man in the back of the knee, but at that distance did little damage. It did buy Dracula a few moments as the idiot hesitated to see whether he was badly hurt, to find his pant leg had taken the most of the strike.

He realized he had made an error in judgement when he saw Dracula had not wasted that time watching him, and turned to sprint away once more. Dracula slammed him into the door of the car he fumbled to unlock. This didn't hurt him, but it stopped him from getting away. The idiot pulled a hastily carved wooden stake from the back of his pants. Dracula grabbed his wrist and crushed the bones.

The idiot gasped when he realized his hand was useless and tried to wriggle free, so Dracula kicked at his ankle and snapped that next. The idiot flopped on the ground and made pathetic whimpering sounds as he tried to crawl away. Dracula stepped on his other ankle.

"Enough," he told him. "You're no messenger, so I suppose I need not treat you as one."

"Wha?" the idiot gasped.

"Surely you've heard the expression, 'Don't shoot the messenger?' It was taken literally once upon a time.

Messengers were sacred. But I can see you have nothing to tell me. So," he knelt and picked up the silly wooden stake. "Nothing sacred about you, is there?"

"Wait wait wait!" the idiot screamed. Dracula raised his eyebrows to indicate mild interest in any information which might be forthcoming. "I—I don't know anything. Honest. He just—"

"He? Does he have a name?"

The idiot shook his head.

"He never told me."

"How did you find yourself in this position?"

"I...it was crazy. I was home, and then I woke up and there were these three people there, and this guy. One of them had duct tape over my mouth, and this guy just bites my wrist. *Hard*. Then he lets the others..."

"I see. Did you get a look at the first man?"

The idiot shook his head.

"It was too dark."

Dracula gripped the stake more tightly.

"Wait! Wait—what do you want? Ask me, maybe I know something."

"Where can I find the man you work for?"

The idiot's eyes pleaded for his worthless "life". Dracula wanted to destroy him right there, but he thought he ought to try something more. He reached into his breast pocket. Malcolm had printed off a picture of Cammy's roommate and delivered it to him in case he stumbled across her or someone who had seen her. He flashed the picture at the idiot. The idiot shook his head.

"Never seen her?"

"No."

Dracula replaced the photograph. At the rate he was going, Boese was likely to incarcerate him again. He was loath to be back in that man's hands.

"You were sent here. What for?"

"To keep an eye on you. Report what I saw."

"Not to make contact?"

"Not unless he told me to."

Dracula made a quick search of the idiot's pockets and turned up his phone and a stylus.

"I shall make your report."

The idiot obliged him by unlocking his phone, and it seemed he was to use "Don't Forget" to report in. Tracing where that information went was beyond Dracula's expertise. He would need Boese's people to do that. Perhaps confirming that this was the method of contact would placate the man. Dracula doubted it, but there might yet be more he could turn up.

"I extended an offer to you," Dracula said to the phone. "It is unseemly to bite a hand offering a chance to talk. Unwise, also. If you should wish to speak, it seems you know how to contact me. Until then, I suggest you make ready your soul, if you still have one."

He kept the phone to turn in to Boese's agents at the next opportunity. He lifted the idiot by the collar.

"You creatures require a great deal of blood to survive. How have you been sustaining yourselves?"

"He never gives me enough," the idiot whimpered. "I had to roofie this chick yesterday, I couldn't take it anymore."

"You had to hunt for yourself?"

"Yeah, what else was I gonna do? Raid a hospital or a blood bank?"

How curious.

"The girl is dead, I presume?"

The idiot nodded.

"I would see to it. Where did you leave her?"

This confused the idiot, and he replied that she was still in his apartment. He hadn't figured out what to do with her body. Dracula could hardly believe his ears. Perhaps the man who created these creatures viewed them as disposable and provided them no resources whatever; but surely even disposable cannon-fodder would be more useful with the smallest of support. No good general ran an army in such a way.

Shortly, he had the idiot's keys and was making his way to the man's apartment while the idiot sat silently slumped in the passenger seat. When Dracula opened the door, he found the girl was up and very hungry; she tried to pounce on him the moment he stepped inside.

She was easy enough to dispatch, and Dracula made a search for more clues. He found nothing, and that was more curious than finding something.

He killed the idiot when he returned to the vehicle and went to find the apartment that had housed the man whose phone he had taken a few nights ago. Malcolm had helped him look up where the man lived, and Dracula had intended to visit when the opportunity presented itself.

He found nothing there either, except that Boese's men had already come and gone. There was the telltale scent of cleaning chemicals and the carpet had been shampooed. The bathroom was scrubbed absolutely spotless. If they had been that meticulous, then the man had things stored in his domicile that Boese's people wouldn't want the local authorities getting wind of. Meaning he was fairly careless. More curious.

Dracula intended to make one last stop on his way back. He had already asked, but given what he had just learned, another round of questions would solidify his theory.

* * *

Cammy peered around the corner to see if Malcolm was still there. He lay draped across the divan like a tossed ragdoll, dead asleep. He also looked like the stupid pose was for a photo shoot. The axe was placed carefully on the floor. She crept forward, but she hadn't gone a few steps before Malcolm started awake and sat bolt upright, eyes riveted to her. He let out a long sigh, rubbed one eye, and glanced at the windows.

"You okay?" she asked him.

"Yeah, it just takes a lot out of me," he said.

"So you don't turn into a wolf."

"I *can*," he said, "but it's hard to use an axe while I've got no hands."

"You couldn't just kill them as a wolf?"

"And chew their heads off while they aim guns at me? No thanks. Plus vampires taste *nasty*. Honestly, being a wolf isn't so useful these days. I guess back in the 1700s it was still a neat party trick." He rubbed both eyes then, and glanced around. "Huh."

"Huh?"

"I called back to give him the all clear, and I thought he'd be back by now."

"Vlad?"

"Yeah. Maybe he found something. I thought he'd come running back here. What time is it?"

"Four. I couldn't sleep."

"Mmm." Malcolm grumped. "I need a drink." He pushed himself up off the divan.

"He doesn't have coffee," Cammy told him.

"I didn't say coffee," Malcolm replied. He sauntered into the kitchen. Cammy was following him when the front door swung open. She turned to see Dracula scrutinizing the part of the person through the window. He spotted her.

"Are you well?" he asked her.

She blurted the very first thing that popped into her mind, even though it wasn't what she thought she was going to say.

"Did you suck my blood?" She waved her hand.

"Malcolm!" he shouted.

"What, old man?"

"You left quite the mess," Dracula said as Malcolm came around to the foyer, a tea cup in one hand.

"Come on, man. You know how it is. Give me a break, there were like twenty of them—"

Dracula grabbed the tea cup out of his hand, set it on the sill beside the body, then fetched Malcolm's wallet.

"Come on," Malcolm protested. Dracula pulled a few bills out and handed it back. "Really? Like you need that for the deposit?"

"I asked a question," Cammy said, and waved her hand in the air. Malcolm grinned helplessly.

"I'll speak with you later," Dracula told Malcolm. He turned to Cammy, who still had her hand raised. "Yes, I did," he said.

She stared, but he just stood there, hands in his pockets, looking at her.

"Um—" she began.

"I will explain that I did it to verify you weren't going to become a rat yourself in a day or two, and as I did not expect to see you again, that would have been my only opportunity," he said.

She stared at him. "And?" she demanded.

"And what?"

She glared. He shrugged, his hands still in his pockets.

"An apology would be nice," she told him.

"An apology for what?" he replied, and nodded at her hand. "You would have your doctor apologize for checking your pulse to see whether you were ill?"

"You should have asked first!" she snapped. "You don't have the right to just—"

"I did no harm to you. Really, you're carrying on."

"Carrying on?! You sucked my blood without my permission."

"I could not possibly ask your permission in that moment," he told her, and she heard that agile condescension again. It was more subtle, but she heard it all the same.

"Yes, you could have," she insisted.

"No. I was on the phone with Boese's people. Had I mentioned anything right then, they would have heard it, and there was a good chance they would have hunted you down afterwards. They are not very interested in verifying whether you would remain human, and you were a witness. They would not likely have been kind to you."

She remembered him mentioning that he was looking for victims but hadn't found any when he kissed her hand. In her mind, she pictured Boese on the other end of the line.

"You could have told me afterward," she told him.

"What is bothering you? That could not possibly have hurt, nor hurt much now, and until my compatriot,"—he glanced at Malcolm—"told you, I suspect you could have gone your whole life without ever realizing."

"Well, that's the point," Cammy told him. "It's sneaky. You never mentioned it even when I came up here and you let me stay."

"I did not see a reason to," he said. "As I said, you could easily have gone your entire life and never known, and I did not see any benefit to having this argument, so I said nothing."

"Well, but, I mean,"—she felt stupid to have to ask, but she had to—"I mean, is it, am I—"

"You'll be fine," he told her. "It's your modern creations which can turn a person with the tiniest exposure. From something like me, it would be virtually inconceivable that you would be in any danger from just one encounter. But I imagine you're tired, and have just had a very trying evening, and that standing in my foyer being angry isn't very helpful at the moment. I thought you might like to know I visited the driver's apartment this evening."

Cammy's heart skipped a beat.

"The driver?"

"Yes. The one whose phone you took."

"No kidding. Anything useful?" Malcolm asked, and pushed the upper part of the corpse out through the window. He picked up the tea cup and sipped its contents.

"Yes. It seems these creatures are, for lack of a better word, complete amateurs."

"Amateurs?" Cammy repeated. Dracula nodded. He strode forward and passed her. He scanned the fireplace.

"No idea how to hide bodies the way the other practicing creatures of the night do," he said. "I found some... unsavory things. Considering how much these creatures need to consume per evening, and the numbers I have encountered, they must be killing a great many people. They must run quite an operation, yet they are sloppy. Hollywood types cannot afford to be this sloppy. I also checked the Underground. No one's heard of them, which means their appearance is a relatively recent phenomenon." He turned to Malcolm, who stood by, sipping from the tea cup. "Can you imagine that? An operation this size and no one has checked in."

"Checked in?" Cammy asked. Dracula considered her.

"There is a society of monsters and the humans who know they exist. They operate outside the usual channels. For creatures like your modern vampires, they are not only a useful resource, but often a *necessary* resource. The Underground can produce blood if they don't desire to murder for it, or else dispose of bodies or provide victims. To run an operation that size and for not a single member of it to even show their noses Underground?" He shook his head. "I don't see how, but these creatures seem to have sprung into existence whole cloth from nothing. I know of no Hollywood type who would go about creating ravenous creatures willy-nilly like this. It draws my employers' attention, and then I have to do something about it." The way he said it, Cammy felt sure no vampire who knew about him would want that. "Then these fools have the audacity to storm my home armed with nothing. No guns, not even knives, only crucifixes and stakes. I took a look out there. Can you imagine."

"Amateurs, yeah," Malcolm agreed. He downed the remainder of the cup. "Makes no sense. But yeah, they didn't seem to have any idea what to do with me, either. And I'm pretty well-known around here."

"You are?" Cammy asked.

"Sure. I'm the only field operative for Ophois for the whole city. Everyone knows my face."

Cammy blinked.

"The only one?"

"Headquarters is elsewhere," Malcolm said. "That's how Ophois usually operates. You contact someone higher up the chain, and they send one of their very few operatives out if they have someone near the problem and it isn't something that requires the head office. Low overhead that way. And the boys like me are only born and bred, not made, so there can't be a lot of us."

"This puzzles me enormously," Dracula said. "To think that somehow or other, an operation of this size sprang up and not a single soul noticed it. My employers didn't, the Underground didn't. No one did. Absolutely baffling."

Malcolm wandered towards the kitchen while Dracula stared at the glowing fireplace.

"Ignoring the how," Dracula continued, "there is also the question of who could have kicked this entire cascade off to begin with, and for what purpose." He crossed his arms and tapped his elbows. Malcolm returned from the kitchen, slurping from a freshly refilled tea cup.

"You know of anybody?"

No one who would benefit from this debacle."

"Did you find anything about Heather?" Cammy interrupted. Dracula looked to her.

"No. Nothing. Nothing at all."

"Oh," Cammy said.

"It is late, and you've no doubt suffered a new trauma," Dracula said, sounding far less condescending. He didn't sound kind or reassuring, but he didn't sound condescending anymore. Maybe that was the best she could expect out of him. "You should rest. I'll work to clean up some of this mess. I doubt you will want to see it once the sun rises."

Cammy hadn't even considered that. She had no idea what that would do to her. Would she end up as cynical and unloving as her two supernatural acquaintances? How long could anyone realistically stare at a bunch of dead people before they started to turn into sociopaths? She gulped. Dracula had told her she'd never been tried. Maybe he just meant that if she had been through what he'd been through, she'd be just like him and care just as little about people and suffering.

Maybe she really shouldn't continue staying here.

She went upstairs to think that over while trying to sleep.

Dracula walked Malcolm to his vehicle.

"When I hire you to do a job, I expect you to do it," he told the young man. He nodded back at the mansion. "Before you go on grousing about me deducting your pay, I'd like you to explain to me that little mess you made."

"Yeah," Malcolm grumped. "But you could have told her. You should have." He walked around to the driver's side and opened the door. Dracula considered the muscle car. Malcolm had purchased it a few years ago and had been modifying it to increase performance. Now it had a new coat of paint. It looked waxed; likely he had done it himself.

"Fine work," Dracula praised, tapping the hood. "Turn it over, let me hear what you've done with it."

Malcolm obliged. Dracula listened to the engine roar to life. He gestured for Malcolm to pop the hood and come alongside.

"The idle's high," Dracula commented.

"Yeah, I'm working on that."

Dracula glanced back at his front door, and Malcolm took the hint.

"We're out of earshot," he said.

Dracula nodded. "It seems to me your job is only half-completed," he said quietly, and tapped on the vehicle with his knuckles.

"Yeah," Malcolm said, and ran a hand through his hair as he gazed down at the engine rumbling in the dark. "I wasn't really prepared for something like that. A full on assault?"

"You never seem to be."

Malcolm tightened his jaw and looked out into the dark.

"You are certainly welcome to be as carefree as you like with your time and your life, but if we are to succeed in this little scheme, finesse and professionalism are required."

Malcolm glanced back, nodded a little.

"This is a deadly gamble. For you, not for me." Dracula fetched a hundred dollar bill out of his wallet and passed it over. "For the future. I would see you succeed."

"Yeah," said Malcolm, and he stuffed the bill in his back pocket. "Yeah, I take all the risk, you reap all the reward."

"I should take that money back, if you think that's true," Dracula growled at him. "There is plenty of risk for me, and everything in the world for you to gain. If left to your own devices, you have no future whatever. Rather, you know what future awaits you in the hands of the Order."

"Yeah sure," Malcolm said. "Still, this is a heck of a lot you want to do all of a sudden, and you haven't done much of anything in decades."

Dracula looked at him.

"Want to clue me in?"

"Have I done so yet?"

"No."

"Then I expect you would understand that meant there was no need for me to do so."

Malcolm glowered.

"I've read our files on you. You don't make bold moves unless you feel pretty confident, but I didn't see any big guns in there."

"Why would you expect to see anything which could be tortured out of you if it came to that?"

Malcolm looked taken aback. "You really think your boss'll go against my people?"

"He's nervous. He gets irrational when he's nervous. And he thinks he has the entire weight of the US government behind him."

"Ophois has *magic*. Maybe he should think about that."

"Men don't think about those sorts of things when they're nervous."

"Is that it?"

"In my experience, despair does most of Ophois' field operatives in. They reach a point when they realize there is nothing for them and no hope, and they simply give up. I would not see you succumb to the same illness."

"Yeah, well, that's what fast cars and hot chicks are for, right?" Malcolm flashed a smile at him. He spread his hands. "What else could a guy want?"

Himself, Dracula thought, *His own soul.* "Be careful, Malcolm."

Malcolm saluted, then shut the hood of his car, got in, and reversed out of the driveway.

CHAPTER 8

FOUND

Cammy turned her phone back on before she went to bed. She'd put it on the nightstand and curled up in the big fluffy bed, trying not to think about Heather, when the phone rang.

"Heather?" she nearly shouted. But she saw the call was from Melissa. She picked up. "Hello?"

"Hey, Cam," Melissa's voice answered. "How are you? Everything okay?"

Cammy sighed. What was Melissa doing calling her in the middle of the night? Then she realized it was getting light out. She checked her phone. Six am. When she usually got up. "I'm fine," she mumbled.

She shifted her head from side to side while Melissa spied for Brian, telling her she was fine, and dodging every question she could about her host. When she detected that Melissa was going to try to guilt more info out of her, she cut her off.

"Look, I'm really tired, all right? I have work today, I really need money. I'll text you later, okay?"

A pause answered her.

"Call me if you need anything, all right?"

"Yeah," Cammy said, "Thanks."

"I mean it."

You mean you don't believe me and you think I'm sneaking out, Cammy thought. But Melissa really *was* worried, unlike her own mother. "Thanks, I know. Say hey to B for me."

She heard the smile in Melissa's voice. "Sure thing, Cam. Stay safe, you hear me?"

To think, she was probably safer staying in a psychopath's mansion than anywhere else. She shook her head.

When she came down for breakfast she didn't feel like asking questions. She ate eggs, and her host joined her this time. She debated asking him about his history, but his threats still loomed in her mind. Especially when he didn't comment on her silence. What was he thinking?

He drove her to work in the Mustang.

"I'll call you when my shift is over. I should be done by six, I think." She told him. "Thanks."

"My pleasure," he replied.

She wondered if it really was, and why it would be if it was.

"Hey, you doing better?" Kenzie asked as she came through the door to clock in. Brandon—Wheat Bran—was already behind the counter. Luna was nowhere to be seen. Cammy nodded. She still didn't want to talk.

Cammy walked behind the counter, stowed her bag, and tied on her apron. As she went to the stainless steel sink to wash her hands, Kenzie sidled up to her.

"So...?" she said.

"I'm still kinda sick," Cammy said. "I can't really talk right now."

Kenzie feigned shock, but backed off. "Just get me his number, okay? If he's cool with that?"

Cammy wanted to throw something at her. Then she realized how unlike her this was. She wanted to throw things at her mother, not Kenzie. Not her friends. Was that all it took? Some stress, and suddenly everything and everyone angered her to the point of violence? She shook her head.

Get over it, she told herself. *You can't let this get to you.* Something about the thought reminded her of her mother. The woman was always telling her to stop blubbering and "act her age." Was that what she was doing?

She bent all her will on her job. Answering questions, making drinks, taking orders. Not wondering about customers, not thinking about people at all.

During her lunch break, she texted Heather again.

If you don't get back to me

She tapped her thumbs on the sides of her phone.

then that's the end. Good bye. You stole my money and got me thrown out. I'm done.

Was it the right thing to do? But she didn't know what to do. Maybe giving Heather a swift kick would get her to wake up.

The end of her shift came, Kenzie divvied up tips, and Cammy clocked out. She took out her phone to call Dracula—she couldn't believe he was going to give her a lift—and saw Heather had called. She checked, no message. She called Heather back.

"You seriously think this is funny or something? What are you doing?" Cammy demanded.

"Cammy! Help!" Heather whispered. Cammy felt her throat tightening.

"What's going on?" she asked.

"Help! I got away, but I don't know if they're going to find me! I'm on campus, in a storage closet. I don't know if they know where I am, and I'm scared."

"Who is after you?" Cammy demanded.

"I don't know, these people." Heather gasped, her voice ragged. "They grabbed me a few days ago. I don't know who they are. They..."

Cammy felt her heart thumping in her chest. The same screaming fear that had gripped her a few nights ago when she encountered these vampires.

"Heather, are you okay? What did they do to you?"

"It doesn't make any sense," Heather sobbed. "They kept... kept... they wanted my blood, Cammy. I don't know; they're sick, or something. Help! I can't call the cops, they won't believe me."

"Where are you? You said campus?"

Heather told her the building and floor.

"I'm on my way. Don't move," Cammy told her. "I'm getting help."

"Not Brian, he's such a cop," Heather whimpered.

"Someone better," Cammy promised. She hung up. "Vlad!" she shouted when he answered the phone.

"What happened?" he asked.

Cammy was hurrying from the Mindful Bean towards campus.

"Heather just called me. She said she escaped, that she was kidnapped—"

"Where is she?"

"On campus. She's hiding from them right now."

"*Don't* go to her," he said.

Cammy froze on the sidewalk.

"Where are you? If you are still at work, wait there. I will be there within the hour."

"The hour? But she said—"

"*Do not go to your friend,*" he repeated.

Cammy swallowed.

"Stay there. I am on my way," he said.

She hung up. She hadn't gone far, only about a hundred feet from the Mindful Bean. Kenzie and Brandon had already gone home, and Luna's nephew was there to help deal with the few people who'd come in the evening when campus was closed. There was a bench not far from the building. Campus lay a few blocks away, barely visible from where she stood.

It was about 6:20, so she had hours of sunlight left. If these Hollywood types couldn't be out during the day, then it should be safe to go. Heather might be the biggest flake of a friend, but she was still a friend. Heather had always listened when she needed to vent about her mother, or the worst teachers. Cammy couldn't just leave her. She continued on towards campus.

Once again, hardly anyone was around. Summer classes should be starting soon, but for the moment the place was a ghost town. Cammy walked under the canopy of trees, past admin, to her destination: the building where all their stupid business classes were. She and Heather had tried lining up a few classes to take together; small perks of going to the same college with a friend who also didn't know what she wanted to do with her life.

The building was being renovated near the big entrance, so Cammy went around the side. She walked the hallway, her steps echoing in the emptiness.

"You lost?"

She jumped, whirled, and stared at the janitor pushing an ancient mop. He squinted at her and twitched his gray mustache.

"No, I'm looking for my friend," she said. Her and her big mouth.

"What's your friend doing here? Classes don't start for a while, yet," he said. "Whole place is shut down. You're not supposed to be in here."

"I won't be long," Cammy promised.

"Your friend and you aren't supposed to be in lecture halls right now."

"We'll be gone soon," Cammy assured him, and walked away.

She heard him coming after her, and quickened her pace. Her eyes scanned room numbers, until she saw the maintenance closet next to one of the drinking fountains. She looked over her shoulder. The janitor was following about twenty paces behind.

Wait, she said they were after her, didn't she? Cammy realized. *Is he one of them?* But it was still daylight out. *Unless, since he's a janitor, he never leaves, and no one thinks about it?* Was she being paranoid? How had Dracula and Malcolm said you needed to kill them? Behead them, stake them? That's what Dracula had done. She had nothing to stake or behead a vampire with. She wiped her palms on her jeans and texted Heather.

I'm here. What do they look like?

All she could do was wait for Heather to reply. The maintenance door swung open, and Heather stepped out. She looked awful, her hair scraggled and unwashed, her flannel shirt stained with old blood near the collar and at the cuffs.

"Heather!" Cammy ran to her and hugged her.

"You girls can't be in here. This isn't a playground, you know," the janitor said. Cammy released Heather and saw her staring at the janitor.

"Is he one of them?" Cammy whispered in her ear.

"No," Heather said.

"We need to get out of here," Cammy said. "My friend is coming to get me at the Mindful Bean. We should meet him there." She took Heather's wrist, and thought it felt awfully cold. She pulled, but Heather didn't come along.

"We should wait until it's safe," Heather said.

"I thought you said they were after you?" Cammy pointed out. "So they're here somewhere, right? We need to get as far away as we can."

"Is there a problem, young ladies?" the janitor asked. Heather looked at him, and the look made Cammy's skin crawl. She released her friend's bony wrist, and Heather turned to her next.

"We should wait," she said. "Until it's safe."

"It's daylight out, so it's safe now," Cammy said. "We can't wait around, come on." She turned to leave, and Heather grabbed her wrist. Hard. Vise-like.

No, Cammy thought.

"We should stay," Heather insisted.

"You can't stay here," the janitor told her. He had come within ten paces and was making his way closer. "The building's shut down. Go home."

"Let me go," Cammy said, tugging her wrist. Heather kept hold.

"You girls need to leave," the janitor told them. Heather eyed him hatefully, then yanked hard on Cammy's wrist, pulling her off her feet and through the air. She tried to catch herself and knocked a bunch of mops and brooms down as she landed in the maintenance closet. One snapped under her as she fell, a broom that might be a hundred years old for all she knew. Painfully, she sat up, and heard the janitor screaming. She crawled to the door to see Heather had pulled him off his feet and had her face buried in his neck.

"No!" Cammy screamed. Heather turned, and it wasn't like in the movies. Blood *shot* out of the janitor's neck in twin spurting jets, spraying the side of Heather's face and hair. Her eyes settled on Cammy, and for a moment Cammy thought the dead look was almost like when Heather was high. But this was different, much worse. Heather considered her, the length of hallway to the door, and then returned her attention to the janitor. His fists beat at her feebly, then went limp all at once. Cammy judged the distance herself. She might be able to outrun Heather. But if she couldn't?

Heather dropped the janitor to the floor and turned around, her face covered in gore.

"I told you to stay," Heather said. "So that's what you're going to do."

Cammy swung the maintenance door shut, only to find she couldn't lock it.

No, no, no, no!

DRACULA'S GUEST

She hadn't told Dracula which room or building. Even if he had arrived and found her missing and figured out she'd gone on ahead, he wouldn't know where to find her. She held tight to the doorknob with both hands, and felt it turning. She tried to grip it tighter, but it was wrenched from her grip. Cammy threw herself back into the closet as Heather stepped into the doorway. Absent-mindedly, Heather wiped blood from her face and licked her fingers.

"You can't," Cammy said. "You can't...."

"It's not so bad, Cammy," Heather told her. "Doesn't even hurt. Kind of tickles, actually. Like getting a hickey."

"It's daylight, how'd you get in here?"

"I came in last night," Heather told her, and stepped inside. "I knew you'd come to work eventually."

"Heather, you don't have to do this. You don't." Cammy swallowed, tried to force her throat and tongue to work. They wanted to seize up on her. "Please. Please, don't."

"I don't think I can help it," Heather said, and started shutting the door behind her. "It's worse than coke, you know. And I *need* it. I'm not supposed to touch you, but I *need* it, and they don't give me any. You'll still be able to talk after I'm done, so no harm no foul, right?"

"Heather, please!"

Heather looked at her, pupils wide portals into nothing. Cammy had heard that when you died your pupils dilated all the way. It was horrifying to see someone moving around with eyes like that. There was no way out. She'd never have time to call for help. Desperately, Cammy looked around the closet. Was there something she could use?

She spotted the broken broom handle.

Heather lunged.

Cammy had no idea how to aim right. She just thrust out the jagged end of wood, bracing it with both hands and all the strength of her arms. Heather fell on it, and the handle slipped out of Cammy's hands, slid past her, and collided with the linoleum floor. Heather gasped, her eyes wide, her bloody teeth glistening in the incandescent light from the lonely lightbulb above.

CHAPTER 9

THEY NEVER DO WHAT YOU TELL THEM

Cammy was not outside her coffee shop.

"*La naiba*," Dracula growled to himself. He'd known she wouldn't listen to him. That meant she'd gone on ahead. He got back into his car and pulled onto the road. He reached the college, parked illegally near a curb, and surveyed the campus grounds. They weren't extensive, but she had neglected to tell him where her friend was supposedly hiding. He tried dialing her phone, but she did not answer.

"*La naiba!*" he seethed.

He had two options: search the campus on foot, or look to see where Special Services had gone.

Suspicious that Cammy would do something stupid, he'd called them as soon as he got off the phone with her. They should be here, like as not.

He didn't drive much during the day, and had not taken into account how much trouble the daily commute would pose to him. This could have proven a fatal miscalculation for Cammy.

He stalked the grounds, studying buildings for any sign that he had found the right place. Then he spotted red and blue flashing lights.

Two encounters with the local police in as many days. What *were* things coming to? He came around the corner of the building with the two patrol cars parked out front to see how they were handling the situation. He needn't have bothered; there was a government vehicle parked just beyond them. The police would be leaving soon enough then, but he still did not know what had become of Cammy. He turned around the way he had come, looking for another entrance. He found one at the side, and let himself in.

The hallways seemed dingy to him. Universities and colleges had once been prestigious places, but to judge from the dreariness of these walls that was no longer the case. He eyed the posters and pinned artwork in the repulsive modern style that peppered the walls. Art was dead, so far as he could tell. Over the previous centuries it had evolved, but now it only rotted, and he was forced to stare at its fetid corpse everywhere he went, since no one had the decency to bury the poor thing. Long gone, it seemed, was any age of beauty or refinement.

For a moment he wondered how Bucharest was faring. He had been pleased to return in the 19th century, and he had swelled with the pride of a father watching his son achieve marvels when he saw how it had developed. He had wanted to return during the nineties, when Boese released him at long last from his most recent incarceration, but there had not been granted him the freedom of movement he had previously enjoyed. He worried about what that blood sucker must have done to the city—the whole country—over the years. Not that Ceaușescu was a literal blood sucker, no, he was a metaphorical one. Metaphorical ones were worse in his estimation; they caused far greater suffering. Some of his modern associates had fled the country when Communism sucked out all its vitality and originality, when the maniac ruling over them would hear no criticism. Fake corn was planted in fields so when he drove by he would be convinced of his country's prosperity; meanwhile the people endured the destruction and privations Communism always brought. He wished to see whether his country had recovered, and dig up a few corpses so he could knock their teeth out in the absence of a better revenge. He half-expected the reason he'd been imprisoned during the Cold War was because the powers that be found it politically expedient to leave his country in Soviet hands and knew he'd never tolerate it.

He passed metal doors, some dented or scratched, until he rounded a corner and spotted a crime scene being erased. There was a corpse on the floor, arterial spray on the tiles and part of a wall, and an open closet. One of the agents from Special Services was pulling down the police tape, while another was wiping away arterial splatter.

He made his way towards the closet, which undoubtedly held the answer of what had become of Cammy. The agents heard him coming, and the one ripping down tape made to intercept until the man recognized him.

"Where were you?" he demanded.

Dracula ignored him and looked inside the maintenance closet.

A young woman lay on her back, her face drawn, her frame unhealthily thin, her hair a tangled mess. She had part of a broom handle through her chest. He recognized the face from the photo Cammy had shown him. No one else.

"Where is the young woman?" he asked the agents.

"She's being taken to debrief," one answered.

La naiba! he thought.

He turned from the closet.

"I should go do the same," he said.

"Yeah, you ought to," the agent agreed with a sneer of contempt. Dracula pushed past him and went the way he'd come until he reached his vehicle and slid down into the driver's seat.

To the devil with that stupid girl, he thought, then pulled his phone and dialed Malcolm. Once he was done with the call, he put the keys in the ignition and made his way south. The local headquarters was an unassuming old building of brick and mortar in the Industrial District, perpetually under the guise of unfinished renovation. It sat nowhere near other businesses, and bore an aged sign that read Cole & Sons. He wondered who had come up with that. There was no parking lot, so he drew his vehicle up to the front door and left it there. There was a basement entrance, which he avoided—it led to a service elevator that went down to the labs, and the padlock on it was more secure than it looked. The front door seemed made of wood—it was not—and no sturdier than any other business entrance, and was unlocked. A single, tired-looking woman with her hair in a bun sat behind a little reception desk that blocked easy access to the rest of the building. This agent was one of Boese's dhampirs. She looked up at him, recognizing him for what he was, and frowned.

"What are you doing here?" she demanded, sitting up straight in her chair. He had the distinct impression she had her finger on an alarm or a weapon, but he walked up to her little desk all the same and leaned over it.

"I'm here to debrief," he told her.

"You needed to come *here* to do that?" she asked, her shoulders tense. If she had a weapon, she knew he could kill her despite it.

"I did," he told her, and nodded to the wall behind her. "Open the door."

"No one told me you were coming," she said. "The director doesn't want you near here—"

"Open. The door," he told her. "I am not accustomed to asking twice."

"I'll have to call it in," she told him. "The director has orders not to allow you inside." She reached for the phone on her little desk. While she called down, he fetched his own phone and dialed.

"I'm at your headquarters," he said. "Let me downstairs."

Shortly, the woman on the phone hung up. She looked up at him with a mixture of hate, fear, and confusion. Without another word, she pushed a worn section of wood on her desk, and a panel in the wall behind her opened up.

"He's expecting you," she told him.

"Thank you," he replied, and she looked more confused. He walked past her desk and into the ridiculous farce of a building.

The more humanity tried to pretend its nightmares didn't exist, the worse things became. When people had *real* troubles, they never needed such elaborate facilities to deal with the occasional supernatural problem. Or perhaps this was simply the bloat the US government enjoyed. It had so much money it could waste a fortune on this nonsense. He doubted even the Vatican had so much as half of this much capital poured into its own single vault of secrets, much less dozens or hundreds sprinkled across half a continent.

The stairs wouldn't tire him, but they would take ages, so he opted for an elevator. Money and technology had made them sleeker, quieter things. More sterile. Even the lights were sterile, their white light devoid of warmth. He ignored the camera in the top corner of the little room, and smiled when he saw who was there to meet him when he reached the bottom.

"Director, how pleased I am to see that you come to greet me in person. It has been so long since anyone treated me according to my station."

Boese glared at him, the white lights above washing away all color from his pale face and eyes. He was flanked by other agents, who would be useless should Dracula decide to kill anyone present, but they were there for show. Boese had his little kill-switch, which would be a terrible inconvenience and slow him down if he had to escape recapture, so Dracula knew better than to push while he was in his enemy's headquarters. That didn't mean he couldn't goad the man.

"We're going to have a little chat," Boese snarled at him.

"Naturally, that's why I've come," Dracula told him, still smiling. He knew how Boese hated that. Boese glowered all the more, and nodded that his agents flank Dracula, as though they could possibly box him in. This was hardly his first time dealing with a greater power who thought to bend him to its will, but this was the most absurd. All the agency could threaten him with was inconvenience and humiliation, not death, torture, and the loss of his entire country.

Dracula's Guest

Give me a Crusade, he thought to himself. *A real war, anything but this tedium.*

"My, my, Director. It seems you've tidied the place since my last visit," Dracula observed. The halls were clean and sterile, the lights all worked, the floor bore not a speck. He didn't hear any unusual sounds reverberating the halls, but this was not the same level where he'd been incarcerated before, so perhaps all the pointless, soulless investigations went on elsewhere.

My word, are these offices? He smirked at the thought as he passed doors bearing nothing more than numbers. Perhaps these were archives. That seemed likelier. Supernatural research required libraries to understand the creatures—if such a thing was possible—and bureaucrats loved paperwork.

They rounded several corners and came to a nondescript metal door with a small, reinforced viewing window. Boese fished a keycard from his pocket, unlocked the door with it, and pointed that Dracula enter. Inside was a plain room consisting almost entirely of polished metal, with one light blaring pale and unfeeling overhead, and cameras at every corner. The only furnishings were a metal table and chairs, beneath which was a drain. Dracula sighed.

"Keep an eye on the cameras, this one's tricky," Boese was telling his agents.

"And would like some tea, if we are to pursue this charade," Dracula added. Boese glared at him, then jerked his head towards the chairs. Dracula seated himself and brushed some lint from the cuff of one pant leg while he waited for Boese to join him at the table. The director took his time readying himself, checking his tie, some files he had needlessly brought. The man flipped through them. Dracula steepled his fingers together and waited for this pointless exercise to end.

At last, Boese seemed to realize his prize asset was not going to speak first, and he glared up from his paperwork.

"So I'm going to hazard a guess that you came down here in person to check on your little friend," he said.

"Why? Has something happened to her?"

"I don't know. You're the one who called ahead to warn us about the situation." Boese scrutinized his face for any hint of what Dracula was thinking.

"I thought keeping the general public safe from the supernatural was something your organization prioritized," Dracula told him. "So far as I see it, I was performing that duty."

"And having her up at your little castle? That part of your duty, too?"

Dracula grinned. "Why, Director, she has nowhere to live. I could scarcely throw her out into the cold."

Boese folded his fingers together and leaned forward. "Oh, *couldn't* you?"

"It's only Christian charity, Director."

"Oh, you're a regular Mother Teresa," Boese said. "And let me guess: you were also concerned for the missing roommate?"

"Certainly."

"Oh sure. You used to burn people like her alive, isn't that right? Dregs of society."

Dracula eyed him.

"So now that we've established your impeccable moral character, why don't you tell me what you're doing down here? Miss the place?"

"I scarcely recognize it," Dracula told him. "You've been earning yourself quite a lot of Christmas bonuses over the years."

Boese didn't blink.

"You want to play games? Why are you here?"

"I came to debrief."

"No, you didn't. What is she to you?"

"A guest of mine."

"You think I'm blind? I saw that bruise you left behind. You been feeding off her? I'm liable to have you locked down here again for that alone."

Dracula didn't answer.

"Why don't we save each other a little time, huh?" Boese asked. "And you tell the truth for once in your miserable life."

"I tell the truth quite often, Director," Dracula informed him, "but no one listens to it."

"Impress me, then," Boese told him.

"I have told you: she is a guest of mine."

"And I say that's a lie."

Dracula grinned. "You see, Director?" Boese clenched one fist.

"Fine, let's play your game. Want to explain to me why you're suddenly so bad at killing vampires?"

"I hardly think I've slipped," Dracula replied. "I told you: I can't be everywhere at once. I have killed any I have stumbled across, which is more than I can say for your people. I told you what I encountered last night. If you need a higher body count, then perhaps your resources are not properly allocated." He leaned forward also. "And besides, if I killed all your vampires for you, where would your Christmas bonuses come from? If there were no more vampires, there'd be no need for you, would there?"

"Well, lucky for me the supply never seems to dry up, does it?"

"I should say that *because* of you, the supply never seems to run dry," Dracula corrected. "I've never spent so much time hunting vampires in hundreds of years."

"That a fact? I suppose you worked for the Vatican as a missionary then?"

"No. Killing much more ordinary adversaries," Dracula corrected. "Surely you've been informed of the work I've done your country over the years? Any undead I have killed have been incidental."

"Much as I'd love to discuss ancient history, you still haven't told me why you're here."

"I believe I've answered you several times. You simply don't like it."

"That's because you're a liar," Boese said.

"Well, it seems we have reached an impasse," Dracula observed. "So I should take my leave now. It'll be dark in a few hours, and I have vermin to hunt."

"I didn't tell you you could leave," Boese said as Dracula rose from the table.

"You think you can stop me?"

"I can have this room sealed off."

"Director," Dracula chided, "I didn't think you had learned to survive hours without air." He nodded at the door.

"And how good is that seal? Suppose that door should be dented?"

"Go ahead," Boese told him. "Give it a try. I think we've got a good idea of the limits of your strength."

He certainly might. Dracula had seen how thick that door was when he entered. He doubted it was titanium, but it didn't need to be.

"And you think that suffocating just to keep me here is worthwhile?" Dracula asked him.

Boese looked at him.

"It's a reasonable question, Director."

"What are you up to?" Boese demanded.

"And you think it wise to question a liar about his motives?"

Boese narrowed his eyes.

"I know you," he said. "You're a lying, deranged, narcissist. You get your jollies torturing people to death."

"Well, that explains why we are such bosom companions, Director." *And if you knew me, you'd have realized the sort of prisoner I make*, he thought. "But while you sit here suffocating, those Hollywood cretins will be out there reproducing like rats and overrunning the city. They're the products of your deranged, modern minds, not mine, and they are no threat to me."

"You have nothing to bargain with," Boese told him. "You're not a 'great lord' anymore. Now you're a joke, Count Chocula."

"Well, I suppose I should remain here, then," Dracula said, taking his seat again and leaning back in his chair. "I doubt a joke would be of any use. Let's see how quickly they overrun your city and expose your little organization.

Perhaps when the secret's out your stock market will crash, followed by some ludicrous, undead apocalypse? Where is my tea, by the way? Can't you afford any?"

"I don't have to take this from you," Boese said, and rose from the table. "You think about your position, then maybe we'll chat again, huh?"

"You as well, Director," Dracula advised him. "I have all the time in the world."

"Well, your little friend doesn't," Boese told him. "What? Nothing smart to say?"

"I could say the same for your city," Dracula reminded him.

"I can *end* you!" Boese snarled. "You keep pushing me, I'll do it. And I'll bury your little friend and your monster sanctuary while I'm at it!"

Dracula grabbed his tie and yanked him down onto the table.

"You don't want to go to war with me, Director," he told the man. "If you knew me like you think you do, you'd mind your manners. You'd step lightly entering a room with *Kaziklu Bey* inside." He pulled the man closer, knowing any moment that door was going to swing open. "You think you know how to scare people so they do what you say, but Director, you are an amateur. You can't make *threats*. Anything you say you will do, you must be willing to do. You must have *teeth*." He tightened his grip. "*I* have teeth, Director."

The door slammed open and he glared up at the agents pouring inside, armed with weapons meant to blast him apart. That wouldn't kill him, but that would keep him from escaping. He pulled Boese over the table and stood him up as a shield.

"Well, Director? What will you have? War, or no?"

Boese pried helplessly at Dracula's fingers. Dracula tightened his grip, and the director started to change color. He signed at his agents to stand down. Once they had lowered their weapons, Dracula released him.

"Now," he said, "Where is my tea?"

CHAPTER 10

UNDERGROUND

Cammy shook so hard the chair rattled beneath her. She couldn't stop. All she could see over and over and over was Heather's dead, staring eyes. She could still feel the weight of her friend's body on her knees, now stained with blood. Her lips tingled, her eyes burned. She couldn't stop gasping.

The police had arrived first; someone coming to repaint had stumbled across the janitor and phoned 911. They had barely begun asking her what happened when three people in suits came and flashed badges, then the police backed down. They had asked her to come with them, and stuffed her in a car with a sack over her head.

After being driven and dragged around, someone had dumped her on this hard, metal chair, and here she sat. In a metal box. She could see the cameras all pointed at her, but no one had come in to say anything. Her teeth chattered. It was cold, but that wasn't the reason why. These people were probably going to kill her. They wanted to keep all their secrets, right? These weren't police, these were people like Boese.

The metal door screeched open, and she jumped. The chair wriggled beneath her and scraped the floor.

She recognized the man's bald head, and the scars notching his ear. Boese took her in, his eyes scrutinizing her sitting there, and he smiled. It was a cold smile, but she thought maybe he was trying to look reassuring.

"Camellia, wasn't it?" he said. "Camellia Lily, that's a lovely name."

It's an old-fashioned, fru fru name, Cammy thought to herself. "I didn't tell you my name," she said, her tongue resisting every syllable. He slid into the chair opposite her, still smiling.

"Didn't you?" he asked innocently. "That's so strange. I thought you had."

At first she didn't know what to say, but it occurred to her that if she *had* told him her name, she would have introduced herself as Cammy, *not* Camellia.

"You're quite something," Boese praised—or said in a tone that affected praise. "Not every day that someone survives several attacks. You must have known what to do, I take it? When did you find out that all this was real?"

She stared at him. What did he want from her? She saw Heather's dead eyes peering out of his colorless ones. He smiled again, and folded his fingers together. He leaned forward, and the image of a principal or school counselor popped into her head. She grinned like a maniac, though she tried not to.

"For some time, then?" he suggested. She shook her head.

"No." Her voice was still small. Like an elementary school student. "Only a couple of days."

"How did you find his place up there?" he asked, nodding up at one corner of the ceiling. "It's not exactly easy to stumble on."

"I just..." Cammy considered him. Why did he care? Was he not going to kill her? He wouldn't be asking her questions if he was going to kill her, right? So what did he really want? She glanced at the metal walls. Was this the place where Boese incarcerated monsters? "I'm human," she told him. "I'm a citizen. You can't keep me here."

He smiled just a little wider. His teeth were coffee-stained.

"I'm not keeping you here, don't worry," he assured. "I just want to understand what happened. Are you feeling all right? You want some water, or pop?"

There were vending machines down here? She couldn't stop the giggles that came boiling up out of her at the thought.

You got holy water down here, too? she wondered. He watched her, his expression fixed and false. She knew that look. Her mother liked to do the same thing: smile coldly, pretending to care. She never reacted when Cammy did anything, just kept on smiling. Because she didn't mean it, and neither did he. Cammy collapsed forward, her forehead smacking the cool metal table as giggles stole away what little air she had. He never responded, just sat there like a mannequin. After maybe a minute, she heard him call someone to bring a glass of water. She had no intention of drinking it. Who knew *what* would be in anything served to her here.

She heard that door *clank* open again, and the sound of shoes on the clean, metal floor. She looked up to see a worn-out guy in his mid-thirties setting down a paper cup filled with water. This stranger had gone prematurely gray at the temples and had bags under his eyes. He left without a word. Boese picked up the cup and offered it to her. Her eyes fell to the cup. She crossed her arms over her stomach and leaned back.

"It'll help," he assured her.

She shook her head. He didn't push, just set the cup down next to his elbow and folded his hands together again. His smile was a little smaller now.

"You work as a barista?"

"Yeah," she said.

"Does it pay well?"

She looked at him.

"You did a pretty good job back there," Boese said. "It's not easy killing something that looks like a human. Or your friend. That was some fine work."

She looked at the wall. She would scream otherwise.

He slapped shut the manila folder he had brought with him and tapped its edge on the table.

"How'd you get up there?" he asked.

"I put my phone in Vlad's pocket, and I tracked it," she said. Boese's pale eyes fixed on her, but she could see him simultaneously doubting her story and being amused at the very idea.

"That a fact?" he asked.

She nodded. "Yeah."

"Why'd you do that?" Boese asked. His amusement was obvious now. She shrugged.

"I dunno," she said. "It was a stupid idea."

"And he didn't kill you when you showed up? He didn't think you were dangerous?"

"At first he thought I was there to kill him, but he didn't kill me. He figured out I was nobody."

"And he let you stay there." She heard nothing but amusement and doubt.

"I guess," she said.

Boese spread his hands. "Help me out, here. Does that story sound right to you? Local barista stalks him up to his little manor house and he just says, 'Make yourself at home?'"

"Look, what do you want from me?" Cammy snapped. "That's what happened, I don't know why! What are you going to do? You going to lock me up? Kill me? What!"

"Whoa, whoa"—Boese raised his hands—"no need to get worked up. I told you: I'm not going to do anything. I'm just trying to put this all together. We want the same thing here: we want everyone to be safe, right? That's all I'm trying to do. But for me to do that job, I need you to tell me what's going on. You understand that, right?"

Cammy eyed the door. She hadn't heard any lock click once he entered, but she had no idea what lay beyond it.

"It's too late for me to care about that," Cammy snapped. "Where were all of you?! I asked you for help *before* Heather—" She couldn't finish. She slammed her hands down on the table and tried not to look at the blood on her knees.

"It's a shame about your friend," Boese said, folding his hands together. "A real shame. But she was likely gone days ago. Maybe a week ago."

"So weren't you guys supposed to do something about this a week ago?"

"If you want to get mad at somebody, get mad at your friend up there." Boese nodded his head at the wall. She wondered if he really knew what direction he was facing and if he was really nodding at the Cascades. "He was supposed to have this under control by now."

"Why just him? He can't be everywhere at once, you heard him. I thought you worked for the government? Why don't you just have all your jackboots in black suits do something?"

Boese considered her, rocked back in his chair, then finally stood.

"Tell you what, you seem like a smart girl, why don't you come with me?"

Cammy eyed the door. Go where?

Boese went to the door and opened it. He waved a hand at it, that she could go. She craned her neck to peer out into the hallway. It was lit with white lights that permitted no shadows on the metal hallway. The floor and walls were some sort of buffed metal that did not reflect light directly back.

"I can go?" she wondered doubtfully.

"No, something better. Come on."

Did she have a choice? She had no idea where she was. She slowly pushed herself from the table and approached the door. She kept out of arm's reach, though. Boese noticed the distance but didn't comment on it. He led the way. They walked down the hallway, alone. She had expected to see a whole bunch of men in sunglasses with earpieces and black suits. There were cameras at the corners and scanning the middle of the walls, but no one else in sight. She might be able to make a break for it if Boese wasn't all that fast. He had longer legs than she did, though, and in her experience that made a lot of difference if someone hadn't spent so much time in front of a screen that their heart had turned to Jell-O. She wasn't certain what sort of shape Boese was in. Politicians weren't exactly known for being stellar physical specimens, but he wasn't a politician.

She just followed him. Who knew where the doors opened to, or where she was? If she ran away, he might just shoot her in the back. Vlad wasn't here to threaten him and make him back down, and even if he was, this was Boese's house. Well, secret lab, but same difference. Maybe worse, actually. She had no idea if Boese would want to chop her up too—especially if he found out Dracula had sucked her blood.

Thinking that, she gripped her bruised hand and stared at the back of his head. He hadn't noticed. And he couldn't read her mind, right? He was human. It occurred to her she was far more frightened of the only human she'd run into during this whole mess than she was of the psychopathic vampire and his werewolf-berserker buddy.

Maybe that was some sort of statement about humanity. She didn't want to think about it. She didn't want to think about anything.

She pressed herself against a far wall when Boese gestured she ride in an elevator with him. At a glance, there were buttons for five floors, and they were going three down. There were no above-ground floors except for the ground-level itself.

The hallway they stepped into looked indistinguishable from the one she'd been on, but it seemed *darker*. Like the lights were slightly dimmed. Were they really, or was it her mind playing tricks on her, knowing she was even deeper underground?

"I think you'll like this, once you get a look," Boese said. She followed him, wondering what he thought she'd like to see.

I'd like to see a check for a million dollars and a one-way ticket to Hawaii, she thought, and had to choke a cackle of laughter. *I'd like never to see you or this place again.*

He came to a pair of doors which slid open Star Trek style when he drew near. They opened to a large, unadorned room with blaring, hateful lights blazing from the ceiling. There were tables strewn with all sorts of objects—mostly phones, now that she looked a little more closely. Some guy in one of those hazmat-looking suits she'd seen people on TV wear to really bad crime scenes was standing in a corner next to some sort of animal trap. She averted her eyes. Whatever was going on there, she didn't want to know.

"What are you doing in here?" Boese demanded.

"Processing," the person responded.

"You..." Boese eyed the hazmat suit, seemed to remember Cammy was there, and turned with a cold smile. "You see all this? This is what we've collated to track down those rats who killed your friend."

Cammy looked at him. He looked at her. It occurred to her this was what he thought she'd be happy to see. She scanned the items again. Most were phones, but she saw some laptops, a few notebooks, and a few folders stuffed with what she thought were photographs. Boese walked to the nearest folder.

"We make meticulous records of anything we find at these people's homes. Never know what'll be useful."

"So you're basically a forensics lab?" Cammy said. Boese's smile looked a little more genuine.

"Sure thing. State-of-the-art down here. Nothing gets away from us for long."

"Why do you need Vlad, then?"

Boese's smile soured straight into a scowl.

"He's legacy tech. Nifty asset from before the Cold War. Haven't gotten approval to retire him yet."

Retire? Cammy suspected that was a serious euphemism. "Tech" seemed a weird term for a vampire from so long ago he resembled nothing she was familiar with.

"You seem to think we've been sitting around doing nothing. Take a look at all this. All we have to do is collate all of it. We'll zero-in on the king rat any day and send in some real pest control. Fumigate the whole city if we have to. In less than a week, this place'll be so clean even *you'll* forget there were ever any vampires running around."

Cammy grunted something. It was almost a swear. But her mother had drilled that habit right out of her, it seemed.

"See, instead of getting used by one of the bad guys, you could work for us," Boese said. "Sit in a place like this. Nice and safe, and help make sure no more people end up like your friend."

Cammy would have performed a double-take if she hadn't already been facing him. *This* was what he thought she'd be so thrilled to hear? That he wanted her to come work for him? Work in a lab and chop people—or vampires—up for study?

She could see her silence hadn't brought his genuine smile back. It hadn't even brought back the cold one he favored.

DRACULA'S GUEST

An old-fashioned ringtone sent her flying towards the ceiling.

"What?" Boese snarled into his phone. It was an old nokia-looking fossil like what Dracula liked. "You're joking. Hang on." He looked at the tiny display screen, bared his teeth at it, and hung up only to pick up again. "What do you want?" His eyes swelled with anger and disbelief. He hung up, dialed. "Let him down. Interview room B. Have someone meet me there. Bring something heavy, he doesn't spook easy." After hanging up, he considered Cammy. She saw something like actual hatred dripping out of the corners of his eyes.

"You stay here," he told her. "Take a look, go ahead." To the person in the corner, "Keep an eye on her. She doesn't leave the room."

The person nodded. Boese pushed past Cammy and disappeared through the automatic doors. Cammy looked the hazmat man up and down. Hazmat man looked back.

"Hi," she mumbled. Hazmat man mumbled something back.

Cammy glanced at the doors. They weren't very noisy, but even if hazmat man's back was turned, he'd probably hear them open. Escape still seemed really unlikely.

All there was to do was wait. She wondered what had Boese in such a tearing hurry. The empusa, maybe? Cammy didn't want to see it, whatever it was. She certainly didn't want to see it get chopped up.

She wandered towards one of the tables and glanced listlessly over the phones. Some were scratched, some looked barely useable. Different makes, models, OS-es. Some had cute covers, some didn't. She realized that each of these represented a person. Or someone who had been a person, but was kidnapped by vampires, turned into one, and probably killed by Dracula.

She squeezed her eyes shut and tried to push the realization back out of her skull, but it was stuck fast. Thoughts had a way of getting trapped like that. One way street into one's brain, it seemed.

She pressed her palms to her temples. Heather was dead. She'd killed her. Vampires were real. She was kidnapped by some government jackboot and was down in a secret lab.

Don't, she told herself, *Keep it together*. It was her mother's voice in her mind.

She looked over the phones, though she didn't want to. The folders wouldn't have anything she wanted to see, either. Probably full of pictures of dead people.

There was a neat little calendar book snuggled right in the middle of the phones. It was pristine, plain maroon-red faux leather. A little pen was hooked into the spine, no doubt designed to fit there. It was so different from the rest of the items that Cammy reached for it. Her mother kept one of those silly old-fashioned appointment books. What sort of vampire would want something like that?

Someone had dutifully written "Bobbi White" on the first page under "This calendar book belongs to" in beautiful, neat, sweeping script. For want of something to do, Cammy flipped through the book. Maybe it would help her take her mind off her situation. She doubted it.

Her eyes roamed the neat little notes and appointments without taking them in. They kept wanting to rivet to the doors in anticipation of Boese's return, so she wrestled to keep them on the little notebook.

DRACULA'S GUEST

The pages were blank. She blinked, realized they'd been blank for a little while. She flipped back a few days and found an appointment for a "Dr. MClure—cold won't go away" about a month ago, then nothing. She flipped back a page to the week before and saw a meeting with "Dr. Dupont." For a moment, she couldn't figure out why that seemed odd. Then she remembered that no one seemed to have any idea where the vampires were coming from. Dracula had said they seemed to appear "whole cloth" from nowhere. But how could that be?

These ones didn't behave like they had any idea what they were doing. Maybe they were being turned—not on purpose by one vampire going around preying on everyone—but by accident? Malcolm had said she ought to be careful nothing got in a cut. There were monsters running around all the time, weren't there? What if there was a doctor or something who wasn't being so careful with his patients? Could that be the answer?

"cold won't go away"

It might be nothing, but it might also be that whoever Bobbi White was, she had turned into a vampire. That's why there weren't any entries afterwards. If so, was the doctor the perp?

Could it be that simple? But surely if it was, Boese's forensic team would have figured that out, wouldn't they?

Cammy fingered the calendar book and eyed the folders and the phones. If she could find a Dr. Dupont in those as well.... Boese thought Dracula was "old tech" and preferred his forensic lab. Maybe hunting the supernatural was like being a cop. Like being Brian. Old-fashioned detective work.

She grinned despite herself. What an idea.

A glance up at hazmat guy revealed he didn't mind her looking through the book. He probably wouldn't care if she looked at the other phones and the folders.

She picked up a phone, found a note taped to the back with the unlock code. The US government probably had an easier time cracking phones than she would. The idea that there were secret jackboots running around who could look in her phone if they thought there were vampires around was a troubling thought. Boese could just kidnap her with impunity, he'd demonstrated that. Who knew what else he could do to her with impunity.

No wonder Dracula hadn't wanted her to get in the middle of this.

She checked the phone's contacts but found no Dr. Dupont. The calendar showed nothing, either. The "Don't Forget" app was installed, though. So this one was one of the drivers.

She checked the next phone. No Dr. Dupont. "Don't Forget."

Maybe she was wrong about her theory. What did she know about anything anyway?

A klaxon blared and she almost front-flipped over the table. As soon as she gathered herself, she saw hazmat man considering the red light blinking above the automatic doors. He looked at her. She looked at the light.

"Stay put," he told her, and hurried out the door.

Cammy stared at the doors. The light. The doors.

No one was there. She could run away. She had no idea where to go, but was she ever going to get another chance?

And go where? To Dracula's place? Boese knew where that was. To her mother's? Same problem, only with her mother thrown into the mix. Brian? Maybe. Brian was a cop. But feds had authority over local cops, didn't they? Could Boese push Brian around?

"Excuse me."

She whirled, found herself alone in the room. But she had definitely heard something.

One of the phones? she thought. What else could it have been?

"Over here."

It was a tiny whisper of a voice. The room was empty, only tables of phones, folders, notebooks, and the animal trap.

The animal trap!

She stared at it. It had solid sides with little air holes, and looked made of steel.

"In here! Help!"

Not an animal. Some sort of supernatural thingamajig. She couldn't move. Was it dangerous? Dracula and Malcolm insisted everything was. But whatever was in that animal trap was asking her for help. Could it really be all that nasty?

Timidly, she approached the trap.

"Hello?" she said.

"It's me!" the voice said. "Help! You were at the mansion, right?"

Wait, not just some random supernatural thingamajig, this thing recognized her. From Dracula's mansion?

The tanuki! she thought. The voice was similar. She rushed to the trap and tried to peer in through one of the air holes.

A yellow, cat-slit eye appeared in the hole, looking out at her.

"Yes! You spoke to my parents," said the little creature. "Help! I went into the city to find food and they caught me!"

"Your parents?" Cammy said. "The tanuki and the fox?"

"Yes! I am Ginko," said the creature.

Was this a trick? *But how?* she asked herself. *Unless it can read my mind, it couldn't know about those animals up at the mansion.* It had to be the real deal.

"How do I get you out?"

"There should be a latch."

Cammy's fingers scraped along the steel, finding nothing but air holes. She turned the cage, found the latch, and opened it.

The little gray fox poked its head out and scanned the room. "Thank you, miss. We should escape."

"I don't know if we can," Cammy said.

"But no one is around," Ginko pointed out.

"But there might be outside," Cammy said. "And anywhere we go, they'll probably know where to find us."

The fox sat on the table beside the cage and tilted its head at the door.

"But I can't wait for them to come back," it said.

That's for sure, Cammy thought. Then it occurred to her that when hazmat man came back he was going to have a pretty easy time figuring out who had let the fox out. *Oh boy.* Boese was going to pitch a fit when he got back.

"What do we do?" she asked the fox.

"I want to run."

"We're five stories down," Cammy told it. "Can you use an elevator?"

"I am not very good at transforming," it said. "Perhaps."

"Wait, you can transform?"

"Yes. Not as well as my parents. And I am able to cast illusions on other things, though not very well."

Cammy was in tons of trouble, but maybe she could buy herself some time.

The hazmat guy came back to find her standing where she was when he left, still flipping through the calendar book. A few minutes later, Boese came back in, looking ready to murder the first thing that moved. He curled a finger for her to follow him, so she did.

It wasn't until they were two floors up that he did his best to adopt his fake friendly demeanor.

"What'd you think?"

"You guys really know your stuff."

He nodded.

"It's a lot safer working down there than staying where you are," he told her. "Pays well. There's a pension."

"You guys get *pensions*?"

He nodded absently.

"I guess it *is* a government job," she mumbled.

"Exactly. See, you seem to be feeling better."

"Yeah." She refused to look at him.

"We're looking into that rideshare," Boese said. "Got nothing so far, but once we bring some court orders to bear, if there's something supernatural we'll flush it out."

"Huh?"

"Sure. Humans lawyer up. Things that go bump in the night run. It's an easy way to flush 'em out. But I don't think we're going to find anything going on behind that. If you'd worked for me for a while, you'd know how ridiculous that idea is. But if there's anything to it, our computer guys will get to the bottom of it."

"Sure," Cammy said.

The door swung slowly open to reveal a pair of agents standing in another well-lit hallway. One had a sack in his hands. Cammy turned to Boese, trying to speak, but she couldn't. She could only shake her head.

"Protocol," Boese said. He pushed her out of the elevator into the two agent's reaching hands.

After another blind car ride, she was let outside and the sack was pulled off her head. She looked around. She seemed to be on the waterfront somewhere in the south of Ballard, if she had to guess. The sky was overcast and deep sunset. There wasn't anyone else around, just piles of trash and a few cawing seagulls. A wooden pier reached out over the water, what looked like warehouses ranged along the street, a fence and a line of trees on the other side hiding what sounded like a busy parking lot from sight.

"We'll be in touch," said one of the agents who had grabbed her. He stepped back into the nondescript car and pulled away. She was left alone.

She pulled out her phone and dialed.

Dracula did not pick up.

She tried again, no answer.

As she tried not to panic, she spotted a new text message. It read *Yo, lots of fun last night. Call me. M.*

Dracula's Guest

M? Who was M? *Malcolm!* she realized. But how had Malcolm gotten her number? The only person who could have shared it was Dracula, and she couldn't imagine why. She dialed the number.

"Hey, so you out of there?" Malcolm asked as a greeting.

"Out of... you knew where I was?"

"Vlad told me Boese had grabbed you and to text you. He figured you'd need a ride once you got out."

"Why can't he give me a ride?"

"Where are you? I'd rather talk in person."

Cammy looked around.

"I don't know. Let me see if I can get it on a map or something."

She shared her location and put the phone back to her ear.

"Got it," Malcolm said. "Be there in a flash."

Cammy waited an agonizing hour before Malcolm's red muscle car came driving hesitantly off whatever road she heard traffic noises from. She hurried towards it before he had even spotted her and opened the passenger door with hands that shook. She slumped down into the passenger seat and shuddered.

"Careful! I just cleaned this thing!" Malcolm said. She glared at him. He held up his hands. "Okay, sorry. Whatever. Just...please. I just finished this car."

"My best friend is dead," Cammy told him.

"Sorry to hear it," he said.

She glared at her blood-stained knees. Her hands balled into fists until her nails bit into her palms. Were they bleeding?

A button under her collar wriggled, turned warm, and popped off her shirt. When it collided with the dash, it turned back into Ginko. Malcolm took a swing at the little fox, who jumped against the window and flopped down on Cammy's lap.

"What is that?!" Malcolm shouted.

"This is Ginko," she explained, and hugged the little fox to her chest. "Vlad let her live at the mansion with her family. I found her trapped down in the labs."

"And you... sprung her?" Malcolm asked, pressing himself against his door and eying the little fox from behind a hand raised to punch it if it drew too close. Cammy nodded. "Boese isn't going to be too happy about that."

"What was I supposed to do?" Cammy said. "I couldn't just leave her there."

"Yeah, you could've," Malcolm grumbled. He shot another suspicious glance at the fox, who had crawled up to Cammy's shoulder to hide behind her head and hair and blink at him. "Where to?"

"I don't know," Cammy said. She didn't. There wasn't anywhere to go. Heather was dead. A hot tear plopped on Cammy's wrist. She blinked at it, then started to cry again. Malcolm sat quietly, fingering the steering wheel and glancing at the waves and biting his lip. Ginko nuzzled her cheek, so Cammy hugged her and thought for a moment how Heather wanted to have a dog, and how dumb it was that here she was, sitting in a werewolf's car, hugging a talking fox.

She spotted Malcolm trying very hard not to comment on her fishing tissues out of her bag and blowing her nose and holding onto the wads afterwards. Once the waterworks started to dry up, she glared at him, opened the door, and walked through the beams of light his car cast in the dark to the dumpster to throw away her collection of damp, gross tissues. She returned, plunked down hard in the seat and slammed the door shut. Malcolm flinched at the sound.

"Okay," he sighed. "You feeling better?"

"Sure," she grumbled.

"What now?"

She shrugged.

"Well, let's get you home."

"Home?"

"Yeah." Malcolm put the car in gear. "I mean, we can't sit out here all night."

Cammy wondered where her home even was.

Malcolm played modern pop music at levels that were probably going to leave them both deaf by the time they were thirty, but at least had some foresight. He stopped at a local café, to pick up an order of take-out he had called in, before driving her up to the mansion. Strange that he thought of Dracula's place as her home. But she supposed she didn't have anywhere else. In movies and books when the main character made the decision to leave their old life behind, they did seem to end up in a new living space. She should have thought through her decision better.

Malcolm carried the three bags of takeout and the cardboard tray of coffee cups into the kitchen without making eye contact with her. Just as well. She couldn't talk right now. Ginko hopped off her shoulder and darted out into the bushes, though she glanced over her shoulder at Cammy one last time before vanishing.

She went upstairs to change out of her clothes and wondered how long it would take for Boese to realize she'd stolen his new little lab animal and what he would do when he figured it out. Also, how long it would take for her host to come home.

After her knees stopped shaking, she wandered downstairs to find Malcolm once again helping himself to some wine out of a tea cup, eating one of the sandwiches he'd ordered—this one was a BLT stacked so thick he could barely fit it in his mouth. He seemed to be scrolling through a dating app on his phone. From what she could see, he didn't turn a single option down. He glanced up at her over a cup of carry out coffee.

"You okay?"

"Yeah." Her voice sounded as flat as a rabbit run over several times on the highway. She saw he'd ordered some vegetarian sandwiches with avocado and eggs, some hummus, and other options. Her stomach protested, so she only sat down. Malcolm returned to his phone.

"Where's Vlad?" she asked.

"I imagine he's down in that lab," Malcolm said. Cammy stared at him, but he only went back to noisily slurping his wine. He had been alternating between that and the coffee.

"But...why? What do we do?"

Malcolm shrugged. "Nothing we can do."

"But, I mean—but how long?"

Malcolm shrugged again. "Dunno. I guess 'til Boese lets him go."

Dracula's Guest

Boese threatened to throw him down there if he didn't make progress, Cammy thought. She felt rage burning right in the center of her chest. Dracula might be a psychopath, but he was out there *doing* something while Boese was sitting around kidnapping people like her and talking foxes and waiting for his "computer guys" to figure it all out.

"He'll let him go if the vampire problem gets solved, right?" Cammy said. Malcolm tilted his head in a lazy sort of "dunno." "I had an idea while I was down there," she said.

Malcolm slurped coffee at her.

"I'm serious," she said.

"You're serious. Fine. What is it?"

She explained her idea about the two doctors from the calendar book. Malcolm scratched his stubble while he listened.

"What do you think?"

"It's half-baked, but it's not a bad idea," Malcolm said. "The modern concept of vampires, with the whole 'virus' thing and such has given rise to the idea it takes a few days of being sick before you turn. I mean, even the traditional ones took a while of being sick." He shrugged. "Could be worth looking into."

"Do vampires work as doctors?"

"Who knows? Vlad was a doctor for a long time."

"What, really?"

"Yeah. Doctors used to like to bleed people. I bet that worked out for him."

Gross.

"So you think we should check it out?"

"Sure. I'm getting paid by the hour this time, so why not?"

"You're being paid?"

"Yep. Vlad offered to pay me to look after you."

"Oh. You're babysitting me again."

"Yep. So far as I see it, it's your time, my money." He winked.

She huffed.

"Well, we ought to start with those names. I don't have any others," she said.

"Sure. First thing tomorrow."

"I have to go to work—" Cammy cut herself off. "You know what? I'll call in. First thing tomorrow."

Malcolm saluted her.

CHAPTER 11

OLD FASHIONED DETECTIVE WORK

She called in first thing and asked Kenzie to cover her. Her friend only agreed when she promised to set up a meeting with her and Dracula. She had no idea if she could fulfill that promise, but if there was any chance that her idea was worth investigating, she had to buy herself the time.

A quick check on the internet revealed that Dr. Dupont was a dentist. Cammy thought a vampire dentist was even creepier than a vampire doctor.

Malcolm had purchased some instant coffee and practically chewed the floating bits in his hurry to suck down a cup. Cammy declined the offer for a serving for herself.

"Did you sleep up here?" she asked.

"Sure did."

"Where?"

He winked. "In a coffin."

"Oh, wow, you should do stand-up," she said flatly. "Wait, does *he* sleep in a coffin?"

"No idea. The only coffin I know about up here is a decoy in case some brave moron manages to get up here with a stake. Lots of beds, though."

Malcolm didn't bother locking the door as they left, so she assumed Dracula didn't either. Maybe he still thought it was the fifties and no one locked their doors.

She scanned the gravel driveway and the bushes for any sign of Ginko, but spotted nothing. Why couldn't any of the supernatural thingamagigs be friendly? She could really use a friend right now.

They drove to the little cluster of medical offices where the internet informed her Dr. Dupont practiced. He had a small suite practically hidden behind some wax myrtle plants. Malcolm opened the door and strode to the front desk. Cammy took a look around the foyer. It looked normal: ugly blue carpet, magazine rack, uncomfortable but sturdy chairs, and one of those bendy, multi-colored bead toys for kids to play with shoved into a corner. A middle-aged lady sat on one of the chairs reading a lifestyle magazine. She spared a glance at Malcolm and Cammy and resumed her reading.

"Hey there," Malcolm was saying to the receptionist—a thirty-something with just a little too much makeup on. Cammy noticed him flashing his winning smile at her. "I need a new dentist; my friend recommended your boss. Don't suppose he could squeeze me in?"

"I don't know about that. Let me get your information. Do you have insurance?"

"Sure do." Malcolm fetched his wallet out of his back pocket, pulled out three hundreds, and laid them down in front of the receptionist. Her brain stripped gears for a moment as she tried to make sense of the gesture.

"I don't," she mumbled. "I don't understand..."

"Sure you do." Malcolm laid down another hundred. The receptionist's eyebrows wriggled at the sight. Malcolm sighed, reached into his other pocket, and produced a portfolio wallet which he flipped open so she could look at what was inside. The receptionist read the contents carefully, looked up at him, and he answered with a nod.

"Let me just go see if he has a moment," she said, and rose from her desk. She didn't touch Malcolm's money, and he slipped the bills back into his wallet.

Cammy came up beside him to peer at what was in the little portfolio wallet. Malcolm showed her an ID that claimed he was a Private Investigator. She raised her eyebrows at him.

"Makes my job easier," he said. "So long as no one double-checks. So far no one ever has."

She noticed the name was "Richard Long."

It took her a few moments of looking at the stupid grin on his face before she got it.

"Really?"

He sniggered like a twelve-year-old boy.

The receptionist returned.

"Dr. Dupont has a few minutes to talk," she told Malcolm quietly. Malcolm winked at her, and nodded that Cammy come along.

"Err!" the receptionist protested.

"My assistant," Malcolm told her. "Lead the way. Time is money, you know."

She opened the door to let them back into the office proper, and led them down a short hallway carpeted with the same, old semi-blue stuff from the foyer. After knocking at the door at the far end, she timidly opened it and waved them inside. Malcolm grinned and bowed his head gratefully at her before stepping inside.

It was a cramped little office—not that Cammy had been inside a lot of dentist's offices, at least, not their personal offices in the back. She'd definitely been to a lot of dentists in her time. Her mother was quite the hypochondriac, not just for herself, but for her whole family.

Bookshelves were jammed up against the walls. There was a tiny desk, and a sad-looking little peace lily sitting on the windowsill. A tangle of computer cables peeked out from the dark beneath the desk, and a human skull—a replica, she hoped—rested on a pile of papers to weigh them down.

Dr. Dupont turned out to be a sweaty, pale man with a considerable beer gut and glasses that kept trying to slide right off his round nose. His watery eyes bounced back and forth between Malcolm and Cammy. His mouth pulled into a painful-looking grin.

"Something wrong?" he asked, and wiped his hands on his pants before rising from his desk and reaching out to offer a welcoming shake. Malcolm took his hand and received a handshake so limp Cammy cringed to see it, and he made absolutely no secret of wiping the man's sweat off on his own pants once done.

"You tell me," Malcolm said. "Not everyday someone like me comes to check on you, right?"

"I...I don't know her name, all right?" Dr. Dupont stammered. "I don't know what it's all about. I just..."

Dracula's Guest

"Just?"

"Needed the money," Dr. Dupont finished.

Huh? Cammy thought. This didn't sound like vampire stuff. This sounded shady, but not the right kind of shady.

"You don't know who she was. Describe her." Malcolm pulled a notebook.

"Uhhh...." Dr. Dupont rubbed his hands on his shirt. "A little older. Attractive, though. I mean, especially for an older woman. Maybe fifty? But looked good. Red hair. Those eyes..."

"Huh," Malcolm said, and scribbled something in his notebook. Cammy wondered if he was really writing anything. For all she knew, the dentist had hired a hooker and thought he was being investigated by someone from vice or his wife's PI. "She approached you?"

"Yeah."

"About your money troubles?"

Dr. Dupont nodded.

"Huh." Malcolm scribbled some more. "Interesting." He kept scribbling. Cammy wondered if he had gone out of his way to find a really noisy pen from how its scratches filled the silence instead of questions. At last, Cammy couldn't take it anymore.

"How'd she know about your money troubles?"

Dr. Dupont shook his head.

"I don't know. Maybe she... she might have talked to...." He wiped his forehead. "I took some loans. I'm in the red. Can't keep up with expenses...."

"So what exactly did she want?" Malcolm asked.

"She offered to help me. Got me supplies for cheaper than market value. I guess she... she got them illegally. But I didn't have much, and I was about to lose the practice."

"Let me see these supplies," Malcolm said.

Dr. Dupont wriggled out of his chair and left the office. Cammy and Malcolm followed him to the nearest examination room. Just the sight of that chair and the movable light that all dentists had gave her shivers. Suddenly it reminded her of that interrogation room down at Boese's headquarters. She might never be able to go to a dentist again.

Brush and floss, she told herself.

Dr. Dupont bent down and fished some plastic bags out of a cabinet. He passed them to Malcolm. Malcolm turned the packet back and forth, held it up to the light, and very unsubtly sniffed the bag.

"Hmm," he said. "Is this all?"

"No," Dr. Dupont moaned. He fished out two cardboard boxes. "Here."

"Hmmmmmm," Malcolm said, glancing inside the boxes. He turned to Cammy. "Here you go, assistant."

She took the boxes. A glance inside one revealed dental putty, the other had those nightmare tools dentists liked to stab you in the mouth with. Malcolm placed the bag he'd been handed on top of one of the boxes. She looked at him.

"We'll take a look at these," he said. "Thanks for cooperating. Don't use anything else she gave you. We'll be in touch."

"What happens now? You're going to arrest me?"

"Let my guys look over this stuff," Malcolm said. "You cooperated, and that goes a long way. Like I said, we'll be in touch." He nodded at Cammy to make for the door. He was able to reach over her to push it open before she had to kick it, and they made their way out of the office to the car.

"I'm going to need to see your patient list for the last couple of months," Malcolm said.

"Wha...my patients? You can't—that's—HIPAA."

"We have reason to suspect that your patients have been infected with a very rare blood-borne disease," Malcolm told him. "If we know who's seen you, we can try to get them treatment."

Dupont's sweaty face grew wetter.

"Disease?" he repeated in a whisper.

"Yep. Your mystery woman got some *very* illegal supplies for you."

"But they...they're sealed... but...." Dupont's eyes dropped to the boxes in Cammy's hands.

"Or you can wait for me to come back with a warrant and tell the DA you weren't very forthcoming," Malcolm told him.

Dupont led them to the receptionist's desk.

"Print off a list of our patients," he whispered to her.

"*What?*" she hissed in answer.

"Just do it!"

Her wide eyes peered into his, and searched Malcolm and Cammy's faces for answers. She scrutinized the boxes, and Cammy saw resignation dull the light of her eyes. Without a word, she typed something on her computer, and turned when the printer started whirring out pages. She passed them to Malcolm.

Back out in the drizzle, Malcolm opened the Camaro's back seat for her to set the stuff down on.

"What was all that?" Cammy asked. "What was he talking about?"

"Dunno," Malcolm said. He looked over his shoulder at the boxes. "But if your theory's right, then this mystery woman gave Dr. Dupont vampire-making stuff instead of medical supplies."

"Is that possible?"

"Dunno. Need someone with a lab to take a look."

A lab. There was really only one lab she knew of which could take care of that. Boese had said he'd be in touch.

Their minds were on the same track, because Malcolm said, "It'll be easier for Boese's people to look at the patient list and see if any of them have this jokester in common."

"Do you think Boese would let Vlad out if we show him this stuff?"

"You want to *bargain* with him?" Malcolm chuckled. He turned the engine over and pulled out of the parking lot.

"He said he wanted to hire me."

Malcolm shook his head and grinned.

"You know, I think I'm beginning to see why Vlad took you in."

"What do you mean?"

"You are a certified wrench in everyone's gears. It's funny. Since you don't know anything, you just come up with the craziest ideas. Ideas none of us would have come up with. Like me, I'd never think of trying to strong-arm Boese. You? You're just wondering if it'll get you what you want." He shook his head again.

"You mean... he wanted me around because I'm innovative?"

"That is definitely not the word I was thinking of, but sure, go with that one."

"Why? What word were you thinking of?"

"I was thinking more: insane." She punched his arm, and he laughed. "All right, unpredictable. Like our vampire buddies. I guess it takes an amateur to catch an amateur in a game full of old professionals like us." She punched him in the arm again, but playfully this time.

"Good to know I'm just a tool for you guys."

"Come on, don't be like that. He called me before going down there after you. He only would have done that if he figured he wasn't going to come back out but you were."

"What do you mean?" Cammy said.

"I mean he probably figured Boese would let you go the moment he had his favorite chew toy back." He looked at her. "I mean, no offense, but you're an amusing oddity. Boese can disappear you whenever he feels like it. Vlad's a problem. Only so many resources and attention to spare."

"He..." *He went down there to get me out?* But he didn't even seem to like her. He barely tolerated her. Heck, he'd threatened to kill her mother, more or less. He said he'd rather be crueler than nicer if he could go back in time. But he'd also let her stay, and he had tried to find Heather— though she doubted he had ever expected to be able to save her. If so, then she really needed to help get him back out. Apparently getting chopped up was only inconvenient, but Boese might do something worse.

"Do you know anything about the woman Dr. Dupont was talking about?"

Malcolm let out a long sigh through his teeth.

"I've got a hunch."

"You don't like it."

"I do not."

"Who do you think?"

"Bathory."

"Bathory? The bathing in girl blood lady?" Cammy said. Malcolm clicked his teeth together.

"She didn't do that when she was alive. But she does now."

"Huh? Why?"

"You know that human belief sometimes affects the supernatural? That's probably why. Everyone liked that story. So it stuck to her."

"Vlad didn't know much about her. But you do?"

"Ophois has worked with her in the past. She was interested in the Occult in life, and after, it seems. Ophois is all about that stuff."

Cammy took a moment to process that.

"You guys have worked with a vampire lady who bathes in the blood of murdered girls?"

"We're not known for our stellar moral code," Malcolm said. "We're known for getting the job done. And these days we're just about the last game in town."

"The last?"

He nodded. "Most of the other Orders are on life support or defunct. The next largest after us are the Pentagrams, a bunch of witch hunters. But think of them like this: the US military Industrial Complex is the biggest in the world, then Russia or China, then basically the rest of the world. Boese and his crew are the US, the Vatican is Russia or China. We're number three, and then everyone else just falls off a cliff into obscurity. Not much money to be made in witch hunting these days, and last I heard those Pentagram boys are a bunch of volunteers. We don't get along, in case you're wondering. We've got all the resources and they're a ragtag group of scrappy wannabes."

That must be why he hadn't wanted to talk much about himself earlier. Was he a psychopath too? He seemed so normal. If she couldn't be certain, then how could she ever tell which of her new allies or enemies were really dangerous or evil?

"Why do you think she's the behind this?"

Malcolm shook his head. "Not certain it *was* her. Just the first high-profile person that popped into my head who matches the description. Could be some Hollywood person who turned in the 50s and disappeared. I Love Lucy-lle Ball, maybe."

"Really?" Cammy was horrified at the idea.

"Not really. Making a joke," Malcolm told her. "Well, let's get back."

All they had to do now was wait for Boese to call.

He called at six that evening.

"I don't think that letting that *tanukitsune* go was very funny," he said.

"Hello to you, too."

"Those things are *dangerous*," Boese growled into the phone. "They can transform and cast illusions—"

"I found more information about all these vampires for you," she said, cutting him short. Dead silence answered her. She tried to picture in her mind if he was enraged, surprised, or something else.

"What? How? What did you find?"

"You'll need to take the stuff down to your lab," she said. "But I'm going to need Vlad's help to get to the bottom of this whole thing and deal with who's behind it."

Dead silence again. She couldn't help smiling at the idea that wherever he was, Boese was stunned on the other end.

"You're playing a very dangerous game, little lady," Boese said.

No kidding, she thought. But really, what did she have to lose at this point? "And I need his help to play."

"I don't think you understand: this isn't some personal vendetta I'm helping you with. *You're* helping me do *my* job."

"Same thing," she told him, and licked some ranch dressing off her thumb. She was finally hungry again. The avocado and egg sandwiches that Malcolm had bought were soggy and dried out at the same time, the way sandwiches got in the fridge, and the coffee was watery now that the ice cubes in them had melted. But she had started eating the wilted salad, and she was drinking instant coffee. Malcom had downed all the coffee from the shop. She chewed the disgusting instant coffee bits that refused to dissolve in the milk from the fridge. The milk seemed thicker and tastier than the stuff from the store. Cammy wondered why the milk was so much better.

The silence this time didn't last as long as the previous two spaces. Boese started chuckling into the phone.

"I see," he said. "I see. You're learning. Fine. You can have your boyfriend back."

"He's not my—eww!"

"Can it. You do more fine work, and I'm going to have a corner office open for you."

DRACULA'S GUEST

"Keep it," Cammy told him.

"Just FYI, you're in some trouble with the local PD."

"What? Why?"

"Anonymous tip came in that they should check your parents' address. They found a body there."

"*WHAT?!*" Cammy jumped to her feet and stared out the window at the trees outside. As though she could see their place from where she was. "Brian didn't—"

"Just 'cuz your other boyfriend works at the precinct doesn't mean he's in the loop for everything. He doesn't work homicide." Cammy's blood ran cold to think Boese knew *that* much about her and her friends. Malcolm wasn't wrong that he'd be able to check the patient list. "Besides, it'd be bad form for him to get involved since he's your friend."

I hate cops, she thought, *and I hate you, too*.

"I thought that was funny. Must mean that whatever or whoever you're after was able to look you up."

Heather, Cammy realized. *Heather was working for the rideshare dude.*

"You can clear that up, though, right?" Cammy said. "You know my parents didn't do anything."

"Not my job to clear that up," Boese said. "Honestly, if they take the fall for this it makes my job easier. Less paperwork."

"What? Your job is to protect people—"

"My job is hunting things that go bump in the night and making sure no one finds out about them. That's it. I'll send someone up there to get what you have."

"You...!" But the line went dead. She slammed her phone on the table.

"Problem?"

She turned to see Malcolm lurking in the doorway to the kitchen. Well, not lurking. Lounging. Leaning on the jamb, one thumb thrust in the pocket of his jeans.

"You were eavesdropping?"

"Yep."

"That's rude," she growled.

"Sounds like a fix," he said. She didn't answer. Malcolm pulled a stick of gum out of his pocket and popped it in his mouth. "Want one?" She shook her head. He cracked a bubble of gum in his mouth. "Well, we've got some time before Boese's people get here. You wanna look at that patient list and see if we can find our problem child before he does?"

She looked up. She nodded.

CHAPTER 12

WHO AND HOW

Almost an hour after Boese hung up on her, a car drove up the driveway. To her disappointment, it was a pair of Boese's goons. Malcolm passed them the dental supplies and the print-out of patients.

"Where's Vlad?" she asked one of them as the agent turned towards his car.

"He'll be released later," he told her.

"Boese was supposed to let him go."

This protest got no reply. The pair of agents dropped back into their vehicle and pulled out into the dark.

She slammed the door and returned to the kitchen. She had taken photos of the printout—if Dracula had a computer, she didn't know where it was—and Malcolm had been looking up names on his phone.

In another twenty minutes they struck gold.

Colston Terry turned out to be the bona fide founder of the stupid rideshare.

"Take a look at that!" Malcolm laughed and slammed his palm on the kitchen table. "We done struck oil! What are they even doing down there at Boese's?"

"Kidnapping foxes," Cammy grumbled. "Can you find any contact information?"

"Let's find out."

They easily tracked down the contact list on the website, but getting the man's personal number was more difficult. Then she struck on an idea.

"Why don't we hire one of his cars?"

Malcolm raised his eyebrows.

"Use the stupid 'Don't Forget' app they have."

Malcolm leaned back in his chair.

"You're jumping into the deep end, you know," he said. "If he's been orchestrating a human murder machine you oughta be a little more careful dealing with him. Vlad would be our big guns. We oughta wait for him."

"This... piece of garbage just made it personal," she told him. "He's going after my parents and *no one*'s going to help."

Malcolm frowned at his phone and the photo they'd found of the man on his company website. Colston was a normal-looking thirty-something with short, sandy-blond hair. He was smiling in his photo. Just a hopeful start-up guy. Cammy tried to understand how he'd managed to graduate to mass murder. Was that just how it worked if you turned into a vampire?

"Does it make you evil?"

"What?"

"Getting, you know, turned into a vampire?"

"This strain seems to end up that way," Malcolm said

"Do they all?"

Malcolm shrugged. "These days in pop culture you've got everything from *Buffy* to *Twilight*, right? Guess it depends."

Cammy realized that Dracula had probably never heard of, seen, or read *Twilight*. She wondered what he'd think of vampires who sparkled.

"Why would anyone give that dentist some sort of contaminated supplies to turn people?"

Malcolm shrugged again. "That's a real good question. If you're a monster, I can't imagine you'd want to draw attention to yourself by just turning a ton of people. That makes people like Boese go to Defcon 1. That in turn creates chaos in the monster world. When there's heat in your area, it makes it a lot harder to get your food, right? And I don't know why any human who knows what's going on would want to just turn a bunch of people into unruly vampires. What's there to gain out of doing that?" He looked at her pointedly.

"Why do you think *I* would know the answer to that?"

"You're the idea person right now. This doesn't seem like the kind of thing any of us old guard would have come up with. So whaddaya got?"

Cammy frowned at the online image of the smiling, normal face. He probably looked almost exactly the same, only maybe little paler than before.

"It's a message," she said. "Or a revolution, maybe."

Malcolm stared. Cursed.

"You're probably right. Someone somewhere wants to upset the whole apple cart." He hugged himself and his eyes burned holes in one of the drawers across the table from him. Slowly, his eyes traced meaningless tracks across the room, and Cammy realized he was thinking about something he'd seen.

"What is it?"

He shook his head. "Let's keep focused on our boy for right now. This guy seems to be an amateur. So that'll give us a little bit of an advantage. But honestly I think we should wait for Vlad. Numbers can make a *lot* of difference in a fight."

"He's that much better than you?" Cammy asked. He glowered at her.

"Hey, you're an amateur too. That's why I have to babysit. And to answer your tactless question, he's got almost six hundred years of experience and is pretty much indestructible."

"Indestructible?" Cammy pressed. Maybe she'd finally learn something.

"I've seen the notes on him. No one's been able to kill him yet, and not for lack of trying."

"So... stake through the heart?"

"If anyone's managed to get one in him, I haven't heard about it. He got hit by a freaking mortar during World War 2. Direct hit. That only seemed to piss him off."

The modern vampires were looking lamer all the time. She couldn't disagree that Dracula would be a *lot* of help, but her parents were on the line and Boese wasn't going to intercede. For all she knew, this Colston person was going to keep after her. He might target one of her friends next. It wouldn't be too hard to look at her social media and figure out who Lindsey and Kenzie and the others were. Brian might be all right because he was a cop, but if this guy didn't care about kidnapping and murdering people, maybe he wouldn't care if someone was a cop. Or worse, maybe he'd try to get Brian involved on purpose to create more chaos.

She tried Dracula's phone. No answer.

"How long before Boese lets him go?" she asked.

"Dunno," Malcolm said, almost apologetically.

She couldn't wait.

"Let's try contacting this vampire guy and getting him to meet us somewhere," Cammy said.

"To try and ambush him?" Malcolm said. He squinted at his own eyebrows to think. "Maybe that would work. Where?"

"Here?"

"Dunno if he's going to want to try up here again after what happened. There were about thirty of them that night. By the time I got out there, lots of them were strewn all over the place."

"How many did you get?"

He shook his head. "My brain gets foggy when I go berserk. Not sure. Six or seven. Definitely the one trying to get in the house."

Malcolm drained what remained of his instant coffee in a tea cup and bared his teeth at the flavor. "Gonna level with you: I don't want to go in without back-up."

"I thought it was your job to hunt monsters."

"When I'm being paid to do it," he said, and poured himself some wine next. "Right now I'm being paid to *not* hunt monsters. I'm being paid to babysit. Honestly, I prefer babysitting. Pays better and it's way less dangerous."

Cammy frowned at him. He glanced at her over the rim of his tea cup.

"You don't care about people?" she demanded.

"Not when I'm not being paid to," he said. She waited for that winning smile of his to appear and prove he was joking. It didn't.

"You're serious."

"Dead serious," he said.

"You don't care whether people die."

"I care whether *I* die," he said. "I'd like to avoid that as long as I possibly can. Hard to spend a paycheck when I'm dead." He rose from the table and put his tea cup in the sink, ignoring the look she kept shooting at him.

"But I need your help," she said.

"Doing what?"

"Taking this guy down."

Malcolm stood in the doorway and crossed his arms.

"You want to take him down personally? That's a bad idea. Never let this job turn into something personal."

"Well, it's not *my* job," she informed him.

"You don't know what you're doing," Malcolm told her. "You'll only get yourself killed. Or worse. Probably worse. Then I won't get a paycheck."

"You said it before: stake 'em, behead 'em, right?"

Malcolm squinted at her.

"I also remember you pissing your pants and getting all weepy about it before." He adopted a whiny little voice, "'*Oh, I'm a vegetarian. I can't even kill an ant! I can't kill a vampire! Axes are too scary!*'"

She glared at him.

"That's what you sound like," he said.

"I do not."

"You do."

"I had to kill my *best friend!*" she shouted at him. "Don't you understand that? And this guy's gone after my family! He might go after my other friends next"

"Well, I'm glad you're finally gonna man up and get serious," Malcolm said. "But I told you before: you don't know what you're doing. That means if we go in, I'm going to have to keep one eye on you the whole time, and the other on the thirty more of these guys he might send, all without Vlad's monster sanctuary as a back-up. That's long odds on either of us making it out alive, and I don't like long odds."

"You offered to help me find this guy before Boese's people did."

"Yeah, because I thought Vlad would be back when Boese's people came to get the files and the lab stuff. Until he returns I'm the resident expert, and I say we don't do anything stupid. You're not going to get revenge or protect anyone if you go and get yourself—or me—killed."

"But we can't just do *nothing*," Cammy insisted.

"Of course we can!" Malcolm shouted. "What are you talking about? We can both absolutely just sit here and wait for the big guns before we go head out into war. Get your head on straight!"

"But you liked my ideas! You said—!"

"No!" Malcolm shouted. "No. You know what? You just sit there and think about what I said. Vlad's gone, so I'm in charge. I say we don't go." He turned to stalk out of the kitchen, pointed that she keep sitting in the chair when she rose to follow him, and stormed off.

You're just like Boese, she thought. *You don't care!* Dracula would have gone to do something, she was sure of it.

She slapped the table in anger and blinked away the stupid, angry tears that came into her eyes.

About half an hour later, she went looking for Malcolm. She found him in an upstairs bedroom, sitting in a chair beside a nice four-poster bed.

"What are you doing up here?"

"Getting alone time," he said. "Turns out I'm not cut out for babysitting."

She considered him sitting in the chair.

"You heard me coming?"

"Hard not to. You stomp around like an elephant."

"You're a jerk," she told him.

"What do you want? I'm not taking you vampire hunting."

"I need supplies," she said. He narrowed his eyes at her.

"You think I was born yesterday, do you?"

"I do!" she told him, and fidgeted. "You know... *feminine* supplies."

"Doesn't smell like you do."

"*Eww!* You don't have to be like that! And not right *now*, but I don't have any and I'm going to need them soon. I got kicked out of my apartment and couldn't bring everything with me!"

"If you don't need them now, why should we go get them now?"

You think I want to ask *Vlad* to drive me later when I do?"

He kept boring his eyes into hers, searching for a lie. Finally, he huffed and rose from the chair.

"Fine," he said. "You do anything sneaky and I'm going to tie you up and leave you in the basement until Vlad gets back."

"Gee, you're such a *gentleman*," Cammy said. "Is this how you treat a lady?"

"If you mean a date, no. But you're not a date. You're my paycheck. And a *pain*. Come on."

He stormed out of the bedroom, flicking the lights off as he went. She followed him out the front door to his car.

"Where do you need to go?" he asked. She told him which Bartell's would be easiest to reach, and they headed down into the city.

It was dark by the time they got there. Dracula had a nice home, but its location made it a long drive to any shops, especially when they hit the tail end of commuter traffic. Malcolm parked his car in an empty space with plenty of room for his doors.

"You that worried about your car?"

"I *built* this car," Malcolm snapped. "Built it with my own hands. Would you leave your baby for people to scratch up?"

"I wouldn't think of a car as my baby," she told him. It was raining—drizzling really hard, actually—so she covered her head with her hood.

"Do you need anything?" she asked Malcolm when they passed through the automatic doors. He glanced at the condoms. What a surprise.

"I need to find the bathroom. I'll meet you at the register?"

"You run off, and I'm gonna go berserk. I mean it," he told her.

"Run off *where?*" she demanded and rolled her eyes. "It's raining and I have no car."

"Fine," he grumbled. He wandered off, and she made for the feminine products. Once he was out of sight, she turned around and scooted out the door before he could realize she'd given him the slip. She darted through the dark and the rain to the restaurant in the same shopping center and checked her phone. The driver ought to be nearby.

She spotted the green sedan under a street lamp and walked towards it. She clutched her purse tight to her side, one hand at the ready. Dracula had a lot of anti-vampire weapons in his little collection, and some even fit in her bag. She tapped on the window.

"Hello. I'm Cammy," she said to the driver once he rolled down his window.

"Yeah?" he said, and nodded at the passenger door.

"Actually, I was hoping I could borrow your phone," she told him. This driver was about forty, and wore a scraggly beard. He frowned in confusion at the request.

"I need to use 'Don't Forget,'" she told him.

"What? How do you know about that?"

"If you let me do that, I'll get out of your hair," she said. "And leave you a good rating."

His face wrinkled up at the request, but he lifted his phone from its cradle on the dash, pressed the app, and handed it over. She took a breath.

"Hey, it's me. I want to meet. Here. I'm sure you can look this place up."

"Hey, what gives? That's proprietary. For my protection," the driver said, and took the phone back. "Who do you think you're talking to?"

"Your boss."

"My boss? Margaret?"

"No, Colston Terry."

"The CEO isn't going to bother spying on all these—"

His phone rang, and he glanced down at the number.

"Who is that?" Cammy asked.

"Don't recognize the number."

"That's him," Cammy said.

"Look, I don't know what you're up to. I'm trying to feed my kids. I don't know what you're doing, but I don't want to get involved in anything weird, okay? I'm out of here."

"Wait!"

He was rolling up his window. She saw his phone screen light up as a text came in. His eyes squinted at the message. Then another came in. He stared at it, looked up at her. The window rolled down.

"Here," he said, breathless. "Take it."

She saw the two messages. *Give the girl the phone.* The second was a photo of the driver and a plump woman who must be his wife, a kid about ten sticking out his tongue, and an infant in the woman's arms. Before she had time to process the threat, the phone rang with an unknown number. She answered it.

"Colston?" she guessed.

"Cammy," said the voice on the other side. "I'm surprised you'd reach out. Wasn't expecting to see your number hiring anyone ever again. How nice to get to talk to you. Heather told me all about you."

"I want to talk," she told him. "I want a truce."

"Ah. Your parents?" he said.

"I don't want my family or friends getting hurt."

"To be honest, I'd like a truce myself. It's getting very crowded in this city. But what about your friend? The dangerous one."

"He's not coming," she told him.

Colston had no response. She wondered what he thought about that. Was he suspicious?

"All right. Get in the car. Give the driver the phone."

"I want to meet you here," she told him.

"Well, I don't," he said. "I can't move around very easily. Lots of people are looking for me, and I can't be anywhere easy to find. If you want to meet me in person, you'll have to come to me."

That sounded like a trap. *Really* like a trap.

"Cammy? What are you doing?!"

She turned to see Malcolm power-walking towards her.

"Here," she handed the driver his phone, then opened the back door.

"Don't you dare!" Malcolm shouted, and started sprinting.

"Drive!" she said and dropped into the backseat.

"Wha?" the driver murmured, staring out the window at Malcolm barreling towards them.

"Drive!"

He reversed out of the parking as Malcolm's hand reached for her door. Cammy could hear him swearing, then he turned to sprint for his car.

"Go!" she told the driver.

"What is going on?!"

She reached forward and tapped the speaker on his phone.

"That's better. You can both hear me now?" Colston said.

"Where are we going?" Cammy asked.

"I'll send the address. See you soon."

"I don't want to be in the middle of this!" the driver protested. "I gotta feed my kids!"

"All you're doing, Robert, is dropping the girl off at a house. Nothing illegal. She hired you. Don't worry. This is personal. I'll send you a bonus."

"I don't—"

"Listen," Colston said. His tone was a strange sort of silky smooth, but she could hear something underneath it, something sinister. Like a snake grinning nicely, but you could see its fangs poking out and dripping venom. "Robert, you're not doing anything illegal. You're taking a fare. And you have a lovely family. Crystal seems like a very good mother. I'd like to meet her."

Cammy could see poor Robert's eyes staring wildly into the dark as he drove. His mouth hung slack.

"You understand, Robert?"

"I..."

"I sent you the address. Don't worry. The girl wants to come. Don't you, Cammy?"

"Yeah," she said.

"So don't worry, Robert. Just drive. Was there someone shouting out there before? I thought I heard something."

"No one," Cammy said.

Colston didn't respond.

"To that address," he said. The line went dead.

They had gotten onto I-90 heading west. Cammy shivered when she noticed the address. Phinney Ridge. Heather's parents' house. Her stomach twisted inside her until it hurt. At least Robert wasn't a vampire, and he hadn't bothered to search her for weapons. She ought to be able to get close to Colston before he realized she was dangerous. She had to stop him. If he was at Heather's parents' house, then he must have killed them. She wanted to sob, but she gripped her bruised hand tight. She couldn't lose it, not yet. This monster had to be stopped. If Malcolm wasn't going to and Dracula wasn't able, then it had to be her.

Dracula had been right. Malcolm had been right. She didn't want to be in the middle of this. She wanted her old life back. But she couldn't ever have it back. And she couldn't wait for Boese to get out of his stupid lab and actually deal with the problem.

Robert drove up to the curb, and she noticed him trembling.

"I'm sorry," she told him. "I didn't want to... I'm sorry."

He didn't say anything. She saw his knuckles stand out as he gripped the steering wheel.

She couldn't think of what else to say, so she got out of the car. The drizzle had let up, but it was still pretty dark. Not so dark that she didn't spot the three people coming for her. She froze. Even in the dark, she saw the pallid complexions. Her heart did five backflips in a row. She needed to close the door, let Robert get away. Her body refused to obey her.

"*Move!*" she hissed to herself, and slammed the door.

Dracula's Guest

"Don't," said one of the strangers, and pulled a gun. Another came towards the front of the green sedan with his own gun, and tapped on the hood. The car didn't move.

"Leave him out of this," Cammy said.

The third stranger grabbed her by the hair and dragged her towards the house.

"Let me go!"

The stranger socked her hard in the stomach and her legs lost all strength. She couldn't breathe, couldn't shout. Her stomach seemed to be kicking inside her, and her lungs refused to take air. She couldn't pry the cold fingers from her hair. The front door appeared in front of her, opened, and the threshold passed under her.

The stranger dragged her to the living room and threw her onto the faded green carpet, then turned and went out the open door. She still couldn't breathe, she could barely move, but she could see the stranger standing over her. She tried to reach into her bag. This vampire seemed to be by himself. She might be able to get him before the others came inside.

He ripped her bag from her hands and dumped out the contents on the floor. When he saw the stakes and the little hatchet he laughed out loud, and she could see his fangs glinting in the dark.

Three more people came in through the front door. She recognized one as Robert, his hands held up in surrender, and saw the vampire behind him holding a gun to his back.

"He doesn't have anything to do with this!" Cammy croaked. She still couldn't quite breathe.

The vampire who'd emptied her bag whooped at the others and pointed out her weapons. One of them found the collection equally amusing and picked up a stake to smile at.

"We got ourselves a regular Buffy, huh?" He grinned down at her.

"Please," Robert said.

Air came back to Cammy all at once. "Let him go!" She lunged for a stake, but the first vampire stepped hard on her wrist and pinned her hand to the floor.

"Anyone else?" he asked the others.

"Didn't see anyone else," the third vampire told him.

"Okay, then." The vampire pressed harder on Cammy's wrist until she squeaked with pain. He pulled out his phone. "It's safe. Doesn't seem like she was followed."

"Let him go!" she shouted. The vampire standing on her wrist knelt down, and she gasped in pain. He pressed a gun to her temple.

"You be quiet, now. Don't want to wake the neighbors."

"And if I don't? That gun's going to wake the neighbors."

The vampire grinned.

"You know I don't need a gun to keep you quiet." He looked to the others and the driver. "Bedroom, I guess," he said. "Leave some for me."

"No! Leave him alone!"

The vampire standing on her wrist pistol-whipped her against the side of her head. She squeezed her eyes shut against the throbbing pain.

"You want some, boss?"

She peered up at the sofa where Vernon had made an indentation. The pale, smiling face she'd seen on the website looked down at her from the space beside where Vernon had sat. The man—vampire—didn't seem to want to touch the impression. He leaned forward, peering down at her, his elbows on his knees, his fingers folded together. As she'd thought—he looked pretty much the same; in the dark it was hard to tell if he really was any paler.

"This one stays alive," Colston told the vampire, who still stood over her, though he'd stepped off her wrist. "If you kill her, our one ticket out of here goes straight to hell."

"Right. Sorry," the vampire mumbled.

Colston returned his attention to Cammy.

"So," he said, "here we are."

Cammy had no idea what to say. Malcolm would be the only one who could get to her, but she'd left him in the dust—or at least the drizzle.

"You have his number?"

"Whose number?"

"Don't be stupid. You-know-who. You're living at his house."

He wanted Dracula? Not her?

"Why?"

"Because I want to call him," Colston said.

"Why?"

Colston rubbed his palms together.

"Okay, we'll play it this way. Because I want to get out of town, and I also want to make sure he doesn't keep following me. That's why."

"He wouldn't be after you if you hadn't killed anybody," Cammy told him.

"A man's gotta eat," Colston said. "Surely he knows that. What is he to you?"

"I don't know," she said.

"Really? He's gone out of his way for you, and you don't know?"

"I'm a guest," she said.

Colston tried to hold back his mirth.

"Guest? How? He rescued you?"

"He said he didn't."

"He didn't. Sure. All right. What's his number?"

She gritted her teeth.

"Look, I'd rather not have to turn you first, because my plan's going to be a lot harder if I do, but I have to be able to call him to start with. It's your choice: tell me now, or after we have ourselves a little taste first. Your call."

Her temple throbbed and she wanted to throw up, but she had her bearings back now. She spotted her wallet, phone, the stakes, and her hatchet on the coffee table in front of Colston.

"Stakes, huh?" he said when she spotted them. "Better luck next time. Guess you're not a secret expert at killing vampires, huh? I was beginning to wonder, especially after all my minions disappeared up at that estate."

"They didn't know what they were doing," Cammy told him.

"Doesn't seem like you know, either," he observed. "I figured you'd have someone following you for back-up. Imagine my surprise when you showed up all alone. I'm tickled." He picked up her phone. "It's in here?"

"You need my thumbprint to unlock it," she told him.

She reached for the phone, but the vampire who had stepped on her wrist grabbed her hand in his iron grip and yanked her forward so Colston could use her thumb to unlock the phone. She tried to wriggle free, but couldn't get loose no matter what she tried. He just gripped tighter until she winced. Colston scrolled through her contacts with a stylus, found what he was looking for, and dialed.

"He's not answering," Cammy told him. Colston ignored her. He pressed the phone to his ear and listened. They all waited. He clucked his tongue, frowned at the phone, and redialed. "I told you, he's not answering—"

"Hello," Colston said. Cammy couldn't believe her ears. Dracula was free? Her heart leaped and clicked its heels. Maybe he'd be able to rescue her after all. Unless it was Boese on the other end and Dracula was still down at the lab getting chopped up. "She's fine, don't worry. Listen: I agree it was a mistake my trying to invade your territory. It was a stupid plan. I overreached. Are you still willing to parlay?" He tapped the stylus on his knee while he listened to the reply. "Yes, she's right here. She's fine. I don't think so, I have some demands first." He grinned and chuckled. "I suppose you're right. It *is* only polite." He set the phone on the coffee table and put it on speaker. "Can you hear us?"

"I can." It was Dracula's voice. Cammy's heart jumped up and down again. He was free, then. Colston looked to Cammy.

"He would like to know whether you are all right."

"Vlad! Are you okay?"

"Perfectly well. It seems I will need to punish Malcolm, however. I don't suppose he died with dignity?"

"I ran away," she said.

"Then I will deal with him later. How are you?"

"This guy killed Heather's parents!" Cammy shouted, and Colston glowered at the noise. "And the driver who brought me here!"

"But you are unharmed?"

"They hit me in the head."

"I see," Dracula said. "But you are still human?"

The question turned her blood into ice. He was so matter-of-fact about it. Basically a "So long as I'm heading out there, should I bring a stake for you, too?" How did he think she was going to answer that?

"We haven't touched her," Colston said. "*Yet.* You can hear that she's all right. Now, I have demands."

Dracula didn't respond to the statement, but Colston continued anyway.

"I want information, and money," he said.

"Money? Truly?"

"Seems I need to vacate the area. I gather I've intruded on your territory?"

"After a fashion, yes."

"I need the funds to do that."

"I see."

"He hates thieves," Cammy told Colston.

"Who's a thief? I'm exchanging goods for cash. A monetary transaction, if you will."

"You think ransom is a *monetary transaction?*" she demanded.

"It is literally a monetary transaction. Now be quiet, the adults are talking." Colston picked up the phone, turned off speaker mode, and pressed it to his ear again. "Let's say three million if you can do it. If not, whatever you've got. As far as information, I'd like you to explain to me how to survive out there in the cold once I leave you alone. And some assurance you won't come after me." He tapped the stylus on his knee again. "I see. That is pretty annoying. I'd like not to have to drag your—" He glanced at Cammy. "What is she to you, anyway? Skinny little bride-to-be?" He chewed the inside of his cheek as he listened to the reply. "If you say so. In any event, I was hoping not to have to drag her around the planet with me as insurance. That's not how negotiating works, you know. You give me what I ask, and I give her back unharmed. Hmm. Well, let's circle back to that once you get here. Obviously, I'd like you to arrive alone. And soon. The sun'll be up and that will throw quite the spanner in my travel plans. I'll text you the...really?" Colston chuckled. "All right, you have something to write with?" He glared at Cammy and put a finger to his lips, then proceeded to give a completely different address. She opened her mouth to shout a warning, but the vampire standing over her wrapped his horrible, cold hand over her mouth and pressed her down into the carpet. "No, she's being naughty," Colston said. "Not harmed, no. You'll see when you get here." He hung up her phone and looked to her, then waggled a disapproving finger. "Don't push me. Like I said, I don't want to have to kill you yet. I need insurance, you see."

"What do you mean, 'drag me all over the planet?'" she demanded.

"Your friend seems awfully attached," he explained, and brushed some dust from his pant leg. "He told me that the only way I'd be safe from him chasing me was if you were a shield. The moment you die, he'll be after me again."

"Wha...?" Why would Dracula say that? Did he *want* her to be a human meat-shield for the rest of her life? *Because he's a psychopath?*

"So it's now imperative that you tell me how to kill him," Colston said. He picked up one of the stakes. "This works on us just fine. Does it work on him?"

Cammy considered the little stake. If she could wriggle free, she might be able to get that in Colston's chest and save herself. *Then the others will get you,* she realized. Stupid plan. Plus, there was no way she could get free anyway. The vampire's grip was too powerful.

"I don't know," she said. "People have been trying to kill him for a long time."

"Anyone manage to stake him?"

"I don't know."

Colston sighed and rocked back in the sofa.

"Well, according to the book, I'd have to behead him too. But if the book is real, then he ought to be dead and gone right now."

She nearly blurted that the book was wrong on a lot of counts, but thought better of it in time. "He said that you guys are wildcards. Some need to be beheaded, some staked."

Colston considered her.

"How'd he know that?"

Oops. She should have kept her mouth shut.

"He's been hunting vampires a long time."

"Why? Isn't he a vampire?"

"No. A strigoi."

"A what?"

DRACULA'S GUEST

Again, she should have said nothing. Colston pulled his own phone and typed in the search field. She realized he was looking up the term. He tapped on his chin as he read the answer.

"If he's got a grave, I have to assume it's back home," he mumbled. "So I can't leave him face down in it. But looks like stakes do the trick. If not, beheading. Okay, then."

Face-down in his grave? Cammy wondered. If that was the only way to kill him, then it made sense why no one had succeeded. As Colston said, he must be a long way from his grave.

"Stakes kill strigois?" she asked.

"According to this," Colston answered, waggling his search results at her.

Was it really possible no one had succeeded in putting a stake through his heart in all this time? What about beheading? If Boese had been chopping him up, had he really never taken Dracula's head off? Being blown up by a mortar should be just as good, shouldn't it? Maybe the grave thing was the only way. But none of this mattered if Dracula was going to a totally different location.

"Did he ever count things around you?" Colston asked.

"What?"

"Count things. Like rice. Get upset when stuff got spilled or untie knots?"

"I didn't see any rice," Cammy said.

"Hey, you chuckleheads get out here," Colston shouted to the wall. After a few moments, the other two vampires emerged from the bedroom. "Go check if there's any rice or sunflower seeds in the kitchen." They went to obey.

"Why rice?"

"Seems some of those older vampires have to count stuff if you toss it down in front of them. We'll see if it works on him."

"But he's not even coming here," Cammy pointed out. Colston looked pained.

"Of course he is. My people will pick him up, and make sure he's only bringing what I asked. And no back-up."

Oh. That made sense, actually. If Dracula couldn't sneak any weapons in, could he still kill these vampires? She hoped so. But there were three—four actually, counting Colston. Malcolm had said numbers still counted.

Colston turned on the TV to pass the time and let her sit up, but still on the floor under the watchful eye of the vampire who kept hurting her. She spotted Colston scrolling through his phone occasionally. He clucked his tongue at some point and stared out the window. She didn't know how long it had been. It seemed like ages. At last, his phone rang.

"You got him?" he demanded. "Good. Hurry up, will you? What took him so long?" He glared into the TV. "Fine. Fine. Just hurry." He turned the TV off angrily and tossed the remote into the depression Vernon had made in the sofa. He rubbed his hands together and glanced at the sliding glass door. The blinds weren't quite closed. It was still dark out.

Please have an ace up your sleeve, she thought.

At long last, the front door swung open and Dracula entered, carrying a little wooden casket with a gold lock on it. Behind him, another of Colston's minions came in and closed the door. He was carrying Dracula's wood-metal sword from before. The moment Dracula set eyes on her, the vampire standing over Cammy pressed a gun to the back of her skull.

"Took your sweet time," Colston growled.

"I don't leave millions lying around," Dracula explained, as though to a child. He dropped the casket down *thunk* on the coffee table. He gestured at it. "Bullion."

"Gold, really?" Colston asked, and flipped open the lid to peer inside. It looked like gold to Cammy. Little bars of it. "Well, that'll be hard to track, at least." He slapped the lid shut.

"How are you?" Dracula asked her.

"You came," she said.

"Not that I should have *had* to," he said, and reached out a hand.

"You're kidding," she told him. He didn't move. At last, she offered her hand, and he kissed it again. The move wasn't lost on Colston.

"A guest. Really?" he said.

"Indeed," Dracula said. "If you weren't an uneducated, culturally illiterate churl you'd understand what that means." He put his hands in his pockets. "You wanted information?"

"That's right. I take it you're the big fish in this pond," Colston said. "I'm new, but it seems I'm hungrier than you. I need to know how to survive. First off, how many other vampires like you are out there?"

"I haven't the slightest idea," Dracula told him. "I don't keep their company as a rule."

"You hunt them?"

"If they show their faces above ground."

"Why? Competition?"

"I happen to despise vampires," Dracula said. Colston's face cracked into a grin.

"You do? Really? That's not hypocritical of you?"

"Why should it be?"

"Because you're the most famous vampire in history?"

"That does not oblige me to care for the species," Dracula informed him.

"How does it work? Is every city like this? There's some big guy and everyone else has to get his blessing?"

"You mean to ask if there are other monsters?"

Colston's eyebrows rose. "Are there?" he asked.

"Thousands," Dracula informed him. "All different species. Different alliances, different needs. And different people who hunt them, as well. There are ogres and witches and dragons and worse."

Colston rubbed his hands together again. "So are there secret societies?"

"Of what? Vampires? In some locations. Some of the older ones have orders to which they belong. That's how they've survived for such a long time."

"What about you? You part of an order?"

"Not of vampires."

Colston stroked one cheek and his eyes roamed over the coffee table.

"And there are vampire hunters?"

"Yes. Many different organizations. One is funded and fielded by the US government."

This drew Colston's attention.

"The feds," he murmured. "They... weren't investigating a serial killer?"

"I imagine they are aware of you," Dracula said.

Dracula's Guest

This news set Colston back and he folded his hands together, his palms pressed against one another. His eyes darted as he thought.

"That means I can't go anywhere in the US."

"Correct."

Colston ran his hands through his hair and pressed his clasped hands to his mouth. He hissed into his fingers.

"What about other countries?"

"I imagine all world governments are aware that vampires exist."

"Do they communicate with each other? About fugitives, maybe?"

"I have no way of knowing," Dracula said.

Colston rose from the sofa and began pacing the room.

"Are there... ways to disguise what we are?" Colston asked. "Any sort of... serum? Sun screen? Can we change shape? I don't seem to be able to."

"I have no idea whether you can do something as useless as turn into a bat, as Stoker imagined."

"You think being able to fly is *useless?*" Colston snarked.

"I think being a bat would be useless," Dracula corrected.

"But not a dog or a wolf?"

"I suppose that depends on how well you can use that to your advantage."

"Same with a bat, moron," Colston snipped. "What about you? You can turn into a wolf, right?"

"Why do you think so?"

"The book said so."

Dracula blinked languidly in response.

"Can't you?"

"No."

Colston stuck the end of his thumb between his teeth and considered Dracula.

"Are you even one of us? I hear you breathing over there."

"You've sharper ears than I have," Dracula said. "And no, I'm not one of you."

"You have anything useful you can tell me?" Colston demanded. "It's late enough now I'll have to camp out in this house all day before I can get going."

"You demanded an absurd amount of money. Even were it day outside, no bank would have let me walk out with three million dollars in hand."

"You could have wired it."

"No, I could not," Dracula said.

"Well, if you really don't have anything more you can tell me." Colston nodded to the vampire standing over Cammy.

"Watch out, they planned a trap!" Cammy warned. Colston tossed a handful of rice he'd put in his pocket across the coffee table and the floor while his partner pulled one of the stakes she'd brought in her bag from his belt. She wasn't sure the rice was going to work, but to her horror, Dracula stared down at the scattered rice, frozen in place, his eyes bouncing from grain to grain to grain.

"Look out!" she shouted, but the vampire standing over her plunged the stake deep into his chest while he stood there motionless. Dracula crumpled backwards to the floor and didn't move. Colston stepped forward, craning his neck, then waved his minion go take a look.

"Seems dead," the vampire said.

Dracula's Guest

"Sure not breathing anymore," Colston agreed. He stepped a little closer, until he was practically standing over Cammy, peering at his fallen enemy.

No way, she thought to herself. But no matter how she stared, Dracula didn't move. No way he could be killed so easily. No way no one had tried this in the last several hundred years.

"That was easy," Colston observed. "Better find something to get his head off with, just to be sure." He nodded at the one who stood lurking in the foyer with Dracula's wood-and-metal sword. Cammy's eyes fell on the other stakes from her bag still resting on the coffee table. Colston was standing right there, his attention on Dracula.

She couldn't let him get away with it.

Her hand wrapped around a stake and she nearly got it in his chest before Colston caught her wrist and stared down at her like he'd forgotten she existed. She punched him in the groin, and the action surprised him more, but she had the impression it was because he had expected that to hurt. Relief that it didn't washed over his face.

"Guess I don't need you anymore," he said, and lifted her effortlessly off the floor. "And it looks like we're not going anywhere for a while. Don't know what he saw in you. You've got the curves of a twelve-year-old-boy."

She punched him in the chest, but he didn't seem to notice. He grabbed her hair and bared his fangs.

Then he looked over her shoulder and his eyes widened and this time he *did* forget she existed. Something knocked a glass down onto the floor behind her and she heard a *thud*. She tried to shake Colston off, but he dragged her with him to the sliding glass door on the other side of the room and ripped the stake out of her hand. She managed to turn to try to run when he wrapped an arm around her and pressed the point of the stake to her throat.

Dracula was on his feet, his sword in hand, the bloody stake that had pierced his chest in the other, and only one vampire near him. The one who had taken his sword was out of sight. Not quite. She spotted his leg draped over the end table that stood beside the sofa where a lamp had also been. Dracula rushed the other vampire. He tried to raise his hands to defend himself, only to get the same weapon he had just used plunged into his own chest. He crumpled to the floor in a heap, and Dracula took his head off with the sword.

Then he turned to face Colston.

"Don't you dare," Colston told him, gripping the stake at Cammy's throat tighter.

Dracula didn't. He stood perfectly still.

"You didn't quite manage it, did you?" he asked. It took Cammy a moment to realize he was addressing her.

"I tried."

He sighed.

"When this is all over, we need to have a very long talk."

"Friend, I think you should consider the position you're in," Colston told him, and squeezed Cammy tighter. "I've still got all the cards here." He pointed for a moment with the stake before bringing it right back to Cammy's throat. "Why don't you drop that?"

Dracula threw the sword. Colston ducked aside, and Cammy heard glass *crack*, then shatter on the ground behind her. As she felt Colston turn a little to check the damage, Dracula rushed the both of them. He push-kicked Cammy in the chest, knocking her wind out. She and Colston crashed backwards through the sliding glass door—the empty space where it had been, anyway. They slammed on the concrete outside and she felt her brain smacking around inside her skull.

Colston burst into flames.

Cammy could barely move, couldn't breathe, and needed to puke. Dracula appeared, grabbed her wrist, and pulled her off Colston as he screamed and thrashed around. She curled into a ball and felt her stomach convulsing and spasming. She could not get any air. Dracula left her on the concrete, stepped over her, and Colston's screaming stopped.

It felt like someone was punching her in the temple over and over and over, and her stomach wouldn't stop doing cartwheels inside her.

"Try to breathe," Dracula told her.

She tried, *tried* to break her mother's stupid conditioning and call him every single name and curse she could think of, and the few extras her throbbing brain could stitch together, but she still couldn't suck in a breath much less shout it back out.

"Stay put this time," he told her, and she heard him crunch over the broken glass back into the house. Another scream a few moments later, some thumping, then nothing.

He crunched back over the glass.

"Can you breathe yet?" he asked.

"You are the worst person on planet earth!" she croaked.

"You should have waited for me," he told her. "And I believe I saved your life."

"You kicked me!"

"And saved your life. Here." He held out a hand to help her up. She slapped it away and managed somehow to get to her knees without throwing up. "It seems to me we should find a doctor to check that you're all right."

"I thought *you* were a doctor."

"Well, if you insist," he said. "Though it has been close to a hundred years since I last practiced any medicine."

"No! Not you!"

He drove her to a hospital, where she had to do as every battered housewife in history and spin a story about being at a wild party where some drunk guys knocked her through a sliding glass door. The bruises on her wrists clearly looked like handprints, and the doctor stared at her when she stuck to her story. When he found out she'd been knocked unconscious for what sure seemed like longer than a few seconds, he told her, "You're lucky to be alive. Brain injuries like that can be deadly. This isn't a movie."

He then handed her some pamphlets about "safe houses" and told her anything she reported would be anonymous.

Not that I'm not tempted, she thought. She took the pamphlets and stuffed them in her bag.

After a battery of tests the doctor concluded nothing was broken and she didn't have internal bleeding or anything too serious beyond the concussion, and she'd probably recover on her own with good rest and follow-ups or therapy. Dracula paid for the visit and ignored the look the nurse shot at him from behind the desk.

A police officer called her to see if she would come in to answer some questions about her parents. She told him no. There was nothing she could tell them anyway. Dracula had already called in the scene at Heather's parents' house to Boese's people, so she couldn't even hope that Colston's body

—whatever was left of it—would do the cops any forensic good.

Before they pulled out of the hospital parking lot, Dracula turned to her.

"You tried to avenge your parents," he said. "Well done."

She glared at him and pressed the cold pack the nurse had given her to her temple. He'd had to help her navigate the stupid parking lot because she had stupid double-vision. Apparently head injuries *were* a big deal.

"*That's* all you have to say?" she demanded.

"And you have now been tried," he said. "Though foolish, you have spirit. Too much, perhaps, but you have it all the same."

"I almost *died*," she told him.

"That you did. Very close, by my estimation. That is something we must address." He looked out over the hood of his Mustang. "Here." He reached under his dress shirt and lifted the stone with the hole in the middle over his head and passed it to her.

"What is it?" she asked.

"Put it on." She did, and he waved a hand at the urgent care's wall. She lifted the stone and peered through it. A teenage girl with a face dripping with blood stood outside. Cammy dropped the stone in horror, and the girl wasn't there. A look through the stone revealed the bleeding girl again.

"What..?"

"That's an adder stone. It can reveal hidden things, or pierce illusions or glamour," he told her. "Use it for a while. I think you will start to see why you should stop running off into danger."

"What about you? Don't you need it?"

"I can manage," he said. "Do not lose that. I would never be able to replace it."

"Where'd you get it?"

"Ireland," he told her.

"Fairies?"

He nodded.

"Why didn't you just kill him when you came in if you were going to kill him?" she asked sullenly, and slid the stone under her shirt to hide it. He put the car in gear and pulled out onto the street.

"It wasn't light out yet," he explained. "I had to stall for time to ensure the greatest chance of success. Had I gone in to kill them all earlier, you might have been killed in the scuffle."

"It was so dark. I didn't realize the sun was out."

"I noticed the windows were heavily tinted when we visited the other day," Dracula said. "I hoped I could use that to trick our enemy."

"Why'd you tell him to drag me around the planet?"

"I didn't. I told him that the moment you died, I would never cease to hunt him no matter where he fled."

"So he'd have to drag me everywhere as insurance?"

"Exactly."

"That's not how negotiation works!"

"I wasn't negotiating. I wanted to guarantee he wouldn't kill or turn you the moment we got off the phone. I had no intention of letting him leave alive, so your safety was the only contingency I had to secure."

She played with her thumbs.

"So stakes through the heart don't kill you."

"Stakes through the heart don't kill all strigoi. He would have done better to cut my heart out if he was being serious. Besides, they missed my heart."

"Would that kill you? If they had gotten you? Or cutting out your heart?"

He eyed her until she looked away.

"You didn't have to kick me."

"I am not going to apologize, if that's what you're trying to elicit by pestering me. You shouldn't have gone there alone in the first place. Let your injuries serve to remind you to be wiser in the future. I will be far less inclined to help you if you do something like this again."

"Wow, you're such a nice guy," she said.

"And you're a fool. I would be remiss not to teach you to be more cautious. The next time, you may not fare so well."

She looked out the window at the street and the cars and the stores passing by.

"So what happens now?" she asked.

"Now? Now, you consider what you've learned and what you intend to do. The trial is over. You told me your birthday is coming soon? That practically makes this a rite of passage."

She studied his face.

"Are you being funny?" she asked.

He looked at her.

"Not at all. You did better than most would have in your shoes. For an amateur, and a crybaby, you did very well."

"I am *not* a crybaby."

"You are. And a sissy besides."

She almost punched him in the arm, but thought better of it. Malcolm might take that from her. Dracula was still Dracula. She really ought to stay somewhere else. But now she knew there were monsters, and she had a magic stone that could show her where they were. She fingered the stone under her shirt. There wasn't anywhere else she wanted to stay. She thought about Heather's unmoving body, and the pieces of the broken mug on a shelf in the room she was staying in. Should she throw them away? She couldn't bear the thought.

"Why didn't you come home earlier?"

She noticed him raise his eyebrows at the little slip of her tongue describing his mansion, and wished she could take that back.

"I wasn't finished... I wasn't whole yet," he told her. "Boese wanted to insert something extra."

"Umm, like what?"

"He put a listening device in one of my molars. It's wired to a small explosive which will detonate if I try to remove it." He tapped at the base of his skull.

"You have a *bomb* in your head?" she demanded.

"It'll only go off if I try to remove the tooth," he explained.

"You are *crazy*," she hissed.

"You are an *idiot*," he snarled back.

They reached the mansion without his head exploding, and all the way into the mansion, where Malcolm stood in the foyer, grinning nervously.

"Hey, um—"

Dracula handed him a crumpled piece of paper from his pocket. Malcolm opened it and read what was written there.

"Yeah, okay," he said. "No problem. Sorry about—"

He caught the look in Dracula's eye and swallowed his words. Dracula turned to Cammy.

"You should rest. And arrange for some sort of celebration."

"What about my parents?"

"I imagine if they are able to hire a good lawyer they'll manage to escape the grinder of the legal system," he said. "I doubt your enemy had the time to plant a real crime scene. Likely as not, the police will find neither motive nor means. Eventually, Boese will need to take the body the police found in order to wrap up his own files. If that happens before a trial date is set—and in all likelihood it will—the entire mess will resolve on its own for lack of evidence."

"My mom will lose her job if she's arrested for murder," Cammy said.

"Unless you can change the past, there is nothing we can do about that. But does that trouble you? Truly?"

"You said I tried to avenge them."

"What I am asking is whether you want me to house them also."

"Oh. *No.* No, thank you. They've got money. It's not like they'll be homeless. My dad can probably keep his job. He's a coder."

"Then it sounds as though there is no real trouble there."

You are such a nice guy, she thought at him. "I don't want to celebrate anything," she told him. "Heather's dead, and so are her—"

"Life is for the living," he told her. "Or so I've heard. By all means, mourn your friend. But also savor the taste of life."

"You are so weird."

"And you're rude. Go on."

Once Cammy had gone upstairs, he turned to Malcolm.

"Hey, man, I'm so sorry. I won't—"

Dracula back-handed him so hard he nearly lost his footing.

"No, you won't." He waited until Malcolm straightened back up. Malcolm shot him a sulky, surly glower and balled one hand into a fist.

"You recall I told you I'd castrate you and slit your throat if my guest came to harm. Since Cammy is still human, I decided to be uncharacteristically lenient with you. However, I am ready to reconsider if you do something stupid right now."

Malcolm looked away, his jaw tight, but he swallowed whatever he wished to retort. Good.

"I got the rest of the—"

Dracula placed a finger across his lips, then tapped his jaw and mouthed the word "*Me.*" Malcolm took the hint.

"I got some intel about who kicked this whole mess off to begin with," he said and rubbed his cheek.

"Oh?"

"Apparently it was some really attractive older woman with red hair."

"Mmm."

"Sound like anyone you know?" Malcolm asked.

"That's not much to go off of," Dracula replied. "But I sense you have a hypothesis you wish for me to confirm?"

"I was thinking Bathory?"

"I've never met her. I never even met her cowardly turncoat of a father-in-law who gave Buda over to the Ottomans. If I had, he would never have had the chance to father the 'Black Knight of Hungary' afterwards. I suppose Providence stayed my hand there."

"I have no idea who those guys were," Malcolm said. "If they were contemporaries of hers in life, that's one or two centuries before Ophois. We were barely the twinkle in some occultist's eye during the *loup-garou* epidemic in France in the 16th Century. If you're going to name-drop, I'll only know who you mean if Napoleon was alive at the time."

"You asked about Lady Widow Nádasdy. The physical description would fit, but you would know more about her than I. Your people have allied with her in the past. As to why she—or anyone—would do anything as pointless as creating a horde of ravenous, incompetent, Hollywood-style monsters...."

Outbreaks of vampirism in the past had originated from some strigoi or other running loose for several months before being put down. To have someone intentionally create and spread the modern sort at random was a puzzle piece he could not yet place.

"Cammy thinks it's a revolution," Malcolm said. "Someone sending a message."

Dracula considered this. He'd experienced revolution. Enemies had goaded the peasants into doing something they should have known was foolish: rebel against their lord, who had a reputation for justice and cruelty, which he had wasted no time making very plain to them. Was this similar? Perhaps. But the question then remained who had orchestrated this revolution, and for what purpose? The revolt against him had been orchestrated to weaken his position—the peasants had merely been used for that purpose. If this was similar, whose position was being weakened?

"I gotta do some shopping," Malcolm said, tapping the note asking him to fetch tarps. Dracula was not looking forward to cleaning up the mess he was going to make pulling the tooth, but it had to be done. He expected Boese knew he was going to do it. The explosive was there just to irritate him and make a mess. A petty gesture. Let him have his petty gestures. So long as they kept the man at a distance, that suited Dracula just fine for the moment. Just for the moment.

CHAPTER 13

WALPURGIS NIGHT

Cammy called at long last to try to put his worries to rest. Brian had heard about her parents, but had to stay far away from the whole mess. She assured him she was fine, and that things should calm down. She broke down when she explained Heather was dead. He had worried that might be the case, but hadn't wanted to say anything. Some chatter had reached his ears about a crime scene, but no details. Feds had swarmed all over it and hushed the whole thing up. Whatever had happened, it had ripped a swath through Cammy's life.

Cammy must be feeling a little better at least. She invited him to her birthday celebration at some restaurant he'd never heard of.

"How'd you hear about it?" he asked. He scratched out another stupid idea he'd come up with for what to buy her and adjusted the phone before it slipped off his shoulder to his lap.

"Vlad knows the owners."

"Vlad. Of course."

"Brian."

"All right, all right," he said. "I'll be there. What kind of food is it?"

"Romanian."

Of course it is, he thought. He told her he was happy she was doing better, and to call if she needed anything. She promised she would and hung up. He had a feeling she wasn't going to. He said so out loud.

"Well, not with that attitude of yours, she's not."

Brian whirled to see Melissa standing in the door with Mexican takeout in hand.

"Come get dinner if you're done in there. Also, just tell her you like her already."

Brian grumbled a non-answer. There was no way he could do that after her friend just died and whatever else was going on in her life. The timing was all wrong. Besides, there was the *other* problem. Dr. FBI, or whatever he was. That was the big problem.

"So what's the plan?"

Brian told her about the restaurant.

"Huh. I've never had Romanian food," Melissa said. "I wonder if it's good. I'll ask for that night off. We can carpool. Save on gas. Save the planet." She wandered to the kitchen to set the bags down.

Brian waffled for a few days about what to buy for Cammy, but landed on a Funko Pop figurine from one of her favorite shows. Melissa bought some gift cards for grocery stores "to make sure that poor girl can finally eat something."

Dracula's Guest

The restaurant was in Kirkland, so it was a little bit of a drive for them, but they arrived about five minutes before seven.

"Peles?" Melissa read the sign as she parked in front. "Wonder what it means." She pulled her phone to look it up as she stepped out of the car. When they reached the door, she said, "Whoa! There's this castle in Romania with that name. You should see it; it looks like a fairytale!"

Brian reached to take her phone. The door swung open and Cammy stood there. She was wearing a black dress that looked new.

"Hey," he greeted her, and she hugged him. "You look great. How are you doing?"

She looked out at the light drizzle and the dark, and answered with a shrug. He supposed that was about right.

"Are we early?"

"Kenzie got here like twenty minutes ago. She won't leave him alone."

Him. Brian tried to smile like he meant it.

"Here," he handed her the gift bag.

"Thanks, B," she said, and accepted it and the little packet of gift cards from Melissa. She hugged her, too.

"I'm sorry, I know it's your birthday, but I heard some rumors at the precinct about your mother."

Cammy looked at him.

"Turns out the guy they found at your parents' place was... involved in some unsavory things, and a witness came forward who placed your mother in a location where he liked to operate. Some more digging revealed it looked like she bought stuff from him. Valium, and... and other things."

"Drugs for Heather," Cammy said. Her voice was like venom.

"I think so. I have no idea if there was more going on than that. But from what little I hear, it sounds like she's going to skate or get a slap on the wrist."

"Yeah, well she can kiss her precious job good bye," Cammy said. "She bought that stuff for Heather. She might as well have killed her. Just to get her stupid claws back in me." Cammy glared her hate at the floor. She wiped one of her eyes and she hugged herself.

"Thanks for telling me, B."

"Sorry it's bad news."

"Sounds to me like karma's come around at last," she said, and turned to lead him and Melissa into the restaurant.

There were fake grape vines climbing the pillars, and paintings of a sweeping, green vista across the walls. Pretty decent art, too. Sunlight pierced dramatic clouds and shot rays of golden light down on fields littered with hay stacks and sheep and cattle.

"Whoa, this is nice," Melissa observed. The place was empty, save for a large table near the back wall. Brian spotted Kenzie's aqua blue hair. It looked almost radioactive in the soft, ambient light. She was leaning almost over the corner of the table to talk to Dr. FBI. Brian made a fist.

"Come on, now," Melissa told him, and poked his hand. "Let me talk to him. I'll see what I can figure out."

"Yeah," he said. Cammy led them both to the table and introduced Melissa. Dr. FBI spotted them coming and gently excused himself from Kenzie's attention to rise and greet them. Cammy made introductions.

"Hey, this is Melissa. She's Brian's sister."

"Charmed."

The creep actually took her hand to kiss it. Cammy eyed him weirdly when he did.

"Oh, uh," Melissa giggled a little.

"It's a little old-fashioned, but some of the men in my country still greet women this way," he said.

"You're Romanian?" Melissa asked.

"You aren't going to believe this," Kenzie cut in. "He's totally related to the real Dracula. Like, *directly* related. Can you believe it?!" Her mouth dropped open in a silent squeal of delight.

Of course he is, Brian thought.

"Officer Warren," the creep said. "How nice to see you again. How have you been?"

"Great," Brian told him. "How's your job?"

"All wrapped up, thanks in part to your help."

"My help?"

"Visiting Miss Blake's parents' house was of enormous help."

Cammy stared at a wall. Brian wanted to go to her, but Melissa beat him to it and put an arm around her shoulder.

"I'm sorry," she said. "You holding up okay?"

Cammy nodded. Brian eyed the creep, who smiled maliciously at him. The door tinkled open, and Brian spotted two young men about his age come inside. One was pale as milk with a head of short, red hair, while the other was tall and sported long, brown hair in waves and a sad little mustache he probably ought to shave off if he wanted to look older.

"Hey, you guys made it," Cammy said, and waved them over. These were the other friends Cammy had made since high school. College friends, Brian supposed.

"This is Andrew." She pulled the redhead forward. He glanced down at the floor at first, and played with his sleeve before he took the creep's hand. "His parents run this totally organic farm just outside the city. Doing really well."

"You are a farmer?" the creep asked.

"Yeah," Andrew mumbled. "Chickens and goats and beans and stuff."

"I have vineyards and animals on my estate," the creep said. "Perhaps you could give me advice if you should ever visit."

"And this is Aslan!" Cammy said, as though to draw attention away on purpose. The creep looked at the tall young man.

"*İyi akşamlar, tanıştığımıza memnun oldum.*"

"You speak Turkish?" Aslan sounded surprised.

"I do," the creep replied.

"I don't speak much. My parents know more than I do."

The creep grinned, but it was more malicious than Brian had ever seen.

"I didn't know you spoke Turkish," Cammy said.

He didn't answer, but he took the young man's hand when it was offered.

"So you've been to Europe and to Turkey?" Brian asked.

"Yes. I have many memories of... Turkey."

"Which part?" Aslan asked. "My parents moved here from Ankara."

DRACULA'S GUEST

"I was very young," the creep said, and deliberately turned his back to regain his seat at the head of the table.

"I'm kind of mad," Kenzie said. "He just told me that castle in Romania everyone says is Dracula's isn't really. I was hoping to visit it one day."

"You should," he told her. "It's a lovely castle. Queen Marie lived there."

"The one who toured here in '26?" Brian cut in.

"The same. A wonderful woman."

"Whoa, hold up. Some Romanian queen visited Seattle?" Kenzie asked. "When?"

The creep began regaling her with a story about the woman—how an old man from some place called Iași had stolen her tub, and she found the incident so amusing she let the peasant keep it—while Brian and Melissa said hi to the newcomers.

"Nice to meet you both," Melissa was saying. Brian kept side-eyeing the creep to keep abreast of what he was up to. He barely registered that the tall young man liked photography and the redhead was too shy to talk about himself—or anything—at all.

"Wait, so is Marie a Romanian name?" Kenzie asked.

"No, in Romanian her name would be 'Maria,' which is how she is known within the country. She was the daughter of Prince Alfred, Duke of Edinburgh, later the Duke of Saxe-Coburg and Gotha."

"Wait, some British lady ended up being queen of Romania?"

The creep hesitated, turning something over in his mind, before he at last answered, "Indeed. Did you know her cousin was Tsar of Russia?"

"Wait, what? The *Tsar* was a Brit too?"

The Russian connection! Brian's brain shouted at him.

"You Americans do seem to struggle to understand nobility," the creep said with a little shake of his head.

"You Americans," Brian's brain shouted louder. So he was definitely a foreigner. And that meant he definitely wasn't FBI. Brian had checked. American citizens only. Well, unless he was naturalized.

The door tinkled open again, and Brian turned to take stock of the most recent newcomer. She was trying to shake some water out of her long, dark-blonde hair. The drizzle must have turned to real rain, because she looked more wet than damp. She wore ripped jeans and some sort of loose T-shirt which said "I love Miami" with a heart for the word "love." She threw her mane of hair over her shoulder, and he stared without meaning to.

She had sun-kissed skin and blue eyes. Full lips, cute dimples in her cheeks, very fit, with a slender waist and toned legs. The newcomer scanned the crowd and brushed an errant strand of hair out of her eyes. She spotted Cammy and came rushing over.

"Ohmygosh!" she gushed. "I was so worried! Are you okay?"

"Yeah," Cammy said, "thanks. I'm glad you could make it."

Brian had always heard girls had that one "hot friend." This one, without a doubt, was the hottest friend he'd ever seen. She was a solid 10 by every conceivable measure. The new girl threw her arms around Cammy's neck and squeezed her tight. This gave him another good view of her waist and back.

He deliberately looked aside to get a hold of himself, and to his surprise, saw that the creep was equally taken by this new girl. His weird, dark green eyes seemed glued to her.

One more thing for him to worry about. Before he could move to intercept, the creep rose to kiss this girl's hand also. Oddly, Cammy beat Brian to the punch and stuck out an arm to stop him.

"It's really not necessary. I mean, it's kinda misogynistic these days," she said.

"What is?" the new girl asked.

"He likes to kiss your hand," Kenzie explained. "He's done it to all us chicks. I mean, it *is* sexist when you think about it. I'll bet Andrew feels left out."

The redhead shrank into his seat.

"Apparently some of the men in his country still do it," Melissa explained.

"Oh, I don't mind," the new girl said. "That's kind of cute. Like a fairytale." She offered her hand. Cammy looked uncomfortable as he took it and brought it to his lips. The newcomer giggled.

"I'm Lindsey," she said. "It's nice to meet you. What's your name?"

The whole group looked at her, and Brian realized she was somehow the only person in the room who hadn't heard.

"My friends call me Vlad," he told her.

"Oh! That's Eastern European, or Russian, right?" Lindsey bubbled. "It's kinda exotic."

Cammy and Brian exchanged a look. What a relief that they still thought that alike, he tried to reassure himself. If Cammy thought that was a problem, she was smart enough to notice the guy was weird. Plus, he was a million years older than the rest of them. What a total creep, insinuating himself in a group of people young enough to be his grandkids.

Or further removed than that... his brain floated the thought up to him.

Maybe. Jury was still out, mostly because the idea had to be stupid. Had to be. But still....

"That's everyone," Cammy said. "Is anyone else hungry?"

"I'm really curious to try something new," Melissa said. "What's good?"

"What do you like?" the creep asked.

"Just about anything," Melissa laughed. "I'm a foodie."

"Then you are sure to like anything you order here. But have you ever eaten carp? Americans don't seem to."

"Carp? You mean like koi fish? Never. Definitely trying that."

"How are you able to afford this?" Brian whispered to Cammy as she scooted by him to get to her seat. Kenzie made a fuss about getting up. Cammy turned back.

"This is his present to me. Besides, he knows the owners."

Brian hated him so much. So very, *very* much.

The creep gestured for him to sit beside him, across the table from Cammy.

You absolute creep, he thought, but took the chair. He had plans that would be easier to execute if he was nearby.

Brian was surprised to see a lot of tomatoes and corn on the menu. He'd assumed they were New World foods, and so wouldn't show up in Eastern Europe. That made it easier to find something he wanted. Unlike Melissa, he wasn't very adventurous when it came to food. Kenzie asked what everything was.

"Eww, you'd eat that with *brains* in it?" she gagged.

"Have you ever tried an omelet with pig brain in it?" the creep asked.

"Never! Gross!"

"Hey, is that okay with the health department?" Brian wondered.

"They don't serve that to ordinary customers. It is how I would order mine."

"You eat brains?"

"Like a zombie," Kenzie teased.

"What is missy? Mickey?" Lindsey asked.

"*Mici*," the creep corrected. It sounded like "meech" to Brian's ears. "A type of sausage. Try it. Do you eat meat?"

"Yeah." Lindsey smiled apologetically at Cammy. "Sorry, I'm too attached."

"You go ahead," Cammy said. "I'm not asking anyone else to be vegetarian."

Pretty soon they all had food on the way, and questions were flying left and right. The owner and her daughter came out, and the creep introduced her as Mrs. Moscu. She seemed nice, but barely spoke English.

"How'd you both meet?" Brian asked.

"We met at church," the creep said.

"Church!" Kenzie said. "But with your name...."

"Wait, so that's your name for real?" Lindsey wondered. "I thought it was a joke."

"Why would you think that was a joke?" Kenzie asked.

"Well, because, that's not a real name, right? I thought you were making a movie joke."

"Nope." Kenzie shrugged her shoulders up to her ears. She returned her attention to the creep. "Church? Really?"

He nodded in answer. Brian tried to picture the man sitting in a pew singing hymns or gospel music. He couldn't. But if the guy *did* attend church, then the crazy idea was even crazier. The creep ordered a bottle of wine for the table.

"I don't drink," Aslan said.

"There is juice available. Or coffee," the creep volunteered. He sounded terse.

"What kind is it?" Lindsey asked.

"Mine."

"Yours?" she said. "You make wine?"

"Yes. From my vineyards."

For days, Brian had tried very hard to get a crazy idea out of his head; then he had tried to figure out a way to put the crazy idea to the test. About halfway through his meal, he got the opportunity he'd been hoping for, when the creep was distracted by conversation.

"We've all read *Dracula*, right?" Kenzie was saying. " So if we were characters in the book, who would everyone be? Cammy would be Mina Harker, and that makes you"—she pointed at Brian—"Jonathan Harker."

"Hey," he protested weakly, and glanced at Cammy to see what she thought. He couldn't tell. Was she uncomfortable?

"Wait, no, that's backwards," Kenzie said, smacking her forehead. "Cammy's the one staying at his place. So *she's* Jonathan Harker. Which means *you're* Mina." She grinned evilly at Brian, then turned to the rest of the table. "And Lindsey'd be Lucy."

"Lucy?" Lindsey repeated. "Why?"

"You're the one with all the suitors." Kenzie pointed at Aslan, Andrew, and lastly herself. Lindsey frowned and Andrew shrank further out of sight.

"Wait, you?"

"I've got a lady-crush on you," Kenzie told her, and wiggled her black-lined eyebrows playfully.

"Oh," Lindsey said dubiously. Brian couldn't believe it. This girl was a unicorn. She was that magical sort of girl who had no idea she was beautiful, so wasn't stuck-up about it. The kind spoken of, but no one really believed existed.

"That makes us three Arthur, Dr. Seward, and Quincey Morris," Kenzie said. "I call Quincey."

Andrew looked ready to melt into a puddle and disappear under the table.

"But you like vampires," Melissa pointed out. "Wasn't Quincey the guy who killed Dracula in the book?"

"Sorta. With a bowie knife. But there's this fan theory that Morris was secretly working for Dracula, because Stoker was planning to write a sequel set in the US. See, Morris just used a Bowie knife and then Dracula turned to dust. Could be he was dead, or could be he misted out of there, right? It was late dusk at the time, so it's possible it was just late enough for him to do that. That would be cool for me."

Brian noticed the creep doing his best to ignore the conversation and just pay attention to the glass of wine in his hand. Brian hated to admit it, but it was *really* good wine.

"But Quincey died," Lindsey pointed out. "You wouldn't want to die for Dracula, would you?"

"I won't die. We can make up a better story than Stoker did."

"So who's Renfield?' Melissa asked. "Though maybe it's better if you don't answer that."

"Yeah, probably," Kenzie admitted.

"And who's Van Helsing?" Melissa continued, thoroughly into the spirit of the game.

"Well, *I* am," the creep volunteered, taking them all by surprise.

"You can't be Van Helsing," Kenzie said. "I mean...."

"Then you ought to be; you seem to be knowledgable about vampires," he told her.

"Uh, I suppose. Ugh. Not cool. Van Helsing *sucks* in the book. I'd be the Peter Cushing version."

The creep made no reply and downed his glass.

"Whoa!" Brian pretended to accidentally knock his own glass over. The contents splashed onto the floor beside the creep's ankle. Brian brought his other hand over the creep's plate, napkin held to disguise what he was doing. His covered hand hovered over the creep's plate of trout and sour cream for a moment.

Mrs. Moscu came running out, apologizing as she came. The creep spent some time assuring her everything was fine—that's what it sounded like he was doing, anyway—and she cleaned up the little spill and righted Brian's cup. The creep refilled it for him. He looked like he didn't suspect anything.

About a minute later, Brian's effort was rewarded when the creep resumed eating, nearly fell out of his chair, and coughed up a mouthful of fish right on the floor. He pushed himself from the table and practically ran to the bathroom, retching the whole way. From what Brian could hear, the creep set one of the sinks running full blast.

Everyone looked at each other, then Cammy rose to go check on him.

"No, I will," Brian said. "Let me."

He rose and went to the door, but the creep was already on the way out, so he returned to his seat. That stupid part of his brain had wanted to see if the creep had any reflection in a mirror. Stupid. But it wanted to anyway.

He sat back down and Mrs. Moscu came running out of the back, apologizing all over again. The creep kept reassuring her. At last, he shook his head and told her, "*Usturoiul.*"

"*Nu!*" she protested. He nodded. She grabbed his plate and stared at it, sniffed it, then gasped. She started protesting vociferously. He caught her elbow and told her something quietly. She stormed back to the kitchen.

"You okay?" Cammy asked.

He nodded.

"What was all that about?" Kenzie asked.

"I have a... an allergy, you could call it. To garlic."

Kenzie blinked.

"That's ironic."

He nodded. "Some must have gotten into my food. Mrs. Moscu knows about my sensitivity, so it must have been by accident. Garlic appears in most Romanian foods ordinarily."

An allergy might explain it, Brian supposed. It was an awfully *convenient* or, as Kenzie had put it, *ironic* allergy, but it was still possible. Not enough proof.

The creep looked at him, smirked, and winked. He knew exactly how that little bit of garlic had ended up in his food. He knew who had done it.

And he knew why. And he thought it was *funny*.

You creep! Brian thought.

"Must be hard to be a vampire in Romania," Cammy was saying. That was something Brian would have expected Kenzie to say.

"Very," the creep replied smoothly. "That's why there aren't any there. They're all here."

Kenzie giggle-snorted.

"But you're all right?" Cammy asked.

"Perfectly recovered." He poured himself a fresh glass of wine and gestured for the conversation resume.

"Wait, so is there someone else who ought to be Dracula then?" Lindsey wondered. She looked to Kenzie. "You can't be two people. You already called Quincey."

The door tinkled. Before Brian even turned to see who had come inside, Cammy jumped to her feet.

"Are you kidding me?!" she yelped.

Cammy's mother stood at the door.

Brian rose also.

"Good evening, everyone," Cammy's mother said through the teeth she bared in one of her classic fake smiles. This one was much faker than usual. She had her hair pulled back tight, the collar of her rain coat up against the heavy drizzle. Her nails were red, pointed, and immaculate, her high heels clacked on the wet floor. Out on bail and she had to dress up.

"How did you even know to come here?" Cammy demanded.

"Camellia Constance Lilly," her mother said in that tense tone Brian knew meant nothing good. "You never even called. You were off screwing your little cop friend" —she gestured at Brian— "and never even *once* thought about how *I* was doing."

"Wait, is that your mom?" Kenzie whispered.

"Do you have *any* idea what I've just been through?" The woman continued. "After I went and cleaned your room so you could come home where you belong, and after I went through all that trouble, you never called. You only showed up to harass me about your worthless little friend—"

"Ma'am, you need to stop right there," Brian interrupted.

Her eyes settled on him without seeing him. She turned back to Cammy.

"After what *I've been through*," she hissed. "You should have come home!"

"You bought drugs for Heather!" Cammy shouted.

"Call 911," Brian whispered to Melissa. He saw she had her phone at the ready.

"Way ahead of you, BB," she told him, and rose from the table so she could retreat to a safe distance where she wouldn't be overheard.

"That is a vicious little lie!" Cammy's mother shouted. "Camellia, apologize at once! But how are *you* able to afford all *this*? Are you taking on more debt? You can't do anything right! You go running around behind my back with all your little friends—"

"Hey, lady," Kenzie said, standing up. "We're trying to have a party here. And last I checked, you weren't invited."

Cammy's mother narrowed her eyes at Kenzie, taking in the ripped tights under knee-high socks, the high-top shoes, the black jeans shorts, the studs, the hair color.

"Listen here, you little slut," Cammy's mother said, "I have every right to come here to reprimand my daughter when she fails to do the simplest thing."

Cammy opened her mouth to shout something, but Kenzie started towards the door.

"Stalking isn't cool, lady," Kenzie said. "Seems to me that's the only way you managed to find this place. I'll bet Cammy never told you. You have any idea how lame it looks that you have to stalk your daughter's friends so you can crash her birthday party? Not good parenting."

"You have no right to take her away from me," Cammy's mother said in a voice like ice. "None of you!"

Brian had made his way to the end of the table. Kenzie might escalate things. Ordinarily, he wouldn't have thought Cammy's mother would get violent, but he had a feeling this was going to get out of hand. Kirkland wasn't in his jurisdiction, and if things went badly, he didn't want Cammy's mother to skate because she could make a case about her daughter's "cop friend" interfering.

"You need to leave," he told her.

"*You* need to sit down, mall cop," Cammy's mother snarled, pointing a red nail at him. "You think you're a big shot now. Well, I remember you. All scrawny and scraggly and your hair down to your shoulders. You think you're respectable? You're *nothing*, and if my daughter wasn't so bad at picking friends, she never would have let you drag her around."

"Drag me around? Do you hear yourself?" Cammy shouted.

"Lady," Kenzie said, "last I checked, Cammy's been an adult for a couple of years now. We're trying to have a 21st–birthday-and-Imma-get-drunk-party, and unless she invites you to stay and you get yourself a glass and shut up, I'd say whining isn't exactly a good look for you. Maybe you should go home and cry into a glass of box wine."

Cammy's mother hauled back and slapped Kenzie in the face, earning a yelp of surprise. Brian jumped forward, to find that it hadn't been a slap. There were fingernail tracks on Kenzie's cheek.

Cammy's mother spat directly in his face when he inserted himself between them.

When the police came, Cammy's mother was straight-up screaming that the entire group of Cammy's friends had raped her and that they should all be arrested and charged with every crime in existence. She even threw in "disturbing the peace". Everyone else had been more than happy to give a statement, except the creep, who lurked in a shadowy part of the restaurant and only gave vague and dismissive answers when questions were posed to him.

Kenzie had gleefully declared that she would *love* to press charges, and proudly showed off the welts on her face. Cammy's mother had drawn blood.

Lindsey was standing beside Cammy, rubbing her arm and occasionally touching her forehead to Cammy's. Andrew and Aslan stood about four feet off, saying nothing. Brian wanted to give Cammy a big hug, but he wasn't sure it would be appropriate. Melissa stood between Cammy and the cops and her mother, clearly protective, shielding Cammy from view. In the middle of saying something reassuring, his sister shot him a look and nodded at Cammy.

He sidled up, and Cammy glanced at him with red eyes. She reached out to take his hand, and he grasped it. It would be all right to hug her now, right? Or was that too forward?

He felt a strong shove to his shoulder, knocking him forward. When he turned, he saw the creep had come up beside and shoulder-checked him. He was wearing an expression of disgust mixed with reproof.

You bumped into me, creep, Brian thought at him.

Cammy wrapped an arm around him, taking him by surprise. She didn't seem to have noticed what had happened. He hugged her back. Melissa rolled her eyes and shot him a thumbs-up.

* * *

"I hope we never have to have this much fun ever again," Melissa said, when she dropped down into the driver's seat. "How do you do this for a living?"

Brian wondered that himself sometimes.

"I guess I like to think I'm making some sort of difference," he answered. Melissa let out a long sigh.

"So do we all," she mumbled. Her keys *clinked* as she stuck them in the ignition. "By the way, the weirdo?"

Brian scowled. "What about him?"

"The jury's still out, but I'm happy he did what he did."

"Huh?"

"You know, when he did the movie thing of pushing you into her arms."

"That is *not* what happened."

"Pshaw, it's exactly what happened. It was romantic."

"No, it wasn't. And never use the word 'romantic' when talking about him, okay? Just, never again. I will flip a table. I mean it."

Melissa shook her head and reversed out of the parking lot.

* * *

The next morning, Dracula was savoring the cup of tea he'd brewed. In an hour or two, he'd head out to church.

All things considered, that had gone about as well as it could have. Worthless as most modern people were, he had learned a great deal over the last few days, though he had no intention of spending that much time with Cammy's friends ever again. Young people were far more tedious than he recalled them being in the past. Somehow, during the interval of his most recent incarceration, they had been reduced to self-serving, incompetent, ignorant deviants, empty of ambition or dignity.

On reflection, that was too unkind a valuation. The overzealous police officer might have promise, though his inability to do the littlest thing for the young woman he cared for grated on Dracula's sensibilities. It was most unbecoming for a man to shrink like a child before a woman in that manner. Then there was Lindsey. He attributed her manner of dress to the depraved modern style rather than to any looseness on her part. Kenzie was utterly insufferable and he had no intention of speaking with her again.

He read a paper off the laptop he'd purchased, grateful that he could still find news somehow. It wasn't the same as reading a physical paper, but he reasoned he'd grow used to it.

The front door swung open, and he sighed. He leaned back in his chair to await this intruder. Boese came strolling into his kitchen, alone.

"Good morning, Director," he said, setting his cup in its saucer. "You'll forgive me for not greeting you properly. I don't often—"

Boese grabbed the cup and threw it against the stove, shattering it. Before Dracula could construct an appropriate insult in reply, Boese pulled out the chair opposite him and set himself down in it.

"Now that I've got some time on my hands, I thought I should come up here to chat," Boese told him. Dracula eyed the splinters of china and the tea dripping on his floor.

"That was a gift," he told the director.

"See, I've been thinking about your little temper tantrum earlier," Boese said, folding his hands together. "I didn't have to let you out, you know."

"Didn't you?"

Boese's pale eyes bored into his.

"You see, you think you're special. I've got news for you: you're not. Once upon a time, it was a lot of fun having a bona fide undead fighting the good fight, but those days are long gone. You notice we didn't call you for help for Operation Desert Storm or the War in Iraq? Did you think we *forgot* that you get hard the minute someone suggests it's time to start killing Muslims? Of course not. Fact is: we've got missiles and planes and drones that do a fine job killing terrorists without your help. You're a fossil; a relic of an earlier time. Science has marched on, my friend, and you're only marginally useful on a good day."

"If you have no further need of my help, Director, I am perfectly willing to depart this country and go elsewhere," Dracula told him, pointedly eyeing the broken cup.

Dracula's Guest

"See, I've been thinking," Boese said, "about what you said, about having *teeth*. Here's the funny thing, my friend. You have to think a few steps ahead. You think I don't know you, that all those decades you were down there I was walking around with my head up my ass. But that's where you're wrong. I've read your letters, looked you up. I know your weaknesses."

"I see," Dracula said.

"For example, I know you just can't help yourself. You've always gotta run off half-cocked with your dick in your hand, showing everyone what a big man you are. And guess what? That always comes back to bite you, doesn't it? You've always gotta show everyone you're a great lord, or whatever. Well, I've got news. You're not, you never were."

Dracula glared at him.

"See, a *real* great lord doesn't have to go around showing everyone he's got a big dick, everyone knows he's got one. That's why I said you're a narcissist. See, I don't take your little hissy fits personally. I know you're just a mad dog that's been whipped too many times lashing out. It's my fault if I get bit. But it's also my job to decide when that mad dog needs to get put down."

Dracula fleered in response.

"You made a big deal about Christmas bonuses. Well, guess what? I pull my weight, and I get things done. If the higher-ups hear from me that you're more trouble than you're worth, they'll let me pull the plug on you."

"Really? You'll kill me? At long last, you'll find your courage and do it?"

Boese stared hard at him. "Here's what I can do: I can load you on a rocket and shoot you into space. You can float around up there with no air, no sound, and not a thing you can do about it for the next billion years or more. If you're lucky, maybe you'll still be close enough so when our sun expands it'll finally burn you up and send you straight to hell."

"Hell? I didn't take you for a man of faith, Director."

"Hell takes no faith," Boese told him, "I see it every day. It's the loving God part that I don't buy. And I see you don't believe I'll do it."

"No, I don't," Dracula told him.

"Rockets aren't that expensive anymore, especially since I don't have to make it safe for an actual human to travel in. It wouldn't even set me back for the year."

"And you think that such a fate would trouble me, Director?"

Boese leaned over the table.

"Here's the thing: I know you better than you know yourself. You think I was messing around all those decades? That I had you hooked up to electrodes and put through MRIs and all that just for fun? I got plenty of readings out of your brain. I know what gets to you. And you know what? Seems you're not completely inhuman, because I found out you *do* get lonely. Imagine that. You put up a brave face, but isolation gets to you, too. You just hide it better than others. I imagine it wouldn't take a week before you went raving insane."

Dracula considered it. Would Boese have the stones?

"The Vatican won't be pleased to hear you've shot one of their assets out of orbit," he pointed out.

"What are they going to do, pray about it?" Boese sneered. "You're not much use to them, either, so I hear. It's been a while since they needed someone to go all 'Onward, Christian soldier' for them. The Crusades are over, buddy, and they're going to *stay* over.

"See, here's the thing about *teeth*, my friend. Lots of things have teeth. Pomeranians, for example. Sharks, for another. If a Pomeranian bites you, you just kick it through the uprights. If a shark bites you"—he smirked—"big difference. See, even when you were at your best, you were nothing more than a teeny-tiny prince of a teeny-tiny country that the surrounding super powers played tug-of-war with, and there wasn't a thing you could do about it. You're a footnote in history. Oh, I've heard people say you never forgave a slight. That's garbage. You went crawling to the man who got your father and brother killed, didn't you?"

"Tread carefully, Director," Dracula warned.

"You went crawling to Hunyadi for help. Even fought alongside him. And before that, you went to the man who took Constantinople. Bet that sticks in your craw, doesn't it? What'd you have to do to get him to trust you? Sell him your kid brother?"

Dracula pulled out his magnum. Boese pulled out the kill switch.

"I want you to think real careful before you do something stupid," Boese said. "My men have orders if you blow my head off. Orders about your little friend, for one."

"I will not sit here and listen to a crawling, ill-bred mongrel insult me," Dracula told him. "I have killed better men for *far* less."

"You'll sit there, and you'll listen to what I have to say, because I have something important to tell you. See, you had us going for a while as the only strigoi that seemed to be willing to work with anyone. But *now*? You're not that special anymore. No one *needs* to keep you around. I made plenty of dhampir out of you while you were down there. I even cloned you a few times, just to see what would happen, see what made you so unique. Now you're a dime a dozen. You're a joke. I'm so silly with dhampir I can loan them out for a *profit*. I'm eating into Ophois and those other Orders with my agents. So if one day you tick me off, you go on the rag and bite my ankles again"—Boese pointed a finger at him—"I'll punt you through the uprights. *No one's* going to miss you."

He let that sit.

"Now, with regards to your new roommate, I've got some questions. And before you congratulate yourselves about that half-baked idea actually panning out, I'll let you know we would have gotten that CEO and the kooky dentist eventually. We were about to do a wider search, and the lab guys would have figured them out. All you did was shave a few days off the timeline. And if you had just done your job in the first place, you wouldn't have needed her little idea, huh? Now, as you pointed out, it *is* my duty to protect the general public from the supernatural. So"—the man fetched an unbroken tea cup and poured himself a serving—"and mind your manners, my son, tell me *politely* what that girl is doing up here."

Dracula considered the broken tea cup. He'd never be able to replace it.

"I'm waiting," Boese told him.

"I didn't realize that rockets were so cheap these days," Dracula said. "I'll have to remember that, thank you."

"You don't have any more chips to play," Boese told him, "so you're going to play my way, *capiche?*"

"Director," Dracula said, "I am surprised you think you can replace several hundred years of experience with something grown in a test tube. I suppose that's the sort of mistake a pencil pusher makes. Unlike you, I never sat back and let others get their hands dirty for me. When I needed a man killed, I went myself. When I needed to spy, *I* went to look. Bureaucrats never understand the value of experience."

"I don't think *you* understand: I came here to tell you how it is. I'm not here for a lecture," Boese snarled.

"For example: a field agent might have asked me about this"—Dracula indicated the laptop—"or might have recalled I've always courted the latest technology if I thought it could suit my needs. Or would have been more cautious when he realized all the bugs in this place went dead."

"So that's what your friend from Ophois was doing up here? Not just the one you blew yourself up with at four a.m. today? You hired him to sweep them? When did you figure out they were up here?"

"I'm not the sort of fool that thinks a man who hates me as much as you do would let me go and live up here without eyes and ears to make sure I don't plot revenge," Dracula told him. "That has hindered my movements until this point. However..." He turned the laptop around so Boese could see the screen. "See anything interesting, Director?"

He watched as Boese stared, disbelieving, at what he saw.

"I don't believe that's *all* the men you brought lurking outside, but I'd wager it's enough of them."

"So you have new security cameras installed," Boese scoffed. "So you can see us coming. So what?"

Dracula smiled. "Why, Director, you miss the point. For all your claims to know me, you seem to have forgotten that I am a quick study. For example, how many languages do I speak?"

"History books tell us nine or eleven."

"I now speak over sixty-four, Director. *Fluently*. I'm very good at accents. That didn't happen because I sat on my laurels and pushed money around. So yes, I have removed your spying devices and installed my own, but you're not seeing the whole picture. If you knew anything about human nature, you'd know better than to threaten a man with nothing to lose. The history books didn't tell you what I am like now. They stopped concerning themselves with me after my head was taken off. They also won't tell you whether I'll go public."

Boese frowned, then his thin lips cracked into a bemused smile.

"Go public? *You?* Some people think you should be put on trial for war crimes if you were still around."

"Perhaps," Dracula agreed. "But imagine what they'd want to put *you* on trial for, Director. Imagine what might happen if, say, this video feed that I'm showing you was uploaded to the Internet? I believe human cloning is still illegal."

"You're not human."

"My DNA disagrees."

Boese shrugged. "You'll upload this? Through what? Your dial-up?"

"Or if your threats to kill that young woman should be leaked as well? If I go public, your department goes up in flames, and you with it. And no, not with my 'dial-up'. I've upgraded. And you may have no family, but your agents do. Do you think they'll be pleased if I expose them?"

Boese squinted at him, no doubt wondering whether Dracula would do it.

"You'll still have to upload it." He waggled the kill switch.

"Do I?" Dracula said. "You assume I've kept all the pieces here, with me. Perhaps this is already uploaded, and all the recordings I've taken of your threats don't require my finger to send them. Perhaps it is only my finger moving that stops them from getting publicized."

"So that's your play? You'll take us all down with some videos that everyone will say are faked?"

"Even if everyone thinks so, the men you have to answer to won't be pleased by the trouble you'll have caused them. And you just admitted that your excuse will be that the videos are faked, which confession I would be pleased to upload as well. And you still haven't accounted for the fact that your agents are not going to be very effective if they've been exposed, or how the rest of the supernaturals are going to react once they see this. Some of them use the Internet or watch TV, and the rest talk. I think you'll find your entire Seattle branch will become useless overnight. I doubt you'll see many Christmas bonuses after that, or much of anything, really. I doubt your masters are going to spend precious resources defending a lost cause, such as a man who pushed me to go to war with them. And, Director, the videos are only one part of my preparations. How do you think your agents will like the idea that I have placed several million dollars' worth of bounty on their heads? Contracts to be activated in the event of my disappearance, *or that of anyone who is my guest*. Am I making myself clear?" He took the tea cup from

Boese's hands. "This set was a *gift*. Keep your thieving hands to yourself."

He let Boese consider his next move.

"Director, you don't play much chess, it seems. When you make a play for the king, you better make certain you can take him."

"You're no king," Boese snarled.

Dracula smirked. "Let's not split hairs, Director. But if none of this has yet convinced you, I have another play that I can make. Consider this: your higher-ups have to justify allocating precious tax-payer money to your pack of spooks hunting things that go bump in the night. Do you really think that they've been throwing money your way because you've been doing such a stand up job? Or do you think, perhaps, someone has been making donations?"

He managed not to smile when he saw Boese piecing it together.

"We have a saying where I come from: *Golden keys open all doors*. Which do you think your home office would prefer? You, or an endless supply of capital?" He tapped on the laptop. "How about your men? Do you think they'd like Christmas bonuses of their own? You seem to forget that my men were loyal to me such that my enemies were amazed. I know how to care for my people. Can you say the same, Director?"

He pulled the laptop back towards himself. Boese chewed on what he'd just learned.

"Let it not be said that I can't be merciful," Dracula said. "Let's make a little deal: you leave me and my guests alone, and everything that I've recorded can be our little secret. You keep your agents, your job, your head, and your bonuses, and I keep my castle. Do you think you can manage that?"

Boese glared at him and gritted his teeth.

"Get bent, you monster," he seethed.

"Glass houses, Director. But now that I can see we understand one another... Get. Off .My. Property."

Boese slowly rose from the table.

"I won't forget this," he said.

"Good. Because I will not give you a second chance," Dracula told him. Boese kicked the chair against a bureau. As he stormed for the door, Dracula said, "And Director, if you *ever* mention my family again"—he eyed the man with all the malice he could level—"there will be no corner of this planet where you will be able to hide from me. Do you understand?"

Boese stormed the rest of the way to the door and slammed it shut behind him.

Amaya Tenshi

EPILOGUE

Erzsébet Báthory blinked angrily at the mess in the living room. Her "little helper" was turning out to be more trouble than he was worth. So far, the only thing he'd been able to do right was kill the wealthy widow in whose apartment they were slumming. The woman had her bills autopaid—a feature Erzsébet viewed as an absolute blessing—and it should be some time before anyone came to check on her.

Her latest helper kept bringing home his disgusting habits, and she was tired of having to remind him to do his filthy business elsewhere—and to sell the spare parts in the Underground for money or information. The man had no head for business.

Erzsébet hated getting her hands dirty, with one particular exception. Fortunately, she and her tool preferred different sets of victims. She liked young girls, he liked young boys.

She was not precisely certain how many corpses were currently in the living room, nor did she care to decipher the number from the pieces.

"Clean this mess up!" she hissed at him. He cast his black eyes up at her. "At once! I have told you never to bring your degenerate habits home with you."

He apologized in Middle French. He knew modern French and modern English, but eschewed them in favor of his native tongue when in the presence of one who understood it as well.

Erzsébet massaged her temples. Long gone were the frequent headaches which plagued her family, gone the bouts of seizures and eye pain, but she resented that men were always so useless. Even that dentist had failed to create the kind of chaos she had hoped for. After all the work she'd done to get him those supplies in the first place.

She had hoped the other monster who lived in this city might be recruited to her little mission, based on his reputation. But it now seemed clear that he would either be difficult to recruit, or else impossible to control. She would have to take the utmost care before approaching him. Unlike her useless brothers, cousins, and current pet, the monster in this city knew how to kill without excess or waste, and how to get things done. She lamented that in all her years she had never managed to find such an ally for herself. At least her little helper had been a decorated soldier in life and had served admirably in that capacity. He ought to be able to protect her if negotiations soured.

Her ancestors had known how to get things done. When that fool György Dózsa had gotten it into his head to rebel and to impale nobles, her great uncle István had had the man roasted alive and fed to the few of Dózsa's followers he had kept alive or the purpose—the others having been impaled themselves. Then the peasants had been made slaves. *That* was how the masses ought to be dealt with, and how to keep unruly subordinates from getting uppity. She had laughed to see that one peasant sewn alive into a horse, though she couldn't remember why it had been done. She had been a young girl at the time.

Her idiot helper kissed the closed eyes of the nearest severed head and took it with him to the kitchen to find a trash bag. She curled her lip at his turned back.

Filth, she thought.

This plan had come to nothing. She would have to construct something else, and she would have to be even more careful.

She wanted to beat some girl to death until the little slut's blood sprayed across her face. Perhaps her otherwise useless helper could help her find the right sort of strumpet for that.

"Once you've finished moving all of this to the Underground," she called over her shoulder, "I'll be sending you on a mission."

She received the rustling of a plastic bag as answer.

THE END

Author's Note

Hello, my dear reader.

First and foremost, I would like to thank you for purchasing my very first published novel. It is my sincerest wish that this book (and the rest in the series) are entertaining and that you'll keep coming back to them.

As this is my first novel, this is also my first Author's Note, so I ask your indulgence as I explain a little about the book in your hands. You've surely realized by now this is an urban fantasy, so I am asking you to suspend your disbelief in certain fantastical elements. Well, one, really. Imagine—and I know this is hard—that nothing interesting happened in the world since 2015, and everything continued on as it had been. That is the universe in which this series takes place, and I know that it is much harder to suspend one's belief in what has actually happened than to accept the idea of vampires, ghouls, fairies and other creatures out of myth, horror stories and folklore.

Now to the really important bit. When I first set out to create this series, I could never have predicted where it would lead me. It was a silly little idea of "Well, Dracula is a well-known, royalty-free character, and I'm just starting, so why not rely on something I know, like, and which might attract an audience?" Dracula—the vampire—has appeared in countless properties since Stoker's book was published at the end of the 19th century. (And that book has never been out of print!) Like many folks in the West, I was vaguely aware of a historical figure of the same name from a country which remains curiously obscure.

After years of research and some travel, I have nearly completely lost my love for Stoker's work, and fallen in love with not just the real-life Dracula, but also Romania. It is my hope that I can pass along some of that love for, as Dracula in my book puts it, "the most beautiful country I have ever seen." Like Queen Marie, I fell in love with Romania—its history, its people, its language, its food, its music.

As a result, I have come to view the unfortunate entanglement of the historical Dracula with Stoker's vampire count as an undesirable development in literature and pop culture. Despite efforts by Elizabeth Miller to "divorce" the two, the bleed over has only become stronger. (Consider the movie *Dracula Untold*.) This puts my series in the same unfortunate boat, given that I began this project without any clear idea who Vlad Țepeș really was, nor about the most beautiful country I had yet to see. However, I hope to help distinguish historical realities from Stoker's gothic horror. In an attempt to redirect the attention of readers who prefer historical accuracy to lurid horror, I have applied the thinnest coat of "vampire" I could manage, and intend to take my readers on a journey of learning slowly but surely about the country and history I have come to love. I cannot deny that my interest in vampires and gothic fiction and movies ultimately lead me here, so for the first part of the series, those elements will shine bright. My plan is for the series to change to a truer historical fiction once my knowledge of history fills in sufficiently. Reality is stranger, after all, than anything fiction can ever present.

In the end, even should these stories, these stepping stones, fail to direct attention away from pop culture's cherished misapprehensions about Vlad the Impaler, I pray that my dear readers grow to love Romania as I do. I thank you again for choosing to read this silly little project. I pray to see you on the second stone, and beyond.

I should mention here that Dracula thinks and occasionally speaks in an archaic manner which may be unfamiliar to readers, and he will have further quirks in books to come. For that matter, I occasionally use archaic phrases myself.

This final paragraphs I dedicate to issues which might draw readers' interest. I am but an historical amateur, and despite my attempts to be true to the facts when I include them, there are some deviations from reality, and I don't doubt I have made an unfortunate mistake or two. There was, to my embarrassment, a version of this book that actually went to market in which I called "Moldavia" "Moldova." I had double and triple-checked the only book I own which details the life of Stephen the Great, in which the country is consistently referred to "Moldova." I confess I became confused by these two names over the years, as my earliest research provided me the historical name "Moldavia", which was incorrect by modern usage, so I was constantly being "corrected". At some point, the names became completely muddled in my mind. I refer to the regions of Moldavia, Transylvania, and Wallachia as part of the "Balkans" but understand this may bother some readers. Alas, modern day Romania, which is made up of these former countries, is in a curious position. It could be considered a part of Central Europe or Eastern Europe, or (certainly in its southern regions) part of the Balkans. I fear no matter how I categorize it, I will always be forced to use some term which will be not quite correct.

There are also intentional deviations. The opening which depicts Vlad Draculea III and St. Stephen the Great fleeing for Hunyadi's help is written entirely for the narrative. I cannot imagine that, in history, the two would have ever been alone and not had a retinue along. The spelling of John Hunyadi's name was chosen for my Western readers, who are likelier to know him by that version. I am also unsure whether the region sometimes known as Transylvania was already called that. I know the insignia of the Order of the Dragon which I included is not correct, but in the interest of the narrative, I made an artistic decision. For those worried that the pewter kettle which Dracula uses in this novel contains lead, have no fear: it is Britannia metal, so it is lead-free. For those curious to know why Dracula should appeal to the "sacredness" of messengers when he infamously disregarded this custom by nailing their turbans to the heads of messengers sent to him, it is because he is making a point, not being honest.

I am also one of those Americans who struggle to understand nobility (as Dracula remarks on in this novel), so although I have scrutinized family trees, it is entirely possible I have misrepresented someone, or applied a title incorrectly. Erzsébet Báthory's "brother Gabor" has no known death dates, but I have chosen to lump him in with István.

Dracula's Guest

Brian's obsession with a Romanian-Russian political connection is a misconception I have intentionally given him. His ignorance of history is a deliberate juxtaposition with Dracula's experiences and observations. Lastly, I reached out to two police departments for help writing about Brian's occupation, but alas, neither of them responded to my inquiries, and I was forced to rely on what research I could glean from secondary and tertiary sources. If there are any mistakes regarding police procedure, it was due to my lack of resources, not to indifference.

Thank you all.
Amaya Tenshi

ABOUT THE AUTHOR
AMAYA TENSHI

Amaya grew up on mythology: Greek, Egyptian, Norse, and of course fairytales from Europe and Japan. She has spent years amassing a nifty little collection of fairytales and legends from as many different cultures around the world as she could find: China, Vietnam, India, Africa, and more. With interest in subjects like history, theology, folklore, philosophy, and humanity itself, she earned two BAs which have been entirely useless since graduating college.

When not reading hard to find history books or trying to decipher a rare tome in yet another language she doesn't speak, she writes, spends time training her two cats to do tricks, and taking them for walks. She also designs illustrations for an indie comic book.

Dracula's Guest

GREEK FIRE
BY
JAMES BOSCHERT

In the fourth book of Talon, James Boschert delivers fast-paced adventure, packed with violent confrontations and intrepid heroes up against hard odds.

Imprisoned for brawling in Acre, a coastal city in the Kingdom of Jerusalem, Talon and his longtime friend Max are freed by an old mentor from the Order of the Templars and offered a new mission in the fabled city of Constantinople. There Talon makes new friendships, but winning the Emperor's favor obligates him to follow Manuel to war in a willful expedition to free Byzantine lands from the Seljuk Turks. And beneath the pageantry of the great city, seditious plans are being fomented by disaffected aristocrats who have made a reckless deal to sell the one weapon the Byzantine Empire has to defend itself, *Greek fire*, to an implacable enemy bent upon the Empire's destruction.

Talon and Max find themselves sailing into perilous battles, and in the labyrinthine back streets of Constantinople Talon must outwit his own kind—assassins—in the pay of a treacherous alliance.

PENMORE PRESS
www.penmorepress.com

Amaya Tenshi

Dragon Blood
by
Bruce Woods

Paulette is sent on a mission to China with the words of her mentor ringing in her ears. "A hot wind is now fanning the flames of racism in China, Paulette." Said Lady Ellen Terry. "And, like dust in a drought, it has blown up an army. They call themselves 'the boxers' society of righteous and harmonious fists,' or some variation thereof, and practice rituals that they claim bestow invulnerability and more. They are ill-armed and poorly trained but potentially numberless.
"Recently an auxiliary movement has sprung up. Reportedly consisting of young virgin women, from the ages of 12 to 18 and accounted uncommonly beautiful. They carry the name "Red Lanterns," and claim the powers of flight, fire-starting, and miraculous healing. It is these I wish you to investigate for any sign of Kindred activity.

PENMORE PRESS
www.penmorepress.com

Dracula's Guest

Assassins of Alamut
By
James Boschert

An Epic Novel of Persia and Palestine in the Time of the Crusades

    The Assassins of Alamut is a riveting tale, painted on the vast canvas of life in Palestine and Persia during the 12th century.

    On one hand, it's a tale of the crusades—as told from the Islamic side—where Shi'a and Sunni are as intent on killing Ismaili Muslims as crusaders. In self-defense, the Ismailis develop an elite band of highly trained killers called Hashshashin, whose missions are launched from their mountain fortress of Alamut.

    But it's also the story of a French boy, Talon, captured and forced into the alien world of the assassins. Forbidden love for a princess is intertwined with sinister plots and self-sacrifice, as the hero and his two companions discover treachery and then attempt to evade the ruthless assassins of Alamut who are sent to hunt them down.

    It's a sweeping saga that takes you over vast snow-covered mountains, through the frozen wastes of the winter plateau, and into the fabulous cites of Hamadan, Isfahan, and the Kingdom of Jerusalem.

    "A brilliant first novel, worthy of Bernard Cornwell at his best."—Tom Grundner

PENMORE PRESS
www.penmorepress.com

Amaya Tenshi

Penmore Press
Challenging, Intriguing, Adventurous, Historical and Imaginative

www.penmorepress.com